HUNGER

The Vampire Syndicate

REBECCA RIVARD

Wild Hearts Press

❦ I ❦

EDEN

What the hell were you thinking, renting a fourth-floor walk-up?

I trudged up the first flight of steps. Turned the corner. Started up the next flight.

Because this is Williamsburg and all you can afford is a freaking breadbox.

I paused on the landing to take a breath. My backpack and canvas shopping bag felt like they were stuffed with rocks instead of groceries. And had the steps gotten steeper?

I switched the canvas bag to my left hand and kept going, using the rail to haul my tired body up the stairs. By the time I reached the top floor, I was lightheaded and overheated. Putting the bag on the floor, I leaned against the white plaster wall, sucking oxygen like a beached whale.

Mrs. Ortiz was cooking burritos again; the mouthwatering scent of chicken and beans filled the tiny hall. My stomach growled. These days, pretty much anything smelled good, a big improvement on those first months when I hadn't been able to keep down much besides yogurt, apple juice and Cheerios.

Straightening from the wall, I staggered as another wave of dizziness hit me. I'd skipped dinner to pick up a couple of extra hours at BVE, the vintage clothing shop where I worked. Not a good idea when you're five-and-half months pregnant.

I slapped a hand on the wall, breathing through my nostrils until the dizziness receded, then picked up the shopping bag and headed across the hall. I had my key out, ready to insert it in the lock, when I realized my door was unlocked.

I sighed and pushed the door open. I'd *told* Rio to keep the deadbolts locked even when he was home. Williamsburg was fairly safe, but it was still New York City.

I nudged the door closed with my hip. The lock didn't catch but I kept going. I'd get the door after I put the groceries down.

I sniffed, grinned. "Is that green tofu soup I smell? I'm hungry enough to eat a horse."

Rio was a runaway from Ohio who'd moved in with me a few weeks ago. Well, technically he hadn't been a runaway since he was eighteen years old, but he'd dropped out of high school and had been living in a closed-off subway tunnel when we'd met.

He slept in an alcove behind a curtain we'd rigged up in the living room, and in exchange paid half the utilities and groceries—and cooked dinner. He was a prodigy in the kitchen. I could forgive an occasional unlocked door when he produced meals that good.

The apartment door shut with a soft click. I glanced over my shoulder, but no one was there. No one I could see, anyway.

A splinter of apprehension worked its way under my skin.

He's here. They found you.

But I'd been careful, using cash and a fake ID, changing cities every few days before sneaking across the Canadian/US border six weeks ago and making my way to New York. A big city seemed like the best place to lose myself in.

I shrugged off my uneasiness, telling myself the door had just been stuck, until I realized Rio still hadn't answered me.

My heart bumped against my ribcage. "Rio? You here?"

The apartment was laid out so the kitchenette wasn't visible from our front door. I skirted the striped Ikea couch—the only thing I'd bought for my new place other than a comfortable bed—and turned left into the kitchenette.

"Becky." Rio stood at one end of the kitchen island, his expression pinched. "I'm sorry. I couldn't—" His bony shoulders lifted in a help-less shrug.

All the spit left my mouth. My gaze swung to the other side of the marbled-laminate island to where Talon slouched on a bar stool in an unzipped leather jacket.

His sensual mouth curved in a nasty half-smile. "Hello, Eden," he said in his deep, growly voice. A voice I used to find sexy.

"Eden?" Rio echoed.

Neither of us looked at him.

The canvas bag slipped from my fingers, thudding to the floor. Apples rolled across the fake wood planks. I ignored them, my gaze locked on the uninvited—and pissed-off—vampire in my kitchenette.

"I wouldn't let him contact you," Talon told me.

My lungs filled my throat. For a few seconds, I couldn't breathe... or even move.

Things weren't supposed to go down like this. I'd hoped Talon would just let me go, but that was wishful thinking, and I'd known it. I'd betrayed not just him, but his syndicate.

So I had an escape plan.

But he wasn't supposed to be *inside* my apartment. He was supposed to come to the door first so I could put my plan into action. I had a go-bag in my bedroom with cash and a change of clothes. I'd figured I'd have a few seconds—time enough to grab the bag and escape down the portable fire ladder which was the first thing I'd bought after subletting the apartment.

Run, damn it!

My breath whooshed in. "Okay," I said, more to say something than because it made sense.

I slid a foot backward.

Talon rounded the kitchen island, all six-feet-plus of him on the prowl. Outwardly calm, but I saw the muscle ticking in his jaw. He was furious with me.

I swallowed dryly. Slid the other foot backward.

My muscles tensed. I readied myself to make a dash for the door.

I couldn't let him find out about the baby. My loose shirt and thigh-length jacket hid the still-small bump. He'd never know.

Out of the corner of my eye, I saw Rio shift to the left and casually reach behind him, feeling for the knife block on the counter behind him. He was going to try to protect me, and Talon would kill him for it.

My stomach bottomed out.

"It's okay, Rio," I said without looking away from Talon. "I know him."

Rio lowered his brow and dropped his chin, a young, naïve bull about to charge. "He can't make you go with him. There are laws about that. Treaties."

Talon was right in front of me now. He had wolf eyes with irises that changed from dark brown at the outer edges to gold as you moved inward until the band around his pupil was almost yellow. They bored into mine.

"Actually, I can," he said. "Eden signed a contract with my syndicate. Didn't you?"

I moistened my lips. I'd never felt so much like prey, even in my first few weeks as a syndicate thrall.

"Becky?" asked Rio, clearly upset.

"Eden," Talon bit out. "Her name is Eden."

Rio flicked him a look, frowned. To me, he said, "You signed a contract?"

He might be young, but he wasn't stupid. He knew how these things worked.

Talon was still staring at me. "Tell him," he said silkily.

His face filled my vision, an implacable mask I couldn't look away from.

"He's right," I told Rio, my voice a thready rasp. I cleared my throat and tried again. "I signed a contract with his syndicate."

"Which she broke," Talon explained in those same silky, dangerous tones. "After she conned me and my primus. Spied on us."

He—Brien—wasn't the primus at that point. But that was nitpicking. I'd known that what I was doing was wrong, and I'd done it anyway.

"Oh, girl." I dragged my gaze from Talon in time to see Rio shake his head. "You're fucked."

"Yeah." My laugh held zero humor. "I know."

Talon leaned closer. I edged backward until my backpack hit the refrigerator.

His dark brows formed an irritated slash. He shoved the canvas shopping bag out of the way with his foot. "Turn around."

When I obeyed, he removed the heavy backpack while I stood passively, letting him move me around like I was a doll with flexible limbs for him to position as he pleased. Inside, my mind worked desperately, searching for a way out.

I couldn't let Talon take me back. If it were only me, I'd woman up, accept my punishment. But this wasn't just about me. There was the baby, too.

And I'd messed up, big time. Rio had no idea.

If I were a man, I'd probably already be dead.

But I was a woman, a former thrall pregnant with Talon's child, even if he didn't know it. If the syndicate found out, they might take my baby away from me. I was in that much trouble.

And if they took my baby, I might as well be dead.

Talon put the pack on a stool next to the kitchen island. I bent to pick up the apples and canvas bag. By some miracle the eggs hadn't broken.

"Leave it," Talon told me, but I'd already put the apples back in the bag. With a scowl, he took the bag from me and placed it on the island.

I sent the groceries a longing look. They represented independence. As a thrall, I'd never even had to step foot in a kitchen. I mean, I'd liked it—who wouldn't? But that wasn't me. Being pampered like that had felt strange, like I was playing at being a grownup.

At least Rio could use the groceries. His job bussing tables at a hipster restaurant paid his share of the bills, but what he really wanted was to be a chef. He was saving up to take classes at ICE, a fancy culinary institute in lower Manhattan.

"Just let me get my wallet and phone." I turned the backpack so I could unzip the outer pocket.

Because when I escaped—and I *would*—a wallet and phone would make things a helluvalot easier.

Talon's strong fingers landed heavily on my nape. "No."

He turned me and marched me toward the front door...which was blocked by a pair of syndicate soldiers in leather jackets and chinos.

I started in surprise.

So there had been someone in the shadows. *Two* someones, in fact—Adrian and Nathan. You'd think after almost three years as a syndicate thrall, I would've sensed them, but I hadn't. I'd been too focused on getting myself, my ever-expanding belly, and the groceries up the stairs.

Talon's grip on my nape tightened. He must think the tiny jerk I'd given was me trying to get away.

My insides clenched. He could snap my neck so easily.

But he wouldn't, unless he decided that was my punishment for running away. Talon didn't act impulsively. He took his time coming to a decision, and everything he did had a logical reason.

Which is how I knew that once he'd decided that all I was to him was a thrall—nothing more—he wouldn't change his mind.

And I'd been damned if I'd stay with a vampire who'd vowed never to love a human. Who believed human DNA would contaminate his blood line.

Not that Talon had asked me to stay.

I cast Adrian and Nathan a beseeching look. Both men were dhampirs with vampire fathers and human mothers. Adrian was a slim, dark-haired guy who was supersmart about tech. He'd probably had a hand in tracking me down. Nathan was a by-the-book guy with short brown hair who looked kind of like Marcus Mumford. Talon would've brought him along as muscle.

Adrian folded his arms over his chest. Nathan just eyed me coldly, like we hadn't grown up together. Adrian was from a small town in New Brunswick, but Nathan was from the island, same as me. We'd played together as kids.

My chest constricted. I suppose I deserved their unfriendly stares, but something about how they were looking at me slapped me out of the stunned hopelessness that had descended on me along with Talon's grip on my neck.

As we passed the couch, I dug in my heels. For some reason, Talon allowed it, and we came to a halt. Outside, the elevated train at the end of the block rumbled by, vibrating the floorboards.

I turned my head toward Talon. "At least let me pack a bag."

Maybe I could still climb out that bedroom window.

His expression darkened like he'd read my mind. He couldn't, but he *could* read my emotions. He'd probably detected my surge of hope. "We'll buy you anything you need."

He palmed the base of my skull, forcing me to look forward. He propelled me the rest of the way to the door. Adrian and Nathan unfolded their arms and moved aside.

Rio shot to my side, his gawky teenager's body tense. He glared across me at Talon. "Promise me you won't hurt her."

Talon just gave him a look and nodded at Nathan. "Open the door."

Rio tugged my arm, trying to pull me away from Talon. "You can't just kidnap her."

Talon stiffened. Adrian and Nathan's expressions turned murderous.

Adrian grabbed Rio by his T-shirt. "This is syndicate business. Get your hands off her before I rip your fucking head off."

I turned slightly toward Rio, all I could manage with Talon gripping my skull, and gave a frantic shake of my head.

Actually, Talon could do whatever he wanted with me. When I'd signed that thrall contract with the Maritime Syndicate, I'd signed over most of my rights for three years in return for a boatload of money. However, they didn't own me. I was a thrall, not a blood slave.

Unfortunately, by taking a bribe to spy on the syndicate, I'd broken the contract. They could legally punish me for betraying them. It was right there in the fine print.

And if I disappeared, no one would ever find the corpse.

Rio ignored Adrian. "I want your promise," he told Talon.

His expression hardened. "Let her go."

Rio's swallow was audible, but instead of releasing me, he gave my arm another, firmer tug. Talon bared sharp white fangs and leaned across me, pushing his face into Rio's.

"Let. Her. Go."

The teenager dropped my arm like it was a hot poker.

"Stay away from the lieutenant's woman." Adrian shoved Rio in the chest.

He reeled backward, arms flailing. When he caught his balance, he muttered, "Lieutenant? Damn," his light brown skin ashen. But he didn't back off. "That doesn't give you motherfuckers the right to drag her out of here like a freaking pet dog."

Christ.

A cold bead of sweat trickled between my shoulder blades. I had to defuse this before Talon decided Rio was more trouble than he was worth.

"It's okay," I told him. "I'll be all right. But call BVE for me, okay? Tell them I won't be coming back to work. That I went...home."

"I will. Of course." His fists clenched at his sides. "But Becky...I mean Eden...whatever. I'll call 911. They won't get away with this."

"The cops won't do anything," I said. "These guys aren't even from New York. They're not even from the United States." Not that the cops would do anything even if Talon was from the local syndicate.

"And everything in my room is yours." I had five thousand in cash in my go-bag. If I couldn't take it, I wanted him to have it.

Rio shook his head.

I sent him a pleading look. "Please, Rio."

I sensed Talon eyeing me. I blanked my expression and tried to blank my emotions as well. But it was too late, because Talon said, "He's coming, too."

"What?" I blinked rapidly. "No! He's nothing—a kid."

Talon jerked his chin in Rio's direction. "Get him," he told Adrian and Nathan.

The soldiers bracketed Rio, each grabbing an arm.

I sucked in a breath, afraid Rio would fight back. He was tough and he didn't take any crap—he'd never have lasted in New York otherwise. He stiffened and drew in a breath, then sent me a look and went along with it.

That was worse. Despair filled me.

"Please." I clutched Talon's leather-clad arm. It was hard for me to beg, but for Rio, I'd do it. "Let him stay here. He has nothing to do with this. We've only known each other a few weeks. He helps with the bills, that's all."

Talon glanced around my tiny apartment, his left brow hitched up. Something he did when he was curious or disturbed.

Probably wondering what had happened to the money I'd left Canada with. But he was a rich vampire who lived rent-free in a goddamn castle. He wouldn't know that in Williamsburg, even a one bedroom went for four or five thousand dollars.

He folded his lips in. "The kid's insurance," he told me.

"Insurance?" I felt the steel bars of a cage closing around me.

"To make sure you come with us, no tricks. Soon as you get on the jet, he goes free. If not—" Talon moved a big shoulder.

The door to the cage started to swing shut.

I searched his face, trying to find a hint of affection, or at least, softening. "Don't do this."

Talon's lip curled. "Don't do what? Take your lying, betraying ass back to Lilith Island?"

I glanced at Rio's tense face. "It's okay," he told me.

But it wasn't okay. Rio had left Ohio to escape the bullies in his small town. He shouldn't have to deal with Talon and company.

"I don't care what you to do me," I told Talon. "I'll go back with you, I promise. But leave Rio. He has nothing to do with this. We just share the apartment."

Talon narrowed his eyes. "He sleeps in the living room." He glanced at the sheet we'd hung across the middle.

"Yeah, of course." I frowned. "Wait. You thought he was sleeping with *me*?" Rio was still a teenager—and besides, he was interested in boys, not girls. "For fuck's sake, he's practically a kid. I'm five years older than him."

"That's why he's still alive. If I thought you were sleeping with him, he'd be dead."

I gulped. "So let him stay. Please."

"He comes," was the unyielding reply.

I briefly closed my eyes. "I'm so sorry," I told Rio. "I never meant for you to be involved in this."

His chin jutted. "Fuck them," he mouthed at me. "I'm not afraid of them."

"Funny," said Adrian under his breath. "You don't look stupid. Now let's go."

"You too." Talon urged me forward after them.

The cage door slammed closed.

My head pounded. Tiny lights danced at the edges of my vision. It was too much after being on my feet all day at the shop, and then picking up groceries. Plus, the last time I'd eaten except for an apple on the way home was at lunchtime five hours ago.

I swayed on my feet.

"Eden?" Talon took me by the shoulders.

I was falling down a dark tunnel. I clutched his upper arms. Even angry at me, he was still an anchor, the man I'd fallen in love with despite that stupid thrall contract.

"What's wrong with her?" Talon demanded. He sounded...worried.

The world shifted, and then I was in his arms, my cheek tucked into the curve of his neck. He smelled so male. So familiar. Leather and earth and crisp autumn air.

"She's pregnant, you asshole." Rio's voice. "And you're stressing her out."

The darkness pulled me under.

❦ 2 ❦

TALON

"**P**regnant?" My jaw unhinged.

Eden's gold-tipped eyelashes rested on her cheeks. Her creamy skin was bleached of color, her heart beating double-time.

My rattled gaze went to her abdomen, concealed beneath her thigh-length suede jacket. My sources hadn't said anything about her being pregnant.

I glanced back at Eden's self-appointed guardian. "With a baby?"

The pink-haired kid actually rolled his eyes. "Of course with a baby."

"Fuck." My stomach dropped. "We have to get her to a doctor."

"She should be okay," Rio muttered, his brow furrowed. "It's not the first time she's passed out."

My back teeth ground together. "She's passed out before?"

The teenager moved his head solemnly up and down. "She said it happens to some pregnant ladies. Something to do with hormones and blood pressure."

"Yeah?" I still didn't like it. What if she'd collapsed on the way up the stairs? Or worse, outside? "When is she due?"

"February."

"February. That's...soon."

Then it sank in. This was November third. Eden had been pregnant when she'd left Lilith Island.

"I need to feed her, ASAP." Rio tried to shake off Adrian and Nathan, but they hung on, waiting for my okay.

"Let him go," I said, and they released him so suddenly, he staggered. He caught himself and stalked into the kitchenette.

I gathered Eden closer. She was a little heavier, maybe five pounds or so, although you couldn't tell by looking at her face, which was too damn thin in my opinion.

Pregnant.

A shaft of awe worked its way through my shock.

My arms tightened around her limp body. The baby was mine. It had to be.

This past year, she'd been my exclusive thrall. She'd been on birth control like all the female thralls, but birth control could fail.

Eden was carrying my spawn—and she'd left without telling me. Maybe that was even *why* she'd left.

The awe darkened, took on a bitter taint.

Because I was pretty sure that if the Krals hadn't tipped us off that she was in New York City, I'd never have known.

Adrian moved up alongside us. "We should take her to a physician. We probably shouldn't put her on a jet until we know she's all right."

That right there was why I'd brought Adrian. He wasn't just tech-smart, he was practical, with street smarts from growing up off-island with a single mother.

"Do it," I told him as I laid Eden on the couch.

He nodded and took his phone out, moving to the other side of the room.

I crouched next to Eden. Her blond hair had been cut short and dyed black at the tips, a surprisingly effective disguise. Finding her had been harder than I'd expected. She was a twenty-three-year-old human who'd never lived anywhere but Lilith Island. We should've located her in a day or two, but until tonight, she'd managed to stay a step ahead of us.

I combed the short, silky strands back from her face, telling myself I was simply making her more comfortable, but my fingers knew different. The tips tingled with the need to touch her—her hair, her lips, her fine-grained skin. To relearn her body, discover how pregnancy had changed it.

I traced a thumb over her high cheekbone. I could've taken her on the street, but I'd deliberately forced my way into her apartment.

A message: Fuck with the syndicate and there's no place you can hide.

The woman meant nothing to me. I was a Maritime lieutenant here to drag a pretty, lying traitor back home. For a while there, I'd forgotten that humans were prey, good only for blood and sex. I wouldn't make the same mistake twice.

The plan had been to take her directly back to Lilith Island. I'd intended to make her as uncomfortable as possible, to march her out of here with only the clothes on her back. Even food would be contingent on her good behavior.

That, of course, was no longer an option.

But what in Lilith's name was going on?

Eden had left Canada with close to a half-million dollars. Even in Canadian money, that was enough cash for her to live more comfortably.

So why was she sharing a cramped apartment with a scrawny, pink-haired kid in ripped jeans? And working long hours at some used-clothes store?

I came back to my feet. Rio hovered a few feet away, an oversized cup of soup in his hand.

I turned an accusing glare on him. "What the fuck was she doing carrying groceries up three flights of stairs?"

His brows lowered belligerently. "Hey, I'm not her boss. She does what she wants. If you know her at all, you know that."

"Yeah." I rubbed the side of my neck.

"Anyway, you heard her," he said, his tone aggressive. "She's hungry. She worked through dinner tonight to make some extra cash. Then you dudes bust in here and scare the shit out of her."

I just looked at him. He puffed up but had the sense to close his mouth.

Eden's lids fluttered. She was coming around.

I eased off her suede jacket and dropped it over the back of the couch. Beneath she wore black pants, low-heeled boots and a simple cream shirt with ruffled cuffs.

Even as a teenager, she'd had a gift for looking both classy and funky.

And yeah, I'd noticed her back then. I hadn't acted on it or acknowledged her in any way.

But I'd noticed.

I ran my hand over her abdomen, unable to resist. The loose, thigh-length shirt hid it, but she definitely had a baby bump.

Beneath my fingers, a tiny heart pulsed. *Thump-thump-thump-thump-thump.*

My throat worked. *Mine.*

Eden's striking blue eyes flew open. "*Don't*," she said, pushing my hand away. As if she had to protect her child from me.

My fingers dug into my palm. I scrutinized her face, looking for something—anything. A hint that I was wrong and she wasn't trying to defend her child against me. An apology, even.

But she closed her eyes, shutting me out.

So that's how you want to play this.

I deliberately opened my clenched hand, retreating to the icy, emotionless state I'd been in ever since I'd realized that Eden hadn't just broken her contract, she'd spied for Brien's enemies.

Eden pushed up on her forearms and, before I could stop her, swung her feet to the floor. "My boots. The couch—it's new."

"Who the hell cares? You're never coming back here."

Her chin jerked back like I'd slapped her. Then her mouth set in a stubborn line and she bent forward, her hands going for the first boot. She could still reach it, but I could tell it was awkward for her.

I brushed her hands away. "I'll do it."

I helped her out of both boots, then grabbed a cushion and put it against the couch arm. "Lean against that."

I waited until she obeyed, then glanced over my shoulder at Rio. "Where's that soup?"

"Right here."

He tried to hand the cup to Eden, but I took it from him and sat on the edge of the couch, facing her. My hip touched her leg, and she stiffened like I was some kind of monster.

My jaw hardened. The woman was carrying a child. *My* child.

I'd cut off my own hand before hurting her or my spawn, which if she knew me at all, she'd understand.

And even if she hadn't been pregnant, I wouldn't have hurt her. Not really. Just...scared her a little.

I pressed the oversized cup into Eden's palms. "Eat." The word came out harsh from the anger pressing on my lungs.

Her gaze flew to mine, her emotions a snarled tangle. Fear, distrust, worry.

"Thank you," she said, the phrase clearly pulled unwillingly from her mouth.

Adrian was texting, his thumbs flying over the screen, and Nathan stood to one side of the apartment door.

"Nathan," I said, "stick with the kid. Adrian, you guard the door."

Nathan immediately took a stance near Rio, who was back in the kitchenette. At the same time Aidan moved to the door, blocking anyone from entering or leaving, his attention on his phone.

Eden's stomach rumbled. Clearly, the woman wasn't taking good enough care of herself. That changed as of now.

"Eat," I repeated, more calmly this time.

She blew on the hot liquid, then a small sip. "Thanks, Rio." She slanted the kid a smile. "This is really good. Better than last time, even."

He moved a shoulder, pleased. "Extra ginger."

"Keep eating," I told her. "I want you to finish that."

She looked past me at Rio. "Can I have a spoon?"

When he brought it to over, I took it, telling Eden, "I'll feed you."

"I can do it." She reached for the spoon.

I leveled her a look. "I said, *I'll feed you.*"

Eden was carrying my spawn. Some primitive instinct had kicked in. I needed to take care of her. It was either that or punch a hole in the fucking living room wall.

"Fine," she said in a toneless voice that was somehow worse than if she'd kept fighting me.

But she allowed me to feed her. At least the soup seemed nutritious—leafy greens and chunks of tofu floating in what my nose told me was a coconut-milk-and-ginger base.

She swallowed every drop, and Rio refilled the cup. When she'd finished that, too, she swung her feet to the floor. "I'm better now."

"Easy, there." I put a hand on her thigh, preventing her from standing. "She should eat more," I told Rio. "What else do you have?"

He looked at Eden. "Apples and peanut butter?"

"That would be great, thanks. And something to drink."

The grateful smile she gave the kid stirred an unreasoning jealousy in me. Rio was just a teenager, and I knew he wasn't anything more than a friend. But I wanted one of those smiles she kept directing at him.

"And milk," I growled, because pregnant humans needed milk, didn't they? For the calcium and stuff.

I jerked my head at Nathan, and while Rio got out the peanut butter and apples, Nathan brought Eden a glass of milk. She took a sip, then rested the glass on her thigh. She had the prettiest eyes, not just the color, but the shape: long-lidded and sultry. Now, though, they had dark smudges under them like she hadn't been getting enough sleep.

She rubbed the edge of her thumb up and down the glass. "How did you find me?"

"You were seen by a Kral soldier."

"What did you do, have an APB out on me?"

"Something like that." In fact, I'd hired a top private investigation firm to hunt for her. The Kral soldier had been pure luck, though. He'd mentioned something to Rafe Kral, who'd passed the intel on to me.

"Food's ready," Rio said.

Eden nodded and stood up. I rose, too, standing close enough that she had to slide past me, her body an inch from mine so I felt her warmth. Yeah, I was being an ass, but she didn't give me the satisfaction of reacting. Her eyes remained stubbornly downcast; her expression unreadable.

She padded to the kitchen island in her stocking feet and sat on a stool. Rio placed the plate of sliced apples in front of her along with a small dish of peanut butter. She dipped an apple slice into the peanut butter and ate it, washing it down with the milk.

Meanwhile, Rio got himself a baguette and a large bowl of soup and took them both to the stool beside her. Before dipping his spoon in, he glanced at me, Adrian and Nathan. "You guys eat human food?"

"Talon's a vampire," Eden said, "but the other two are dhampirs."

"Help yourself." Rio pointed his spoon at the pot on the stove.

Adrian was on a call with someone now. He shook his head at Rio.

"We already ate," Nathan said with a grin that showed his fangs.

Rio's cheeks reddened. He hunched over his soup. "Suit yourself," he muttered and started eating.

I roamed restlessly around the tiny apartment. The single bedroom was barely large enough for a bed and a night table. A dresser took up most of the small closet, and a lightweight escape ladder was rolled up beneath a bedroom window.

I eyed it. Did Eden really think she could outrun me, a vampire? Even so, I shoved the ladder into the closet in the narrow space between the wall and the dresser, then grabbed the small, packed duffel bag tucked into a shelf above the dresser.

I unzipped the duffel bag, upending it onto her bed. A cotton sweater, a couple of T-shirts, and a pair of leggings spilled onto the worn flowered quilt along with underwear and socks. The bag also held a hairbrush, a toothbrush and an envelope of cash.

No jewelry. When she'd run away, she'd left behind every piece I'd given her. Like I gave two fucks about trinkets.

Still, I'd wondered why she'd take a traitor's money and not my gifts. If she was so easily bought, why leave behind diamonds and sapphires?

The cash went into my pocket, then I repacked the bag and took it with me into the kitchen.

Eden was finishing the last apple slice. I handed Nathan the duffel bag. Her gaze tracked the bag but she didn't say anything.

Adrian ended his call. "Any luck?" I asked him.

"The Krals have an OB-GYN in Manhattan who can take a look at her. They suggested you bring Eden to the Hotel Garnet."

Eden's color had improved but she was still drooping. There was no rush to return her to Canada, and for my own peace of mind, I wanted her to be seen by a doctor as soon as possible.

"All right," I told Adrian. The Garnet was a vampire hotel owned by the Kral Syndicate. I'd already received permission to enter their territory to extract Eden. "Book us a couple of suites, too. We'll leave tomorrow night instead. And get the kid a room."

Rio put down the dish he was rinsing. "I guess I should pack my bag."

I jerked my head in assent.

Eden's head snapped up. "Talon, no. I'll come with you. I swear I will. But please don't make him come."

Rio turned off the water and circled the kitchen island. "Hey." He wrapped a skinny arm around her shoulders. "I'm not letting you go with them alone."

"Oh, God. I never thought you'd get dragged into this. I'm so sorry." She pushed her empty plate away and scrubbed her hands over her face.

The kid shot me a dirty look. "*You* have nothing to be sorry for," he told Eden.

"Pack a bag," I ordered. "Now."

Her shoulders sagged. "You'd better do what he says."

Rio gave her another hug and whispered something in her ear, then disappeared behind the curtain dividing the living room. Meanwhile, I texted the pilot of the syndicate jet waiting at a private airport in New Jersey, letting him know we'd be flying out tomorrow night instead.

"I have to use the bathroom," Eden said and pushed past me. It was off the living room. I followed her and, after making sure the window was too small for her to climb out of, waited outside the door.

Rio reappeared in a baggy purple hoodie, a backpack slung over his shoulder. "I have to get something from Eden's room," he said, darting around Adrian and Nathan.

Nathan made to go after him, but I gave a slight shake of my head. Rio reappeared with a sleeveless beaded shirt, a velvet skirt and a plastic box about the size of a book.

"What's in the box?" Nathan demanded.

"My sewing kit," Eden said, coming out of the bathroom.

My brow creased. I didn't even know she sewed.

"Let me see," I said gruffly, and Rio opened the box to show me the neatly arranged needles, scissors, thread and other sewing gear. All the metal items were stainless steel, so I shrugged a shoulder. "Fine. Bring it."

Rio rolled up the shirt and skirt, taking care not to wrinkle the fabric, and stowed them in his backpack along with the sewing kit. Meanwhile, I helped Eden into her boots and jacket, then pointed her toward the hall. She yawned and shuffled along beside me like a zombie—and stumbled right as we reached the stairs.

She would've tumbled down the steps if I hadn't been holding her arm.

Swallowing a curse, I swung her into my arms and started down the stairs. This time, she didn't clutch at me, just slid an arm around my neck, the other hand resting lightly on my chest, as if she was only touching me because she had to.

It pissed me off enough that I gathered her closer, tucking her head into the space between my chin and shoulder. Unfortunately, that gave me a nose full of her sweet, sugar cookie scent. My favorite cookie before I was turned.

My mouth tightened. I turned my head, but it didn't help much. I could still smell her, warm and sweet, with an overlay of salty perspiration from her long day.

Outside, I bundled her into the waiting SUV. Adrian pushed Rio in next to us and took shotgun in the front seat, with Nathan driving. On the way from Brooklyn to Manhattan, Eden dozed off, her head on my shoulder.

On my other side, Rio's thin body practically vibrated with tension. He stared out the window as we crossed the Williamsburg Bridge, then turned to glare at me.

"Which syndicate are you guys from, anyway?"

I eyed him and, after a couple of beats, decided to indulge him. "The Maritime Syndicate."

"Not the Kral Syndicate?"

"No."

"And where are you from? I mean, your base or whatever you call it."

"Nova Scotia."

His brow scrunched. "Where the fuck is that?"

"Canada."

"Oh. Well, I want to come too. I don't want to get left at the airport."

"That so?"

"Yeah. And if you try to leave me, I'll raise all kinds of hell."

"We'll see." But I'd already decided the kid was coming with us. Eden clearly cared about him; I could use that.

And the kid had a pair of balls on him. I liked that in a man.

Adrian leaned over the front seat, and in a swift move that had Rio blinking, gripped the teenager around the throat. "That's a lieutenant you're speaking to," he growled. "Show some fucking respect."

Rio's face darkened. Anger radiated off him. The idiot was actually considering fighting back. "Sorry," he muttered.

Adrian gave him a rough shake. "I can't hear you."

A beat passed. "I'm sorry," he said, louder this time.

"I'm sorry, Lieutenant," prompted Adrian.

"I'm sorry, Lieutenant." The last was a gasp. He'd run out of breath.

"Good boy." Adrian released him and faced front again.

Rio's breath rushed in. He sat beside me, fingers digging into his thighs, dragging in oxygen. Out of the corner of my eye, I saw him mouth "prick" at the front seat.

I turned my head so he wouldn't see my smile. Yeah, the kid definitely had balls.

⚜

G reenwich Village was coated in a pale, moody mist. The tree-lined streets were scattered with glistening autumn leaves, and the sidewalks crawled with humans out clubbing. Nathan halted the

SUV in front of the Hotel Garnet's entrance, an anonymous metal arch flanked by potted flowers.

A Kral soldier stepped up to the vehicle, trying to make us out through the tinted windows. While I nudged Eden awake, Adrian exited and explained who we were and what our business was.

I helped Eden from the backseat after Rio. "Can you walk?" I asked.

She blinked sleepily up at me, clearly exhausted. "Of course," she said, a stubborn set to her chin.

"I can see that," I said dryly and swept her into my arms.

She heaved a breath, then relaxed against me. "This isn't necessary," she muttered against my chest as I carried her through a brick courtyard lined with more potted plants. I pretended I hadn't heard.

Nathan followed with our bags—we'd come prepared to stay a few nights in New York if necessary—and Adrian took charge of Rio. The Kral soldier strode ahead to open the brushed bronze door.

Inside, the pretty, middle-aged human behind the front desk turned a professional smile on us. "Lieutenant Talon and party?"

Adrian stepped forward. "Yes."

"Your suites are ready." She handed Adrian two sets of key cards along with the room numbers.

"We're expecting a physician," he told her. "Dr. Perez."

"Very good. I'll let you know as soon as she arrives. Charles will show you your room." She nodded at the bellhop standing at attention against the wall, and he hurried forward with a cart for our luggage.

"Right this way, sirs. Miss."

Our suites were two floors below ground level at one end of a short hall. At my direction, the bellhop left all the luggage in one suite. Adrian tipped him and he left.

"Eden stays with me," I told Adrian and Nathan. "The kid goes with you." To Rio, I said, "Behave and you'll be all right."

He clenched his fists, his mouth hard. But beneath the posturing, he was afraid. The fear rolled off him. I didn't just sense it, I smelled it.

But he still jutted his chin. "I want to stay with Eden. Lieutenant, sir," he tacked on.

I eyed him, equal parts exasperated and impressed. It's not easy for a human to stand up to a vampire. That didn't mean I was going to indulge him any further.

"No," I told him, and nodded at Nathan. "Bring Eden's and my bags to the other suite."

I waited only long enough for him to deposit the baggage inside the suite door, then closed the door behind Nathan, leaving me alone with Eden. In the hall Rio sputtered angrily until he was cut off mid-sentence. Adrian had probably applied some kind of hold to his throat. Adrian wouldn't hurt Rio, just rough him up enough to teach him that when we gave him a direct order, he obeyed—or else.

I put him from my mind and turned to my sleepy-eyed prisoner.

❧ 3 ❧

EDEN

Talon's wolf-brown eyes roved over my body. He unbuttoned my suede jacket and gathered my loose cotton shirt in his hands. It pressed against my abdomen, revealing what the looseness had concealed. The lighting was low, but vampires have vision like cats. I knew he could see every detail—my full breasts, my noticeably rounder belly.

"When were you going to tell me?" he asked.

I lifted a shoulder, let it drop.

"Yeah," he said. "That's what I thought."

My gaze slid from his. I wasn't proud of what I'd done. Leaving without telling Talon he was going to be a father had been wrong. Yeah, I'd been desperate, but it had still been wrong.

"I've got to pee," I muttered.

He released me and I turned, making my way down the dimly lit hall and pushing open the first door I came to. A frosted-glass sconce came on, illuminating a lux silver-and-black bedroom. I dropped my jacket on the massive black-lacquer bed and hurried into the attached bathroom.

When Talon tried to follow, I shut the bathroom door in his face. He rapped on the thick wood.

"*What?*" I jerked down my pants and underwear, lowering myself to the toilet seat with a sigh of relief.

"Just...tell me if you feel faint or anything."

I briefly closed my eyes. *Now* he was being nice, but I knew it was only because of the baby. Somehow that hurt more than the cool disdain.

"I'm fine," I gritted. "You didn't have to call a doctor."

He grunted and didn't say anything else, but I knew he remained outside the door. Standing guard.

I finished and zipped up my pants, leaving the button undone. I was tall and wide-hipped enough that I wasn't in maternity clothes yet, but it wouldn't be much longer.

I took my time in the bathroom, washing my face, running my fingers through my hair. Then I placed my hands on the marble counter and stared at my reflection.

Jesus Murphy. I looked like crap. Pale, with purple smudges under my eyes and a pinched look around my mouth, like I was forty-three, not twenty-three.

Stress and pregnancy weren't a good mix. Talon showing up out of the blue tonight didn't help, but I couldn't blame it all on him. I'd been stressed for months.

First, I'd found out I was carrying the baby of a vampire who'd vowed never to mate with a human because he didn't want a dhampir spawn. Then I'd let myself get roped into spying on the other thralls, including a thrall that Brien, now the syndicate's new primus, had fallen in love with. And after that, I'd run, leaving everyone I loved behind.

Talon knocked again. "Eden?"

I heaved a breath, weary clear to my bones.

"*You made your bed, now lie in it.*" Why did I hear my mom's voice whenever I messed up?

I wiped my hands, straightened my spine. "Coming."

The duffel bag was on a plush armchair, my jacket folded neatly on top. It was the only chair in the bedroom, so I sank onto the bed's velvet coverlet instead.

Talon dropped his leather jacket on top of my stuff and prowled closer, stopping with his booted toes an inch from mine. God, he was sexy. Dark-haired and broody, his jaw shadowed with stubble. A navy T-shirt hugged his powerful torso and biceps, and a menacing shark tattoo, the mark of a "made" man in the Maritime Syndicate, curved around the side of his neck.

I felt the usual tingle in my belly at having him so near. I'd missed him, which was so fucked up.

I hated how susceptible I was to him, how starved I'd been for his touch, his earthy male scent. His rare, slow smile.

"My mom and dad?" I blurted before he had a chance to read me. "They're okay?"

His heavy brows pulled together. "Yeah."

"And my sister?"

"Freya? She's fine, I guess. Still in Halifax as far as I know—I don't keep tabs on her."

"Good." Tears filled my eyes. I was just so relieved. Plus, I cried a lot these days. I swiped the moisture away. "That's good."

He took hold of my chin, making me look back up at him. "You're crying."

I drew a ragged breath. "It's nothing. Hormones."

His expression darkened. "You thought I'd hurt them to punish you?"

I swallowed, the sound loud in the quiet bedroom. "No."

"Don't lie. You know I can sense it."

"Fine, then. I wondered, all right? I know how angry you and Brien must be with me. How bad I made you look, and I was afraid you'd take it out on them—"

Talon released me. "The *primus*," he said, emphasizing his friend's title, "has kept what you did quiet. Everyone thinks you left with our permission."

I blinked. "He did? But why?"

"We would've looked weak." His mouth twisted. "You spying on us like that and then escaping without punishment."

"Oh." The faint hope that I'd been forgiven shriveled. My shoulders slumped. "Of course. And the baby?"

His gaze dropped to my abdomen. I covered it protectively.

I didn't mean to. Instinct made me do it, just like when I'd come back to consciousness at my apartment and found Talon touching me, his expression possessive. I'd spent the past few months terrified that when the syndicate found out about my baby, they'd take him or her away to punish me.

Talon's gaze snapped back to mine. "Fuck, Eden. I'm not going to hurt you or the baby."

I rolled my lips in. I couldn't seem to help messing things up with this man. "I know."

At least, I knew he wouldn't hurt either of us physically. But would he let me keep the baby? That was the fear that had made me run, that still had me jolting awake, heart racing, sweat beading my forehead.

He expelled a breath through his teeth. "You're tired. We'll continue this tomorrow. Just tell me one thing. The child—it's mine, isn't it?"

It wasn't really a question. His voice barely went up at the end. But I knew he still wanted an answer, and he'd know if I lied. Like he'd said, he could sense it; vampires have built-in lie detectors where humans are concerned.

But damn him for asking. He *knew* it was his.

He *knew* there'd been no one but him for the past year.

He might've well slapped me. I recoiled, my hand flying to my abdomen.

"Yes," I said between tight lips. "There was no one else, and you know that. When would I have even had a chance to—?" I shook my head. "And if you don't believe me, check your goddamn cams."

He nodded, satisfied. "I believe you."

I ground my back teeth together. "That was some kind of a truth test, wasn't it?"

An unapologetic shrug. "I had to know."

"Well, fuck you, too."

His jaw set. "You know the syndicate takes full responsibility for any spawn born to a thrall."

"Maybe I don't want my baby"—I deliberately used the word *baby*, not *spawn*—"growing up in a syndicate."

My *dhampir* baby—half-human, half-vampire. Talon wasn't the only vampire who looked down on dhampirs. My kid wasn't going to be raised as a second-class citizen. A child whose mother wasn't even his father's mate, but a disgraced thrall.

His frown deepened. "Is that why you ran?"

I dug my fingers into my thighs. "It's part of the reason, yeah."

But mostly because I was afraid that when you found out what I'd done, you'd take the baby from me.

I didn't say it aloud, though. It was a weakness, one Talon might use against me like he'd used Rio.

He pursed his lips, considering me in that way he had of peeling back the bullshit to see straight into my soul.

I shifted, feeling itchy, exposed. "But I was always planning to leave. I was just marking time until my contract was up."

It was a bitchy thing to say, and I knew it.

Still, I didn't expect my jab to hit, but something flickered way back in his eyes. Something that looked like hurt.

But that couldn't be right because I'd always known I had an expiration date. He hadn't made me any promises, and he sure as hell hadn't asked me to extend my contract. As soon as my time was up, he would've turned to another thrall...or three. He was a vampire, after all.

Even this past year, I might have been his favorite, but I'd known we weren't exclusive. Actually, that wasn't true. He'd called dibs on me, and he was high enough in the hierarchy that the rest of the syndicate had left me alone.

However, it hadn't worked both ways. He hadn't flaunted other women in front of me, but it was no secret. I knew...which was a special kind of torture.

His eyes hooded, hiding whatever I'd thought I'd seen. "Yeah, I know."

I opened my mouth to say something—maybe even apologize—but he put his fingers on my lips. "I told you, we'll talk tomorrow."

He crouched at my feet to remove my boots. I stared down at him, confused and wanting.

Don't read too much into it.

But it was such a gentlemanly, caring thing to do.

He stood up, my boots in his hand. As he set them next to the chair, Adrian knocked on the outer door to say the doctor had arrived.

"Stay here," Talon told me, and let her in.

The two had a low-voiced conference in the hall, then Dr. Lopez appeared, a small, motherly woman who seemed unfazed at being called out at eleven p.m. to examine me. She won me over when the first thing she did was to shoo Talon from the bedroom.

He started to object until I frowned at him and mouthed, "Go."

His lips lifted in an almost-smirk, like he found me amusing. But he left, saying, "Call me if you need anything."

Dr. Lopez set a leather bag on the bed. "I'm Carla," she told me with a warm smile. "And your name is Eden? May I call you that?"

"Yes." I relaxed enough to smile back.

"So, I hear you're pregnant, sweetie. How far along?"

"Five and a half months," I told her. "I think. I...haven't been to a doctor yet."

She clucked her tongue, not to shame me but more like my mom would've—commiserating with and scolding me at the same time.

"I suppose you had your reasons," she said. "You need a proper exam—blood tests, an ultrasound—but let's look you over, check your vitals. I understand you've fainted more than once?"

"Yeah, but I thought that was common."

"It is, but you shouldn't ignore it. It could be a sign of something more serious."

"Oh," I said, feeling like the worst mom in the world. "It was only three—no, four—times."

"Okay." She took out a blood pressure cuff from the leather bag. "Blood pressure is great," she said after checking it. "And your pulse seems normal."

She had me remove my clothes and lie on the bed. After some poking and prodding, she announced that everything seemed fine. "And you're right, you're about somewhere between five and six months pregnant."

"You can tell?"

"The size of your uterus confirms it." She looked sideways, calculating. "It's early November, which means the baby is due in February. You can put your clothes on now."

She pulled off her surgical gloves and dropped them into a trash can. She waited until I was dressed, then said, "I assume the lieutenant is the father?" She waited for my nod, then said, "Well, you're a healthy pregnant woman, and your baby is doing great."

"Yeah." A relieved smile bubbled up from my chest. "That's good to know. Thank you."

"You're welcome." She handed me bottle of prenatal vitamins. "Start taking these as of now. And no more skipping meals," she added sternly. "That's not good for you or the baby."

I gripped the bottle. "I'm sorry."

"You should be." Her hug softened the scolding words. "You have to take care of yourself. If not for you, for your baby."

"I will," I promised.

Her arms tightened on me. "Are you safe?" she asked in my ear. "I can arrange something..."

Heat pressed at the back of my eyes. I bit down hard on my lower lip.

She was a brave woman, to offer to interfere in a syndicate matter. And a good one.

"It's not like that. Talon—I'm in the wrong here, not him."

"You're sure?" She pulled back to examine my face.

I formed my features into what I hoped was a reassuring expression. "I'm sure."

The bedroom door opened as she was packing up her medical bag. "How is she?" asked Talon.

"She's in excellent health—and as far as I can tell, so is your spawn —but she needs a full exam as soon as you can arrange it."

"I'll make sure of it," he said with a frown in my direction.

Talon followed the doctor into the hall. He thanked her for coming out tonight, then they had a short conversation in voices too low for me to overhear. But from her tone, she was scolding him, too.

When Talon returned, his face was carved into rigid lines.

"What?" I asked.

"You haven't even had a fucking exam?" His measured words made me wince.

"I should've. I've been meaning to. But I didn't want to be traced, and I was afraid that would make it easier…"

He pinched the bridge of his nose. "Come here."

I padded over to him in my stocking feet. His fingers went to my shirt.

I tried to push him away. "What are you doing?"

A dark look. "Undressing you." In a few efficient moves, he stripped off my shirt and pants, leaving me in my bra and panties.

We both stared at my naked abdomen. I looked like I'd swallowed a rugby ball.

Talon laid a hand on my rounded stomach. "This is mine, Eden."

I frowned up at him, uncertain of his meaning. "And mine," I said, just so we were clear on it.

"Mm," he said, which wasn't really an answer. His other hand curved around my nape, pulling me closer so that my nearly naked body touched his fully clothed one. Beneath my bra, my nipples hardened and pressed against his T-shirt.

He felt it, of course. His hand skated up to my breast, squeezing it. "That means you're mine, too."

A treacherous thrill went over me at hearing him claiming me so explicitly. I tamped it down.

He doesn't want you.

He didn't even want the baby, not really. I'd overheard him telling Cain he didn't want to sire a dhampir, that he only wanted a pureblood spawn.

I tried to pull away, but his fingers tightened on my nape. His eyes dropped to my mouth at the same time mine went to his.

He had such a sexy mouth, with a full, sensual lower lip.

I moistened my lips. He made a sound low in his throat and lowered his head. His clean, woodsy scent enveloped me, a reminder of everything I'd left behind in Nova Scotia.

My family, my friends—and Talon himself.

Yearning knotted my chest, a tight ache that made it difficult to breathe.

His tongue slid over the seam of my lips. I swayed into him, my pregnant belly resting against his rock-hard abs.

"Open for me," he coaxed, his tongue licking my closed mouth. Sweet, wet temptation.

I swallowed a moan. It would be so easy to part my lips and let him in. To go back to how we were, vampire and thrall. To be Talon's willing hostage so that I could be with my baby.

But I didn't want Talon like that.

I wanted Talon to want me for myself, not my baby.

I wanted Talon to love me for myself.

"Don't." I turned my head to the side.

He straightened from me and craned his neck, trying to make me meet his eyes. "Eden?"

"I'm really tired." I kept my gaze angled down and away from him. "I just want to go to bed."

"Of course." The warmth in his voice evaporated, leaving me feeling hollowed out and lost.

He pulled back the coverlet and sheet and waited as I climbed into the bed. My cheeks heated. I felt awkward and very pregnant, having him watch me with that intense focus. I dragged the sheet up to my neck, and he tucked the coverlet around me.

Without saying anything, he left the bedroom, returning with a bottle of water, which he put on the nightstand next to me.

"Thanks," I muttered and struggled back to sitting. This time, he just watched without trying to help.

Uncapping the bottle, I took a drink and put it back on the nightstand.

Talon waited until I was under the covers again, then stowed the duffel bag in the closet and settled on the armchair.

I eyed him. "What are you doing?"

"Making sure you sleep."

"What if I don't want you to?"

He stared back, unblinking.

"Whatever. Suit yourself." I rolled onto my side, giving him my back.

I thought I was too churned up to sleep, but I was wrong. I was out within minutes.

Right before I dropped off, I thought I felt Talon brush a hand down my face from my forehead to my chin, soothing me in a way he knew I liked. "Sleep, now. Everything's going to be all right."

But I might've dreamed that part.

❧ 4 ☙

TALON

I settled onto the chair, watching Eden sleep.

I'd meant what I'd told her. She was mine now. I was a possessive SOB, and she wasn't just the woman I couldn't get enough of, she was the mother of my spawn.

Yeah, I was taking advantage of the circumstances to have more involvement in everything about her, and the Talon who remembered what it was like to be human and desperate felt guilty—but the vampire? It was coldly satisfied.

I hadn't wanted to allow Eden to leave in the first place. If I'd had my way, I'd have kept her with me on Lilith Island even after her contract was up. But she was so young. She'd made it clear she couldn't wait to escape the island and small-town life. She'd saved almost everything she made as a thrall to finance her big move.

I'd figured I'd give her a few years to get it out of her system, then go after her. I'd even told myself I'd have given her a choice, although when it came down to it, I'm not sure I would've.

Eden muttered something scared and broken. I was instantly on my feet.

"Easy." I feathered my fingertips over her downy cheek. "It's just a bad dream. You're safe."

"No…" Her heart rapped out a panicked beat. She moved her head back and forth on the pillow. "Please, don't…"

My gut squeezed. I'd wanted the upper hand. Wanted her punished.

Lilith knew, she deserved it.

It shouldn't bother me that she was frightened, upset. But it did, damn her anyway.

I gripped her chin. "Eden. Look at me." When she did, dazed and afraid, I captured her gaze and put a compulsion on her. "*Sleep*. You're safe. You will sleep deeply, without dreams."

Her breath shuddered in.

"Sleep," I repeated, low and firm.

With a sigh, she curled into a ball and was out.

I stared down at her, every muscle in my body strung tight, a germ of an idea teasing me.

I wanted her safe, yeah.

I also wanted to own her, to guarantee she never left again. Having her off-island had gutted me. I'd been obsessed with getting her back.

That was unacceptable. I was a syndicate lieutenant now, and Brien was still establishing himself as the new primus. He needed my full attention.

Yeah, the baby would ensure Eden stayed for the next eighteen years, but after that, there'd be nothing to hold her on the island… unless she accepted my blood bond. Then she'd be mine for the rest of her life.

Gradually, her breath slowed as she drifted into a deep sleep. I left the room, keeping the door ajar so I could monitor her.

The suite had two bedrooms and a large living room with more black lacquer furniture. I stretched out on the velvet couch, my head against the arm, and took out my phone to report to Brien.

He answered on the first ring. "Talon."

"It was Eden, all right," I replied.

"You have her?"

"Yeah. But there's been a change of plans. We're not flying back tonight. We checked into the Hotel Garnet."

"Why? What happened?"

My fingers tightened on the black case. "She's carrying my spawn. Five or so months along. I asked the Krals to arrange for a gynecologist to look her over. She passed out when she found me in her apartment. The doctor said she's okay, though."

He whistled. "You sure it's yours?"

Anger heated my chest. But it was a legitimate question. Eden had proved she wasn't trustworthy.

"I'm sure. You know we were exclusive this past year. I would've known if she'd been with another man."

If nothing else, I would've smelled him on her. You can't hide who you're fucking from a vampire.

When the silence stretched, I added, "And yes, I asked her straight out. She confirmed it."

A heavy exhale. "Well, bring her back and we'll decide what to do with both of them."

My hackles lifted at that "we'll decide what to do with both of them." Brien might be my best friend, along with Cain, his other lieutenant, but he was also my primus. He could order me to slit Eden's throat and I'd have to obey.

No. Fucking. Way.

Eden was *mine*. And so was her baby.

I'd vowed never to have a child with a human. In a syndicate, vampire blood, and how much of it you carried, was everything.

But now all I could think was that this was my woman...my spawn. And I was damned if I'd let anyone take either of them away from me.

That germ of an idea sprouted, grew roots.

And then, for the first time ever, I lied to Brien. "I offered her my blood bond, and she accepted."

"Did you?" His tone was neutral.

"Yeah." I sat upright on the couch. If I were still human, I'd be sweating.

This was the tricky part. If Eden accepted, I'd basically own her— her body, her blood. Just as important, her punishment would be left to me; a primus almost never got between a vampire and a blood-bonded thrall. Eden, however, was a special case. She'd disrespected Brien and the syndicate, and as his lieutenant, I should be backing him up, not taking her under my protection.

"I know she fucked up," I said, "and I'll address that. But she's carrying my spawn, Brien. I want to handle it."

"I see."

A beat passed. Two. Three. I forced myself to wait him out.

I hadn't come to New York planning to blood-bond Eden. Hell, it had been the farthest thing from my mind. Still, now that it had occurred to me, I liked the idea.

Actually, I fucking loved it.

If she accepted, she'd be mine—permanently. My exclusive thrall for as long as I desired. She could never leave me again.

And she'd be under my protection. Even Brien, my primus, would think twice before harming her.

Not that she wouldn't be punished. She would. But I'd be in charge, the man who decided what form the punishment would take.

"Your call," Brien said at last. "But make sure she knows this is her last chance. She'd better behave herself or I *will* take action."

"Understood, and thank you." I knew he'd only agreed because of our friendship, and I appreciated it. "FYI, I'm also bringing a kid back. Seventeen or eighteen. Name's Rio. He was living with her, and she cares about him—he's insurance that she'll behave. If he works out, I might use him as a PA, too."

"I trust your judgment," he said. "Is that it? Twilight's waiting." Twilight was Brien's new mate.

"Only that I want to put Eden in the garden suite. She needs fresh air, being pregnant and all."

He grunted assent, clearly uninterested in where Eden slept, and ended the call.

My next call was to the Hotel Garnet concierge. A blood-bond ritual required a bracelet. As I expected, the concierge was happy to compile a selection for me to choose from.

"Something simple," I told him. "Nothing too fancy. And I want blue stones."

Because despite everything, I wanted to please her, and Eden wasn't a fancy, frou-frou type. The blue stones were to match her eyes.

"Of course, Lieutenant," said the concierge. "I'll have it to you within the hour."

I thanked him and looked in on my prisoner. She was sleeping peacefully, so I locked the suite and went to inform Rio of his new employment. He was sitting straight-backed on the couch, Nathan on a chair nearby.

Nathan jumped to his feet. "Adrian's in his bedroom working."

Adrian appeared in the bedroom doorway. "I ordered thralls for the three of us."

I nodded my thanks. Unlike Adrian and Nathan, my only meal tonight had been a half-bottle of blood-wine. Unfortunately, I wouldn't be feeding from Eden for the foreseeable future. And although I would be fucking her, that clearly wasn't an option tonight, either.

Rio was next. "How would you like a job?" I asked him.

A suspicious squint. "What kind of a job?"

"I could use a PA."

"What's that?"

"A Personal Assistant."

"Yeah? What would I be doing?"

"For now, you'd be Eden's personal chef and companion. Later on, we'll see. You'll have to prove I can trust you."

His chin lifted. "I won't spy on her for you. I don't care how much you're paying."

"I wouldn't hire you if I thought you'd spy on a friend."

"Yeah? That's all right then. How much are we talking about?"

I named a figure and his brows shot to his dyed-pink hairline. "And all I have to do is hang out with Eden?" he asked, clearly expecting a catch.

"That and cook for her. You'll sign a contract with us—one year. After that, you can leave or stay. Your decision."

He rolled his tongue around his cheek. "All right. Sure. I'm in."

I suspected he'd only agreed because he thought he might get to play the hero. The kid clearly worshipped Eden. But if he helped ensure her good behavior, it was a win-win.

I glanced at Nathan. "Have Smythe work up a contract for Rio. A digital version so Rio can sign it before we leave." Smythe was Brien's new PA. "Standard terms. That means you won't share information about us with anyone," I told Rio.

"And if I do?"

"I wouldn't," I said. "Not if you want to leave the island with all your fingers."

Rio nodded. "Understood." To his credit, he didn't appear afraid. If anything, he seemed to respect me more for the threat. He even tacked on a *Lieutenant* without prompting. Then he frowned. "But if we're going to Canada, I don't have a passport."

Adrian's lips twitched. "We won't be going through customs."

Rio's cheeks reddened. "Right," he said.

While Nathan contacted Smythe, my own phone buzzed with a call from Cain. I refused it. If I knew Cain—and I did—he just wanted to tell me to get my head out of my ass.

A few seconds later, a text arrived.

Cain: *You sure she's not fucking with you?*

I growled and shoved my phone back into my pocket without replying.

Cain and I went way back, further even than me and Brien. We'd met soon after he'd come to the island as an orphaned ten-year-old to live with his aunt and SOB of an uncle. The friendship came after he saw me steal a candy bar from Mrs. O'Brien's store but didn't report me. I wasn't an orphan, but I might as well have been with a mom who liked wine a little too much and a father who spent more time on the mainland than at home.

So yeah, Cain was my oldest friend, but I wasn't in the mood to listen to him chew me out for impregnating Eden. Not that I'd done it deliberately, but still. I could've been more careful, worn a condom like I did with other thralls.

Cain and I had made a pact to never sire a spawn with a human. To kids like us, who'd had to fight for every scrap of respect, power was important. With it came status. Dignity.

A knock on the door announced the arrival of the thralls. Rio gulped audibly as three chic, beautiful women sauntered into the suite.

He stood up, stretched. "Think I'll go to bed now."

Behind his back Adrian and Nathan exchanged amused glances. Adrian pointed to the room on the left. "Take that bedroom."

He and Nathan would take turns sleeping, since one of them had to be awake when the day sleep knocked me out.

I looked the trio of thralls over with a jaded eye. They were all gorgeous, with lush, fuckable bodies, but none were a sexy, prickly, blue-eyed blonde.

Adrian and Nathan waited for me to make my choice. I held out my hand to the nearest thrall, a dark-haired, brown-skinned woman who was basically Eden's opposite.

When she came to me, I put my hand on the small of her back and guided her out the door. "I'm Talon."

Her lips curved in a practiced smile. "Call me Coral."

I gave her a small smile back. "Coral. That's pretty," I added absently.

"Thank you," she murmured.

She was obviously a pro, which made things easier. I needed fresh blood and a quick fuck to take the edge off.

Back in my suite, I glanced at Eden's door. The compulsion should keep her out until morning, but I amped up my senses for a few seconds just to make sure. Her breathing was slow and even, the sound of a someone deeply asleep.

Coral wrapped herself around me, but I disentangled her fingers from my neck and set her away from me with a shake of my head.

"In my bedroom." I indicated the open door on the other side of the living room.

"Of course." Unperturbed, she strolled through the living room and into my bedroom, where she stepped out of her heels and turned to face me.

She wore a red body-con dress with a plunging neckline that bared her throat. Her lips were glossy, her eyes smoky. "Where do you want me, sir?"

I'd been hard for hours. I needed this release so I could think straight.

But damn if I didn't hesitate, tempted to tell Coral I'd changed my mind. It felt...wrong.

She laid a hand on my chest. I brushed it away. "Take off your dress and bend over the bed."

I sensed her spurt of arousal. She liked being ordered around.

Good. I wasn't in the mood to be polite.

She unzipped the side of the dress and stepped out of it. She wore no bra, and her panties came off along with the dress.

She put her hands on the mattress and eyed me over her shoulder. "Like this, sir?"

"Yes." Stepping closer, I pressed her head down so I couldn't see her face.

Not because she wasn't beautiful. She was.

But she wasn't Eden.

I fed from Coral as we fucked. After, I zipped up my pants and waited as she cleaned up in the bathroom. When she came out, I handed her a couple of large bills.

"A tip," I said and walked her to the door.

As I reached for the doorknob, she moved closer, fingering my bicep. "Next time you're in New York, get in touch. The front desk has my details."

I grunted noncommittally and pulled the door open. Behind us, I heard a click.

My nape tightened. The compulsion I'd put on Eden must've worn off. Coral glanced down the hall, clearly curious.

"Goodbye," I told her.

Eden drew a tiny, pained breath. Her hurt and anger radiated down the hall.

I blocked her.

She knew what I was. I didn't have to explain myself to her.

So why did the tightness spread from my nape to my chest?

Coral was still standing there. I gently but firmly pushed her through the door, closing it behind her.

Eden's door was shut again. There wasn't a lock or she probably would've turned it.

I stopped in the hall outside her room. I could hear her breathing on the other side of thick wood. I grasped the handle, then released it.

"Get some sleep," I growled and continued to my own room.

5

EDEN

It was quiet. Too quiet. No barking dogs, no car doors slamming, no people calling to one another. No M Train rumbling by.

My eyes popped open. For a panicked moment, I didn't know where I was. How had I ended up in this swanky bedroom with deep gray walls and lacquer furniture?

Heart pounding, I sat up and frowned at the silver wolves embroidered on the velvet coverlet tucked around my legs.

Kral Syndicate wolves.

Everything came rushing back: Talon in my apartment last night, grim and authoritative.

Talon and his soldiers bundling me and Rio into an SUV and bringing us to a Kral hotel.

Talon with his hand on my abdomen, claiming the baby. Claiming me.

And my traitorous body softening, leaning into his. Craving him even when my heart knew he was bad for me...

Then as soon as I fell asleep, he'd fucked another woman.

Pain ripped through me, a tearing ache almost too big for my chest to contain. I moaned and rocked back and forth on the mattress, hugging myself.

Stupid, stupid girl.

Why hadn't I kept moving every few weeks? Made it harder for him to find me?

But I'd been so tired of running, and the job at BVE had been perfect for me. The owner had taken me under her wing, teaching me the vintage clothing business from the ground up.

And there was the baby to consider. I couldn't keep moving from place to place. I required medical care and a safe place to bring my child back to after they were born.

I needed a home. *We* needed a home.

Then one morning, Rio had sauntered into BVE to sell some of his clothes, and I'd read his desperation on his face, his eyes hostile with knowledge no teenager should have. He'd dragged the clothes from a tattered backpack and piled them on the counter. "How much?" he'd asked.

Our eyes had met and I'd *known* those clothes were the last thing he had to sell. Unfortunately, they weren't vintage, just ordinary, off-the-rack T-shirts and a pair of jeans. They'd bring him a few dollars at most.

I'd pushed the small pile back across the counter and invited him to have lunch instead—and we'd clicked. That was the only way to describe it. Two desperate, lonely people. Neither of us trusted easily, but something made me take a chance, ask if he wanted to share my apartment.

Rio said no, of course. The idiot was too proud to take charity. That's when I'd made that deal with him, a deal that benefitted us both, although I told him he'd be doing me a favor.

So I'd stayed in Brooklyn for Rio, too. Because he needed me, even though he believed it was the other way around.

A rapid fluttering, butterfly-light against the inside of my abdomen made me still. A fierce love welled up in me, pressing hotly against my throat.

I covered my uterus with my palm.

This was what was important. Not me. The baby.

I'd die to keep this tiny being safe.

"You'll be okay," I said aloud. "I swear you will. It's me they're mad at. Me who fucked up."

Another flutter, this one harder, like the kid was saying, *Yeah, yeah. Now get moving and feed me already.*

My mouth twitched in spite of myself. The kid was definitely half-vampire—already demanding as fuck. Although I wasn't exactly bashful and retiring myself.

"Good morning to you, too," I said and climbed out of bed.

Twenty minutes later I was showered and dressed. I left the bedroom, hunting for breakfast. The door on the opposite side of the living room (which I assumed was Talon's bedroom) was shut, but a cart next to the wet bar held a trio of covered plates with enough food for two or three pregnant women—scrambled eggs, hash browns, buttered toast, pastries, a bowl of fat red strawberries, a small bottle of cream, coffee, orange juice.

I ignored the coffee and poured myself a glass of juice. Normally, I was a coffee drinker, but these days, I could barely stand to smell it. The orange juice was as good as it looked, tart but sweet and refreshing. I carried the glass with me to the closed bedroom door and gave the handle an experimental wiggle.

The door was locked. Of course, it was.

Talon wouldn't trust me to walk in on him when he was deep in the day sleep, even if I was still an ordinary thrall, not a prisoner. That was standard Maritime Syndicate procedure.

Today, though, it bothered me—a symbol that Talon had all the power. He could've locked me into my own bedroom and no one would've stopped him. I suppose I should be grateful that I had the freedom of the suite, but I wasn't.

I felt angry. Trapped.

I was three years younger than my sister Freya, but I'd always been the together sister, the one with the plan: Finish high school and apply to be a syndicate thrall. Put in my time, then take the money and travel. Somewhere along the way, I'd started dreaming of opening my own vintage clothing store. Then I'd expand into styling outfits for actors and artists or even rich vampires.

Well, I had no plan now but to somehow make this better so the baby wouldn't suffer for what I'd done.

On cue, I felt another sharp kick.

I filled my lungs and slowly released the air. "Okay, okay. I know you're hungry."

I piled food on a plate and took it to a small round table along with my orange juice. When I'd eaten my fill, I tried the outer door. It was locked. I swore under my breath and smacked a palm against the silver-reinforced wood, that trapped, angry feeling returning.

To my shock, the lock clicked. I jolted and stepped back as Nathan opened the door, Rio bobbing behind his shoulder, trying to get a look at me.

I brushed past Nathan to fling my arms around my friend. "You're okay?"

"Yeah, no worries." He squeezed me back. "And guess what? I'm coming with you. They're giving me a contract and everything."

"A contract?" I released him. "But Talon said that you were only coming as far as the airport. That as soon as I got on the jet, he'd let you go free."

"Change of plans. Talon hired me as his PA." Rio bounced on his heels in excitement. "For now, I'm going to be your personal chef and companion. Sick, huh?"

"Oh." My heart dipped. The last thing I'd wanted was to drag Rio into the world of vampire syndicates. I glanced at Nathan for confirmation.

"It's true," he said, unsmiling. "The contract's already been signed."

"Hey, it's okay." Rio gave me a meaningful look. "I want to come."

I lowered my voice, although Nathan could probably hear me anyway. "If this is about me, then don't. I'll be okay."

"It is and it isn't. By the time the year's up, I'll have enough to pay for the first year of culinary school."

"Oh." I had to admit it was nice seeing Rio so pumped about something, and he could certainly use the money. "You sure?"

"Yes." His head dipped in a decisive nod. "Now stop worrying, Mom."

Nathan shifted impatiently on his feet. "Where's your coat? I'm here to take you two out."

"For a walk?" I'd assumed they wouldn't let me leave the hotel today.

"And shopping."

"Shopping?"

"For clothes." The expression on Nathan's square face was hilarious, like he'd rather chew off his own foot than go clothes shopping. "Because..." He gestured at my pregnant belly.

"For maternity clothes?" I clarified, straight-faced. "Because, you know, I can't button my jeans anymore? I'll need panties, too. And nursing bras..."

Rio choked. "Hell, Eden. TMI, okay?"

Nathan's mouth thinned. "Just get your damn coat."

I rolled my lips in, suppressing a smile. "Yes, sir."

We took an elevator to the lobby. As I followed Rio out of the elevator, Nathan grabbed my upper arm.

"Behave, understand?" he said in my ear. "You run now and you won't like what Talon will do to you."

"Let me go." I tried to shake him off, but his fingers tightened painfully.

"I know what you did," he said, low-voiced. "You're lucky Talon doesn't drag you back home in chains. Smart, to get pregnant so he can't just off you."

I drew myself up to my full height. "Go fuck yourself."

Rio was halfway across the lobby. He turned and started back to us, frowning.

"I won't chase you." Nathan nodded at Rio. "I'll go after the kid—and nothing says I have to leave him alive."

My look of loathing should've fried him where he stood. "I'm not going to run, asshole. I mean, look at me. How far do you think I would get?"

I meant it. I was through running.

Even if I could escape Talon a second time—which was about as likely as me sprouting wings and soaring over the Empire State Building—I couldn't live like this any longer. Looking over my shoulder. Wondering if this would be the day they'd catch me. Last night had been the best sleep I'd had in weeks.

Dr. Lopez was right. I needed to take better care of myself, not just for my sake, but for the baby's, and that included a home and regular medical care.

For now, my best option—okay, my *only* option—was to return with Talon to Lilith Island and hope for the best.

"Just so we understand each other," Nathan said, releasing me.

Rio was almost upon us now. "What's up?"

His gaze moved between me and Nathan, a tiny groove between his brows.

"Nothing." I conjured up a *nothing to see here* smile and grabbed his hand. "Let's go spend some money."

$\approx$ 6 $\approx$

TALON

When I emerged from my bedroom that evening, Eden was kicked back on the living room couch, a silky black sweater slipping off her shoulder, watching Japanese anime on the big-screen TV mounted in a lacquer cabinet.

"Hey." She turned off the TV and straightened, a smile pinned to her face.

She appeared relaxed, but I knew this woman. I saw the tension tightening the corners of her eyes, *felt* her apprehension—and knowing I was the source made me want to break something.

I'd wanted Eden back. Hell, I'd visualized her punishment in detail, starting with spanking that round ass of hers red. But now that she was here, completely in my power, I found myself at a loss. This wasn't *my* Eden—a little sassy, a little jokey. Easy-going but not taking shit from anyone, including me.

That didn't mean I wasn't still angry at her, which left me confused and irritable.

I stopped a few feet from the couch. "Hey," I said stiffly. "You get out today?"

"I did, yes. Nathan took me shopping." She tipped her head at a trio of sleek gray bags next to the couch. "He said you told him to buy me some maternity clothes. We found a secondhand shop with some really pretty things."

A perplexed line formed between my brows. "You didn't want new clothes?"

She shook her head. "These are fine. It was an upscale shop. The clothes were like new, and trust me, they weren't cheap."

She said that like I cared how much she spent. "I can afford it. But I wanted you to have new—"

"I'm good," she insisted. "I did buy new underwear." A corner of her mouth hitched up. "I draw the line at used panties."

And there was my Eden. A hint of her, anyway.

My anger melted around the edges, like her smile was heat applied to the iceberg in my chest. "I fucking hope so," I returned gruffly. "Are you ready?"

"Yes." She rubbed her hands down her thighs. "But...don't make Rio come. Please?"

"I'm not making Rio do anything. He wants to come. We'll pay him triple what he was making bussing tables."

She hunched her shoulders. "I wanted to help him, you know. Not drag him into this."

I hardened my heart against her forlorn expression. Maybe I was using Rio to ensure her good behavior, but I was paying the guy, wasn't I? I could've just kidnapped him. It's not like anyone would notice he was missing.

"He signed a standard service contract. He'll be your companion and personal cook, not a thrall. If he works out, I can use him part-time as my PA, too. As soon as the contract is up, he can leave, or sign another contract. His choice."

"Yeah?" Her eyes moved between mine like she was trying to see into my brain. "I guess that's all right, then."

"Not that it's your business," I added. "Just so we're clear—he's under contract to me. Which means, he answers to me—not you. Now, let's go. Where are your boots?"

She'd gone stiff at my mini-lecture. "I can get them myself," she said, starting to rise. "I'm not that big yet."

"Sit," I said between my teeth. "Sweet Lilith, do you have to fight me about every little thing?"

She sank back down. "Sorry," she said, her glare making it clear she was anything but.

The boots were a soft, slouchy leather. I slipped the first one on and ran a palm beneath her wide-legged pants, caressing her calf.

She sipped a breath. Our gazes snagged. Her pupils were big and dark.

My heart gave a single hard thump. It seemed like a year since I'd last touched her, not a couple of months.

A decade since I'd drawn a lungful of her sweet Eden-scent.

And a fucking century since I'd had her beneath me, crying out my name, begging for more.

She might not like me much right now, but she still wanted me. It was etched on her face, visible in her heavy-lidded eyes.

Gods, I wished we weren't on a schedule. But the primitive part of me itched to get her and my spawn safely back in my own territory.

She dragged her teeth over her lower lip. "Talon?"

"Mm?" I stroked the warm, firm muscles beneath my fingers, my gaze on that soft pink lip she was mauling.

"What do you want from me?"

You. Coming with me willingly. Accepting my blood bond because that's what you want, too.

Now where in Hades had that come from?

Frowning inwardly, I shoved the thought down deep where I wouldn't have to think about it and skated my fingers down to where her calf narrowed above her ankle, chaining it between my thumb and fingers.

"After you fell asleep last night," I said, "I called Brien."

Her leg muscles tautened. "And?"

"He said to make sure you understand this is your last chance."

She nodded rapidly. "I do. And I appreciate that you're giving me a second chance. I promise I won't mess it up."

"I hope not." I released her calf. "There's something you don't know—Brien and Twilight mated. She's his prima now."

"His...mate?"

I nodded. "And his prima. It's official—he wanted it that way."

Her mouth moved in a soundless, "Oh, no."

"Yeah." I amped up the pressure. "Brien's letting me take the lead on this, but I don't know how far his goodwill will extend. Then there's the fact that you're pregnant with my spawn..."

Her hands fisted on her thighs. "And—?"

I moved in for the kill. "You're going to accept my blood bond. Tonight—before we return to the island. It's the only way I can protect you both. You'll answer to me, not Brien or Twilight."

She recoiled like I'd slapped her. Not the response I was looking for, and I had to admit, it pricked my temper.

"I thought that a blood bond can't be forced on a thrall," she said. "That it was my choice."

My back teeth set. "Most thralls don't spy on the syndicate that employs them and expect to live."

"How is this giving me a choice?"

"You do have a choice. But think." I aimed a pointed look at her abdomen. "Do you want to return to Lilith Island under my protection—or not?"

She went white around the lips. "You think Brien would hurt the baby?"

I hesitated, tempted to lie if it got her to agree. But that wasn't fair to Brien.

"No," I admitted. "The child is my spawn—I've made that clear. Brien will welcome them into the syndicate. But after they're born, I can't make any guarantees where you're concerned. My spawn belongs to the syndicate now. But you—?"

I let the implications hang there. Eden was smart; she'd understand. After she gave birth, she'd be expendable. Brien would be justified in locking her in the cell for the next decade...or even expelling her from Maritime Syndicate Territory. Some primuses would even make sure she suffered an "accident."

"He wouldn't," she said hoarsely.

"D'you want to chance it?" I was being the worst sort of bastard, threatening a pregnant woman, but fuck ethics. Being nice had gotten me fuck-all with Eden.

Her throat muscles worked. She glanced at her fisted hands, and then back at me. "Why do you want this so bad? What do *you* get?"

Did she really not know? "You, Eden. I get you."

Pain ghosted across her fine-boned features. Her mouth twisted. "You know I saw you last night with that woman."

I lifted a brow. "And?"

Eden was a thrall. A warm body, one the syndicate had bought and paid for. She knew better than to expect me to be faithful.

"So is that how it's going to be if I accepted your blood bond? You get to fuck anyone, but I only get you?"

I considered her. I'd regretted putting my dick into Coral almost as soon as I'd removed the condom. I wasn't making Eden any promises. Hell, she was lucky I hadn't made her watch. However...

"I need to feed from other thralls. You know that. But you don't want me to fuck anyone else?" Catching her chin in my hand, I rubbed my thumb over her lower lip. "Then you know what to do."

She drew a slow inhale. Her body inclined subtly toward mine.

"Say yes," I coaxed.

Her eyes squeezed shut. "I—I need to think."

I sat back on my haunches, baffled. "You want me. And you want your baby safe, don't you?"

The gaze she sent me was pure blue fire. "Of course I do."

"Then what's the problem?"

She pressed the heels of her hands to her eyes. "The problem is it's my *life*—and the baby's. So I just don't *know*."

The hell with this. I'd all but promised to be exclusive with her. For an unmated vampire that was a major commitment. Before we returned to Lilith Island, I wanted her under my protection.

I shoved her foot into the second boot and stood up.

"I already told Brien you accepted my blood bond. It was the only way. A blood-bonded thrall belongs to her master, not the syndicate. If you want to tell him I lied, that's up to you. So." I held out my hand. "What's your answer? Yes or no?"

She looked from my hand to my face. Her chest rose and fell in a quick, tight inhale. The silence stretched until I actually wondered if she'd refuse—and then what would I do?

But she took it. "All right. Yes."

Thank fuck. Relief shuddered through me, shocking in its strength.

"Now." I drew her to her feet, then released her to text my companions. "Adrian and Nathan can be our witnesses."

While we waited, I retrieved the bracelet from my bedroom and slipped it into my pocket. When I returned, Eden was still standing next to the couch. When she saw me, she ran her fingers through her hair and squared her shoulders.

The two dhampirs arrived, Rio in tow. They must've put the fear of God into him because he didn't challenge me, just pulled Eden into a hug while giving me the side eye over her shoulder.

"Just remember, I got your back," he said, not even trying to lower his voice.

"It's okay." She squeezed him back. "I...want to do this."

It wasn't a lie—her words tasted of truth—but that hesitation said a lot.

I pressed my lips together and extricated her from Rio.

And there in the opulent but impersonal suite of a Kral Syndicate hotel, we spoke the words that bound her permanently to me.

I went first, offering her my protection in return for the bond. Then it was Eden's turn.

"I accept your blood bond, Talon of the Maritime Syndicate," she said, her voice low and a little shaky, "and bind myself to you in return. To be yours, and yours only, for the rest—" she stumbled over the words—"for the rest of my life."

I took out the gold cuff and, pushing up her sweater sleeve, snapped it around her left wrist. It was inlaid with lapis lazuli, five asymmetric pieces the same saturated blue of her eyes.

She fingered it, then glanced up at me, leaking sadness. "It's...pretty."

I gave her a hard kiss, then picked up her suede jacket and held it out for her. She tried to take it from me, but I shook my head at her.

"I'll do it," I said, emphasizing that her independence was something I could grant—or take away—at will.

She understood. She turned and allowed me to help her with it.

When the jacket was on, I remained behind her, my hands on her shoulders, and pressed a kiss to the sensitive spot below her ear. A quiver ran over her.

"Mine," I whispered and closed my teeth around the cord of her neck—not hard, but enough to leave a faint red mark. I wanted her to feel my teeth on her all the way to Lilith Island.

❦

Eden slept for most of the two-hour flight. I eased her out of her seat and onto my lap. She woke up enough to give me a startled blue-eyed look, before curling into me with an incoherent murmur.

I gathered her closer and brushed my lips over her silky temple, taking advantage of the fact that she was too sleepy to fight me.

Rio had roped Adrian and Nathan into playing poker with him. They were gathered around a round table at the other end of the cabin, and from what I could hear Rio was winning. The kid was smart. Bringing him with us had been the right move. For now, I wanted him where I could see him, not making trouble back in New York.

Besides, I remembered what it was to be young and fighting to survive. Not that I was Mother Teresa or anything—I expected Rio to work hard and keep his nose clean—but by the end of his contract, he'd have a nice chunk of cash.

Eden's breath sighed out. She went boneless, deeply asleep.

I slipped a hand beneath her sweater and widened my fingers, taking in the size of her uterus, which extended from the tip of my thumb to my littlest finger. The surface rippled beneath my palm.

An overwhelming protectiveness hijacked my brain. I swallowed over what felt like a pack of razor blades.

A new being was growing in there, a spawn of my bloodline. For a young vampire like me, that was almost unheard of. We often went a century or more before siring our first offspring.

It shouldn't have happened. We'd been careful. No condom, but like all thralls, Eden had received a yearly birth control shot.

I'd thought I didn't want a spawn with human blood, but now I didn't know what to think. I skated my palm over Eden's abdomen, learning the new shape of it. Trying to wrap my mind around the idea that I—we—were going to have a child.

The flight attendant appeared, asking us to buckle up for the descent. Reluctantly, I eased Eden back into her own seat. She woke up, yawning and rubbing her eyes, looking barely older than a teenager herself.

I felt a clench of guilt. But the choice to have the baby was hers; I hadn't forced her into it.

But you did use it to your advantage, my conscience pointed out.

For her own good, I returned.

But was it?

I told my conscience to take a hike and focused on Eden, securing the seatbelt beneath her belly as the attendant had directed.

"Here." I uncapped a bottle of water and handed it to her. "Lopez said you need to drink plenty of fluids."

"Thank you," she said, so politely it set my teeth on edge, and took a drink.

"We're landing in a few minutes," I told her.

Eden slid the bottle into a cupholder and straightened her spine, her predominant emotion resignation. You'd think I was bringing her back for her execution, when instead, I'd bonded her to a syndicate lieutenant.

Still, I supposed it was for the best. I couldn't have her fighting me at every turn—I'd lose face within the syndicate. Vampires didn't respect a man who couldn't control his woman, especially a blood-bonded thrall.

The hierarchy was still in a state of flux after all the changes in the past few months. I'd been a lieutenant less than three months; if someone was planning to challenge me, now would be the time.

"So," said Eden. Her fingers went to her bracelet, toying with the clasp.

I lifted a brow. "I'm the only one who can remove it."

She released the clasp. "I know."

"I won't," I added. "In case you're wondering."

Her shoulder hitched in a jerky little move. "Whatever."

Now what the hell did that mean? But I let it drop. I'd pushed her enough for one night.

Adrian and Nathan retook their seats a little behind us, with Rio in between them. Her gaze flicked in their direction. "How many people know about me, anyway? You said Brien didn't tell anyone."

I lowered my voice so the others wouldn't hear over the vibration of the engines. "All they know is that you ran out on your contract. That's all anyone knows."

She leaned closer, speaking in an undertone as well. "You're wrong. Nathan knows. And if he knows, so does Adrian."

I frowned. "Nathan said something?"

"He just wanted me to know that you were treating me better than I deserved."

Fuck. "I'll talk to him."

"No, don't. He'll know I told you and it will only make things worse."

"It's not his place to reprimand you."

She shook her head and changed the subject. "And the man who made me do it in the first place? What happened to him?"

"Kuro? He's in his final grave."

She stared at me. "For real?"

"Yeah. It happened the night you left."

Her breath leaked out. "Thank God. I... Thank God."

That answered one question. She hadn't planned on taking up where she'd left off; her relief was obvious.

Then I replayed the rest of what she'd said. "What do you mean he made you do it?"

She scraped at the water bottle's label with her thumbnail. "I'm not trying to excuse myself. I took his money to pass a note to Twilight—that was on me. But then he had me." She squeezed her eyes shut. "I was so stupid. He said if I didn't do exactly what he said, then he'd go to the primus and tell him I was a double agent. I'd have been fucked. Maybe even dead. So—"

The hairs on my nape lifted. The former primus, Jules Leclerc, had been going blood-mad. He'd already killed one thrall, maybe more.

Eden was right. If they'd turned her over to him, she'd probably be dead now.

"How did you find out about Kuro, anyway?" she asked.

"He was actually Eugene Smith. Matthew's spawn."

"Seriously? I had no idea."

"Yeah. *He* was the double agent. The bastard was on the Slayers, Inc. Board of Directors. And his sire knew—was behind it, actually." Which was why Matthew Smith was also in his final grave.

"So Matthew's also—?"

"Yeah," I told her.

"Huh." She sat back. "Kuro didn't look anything like Eugene."

"A glamour."

"But he didn't even sound like Eugene. Not that I knew Kuro that well—he mainly communicated with me through notes." She rubbed her upper arms. "Whatever. I'm just glad he's gone. I thought I'd never be free of him. He would've come after me."

Ice sheeted my spine. If Eugene had somehow escaped, what would he have done to Eden?

"He's the one who got you a new ID?" I asked.

"Yeah. I threw it away after I crossed into the States. The store was paying me under the table, but they couldn't do that forever. Sooner or later I would've had to get a new one. I was asking around, actually." She shot me a look. "But why would Brien keep what I did a secret? I mean, no one knew I was carrying your spawn."

"Feeling generous, I guess."

Actually, I suspected Brien had done it for me, not her. He'd wanted to leave my options open.

Moving closer, I curved my fingers lightly around her throat. The pulse at the base of her neck hitched.

I skated my tongue around the shell of her ear, enjoying her shiver of arousal. "That doesn't mean you're off the hook."

She swallowed and squeezed her thighs together.

Gods, I'd missed this. I fucking loved how easily she got hot for me.

"What d'you mean?" she asked thickly.

"It means I'm still deciding what your punishment will be."

✣ 7 ✣

EDEN

Talon settled back into his seat, watching me from beneath thick dark lashes. His words bounced around in my brain, menace wrapped in silk.

The small jet banked right over the coast of Nova Scotia. Lilith Island came into view, a chunk of black basalt coughed up by a long-ago volcano. My family had lived here for generations, pirates who'd staked a claim back when the French and British were still fighting over Canada. The First Nations people had known about Lilith Island and its neighboring islands, of course, but nobody except the pirates had been willing to cross miles of rough, shark-infested seas to settle them.

To Jules Leclerc, Brien's father and the first Maritime primus, the island's isolation had been ideal. He'd struck a deal with the pirates—sell Lilith Island to him and they and their descendants could live on the land rent-free. My ancestors' stolen treasure had been plowed into legit businesses like farms, fishing boats and shops, while the Maritime Syndicate grew into a powerful conglomerate with its fingers in pies across Eastern Canada.

And Talon was one of their two top men, answerable only to the primus.

I'm still deciding what your punishment will be.

The way his voice had dropped lower... That touch of his tongue to my ear...

I squirmed on my seat, a tiny bit afraid and a whole lot aroused.

Of the three friends—Brien, Talon and Cain—people said Talon was the laidback one. I knew better. With him, like with the ocean, you only saw the surface of something dark and deep and dangerous. Running from him had been a huge miscalculation. I'd triggered his alpha instincts. He would've never stopped hunting until he'd found me.

And now, I was blood-bonded to him. My thumb worried at a piece of lapis lazuli in the gold cuff encircling my wrist. A part of me was thrilled, the part that had missed Talon every single day I'd been gone. Which was messed up, but there it was.

Sensible Eden, though, had thrown up her hands, yelling, "What the hell, girl? He *owns* you now." That cage door wasn't just shut, it had been padlocked and reinforced with heavy chains.

He'd known just how to work me, too. I would've crawled naked through broken glass to keep my child. It was why I'd run. I'd been so afraid they'd punish me by taking the baby.

You did what you had to.

My mom's voice again.

But that practical tone centered me, reminding me that this wasn't about me, it was about the baby.

The jet dropped lower. It was long after midnight and the island was cloaked in darkness except for a few scattered lights in the windows of Castle Leclerc.

Two months ago, dragging me back to Lilith Island would have been a punishment in itself. Now I put a hand on the window, straining to catch a glimpse of Bluebeard's Cove and the street where my parents lived, but the thick forest between the castle and the town blocked everything except the light burning in the church tower.

Guilt compressed my chest. Mom and Dad must've been going out of their minds wondering if I was all right.

On the ferry to Halifax, I'd dropped my phone into the Atlantic so it couldn't be used to track me. The next day, I'd bought a burner phone and texted my parents to tell them I'd left the island and would be out of touch for a while. When they'd called back, I'd blocked their numbers, and the same with my sister Freya.

"It's not New York." Talon spoke in my ear. When I turned to look at him, his jaw was rigid. "I would've taken you there, you know. All you had to do was ask."

"It wouldn't have been the same."

"Yeah. You wouldn't have been shoehorned into a tiny apartment with no elevator. You'd have been in a big suite in a nice hotel, wearing pretty clothes and eating food you didn't have to buy yourself and carry up four fucking floors after working a long shift."

I shook my head. "It wasn't like that."

"Then how was it?"

"You wouldn't understand."

His mouth compressed. "Try me."

"I needed to do something myself. Make it by myself."

"And how did that go?"

Pride made me lift my chin. "Great. Wonderful. I'd still be there if it wasn't for you."

Actually, I hated it. I missed you. I missed my mom and dad. I was so homesick I spent most of my free time watching Nova Scotia travel vlogs.

The city was too noisy, too busy, too dirty, too...everything.

I'd wanted so bad to call my mom or dad or even Freya. But I couldn't do that to them, couldn't put them in the position of having to lie to the syndicate.

Talon narrowed his eyes, no doubt sensing the lie. Tough shit. He might own my body, but he didn't own my thoughts.

I turned my face toward the window.

"Look at me," he growled.

I did, taking my time about it.

His fingers curved around my throat. Not hard, just showing me who was in charge.

My nipples tightened and a shiver went over me.

The man exerted some kind of sexy black magic on me. More than the usual vampire magic pheromones, I mean. Or maybe it was just that I knew how good he could make me feel.

His nostrils flared in a slight inhale. He knew exactly how he affected me—you can't hide that sort of thing from a vampire.

Still with that light grip on my throat, he rubbed his lips over mine, his thumb caressing the sensitive skin over my pulse.

My insides heated. It was like a pinball zinged from my mouth to my breasts to my sex and back again, setting off flashing lights and ringing bells all along its path.

My lips parted, and his tongue swept inside, deepening the kiss until I was dazed with lust.

Talon released me. I touched my tongue to my lips, shaken.

His sensual mouth curved in an arrogant smile. "I wouldn't fight me if I were you. You won't win."

Fortunately, the jet touched down at that moment, saving me from responding, so I settled for a glare. I wasn't sure what I would've said anyway.

I want you but I also hate you for making me want you?

I love you but I can't tell you because holding it in is better than seeing that smile morph to pity.

God, I was pathetic.

The pilot cut the engines, and Talon unbuckled my seatbelt and pulled me to my feet. "Let's go."

❧

The foyer of Leclerc Castle had been built to impress, but in a tasteful way, like a museum or a cathedral. A temple to the Maritime Syndicate's wealth and power.

As Rio and I followed Talon and the soldiers inside, sea-serpent sconces, their metal teeth clamped around frosted glass pearls, glowed to life, illuminating the French tapestries hanging on the rough stone walls.

"Holy shit." Rio hitched up his backpack. His gaze traveled from the tapestries to the arched ceiling, where a bright crescent moon shimmered in a star-drenched sky.

"My mom says it was painted by a vampire artist," I told him. "She says it's how they see the night sky."

"Wow." He spun in a slow circle, awe on his sharp-boned face.

My gaze was drawn to Talon, who'd turned aside to talk to Adrian and Nathan.

He looked so in control. So darkly handsome. So out of my league.

I recalled what else my mom had said. "They may look human, but they're not. They see things we don't, hear sounds we can't. To them, we're pets. They take care of us, they may even feel affection for us, but we're still pets. Don't ever forget that."

A former thrall, she knew what she was talking about.

Too late, Mom. I did forget. I fell in love with a vampire and now I'm fucked.

Rio eyed the curved mosaic of a great white shark that bisected the marbled granite floor. "This is something. It's an actual freaking castle."

I grinned despite my tangled emotions. "They didn't tell you?"

"Nathan said something like that, but I didn't figure it for a real, live castle. I thought it'd be more like one of those big-assed, Real Housewives of Whatever mansions. The outside is so Goth—all that black stone. I mean, who lives like this?"

"Vampires," I said.

"Right."

We exchanged wry looks.

"So." He hitched up his backpack. "Where are we staying?"

"*You'll* be upstairs," I told him. "That's where the humans who work at the castle live—the second and third floor. Everyone except the thralls."

"So where will you be?"

"The vampires live below ground. That's where the thralls stay."

His brow lowered. "I thought I'd be with you."

"You can't. You're not a thrall. But it's okay. I'll be fine."

"Fuck that." His fingers tightened on the straps of the backpack. "What if you need me?"

I briefly closed my eyes. "Look, just go with it all right? Don't cause trouble for me."

His chest lifted. Fell. Then he gave a reluctant nod. "Fine. But I don't like it."

"I know, but it's better this way."

He grunted. "I can't believe you were a thrall."

"For two-and-a-half years. It's just what you do if you grow up here," I added, aware off-islanders didn't always understand us. "Or a lot of us, anyway. There's no pressure—it's up to us. But you can make triple what you can make doing anything else. And the sex is—well..." I shook my head, my gaze tracking to Talon again.

"Huh." Rio jerked his chin in Talon's direction. "The baby's his, isn't it? That's why he's gone all caveman on you."

"She's carrying my spawn, yes." Talon turned back to us as Adrian and Nathan left the foyer.

He placed his hand on the small of my back, this time under my sweater, his fingers splayed possessively over my exposed skin. I stiffened as my screwed-up, uncertain emotions reared up again.

But Talon must've thought I was fighting him because his fingers flexed on my back. "Come," he bit out. "Rio, you go with Kerry. She'll show you to your room."

The castle's tall, grim housekeeper had materialized from somewhere. Heck, maybe she'd been hanging upside down in a closet. If I hadn't known for a fact that Kerry was human, I would've sworn she was a dhampir—the woman had a creepy gift for finding the darkest part of any room.

Rio planted his feet. "I'll see you in the morning," he told me as Talon propelled me across the foyer.

I sent the teenager a reassuring smile over my shoulder. "In the morning," I mouthed.

He nodded, his lips in an unhappy line.

Talon ushered me through the heavy door to the syndicate's lair and closed it, leaving me alone with him on the dimly lit landing. A flickering gas torch painted one side of his face gold, leaving the other side in shadows.

He'd never looked so much like a vampire.

Stern. Remote. My judge and jury.

My throat felt like I'd gulped down a dry, cactus-filled desert. "What?" I croaked.

Why had I stiffened when he touched me? It's not like I didn't like it. I was...conflicted. But Talon was interpreting it as resistance, maybe even dislike.

"Your punishment starts now, Eden. You're not under contract anymore. You're a prisoner."

Okay, that didn't sound like a sexy punishment.

I forced some steel into my spine. Vampires respected strength. He might be able to sense my fear, but I was damned if I let him see it.

"I know I messed up. I'm sorry. Spying on Twilight was wrong, and I apologize."

His expression didn't soften. "Apology noted. But it's not enough."

"I understand." I grimaced, feeling bruised inside, even though it was my own fault. I'd lost Talon's trust, and I wasn't sure how to gain it back. Or if I even could. "I didn't think it would be. I just needed to tell you."

"Follow me." He started down the narrow flagstone steps that led to the Leclerc lair, two flights below.

Since signing my thrall contract, I must've descended these steps a few thousand times. But never like this, my chest tight, my stomach a mass of knots.

I'd never seen the dungeon, but I knew it existed, a level below the main lair.

He won't lock you in a cell. He bought you new clothes, brought Rio along to keep you company. And there's the baby.

Still, I wasn't a hundred percent sure.

We came out on the lair's main floor and wound our way through its torchlit tunnels. Talon passed the turnoff to the thralls' section where my old apartment had been located. So I wasn't going to be with the other thralls. On the plus side, we hadn't turned toward the passage that led down to the dungeon.

He unlocked the door to the garden suite, and I followed him into the pretty one-bedroom apartment. When Brien had first brought Twilight to the island, he'd moved her into the garden suite. All the thralls had known that meant she was different.

I took in the sea-green walls and warm tropical-wood furniture. "This is where you're putting me?"

It was way better than I'd expected. There was even an enclosed garden attached to the suite, accessed through a French door at the other end of the living room.

And Talon's apartment was right around the corner.

"Yes. Cain thinks you should be thrown in a cell for the next decade, but Brien said it's up to me."

I flashed him a relieved smile. "Thank you."

A shrug. "Don't thank me. You need fresh air and sunlight...for the child."

My stomach twisted with hurt. Of course, he was doing this for the baby, not me. He wanted to keep his spawn's mother healthy.

He frowned at me, no doubt sensing my pain, but all he said was, "For now, you're confined to these rooms and the garden outside except for a daily walk, where you'll be accompanied by a guard."

"I see. That's...fair."

"Your bags should be here soon. I can tell Kerry to have your old clothes transferred to this suite but—" His gaze flicked to my abdomen.

"They probably won't fit much longer," I agreed. "But I could use my runners and things like sweaters and sleepshirts. If you let me into my old apartment, I can get them."

"No trips outside this suite," he reminded me. "Except for your daily walk. I'll have a maid pack up your room and bring your stuff here."

"Okay. Sure." I massaged the bridge of my nose. God, I was tired.

He nodded at the bedroom. "You're asleep on your feet. I'll see you later."

I peered at him. Was his tone softer, less cold?

Then he added, "And Eden? Don't fuck up, okay? Or even my blood bond won't protect you."

I grimaced wearily. "Got it."

8

TALON

"You're back." Cain emerged from his office dressed in a white button-down shirt and black pants. It was like a uniform for the guy.

After leaving Eden, I'd come straight to the war room to check in with him and Brien. "We arrived about half an hour ago," I said, automatically lifting my hand.

We bumped fists, a leftover ritual from when we'd been two neglected, half-feral ten-year-olds united in our anger against the world. Habit kept us doing it even now, nearly thirty years later.

"You have any trouble in New York?" he asked.

I slanted a look at Diane, the wiry, black-haired dhampir monitoring the video feed nearby. "Nothing unusual."

"Let's take this into my office," Cain said, following my gaze.

I nodded and led the way. "Brien's not around?" I asked as we passed the primus's office.

"He's with Twilight." Cain closed the door behind us, his hard mouth edging up in a half-smile. "You know."

"Ah." We exchanged he's-a-newly-mated-man-so-what-d'you-expect smirks.

Cain leaned a hip against the edge of his glossy black desk. Whenever possible he stayed on his feet, another remnant of when we were kids. If he kept moving, his abusive SOB of an uncle couldn't catch him.

"So you knocked up Eden," he said.

"I did."

Cain pressed his lips together. "What about that promise we made each other?"

I met his glare with one of my own. "Things happen."

He scraped a hand over his short blond hair. It fell back into place, every strand perfectly aligned. That was Cain—precise, controlled, polished—from the buttoned-up collar of his crisp cotton shirt to the hem of his perfectly pressed pants. "You sure it's yours?"

Anger flared in me. First Brien, now Cain.

"Yes," I said shortly.

"You'll have her tested anyway." Cain's office was too small to pace in. Instead, he put his hands on his desk on either side of him, jiggling his right leg.

"A paternity test? No. The spawn's mine. She told me straight out. She was telling the truth—there were no ambiguities or half-lies."

For me, lies came entwined with curlicues and embellishments, and even a half-lie had an oily twist to it. A troubling vibration in my gut.

"You're trusting that—?" Cain halted mid-sentence, and I realized my fangs had elongated.

"She's the mother of my spawn," I gritted out. "And before you say anything else, she accepted my blood bond. Adrian and Nathan witnessed it."

I waited for him to tell me she was playing me. Hell, maybe he was even right, although I didn't think so. She wanted this baby—that came through loud and clear.

Even if she had some hidden motivation, I could handle her. She was only a human, after all.

"Sorry," muttered Cain.

I took a deep breath. Retracted my fangs. "I believe her, yes. A human has to be trained to lie to us. You know that."

He snorted. "She conned you into thinking she was a fun, party-loving thrall who only wanted to fuck you, didn't she? When all the time she was a greedy you-know-what spying on us for pay."

Uneasiness settled in the pit of my stomach. Cain was forcing me to face my own fears, and I kind of hated him for that.

But damn it, Eden seemed to genuinely want to make things right between us. Her apology had been sincere. She was truly sorry.

I just had to establish a clear boundary and make sure she kept to her side: Vampire and his blood-bonded thrall.

Boundaries were good. They kept things...safe. Unemotional.

They didn't screw with your head.

"You said yourself she didn't do any real damage," I pointed out. "And she wasn't spying on me—she was spying on Twilight."

Cain's leg jiggled faster. "As far as we know," he said under his breath.

"What the fuck's that supposed to mean?"

"That she wasn't spying on you as far as we know."

"She wasn't, okay?" I said, even though I wasn't completely certain myself. "And none of this is your goddamned business."

He stiffened. Even his leg stopped moving.

I'd offended him. I didn't apologize, though, because there are some lines even an old friend didn't cross.

"No?" he retorted. "Her spying put us all in danger."

We glared at each other. I looked away first.

"I'm handling it, okay? Now tell me what's happened since I left." I dropped into a gray leather chair he'd bought at some chichi French store in Montreal. "Any word about Lemaire?"

A high-ranking Quebec City soldier, Lemaire and another vampire named Fleur had helped place Twilight on Lilith Island so she could stake Brien. When the truth had come out, Brien and Twilight had gone after them, taking out Fleur and a couple of other coven members—but not Lemaire. He'd managed to escape in time.

"Hasn't been seen since Brien staked Fleur," Cain told me. "We have intel that he may have fled to France, but I haven't been able to confirm that."

"I'd like to find the motherfucker who tipped him off."

A tight-lipped nod of agreement. "Now that you're back, I'm

putting Adrian on it full-time, just in case Lemaire is thinking about staking Twilight in retaliation."

"Brien amped up security on her?"

"Yeah. But FYI, Twilight doesn't know. Insists she doesn't need it."

"Understood."

We discussed a couple of other current projects, then I started to rise. "If we're done here, I have some work to catch up on."

Cain grunted. A suspiciously vague grunt.

I sank back into my seat. "What?"

"Nothing." His eyes focused on the door behind me. "It's been pretty quiet, actually."

"But?"

Cain adjusted the left cuff of his dress shirt. Then he fiddled with the right.

"It's your father," he said, still without looking at me.

The back of my neck crawled. The last time I'd seen my 'father'—and I used the word loosely because as far as I was concerned, Marco Esposito was my sperm donor and nothing else—had been five years ago in Montreal. Somehow, he'd found out I was in the city with Brien and had talked his way into a vampire speakeasy.

The man could charm anyone; it was his superpower.

Anyway, Esposito had hit me up for ten thousand dollars—a "loan," he called it, even though we both knew I'd never see that cash again. I paid up and told him to get lost. He hadn't, of course. Every six months or so, he sent a request for more through his friends or family on the island—or worse, my mom.

I willed the tension lifting my shoulders to loosen. "He just wants money."

"You shouldn't keep paying him."

"It's worth it if it keeps him away from Lilith Island."

Maybe it wasn't reasonable, but deep down, I was afraid that if he ever moved back, he'd somehow fuck things up for me. I'd come a long way from that angry kid with a deadbeat father and an alcoholic mom, and I wanted to keep it that way.

"Besides," I said, "if I cut him off, he'd only hit my mom up and she'd give it to him."

Even after all these years, she was still in love with the SOB. As for me, I didn't even use his name. The night I'd been made in the syndicate, I'd dropped the Esposito to go by my first name, Talon.

Cain shook his head. "It only encourages him to keep coming to you, his hand out."

"It's my money."

"You should just off the asshole."

I lifted a brow. "Like you should off your uncle?"

Cain's mouth bent down, but he stopped pushing me. "Anyway, while you were in New York, I heard from the PI we hired to keep track of your father. Esposito's in Halifax. The PI thinks he's on his way back to the island. Something about him owing a shitload of money to a loan shark."

I worked my jaw from side to side. "I see."

"Why don't you have Brien ban Esposito from the island? Who cares if the man's family has been on the island for practically forever? He's a leach. Half of his family doesn't even talk to him."

"Two reasons." I held up a finger. "One, the humans are touchy about things like that, and Brien's just ascended to primus. Why piss them off when it's something I can handle?" I raised a second finger. "And two, if we ban him outright, he might sneak onto the island anyway. This way, we can keep an eye on him."

"You forgot number three."

"What?"

"Your mom would come crying to you."

"So?" I met him stare for stare.

He broke first, shaking his head and looking away. We were equal in dominance, but on this, I'd wouldn't back down. Ever.

Cain didn't remember his own mother—she'd died giving birth to him—and he'd lost his dad while still a toddler. His aunt and uncle had been more like prison wardens than parents. It was easy for him to say that as a vampire, I should break my human attachment to my mother.

Maybe my home life had been screwed up, but I'd always known my mom loved me.

"Does Brien know?" I asked.

"No. I figured I'd tell you first."

"Thanks, bro. Don't tell him, all right? Give me a chance to look into it."

The last thing I wanted was to drag Brien into another of my messes, especially with Eden still fresh in his mind.

"This isn't syndicate business," I added when Cain looked like he was going to object. "It's personal."

His knee was jiggling again. "Fine. But I hope it doesn't come back to bite you."

9

EDEN

I wasn't used to late nights anymore. By the time I crawled into the four-poster bed, I was dizzy with tiredness. The mattress was super-comfortable, and the castle's deep silence enfolded me like a familiar pair of arms.

I should've gone right to sleep, but instead, I stared up at the bed's gauzy white canopy, thinking about my parents and wondering when I'd get to see them again.

Dad was a lobsterman, Mom a teacher. They kept early hours. They would've been asleep now for hours in their white clapboard house, the one with blue shutters and a creaky front step and flowers everywhere.

They wouldn't even know I was back on the island unless Talon let me out of the castle, and I had a feeling that wasn't going to happen—not for a while, anyway.

I gave a teary sniff, missing them so bad. It was hard, knowing they were just a few miles away but I couldn't see them.

Suck it up, buttercup. You did this to yourself. It's up to you to fix it.

Not my mom this time, but it worked.

Things *would* get better.

I had to believe that.

With one last sniff, I snuggled deeper into the covers and resolutely shut my eyes.

In the morning Rio brought me breakfast on a tray, and we took it into the enclosed garden outside my suite. It was sunny out, the garden's weathered walls blocking the wind off the ocean. Autumn leaves still clung to the branches of the small fruit trees, and pots of cheerful mums, asters and stonecrop were scattered among clumps of golden ornamental grasses.

I directed Rio to put the tray on a small cast-iron table beneath an apple tree. While I devoured an omelet and home fries, he told me about his day so far. It turned out that, after I'd left, Twilight's grandmother had moved into the castle.

"Her name's Mrs. Park and she's a freaking badass." Rio's admiring smile reminded me he was still a teenager and impressed by badassery. "We're all a little afraid of her."

"What d'you mean? Isn't she like three times your age?"

"She could still kick my butt. William—he's the castle butler or something—said she used to be a slayer."

Okay, that was impressive. "Twilight's grandmother?"

"Yep. And so was the prima—Twilight. It's kinda the family business. They have a slayer in every generation."

My jaw unhinged. "No way."

"Way. Nathan told me."

"Jesus Murphy." My stomach sank to the soles of my boots. Shoving my plate aside, I put my elbows on the table and covered my face with my hands.

"Hey." Rio put down his can of pop to pat my arm. "You okay?"

"No," I said from beneath my hands. "Last summer, I did something bad. Something to do with Twilight."

"How bad?"

"Bad enough. And don't ask—it's better if you don't know. But now I find out the woman I messed with is the new prima and also a former slayer?" My voice went up at the end of the sentence. "I. Am. So. Fucked."

Rio sat back. "What about Talon?"

"What about him?" I peeked through my fingers.

"Won't the dude defend you? I mean, you're his now, right? That's what this blood-bond thing means."

I snorted. "Because he knocked me up."

"Nah, it's more than that. He chased you all the way to New York, didn't he? And he was seriously worried when you passed out. You didn't see his face."

"Yeah?" I lifted my head.

God, I wanted to believe Talon cared about me. Then I flashed on the woman in the Hotel Garnet and swallowed over the shards of glass that suddenly filled my throat.

"And he hired me, didn't he?" Rio pointed out. "He didn't have to do that."

"You still don't get it, do you? He brought you along for one reason —to put pressure on me."

"Maybe," Rio allowed. "But he didn't have to hire me. He could've just dragged me back here. It's not like I could've fought off all three of them. And I think he did it to keep you happy."

"I suppose so. Or maybe he figured it was the most efficient way to get what he wanted," I said a little bitterly, recalling how he'd pressured me into accepting his blood bond.

"Whatever. I would've come for free anyway. This way, they're paying me a shit-ton of money. So what's this about this Twilight woman?"

"She's Talon's prima now. That means what she says goes. A vampire syndicate isn't a democracy. They might run it like a business, but the primus isn't the CEO, he's the king. Which makes the prima Talon's queen."

Rio's brown eyes went round. "And you fucked with this bitch?"

"The short answer? Yeah."

"But why? What did she do to you?"

Guilt tightened my throat. "Nothing," I admitted.

"Then why?"

I shook my head, embarrassed to tell Rio I'd pretended to be Twilight's friend when instead, I'd been feeding information about her to Kuro, AKA Eugene Smith. I'd ratted out a woman who'd been nothing but nice to me. A woman who'd seemed like she could use a friend.

He frowned. "Tell me. I promise I won't judge, but I don't like going in blind about something like this."

I forked up more of the omelet. "I did it for the money, all right?"

"I thought they paid thralls a lot."

I swallowed the food in my mouth. "They do. Maybe I wanted more, okay?"

He considered me. "That doesn't sound like you. There's something you're not telling me."

A knot formed in my chest. "Busted by a teenager."

"So there is something," he said, refusing to let me dismiss him like that.

I looked away, ashamed I'd tried. Rio might be only eighteen, but he had an old soul.

"Tell me," he pressed.

And I found I wanted to tell him. Keeping the hurt and humiliation locked inside hadn't helped.

"I wanted out. And I wanted to hurt them."

I wanted to hurt Talon.

"Whoa, back up a little," Rio said. "First, why did you want out?"

"Because Talon said he'd never take me as a mate. He wanted a pureblood mate."

"He straight up told you that?"

I shook my head. "Not me, no. His friend Cain. They didn't know I was close enough to hear. But he said it all right."

It had been at a party in Quebec City. I'd gone outside for some air, and I guess Talon had come looking for me, but Cain had stopped him. I'd heard my name, then they'd paused on the other side of a thick hedge, arguing in low voices.

I'd stilled, straining to hear. Instinct told me this was important. I hadn't even dared to breathe.

Please don't notice me. Please don't notice me.

"Remember the pact," Cain had said. "We mate with vampires or nobody. Especially not a thrall."

Talon had growled. "Drop it already. Eden's a thrall, nothing more.

And the last thing I want is to sire a dhampir. I want a pureblood spawn, same as you."

"There's Brien," Cain had interrupted. "Something must be up." They'd returned the way they'd come.

"I'd only just found out I was pregnant," I told Rio. "He—I felt like I'd been sucker punched." Remembering, I pressed my arm to my stomach. "So yeah, I wanted to hurt them, especially Talon. I'm not proud of it, but... Anyway, then this guy came to me, asking if I wanted to make some easy money. All I'd have to do was pass a note to a new thrall—who turned out to be Twilight. I had second thoughts, but by then it was too late. He told me that if I didn't do exactly as he said, he'd out me to the old primus and his lieutenant. If he had, I'd probably be dead now."

"Christ." Rio reached out and squeezed my hand.

"Yeah," I said grimly. "The old primus—Brien's father—was going blood-mad, although the syndicate kept it quiet. If he'd gotten his hands on me, that would've been the last anyone saw of me until my body washed up on a beach somewhere, drained of blood and chewed on by sharks."

"No wonder you ran."

"Yeah." I studied the remains of my breakfast. "Before that, I thought Talon was starting to like me. You know, *really* like me. He treated me different than the other thralls, you know? That last year, he took me as his special thrall, told the other vampires I was his. I was even thinking of asking him if he wanted me to stay with him after my contract was up. God, I was an idiot. Only outcasts mate with humans. And their spawn have low status because they're only half-vampire."

My friend was silent for a couple of beats. "But those three brothers—you know, the Dark Angels—wasn't their mother a human? So they're dhampirs, right? And they say the oldest one is going to succeed his father as Kral primus."

"That's what I've heard. But their father had to strongarm his people into accepting them as his heirs, and he's a primus."

"Seriously? That's fucking medieval."

I huffed a humorless laugh. "Welcome to my world. They're not like us—they're more...primal. Like a wolf pack. Status is determined by raw power, and the more vampire blood you have, the more powerful you are. All I know is Talon never wanted to sire a dhampir." I paused, the pain still sharp and bright. "And I was damned if I was going to stay where me and my baby weren't wanted."

A groove formed between Rio's dark brows. "So why did you accept his blood bond? It's permanent, isn't it? You can't ever leave without his permission."

I moved my shoulder in a despondent shrug. "Because it's the only way I can make sure I stay with my baby. And yeah, he pretty much told me that."

And because if I hadn't, he'd never trust me again.

"Fuck. That's cold."

I barely heard Rio's muttered comment through the ringing in my ears. I'd just realized I was still hoping, still trying to win Talon's love.

And it would never happen. He didn't care for me in that way, and the sooner I got that into my head, the happier I'd be.

"You sent for me?" Eden hovered in the doorway to my apartment.

When she'd been my thrall, she'd dressed in tight, sexy clothes, usually in a fuck-me red. Kept her blond hair long because I liked it that way. And her makeup had always been perfect—not too much and not too little, her lips a hot scarlet.

Tonight, however, she'd shown up in another slouchy sweater, this one a soft blue that reached to her thighs. Her jeans had the knees ripped out and her purple-and-white Adidas trainers looked like something Rio might wear.

Combined with no makeup and the new, boyish haircut, it felt like a subtle *up-yours*. Or maybe a message: *This is me. Take it or leave it.*

If so, I was definitely taking it. On Eden, edgy was sexy as hell.

"Shut the door." I closed my laptop and moved it to an end table.

She obeyed and leaned against the thick, silver-reinforced wood, arms crossed, her expression composed, her emotions a difficult-to-read jumble. "What's up?"

I sat back, spreading my arms along the couch's leather back. "Come here."

She didn't like that. Her eyes narrowed, but she uncrossed her arms and left the relative safety of the door, stopping a few feet away, her unpainted lips pressed together, the challenge on her face irresistible.

I shouldn't enjoy that challenging look so much, but I did.

This is about teaching her a lesson. About establishing control.

I schooled myself to remain tough, reminded myself what she'd done. How she'd left even after she'd known she was pregnant. That she was only a thrall.

"Sit down." I cut my eyes at my lap.

She drew a breath and I thought she might refuse, but she obeyed, perching sideways on my thighs, stiff backed, mouth cinched tight. She could purse that beautiful mouth at me all she wanted. That only made me want to do dirty things to her puckered lips.

I wrapped an arm around her, pulling her up against my chest. My free hand slid between her thighs.

"Is this where you punish me?" Her stubbornly lifted chin dared me.

My already erect dick thickened.

I rubbed the seam of her jeans. "You're already wet, aren't you?"

She shook her head but couldn't quite bring herself to lie out loud. Meanwhile, her inner thighs squeezed my hand, and I felt the heat at her center.

I dug my fingers into her thigh. "The truth, Eden."

"Then don't ask me questions I don't want to answer."

"You'll answer anything I ask."

Her chin lifted. "Yes, Talon." The words were obedient, the tone anything but.

I could've called her on it but I didn't. Her attitude, her willingness to push back at a man who could snap her in two without even trying, was one of the things that had drawn me to her in the first place.

I ran my hand over the firm curve of her abdomen. "How are you feeling?"

She slanted me a look like it was a trick question. "Okay, I guess."

"You're eating okay? Taking your vitamins?"

She bristled. "Yeah."

I lifted a brow. Was she really going to give me attitude about this? "You should've been doing that all along."

She absorbed that, biting her lower lip. "You don't think I hurt the baby, do you?"

"No," I said, some of the sternness bleeding out of me at her obvious worry. "But let's see what the midwife says. I made you an appointment—tomorrow afternoon. She's got the equipment for a proper exam."

"Olivia? That was fast."

"I'm paying her extra to fit you in." I rubbed her stomach reassuringly. "I want you both to have the best care."

"Yes, of course." She deflated, no longer bristling or even challenging me. Instead, sadness wafted from her...sadness and disappointment. "Thanks," she added, picking at a hole in the knee of her jeans, evading my eyes.

A groove formed between my brows. What had I said?

"You don't believe I want you healthy?"

"No. I mean yes, I believe you."

A beat passed while I mentally replayed her words. Then it hit me. She thought I only cared about her health because of my spawn.

I covered her hand with mine, halting her from worrying the frayed blue threads. "Look at me." I waited until she raised her gaze to mine, then said, "*Both* of you. I want you both to have the best care. If Olivia finds anything—anything at all—I'll fly in an OB-GYN from Halifax. Or from Toronto or Montreal—wherever Olivia recommends. I'm not taking any chances with either of you."

I waited for her nod before adding, "As for your punishment..."

She stilled. "Yeah?"

"I appreciate that you apologized." I stroked a finger down the length of her throat. "But I can't just let you off. You disrespected me and the syndicate. Not to mention Brien, the man I swore a blood-vow to protect. The man who's like a brother to me."

Actually, in the eyes of the syndicate, Brien was literally my brother. We shared a sire, Prima Lenore, although he'd been born of her body while I'd been turned by her.

Eden's throat worked. "I know."

My eyes locked on the pulse beating at the base of her neck. Sweet Lilith, I ached for a taste of her hot, tangy blood on my tongue. No human's flavor was exactly the same, and Eden's was...perfect.

It had been too damn long since I'd fed from her. And tonight, I couldn't even fuck her. Not until I got the midwife's all-clear.

Yeah, I was a masochist, ordering her to sit on my lap like this. But I'd rather hold her than fuck another thrall, something I refused to examine too closely.

She was watching me watch her. She waited until I raised my gaze to her face, and whatever she saw in my expression made her blush and squirm on my lap.

"What are you going to do?" she asked in a scratchy voice.

I stifled a groan. She looked so young with no makeup, her pupils dilated, hot color painting her cheeks. My dick was iron-hard now, pressed against the side of her ass.

"You'll see."

I wasn't going to hurt her. Just make her sweat a little.

Although right now, having her on my lap, equal parts confused and turned on, I could almost forget all the trouble she'd caused.

Almost.

I tugged at the hem of her baby-blue sweater. "I want this off."

She had to stand to remove it. I dropped the sweater on the couch arm, then stripped her pants and shoes off until she stood before me in dove-gray bra and panties.

I pulled her between my thighs, running my hands over her curves. She was so fucking sexy, her breasts full, her belly rounded with our spawn. I pressed a kiss to the silky V of her cleavage, drawing her fresh-cookie scent deep into my lungs.

"Damn, you're beautiful," I ground out, the words torn from the dark place in me that had gone a little crazy when she'd left.

Those first few hours, I'd been terrified that she'd been hurt or even kidnapped—I'd been that sure of her, that certain she wouldn't have left me willingly. Then when it had become clear that I was wrong, that she *had* left of her own free will, my terror had turned to a black fury.

"You think so?" Eden asked. "Even now?"

I didn't like the uncertainty in her voice. She was still Eden—a tall, curvy goddess of a woman—just pregnant.

But I also remembered that black fury. So I nipped the curve of her breast, not breaking the skin but as a tiny punishment.

She squeaked and jumped.

"Fuck yeah, I think you're sexy," I told her. "But don't think you can get around me with that sexy body. You're still in trouble."

I dragged her back onto my lap, half-expecting her to fight. But she didn't. Instead, with a leaky sigh, she leaned against my chest, a small surrender that went a long way to appeasing the darkness.

Still, I was far from finished with her. She needed to be taught a lesson about messing with the syndicate—and the vampire who'd made a favorite of her.

I smacked the side of her ass. "Open your thighs."

I waited until she'd spread them on mine, then deliberately didn't touch her there. I wanted her to feel open, vulnerable while I explored her body.

Her spine went rigid. "Yes, Master," she said, the attitude back in full force.

My grin had sharp teeth in it. "You think that bothers me? You can call me Master all you want. Maybe I'll go easier on you, in fact."

Her head snapped around. If she'd had a dagger, I probably would've found myself facing the business end. Her blue eyes smoldered. "You—"

I wrapped my hand around her throat, knowing it was a sure way to shut her up. She liked that. We both did, the light pressure telling her I was in control.

She gasped. An aroused intake of air, the muscles of her ass flexing on my thighs as she tried to pull her thighs together. Beneath my fingers, her pulse kicked up.

Unable to resist the rounded 'O' of her lips, I kissed her. She moaned into my mouth, her fingers curling into my T-shirt.

Then she stiffened again and tried to pull away.

Hell, no. She wasn't going to get away with that.

"Kiss me back," I ordered against her lips.

Her mouth moved beneath mine. At first, she was play-acting. I went along with it, deepening the kiss, stroking my tongue into her mouth.

Her breath sped up. I mouth-fucked her, drinking her in like a fine blood-wine. She sucked on my tongue, all-in now.

My balls tightened painfully.

Gods, I wanted this woman. Too much. Like I'd stumbled into quicksand and was sinking fast, the sticky, quaking mass up to my chest before I knew it.

I tore my mouth from hers, breathing hard.

Eden looked at me, wide-eyed. Inhaled slowly. Licked her lips as if tasting me on them.

Sweet fucking Lilith.

Boundaries, I reminded myself, and forced my fingers to release her throat.

"That's better," I managed to say. I even accompanied it with a got-you lift of my brows.

She drew another breath. Let it out. "Fuck off," she said without heat.

"Oh, I will," I returned, "as soon as Olivia says it's okay."

Just not tonight.

I wasn't waiting simply because Eden hadn't seen the midwife. She was fine, and so was my spawn. Dr. Lopez had confirmed that, although I wanted a second opinion based on state-of-the-art equipment.

No, I was doing it to prove something to myself. That I could remain in control where Eden was concerned.

Boundaries.

"Oh." She looked way too disappointed for a woman who'd just told me to fuck off.

"That doesn't mean we're done here." Tonight I was going to tease the hell out of her. "I can be all kinds of creative with my punishments."

Another "Oh," this one breathy.

I massaged a firm breast through the silky gray bra. "Your tits are larger."

I'd heard that happened, but I'd never had a woman of my own on which to test the theory, so to speak. Eden's had increased at least a cup size, and she'd been a C cup. "And no, the changes in your body don't bother me. Not at all. You're even more beautiful."

She tilted her head, scrutinizing me. "You really think so, don't you?"

"Yeah." I pinched a nipple through the gray satin. "I do."

"Ouch." She squirmed on my lap. "I'm also more sensitive."

"Mm." I toyed with the other one, then pinched that, too. "Consider it part of your punishment, then."

"Talon..." She wiggled again, this time right against my erection.

I groaned and shifted her forward so I could undo the top button of my pants. I eased the zipper down to relieve some of the pressure. My dick pressed against my boxer briefs, and Eden skimmed a hungry gaze over the hard ridge.

I ran a hand down myself. "Like what you see?"

She lifted a shoulder. "Maybe."

My mouth twitched up. "I can smell you, you know—and feel that hot little pussy on my leg. You're wet, baby."

Her cheeks pinkened again, but she managed an eye-roll. "Thanks for the play-by-play."

I almost laughed aloud.

How did she do that? Make me want to smile even when I was angry at her?

Shaking my head at myself, I arranged her on my lap so her back was to me, her legs open on my thighs. When I slid my fingers into her panties, she was even wetter than before.

"You're so ready." I teased her with my fingertip. "Tell me you want to be fucked. Tell me you want my dick inside you, making you scream."

She swallowed and pressed back against me, her panty-clad ass brushing over my erection. "It's...nothing personal," she choked out, still fighting me. "I'm just...so damn horny these days. Hormones."

"Nothing personal, huh? Oh, baby, you're going to pay for that."

I'd already intended to tease her, then send her away needy and wanting. Payback for the past two-and-a-half months.

Now I intended to draw out the torment. I undid her bra and removed it.

"Put your hands around the back of my neck."

We'd played games like this before. She swallowed, like she was thinking of disobeying me, then apparently thought better of it and complied.

The position arched her back so her breasts were displayed for my greedy gaze. They weren't just bigger, they were rounder, the nipples larger and darker.

"So fucking sexy," I said under my breath.

I pinched each nipple again, harder this time. She moaned a protest at the same time she pushed her breast into my fingers, wordlessly showing how much she liked it. On my lap she widened her thighs even more, seeking my touch there, too, while still keeping her hands linked around my neck.

I put my hand on her mound over her panties. The satin was soaked now, my brain filled with the sexy ocean scent of her.

I cupped her firmly, possessively. "What do you want?"

I sensed her inner struggle, but she caved. "You," she admitted lowly.

I grazed my fingers over her clit. "D'you like that?"

A rapid nod. "Yes. You know I do."

"Hm." I teased her for a minute, maybe more. Waiting until she gave needy mewl.

"What's the matter?" I rasped against her temple.

"You know." Her fingers dug into my nape. Her hips lifted, straining for more.

"Do I?"

"Please," she whispered brokenly. "Please, Talon. I want you inside me. I want you to fuck me."

Normally if she begged me for something, she'd get what she wanted. That was how the game went. She liked begging, and I liked granting her wishes.

And gods, I ached to bury myself in her.

Boundaries.

Although at that moment, I was having trouble remembering—or caring—why the hell they mattered.

Somehow, I managed to stick to the plan. Sliding my fingers back into her panties, I teased her sex until she was flushed and writhing and sobbing with need. "Please, please, please. Let me come. I'm so close..."

Then I stopped.

She blinked up at me, breath coming in short huffs, pelvis still moving in that hungry way. I licked her juices from my fingers, then untangled her hands from around my neck and moved her to the couch beside me.

Dragging my boxers and pants off along with my shoes and socks, I took my cock in hand and reclined against the couch arm. "Watch me."

Her gaze jumped dazedly from my dick to my face. "What—?"

"That's your punishment. You don't get to come. But you have to watch."

I fisted my heated flesh and began stroking myself. A slow, hard glide.

She made a small moan, but she focused on my lap as I began working myself.

It was a special kind of hell, making her watch, that ripe body half-naked and flushed with desire, knowing I wasn't going to finish inside her. My whole lower body throbbed with a painful pleasure. Hating me for not bending her over the couch and taking her, hard and dirty.

Stunned understanding dawned on her face. "Talon. Please. Don't..."

I gazed back steadily. "No."

She licked her lips, arousal and confusion radiating off her, but she couldn't take her gaze off what I was doing. Her hand inched toward her panties.

I growled. "Hands behind your head. Now."

She stared at me so long, I thought she wasn't going to obey, but she did it. Maybe she thought I'd relent if she complied. Her back arched against the couch, the nipples tight and red.

"Good girl." I pulled harder, squeezing and twisting, my balls close to exploding. "Don't move. You're going to stay there until I finish."

She groaned, irritated now. "Why are you being such a dick?"

My hand didn't stop. "Because."

Her fingers flexing on her head. "Please. I'm so..."

"Don't. Move."

She shook her head, eyes closed tight.

"And keep those eyes on me, or we'll do this every night for a week."

Her chest heaved. Her eyes blazed at me through slit lids.

Her knees had fallen apart and I could smell her, see how soaked her panties were. She was as turned on as I was.

Good.

I hoped she was in pain. Hungry. Itchy. Needy.

I wanted her to hurt. To want like I did.

How many nights had I jerked myself off since she'd left, picturing her face and those round, creamy tits? Too damn many, that's for sure.

I squeezed harder, faster. "Like what you see, baby?"

She rasped an assent, completely focused on me now. Then she touched the tip of her tongue to her lower lip, and I could've sworn I felt that tongue on my dick. A phantom touch that set me off like a match to a skyrocket.

A blinding heat detonated up my spine and I groaned as hot semen spurted, coating my hand and stomach. I kept working myself until I was spent. My head dropped back, my lungs sucking in air.

When I looked at Eden again, she had brought her hands down. "You—that was..."

She inhaled raggedly, her hand skating down her stomach to her panties.

I made a warning noise low in my throat. "Touch yourself and you'll be sorry."

Her lips thinned, but her hand stopped moving. She sat up. "Definitely a dick," she said in an undertone.

I pulled off my T-shirt and wiped myself clean, then pulled her to her feet. "Get dressed."

I swatted her round butt, enjoying how it bounced a little beneath my hand, then did it again for good measure before scooping up her clothes and handing them to her.

"So that's it?" She scowled up at me. "Now I leave?"

I nodded. "I told you, that's your punishment."

I should've felt satisfied. Cain would probably say I'd let her off easy. But as good as that had been, it hadn't been…satisfying.

I wanted to see Eden come, too. Wanted to give her pleasure.

The woman was definitely messing with my head, and the fucked-up part was, she wasn't even trying to. She didn't have to. She did it simply by being herself.

She sat on the couch again, dragging on her pants and shoving her feet into her socks and shoes. Then she pulled on her sweater and stood up.

"Good night," she muttered.

"Eden?" I gripped her arm.

"What?"

"Don't touch yourself. You don't get to come when it's punishment. Is that understood?"

"Go to hell," she muttered.

"Oh, I probably will." I released her. "But I mean it. I'll ask you tomorrow night, and if you lie to me, I'll know. Now, go." I gave her another swat and turned her toward the door.

Her growl had actual teeth in it. She exited, head high, hips swaying.

I crossed to the wet bar and poured myself a stiff blood-whisky. Tossing it down, I stared at the closed door, wondering why it felt like she'd taken all the energy in the room with her.

⁂   I I   ⁂

EDEN

I didn't touch myself, didn't make myself come.

I wanted to. God, I wanted to.

I'd gone to Talon's apartment not sure what he had in store for me.

And *Jesus Murphy*, watching him fuck his fist was going to be seared in my spank-bank forever. The way he gripped himself, moving his hand up and down his smooth, hard flesh. The way he sprawled on the couch, eyeing me in that stern, you-will-obey-me way.

My pussy had clenched over and over, aching to have him inside me. Weeping with readiness.

He'd gone easy on me. I knew he had, but I'd had been so close to climaxing myself. So wet, so primed—and he'd still told me no.

I'd seen that smile he'd tried to hide. He'd enjoyed teasing me, enjoyed making me beg and then sending me away.

He really had been kind of a dick, but on the other hand, I'd never expected to get off scot-free. And if this was how he wanted to punish me, then I'd take it. He could've done so much worse to me, and we both knew it.

Now, though, I was so worked up, I hurt. I had to take a shower to cool myself off. After, I padded to the walk-in closet and pulled on a sleepshirt.

Kerry had brought a laundry cart of my clothes to me—things I

89

could still wear like sweaters, joggers and yoga pants, along with shoes and outerwear. I'd stowed them in the closet alongside the clothes I'd bought in New York.

I flipped through my shirts, stopping on a new black top. I fingered it, a small, wicked smile formed on my lips.

Perfect. Especially paired with my leather-look pants, the pair Rio said made my ass look amazing.

Yeah, they were maternity clothes, but they were still sexy in a downtown New York kind of way.

If this was war, then I refused to be on the losing side.

❧

Rio spent the morning with me, then left, saying, "I have to get back. Mrs. Park's going to teach me how to make Korean shaved ice. She says she never learned how to cook, but anyone can make shaved ice—even a skinny white kid like me."

He chuckled. Twilight's grandmother had made a conquest.

"Have fun." I'd have liked him to stay longer, but I was happy he was making friends. "And I call dibs on whatever you come up with."

"You got it," he said and took off.

A few minutes later, a soldier named Jasper arrived, a dhampir who'd grown up off-island.

"Hey, Jasper." I grinned, genuinely happy to see him. Jasper was kind of like a puppy, friendly and eager to please—all the thralls liked him. "How's it going?"

I stepped back to allow him into the living room, but he stopped in the doorway. "Get your coat," he said, unsmiling. "I'm here to take you for a walk."

My smile just hung there for a second. Then I pressed my lips together, confused and a little hurt. "Oohh-kaayy," I said, and got my hiking boots and puffer jacket.

Castle Leclerc squatted on the island's northernmost cliff, a four-tower square enclosing the courtyard. Usually at this time of day, at least a couple of other thralls would be out walking, too, but the courtyard was conspicuously empty. Apparently, I wasn't allowed to see or speak to anyone but Rio and my guards.

The silver-reinforced main gate was closed, but Jasper unlocked the smaller door next to it, and we followed the cobblestone road until we reached the path that ran the cliff.

Sixty feet below, the ocean hurled itself against the rocks: smash and retreat, smash and retreat. A stiff breeze lifted my hair, stinging my eyes and nose. Sunlight glinted off the deep blue water, and seagulls wheeled above stark black cliffs softened by beach grass and velvety moss.

I drew a lungful of the salt-scented air.

This was Lilith Island, a mass of contradictions: Sunshine and darkness. Soft sand and stony paths. Humans and vampires.

When I was Rio's age, I couldn't wait to escape this fifteen-kilometers-long, three-kilometers-wide rock in the middle of nowhere. I was the kid who was going to get out of here, make something of herself, but living in New York City had given me a new perspective. Lilith Island was beautiful in a way that a city could never be.

Still, I felt a tug of sadness for that girl who was going to make something of herself.

Jasper had dropped back so that he was a few steps behind me. It made me itchy, so when we reached a path that led down to the ocean, I shoved my hands into my coat pockets and turned to face him.

His spiked-up, reddish-blond hair gleamed under the sun, and his freckles stood out on his pale skin. "So you're my babysitter today," I said.

His dark glasses made his expression hard to read. A dhampir can tolerate an hour or two of sunlight, especially in the fall and winter, but it's painful to their sensitive eyes.

His only answer was a shrug.

Inside my pockets, my nails dug into my palms. "So you're not allowed to talk to me? Or are you pissed off at me for some reason?"

Jasper was only a few inches taller, but he managed to look down his nose at me. "You got greedy, Eden. What—they weren't paying you enough? Because I know you were making the same as me, and that's a helluvalot more than you'd make anywhere else."

"You've been talking to Aidan and Nathan."

A cool stare.

My jaw set. "Does everyone know?"

"The soldiers do, anyway." Jasper's mouth twisted. "You're lucky Talon didn't slit your throat. But you got pregnant, didn't you? Smart."

"Who told you I was pregnant?"

"William, when he assigned me to guard you."

I blew a breath out through my nose. "So that's what you guys think? That I got pregnant to weasel my way out of this?" Nathan had said something similar.

"Didn't you?"

"It wasn't like that. But you know what?" Removing my hands from my pockets, I drew myself to my full height. "I don't have to explain myself to you."

"No, you don't. But—" he cast a pointed look at the gold cuff peeking out from beneath my sleeve—"Talon's treating you better than you deserve."

"I thought we were friends," I returned, then rolled my lips in. That had come out more forlorn than I'd intended.

"*Were*," he returned. "We *were* friends. Not anymore."

"Suit yourself." Still, things were bad if even Jasper no longer wanted to be my friend. He was the nicest soldier; all the thralls liked him.

"And now you're carrying a dhampir. You know I'm a dhampir, right?"

I frowned. "Of course. So?"

"Do you know how hard it is for us in the syndicate? Yeah, your spawn's father is a lieutenant, but what you did is going to leave a stain. Your kid's going to have to work even harder to find their place."

I flinched. I'd accepted Talon's blood bond for the baby's sake, and for Jasper to imply I didn't have my child's best interest in mind was like a jab to the solar plexus.

"Did you even think about what you were doing?"

Okay, I was officially angry now. "You know what? Attack me, sure. Maybe I deserve it—but not for getting pregnant. That was an accident, not that it's any of your business. And I'm doing my best to roll with it. And yeah," I added, "I do know how hard it is for a dhampir. Maybe that's why I left. Maybe I don't want my baby to grow up in the syndicate. Maybe I didn't want my baby to have to fight for their place in a hierarchy that's rigged against them."

Maybe I wanted my baby to be wanted—not tolerated—by his father.

Jasper huffed a scornful breath. "You really think it's better out in the human world? I grew up with a human mom, remember? The other kids treated me like I had two heads, and their parents were afraid to let me play with their precious babies in case I dragged them somewhere and drained their blood. It didn't help that when you're pissed off or excited, your eyes change and your fangs slide out, something I couldn't always control. I mean, what four-year-old can?"

Holy crap. I stared at him, shocked and a little ashamed. "I'm sorry. I…didn't know."

"Because you're a human."

"Because it wasn't like that here on the island. Nathan—back when we were kids, everyone knew you didn't want to mess with him, but we accepted him."

"This is Lilith Island," Jasper said. "Trust me, the real world is nothing like this."

⁂

Olivia's office was in a little stone cottage nestled beneath an ancient oak at the edge of Bluebeard's Cove.

I was conveyed there in a syndicate SUV by a stocky, silver-haired driver named Mr. Jones. The thirty-minute drive passed in silence, me staring out the window as we drove around the southern end of the island as the thick forest that surrounded the castle gave way to farms and vineyards.

Mr. Jones parked the SUV and exited to open my door. "I'll be out here," he told me.

I thanked him and walked up the cobblestone path through a yard crammed with wildflowers. They were dormant now, their leaves shriveled by frost, the seedheads picked clean by the birds.

A certified nurse-midwife, Olivia lived on the cottage's second floor, using the first floor for patient visits. Her purple door was unlocked, and inside, the waiting room was deserted. Talon must've arranged that, too. Even the receptionist's desk stood empty, her computer off.

As I hung my jacket on a peg, Olivia strode into the waiting room, short brown curls bouncing, a smile on her round, pretty face, and pulled me into a hug.

"Eden! It's so good to see you."

"You, too." I hugged her back.

Inside my chest, something tight eased. I'd known her since I was a kid, and it was nice to see someone who seemed happy I was home.

"So," the midwife said in her blunt way. "I hear you're preggers. Come on back."

Leading me into the examining room, she asked me a few questions, then had me undress so she could "check things out," as she said, joking with me the entire time like we were having a girls' night out or something.

For the first time, I saw and heard the baby's heartbeat. I stared at the ultrasound image, awed at this evidence of a person growing inside me.

This was really happening.

I was having a baby.

Talon's baby.

Olivia moved the ultrasound wand to another place on my abdomen. "Would you like to know the gender?"

My mouth hitched up. "I think I figured it out." That appendage at the base of his belly was unmistakable.

"A boy," she confirmed. "Sometime in the middle of February, give or take a week."

"A boy." I drew a slow inhale. "Okay."

Somehow, I'd figured I'd was having a girl. Growing up, it had been just me and Freya.

"Congratulations." A grinning Olivia shut down the machine and wiped the gel off my stomach.

"Thank you?" It came out like a question because panic had

screwed itself into my insides. What did I know about raising a boy? And a half-vampire boy at that?

My conversation with Jasper came back to me. I'd been thinking about it ever since this morning, actually.

This is Lilith Island. Trust me, the real world is nothing like this.

I'd be a human mom with a dhampir son. A little boy who could eat human food but required blood to thrive.

Maybe I'd been wrong to think we'd be better off elsewhere. I mean, I would've figured it out. Whatever my baby needed, I would've given it to him. Hopefully.

But maybe staying on Lilith Island, trying to make a family with Talon, was best for my baby.

"He's a dhampir?" Olivia asked, echoing my thoughts.

"Yeah."

"Lieutenant Talon's?"

"Yes." I caught her hand. "But promise me you won't tell my mom and dad. I want to tell them myself. Don't even tell them you saw me, okay?"

I did want to tell my parents myself, but I was more worried about my dad, and what he'd do if he heard I was home. Nothing scared him, especially where me and Freya were concerned. He'd come to the castle and raise hell, demanding to see me, and if the syndicate refused, God knew what he'd do.

"Who you tell is none of my business," Olivia said. "I'm here to make sure you have a safe, healthy delivery, and that's all. Right now I can tell you that you and your little guy are doing great. Now get dressed and we'll talk about what comes next."

A few minutes later I exited her office armed with pamphlets and more prenatal vitamins—her special blend for dhampir babies—as well as instructions to eat right and get moderate exercise.

She followed me into the hall. "I'll want to see you again in four weeks. I'll set it up with Talon. And Eden?" Her gray eyes creased in a reassuring smile. "It will be okay. You'll see. Call me anytime you need me—I'm here. Night or day."

"Thank you," I said, still absorbing the fact that I was going to have a baby boy. Clutching the small bag with the vitamins and pamphlets, I headed back into the waiting room—and froze.

My mom was ensconced on one of Olivia's comfortable lavender chairs, flipping through a magazine, her thick blond braid falling forward over her shoulder.

"Mom?" I asked at the same time she exclaimed, "*Eden.*"

Tossing the magazine aside, she stood up, arms open wide. I walked into them, bag of vitamins and all, and she enfolded me in a hug, her cushiony breasts pressing against mine. The familiar scent of coffee and cinnamon and Mom—of *home*—enveloped me.

My heart constricted. I hugged her back.

"Where the *heck* have you been?" she demanded in a voice rough with tears.

My own eyes stung. I swallowed hard. "New York. Well, that's where I ended up anyway."

"The *city?*"

"Yeah. Brooklyn."

"You're okay?" She stepped back, holding onto my upper arms. "You never called. We were so worried."

"I'm sorry. I wanted to call, so bad, but I was afraid."

Her brows scrunched together. "What d'you mean you were afraid?"

I blinked. Why had I said that? "I mean, I didn't want you two involved."

"Involved?"

Damn, I was only making things worse. I shook my head without speaking, and she palmed my cheek.

"It's okay, honey. Whatever's wrong, we'll fix it. C'mon, let's go."

She plucked my jacket from the coat rack and held it out. I took it, hugging it to my stomach instead of putting it on. In the little bag, the vitamins rattled.

"I can't, Mom. I have to get back."

"You don't have time for a short visit? What's going on? And why are you here?"

"Just a routine checkup."

Olivia entered the waiting room in time to hear that last part. She looked from me to my mother, clearly sensing the awkwardness, then smiled. "Hey, Gigi."

My mom flicked her a look, but she was too polite to ignore the midwife. "Hello, Olivia."

"She's fine," the midwife said. "Nothing to worry about."

"See," I told my mom. "It was routine. Now I have to go. My ride is waiting..."

Mom's blue eyes scraped down my body. Then her mouth dropped open. Drawing my jacket to the side, she touched my abdomen.

"You're pregnant, aren't you?" She snatched the bag from me and pulled out the prenatal vitamins, eyeing the bottle like it was a hand grenade. "That's why you're here."

I swallowed. "Yeah."

My mom read the vitamin label and inhaled sharply. "With a dhampir?"

Olivia shifted on her feet. "Maybe I'll give you two a few minutes alone."

"Please," said my mom without taking her gaze from me, and Olivia withdrew.

"Well?" Mom demanded.

I heaved a breath. "Yes, the baby's a dhampir. Talon's."

"But why did you leave, then?"

"It's...complicated."

"Why?" She puffed up, a mama bear ready to defend her cub. "Is he giving you trouble about it?"

"No. I mean, not because of the baby. Actually, he seems okay with it."

"Then what's the problem?"

"Don't ask. Please? It's syndicate business. And don't blame Talon. I messed up and it's up to me to fix things."

She stared at me, her eyes moving between mine. "What d'you mean, you messed up? And don't give me that "syndicate business" crap. You're my daughter and I want to know what's going on."

The doorknob turned and we both started like we'd been caught doing something wrong.

Mr. Jones poked his head inside the room, his bushy brows

lowered. "Time to go, Miss. The lieutenant said to bring you straight back."

"I'll be right there," I told him, and he withdrew, leaving the door ajar.

I gave my mom a last, hard hug. "I love you, Mom."

I tried to step back, but she hung on. "Wait. What am I going to tell your father? He's been so worried. We both were. In fact, he's in Halifax right now trying to find out what happened to you."

Guilt fisted my lungs. "I'm sorry. I told you I'd be out of contact for a while."

Which was a lame excuse, and I knew it—and my mom called me on it. "What did you expect? You just disappeared. One text, and you were gone."

"I'm sorry," I said again. "But tell Dad I'm all right. Because I am. Really."

Was I protesting too much? Probably.

"I don't like this." Mom released me, shaking her head. "And to be honest, I don't know if I can stop him from coming up to the castle."

My stomach bottomed out. This was what I'd been trying to prevent. The last thing I wanted was my parents involved in this.

"No!" I blurted. "You have to stop him. If he shows up, he'll just make things worse for me."

She put her hands on her hips. "What aren't you telling me?"

That I spied on the syndicate and I'm under house arrest until Talon decides I've been punished enough.

Yeah, that would go over real good.

"Please." I edged toward the door. "Just let it go for now, okay? I promise I'll visit as soon as I can. Just...give me a little time to work things out with Talon. I'm not in any danger—I mean I'm pregnant with his spawn, after all. He's not going to hurt me."

"Fine," she said, tight-lipped. "But you tell Talon that if anything happens to you—anything at all—we will tear this damn island apart and take our story to the world. They won't be able to hush us up like they did Gwen's family." Gwen was the thrall Jules Leclerc had murdered in a fit of blood-madness.

I nodded several times. "I will," I lied.

"I mean it, Eden Montgomery." She grabbed my arm, determination in every line of her body. "You tell him, or I will."

Mr. Jones opened the door again, preventing me from making my mom any promises. "Time to go," he said firmly. "I should have had you back already."

"Coming," I said and brushed my lips over my mom's soft cheek. "I love you, and everything's going to be all right. Promise. Give Dad my love, too, okay?"

"Wait!" She gripped my hand. "When are you due?"

"Middle of February."

"Yeah?" Her face softened. "A Valentine's Day baby."

"I guess." That hadn't occurred to me, actually.

Now it hurt my heart.

A Valentine's Day baby implied love, commitment. I suppose Talon was committed to me and the baby. He'd offered me his blood bond, after all.

But love?

I swallowed over the goose egg in my throat. "Love you both," I said again.

Mom heaved a breath and squeezed my hand. "Love you, too, honey," she said and helped me into my coat, then followed me out the door to the curb.

Mr. Jones was holding the SUV's back door open.

I climbed inside. Mom leaned past him to ask, "When are we going to see you?"

I moved a shoulder in a helpless shrug. "I don't know."

"Text me then. I want to hear from you every day."

"Can't. I...lost my phone."

"Eden." Her mouth tightened. "I don't like this. I don't like this at all."

"I know, but promise me you'll give me a week or two, okay? If you do anything, you'll only make things worse."

"Make things worse?" she asked, her voice rising.

"Promise me, Mom. You were a thrall. You know how it is."

"Damn it, Eden."

"*Please.*"

Her lips pressed together, but she nodded. "A week. That's all. And it's going to be hard enough getting your father to agree to that."

"Two weeks," I said. "Please, Mom. This is important, okay? You have to let me work this out myself."

I sat back before she could tell me no. Mr. Jones shut the door and got behind the wheel.

The last thing I saw was my mom dragging a hand down her braid, her worried, unhappy expression causing an answering lump to congeal in my stomach.

❦ 12 ❦

TALON

"Mom?" I tried the doorknob of my mother's white clapboard cottage. Finding it unlocked, I let myself inside. The tiny foyer was dark, but there was a light in the kitchen. "Mom? It's me, Talon."

"In the kitchen," she called in a voice raspy from too many cigarettes. She was smoking one now, a shot glass and a half-empty whisky bottle on the kitchen table in front of her.

All my memories of her were infused with the odor of tobacco and whisky.

Back then, the small cottage had been falling down around us while Esposito tossed away his pay—and most of my mom's, too—playing poker or on get-rich-quick schemes. These days, the building was freshly painted and in good repair. I made sure of that, just like I'd hired a woman to come in a twice a week to clean and cook dinners for her. It was the only way I could be sure my mom was eating regularly.

"Hey there, sweetie."

Smiling up at me, she nudged the shot glass and bottle to the side, like I wouldn't realize she was drinking alone and in the dark except for a light over the stove. At least she was awake and relatively sober.

I dropped a kiss on her lined cheek and leaned against the counter, my hands braced on the countertop behind me. "How are things?"

"Not bad." She stubbed out the cigarette in a dented brass ashtray that was older than me. "How about yourself?"

"Not bad."

"I thought you were away."

"Yeah? Where did you hear that?"

Her eyes shifted sideways. "You know. Word gets around."

I grunted. No one but Brien, Cain, Twilight, and a few of the castle staff had known I was off island.

"Was *he* here?"

"No. You said yourself he'd better not come to the island."

"So you went to him, then."

She shrugged, fiddling with her shot glass.

Of course she'd been to see him. Now that I looked closer, I saw the signs. Her salt-and-pepper hair had been recently cut in a stylish cap that feathered around her face; she was wearing an outfit I'd never seen before —a soft cream sweater and khaki pants—and she was trying not to drink.

When Esposito crooked a finger, she went running—to Montreal, Toronto, Vancouver. I knew about it, of course, but she was an adult. Yeah, I could've stopped her, but she was still my mom, even if she was piss-poor at mothering.

The only good thing about it was that when she was with Esposito, she drank less. Sometimes she even stopped altogether for a few months.

I folded my arms over my chest. "Where is he?"

And how the hell had he known I was off-island, anyway?

Her mouth pinched. "Is that the only reason you came to see me? To grill me about Marc?"

I clenched my back teeth. "You know that's not true. I check in on you every few days. I was here Tuesday night, and the Friday before that."

Instead of replying, she patted the chair to her right. "Sit down. Tell me what you were doing on the mainland."

"Mom—"

"I said, *Sit*."

When she took that tone, I knew she'd dug in. I wasn't getting any more information out of her until she was ready.

I lowered my ass to the damn chair. "I wasn't on the mainland. Well, not in Canada anyway. I was in New York. Syndicate business," I added to forestall further questions.

She snagged the whiskey bottle and glass and poured herself a double shot. "The primus sent you?"

I looked at her without speaking.

"Hm." She fingered the glass.

She took her whiskey neat. Ice melted and diluted the alcohol, she said. I expected her to toss it down, but she only ran a fingertip around the lip. Yeah, my father was definitely in the picture.

"I always wanted to go to New York," she said. "See a Broadway show, go to the museums."

I reached for her hand. It was lean and strong, but she had age spots and a few wrinkles now. Sometimes I forgot she was almost sixty-seven.

"You want to go, then I'll take you. Say the word and I'll arrange it."

She squeezed my fingers. "I'd like that."

"When, then? Would you like to go for the holidays? See the decorations?"

"Next month?" She wrinkled her nose, then made an excuse like always. "I don't want to miss Christmas with you and my friends. Maybe in the spring, when it's warmer."

"Okay. Sure. The spring."

I probably shouldn't be leaving the island right now anyway, not with the way things were with Eden.

"You're good to ask," she said. "You always did your best. I know I wasn't a great mom."

I moved uncomfortably on my seat. "You did okay."

"No, I didn't." She stared at her whiskey. "You ran wild and we both know it. Everyone knew it."

I rolled a shoulder. "It worked out in the end."

"Yeah. The prima made you a vampire, didn't she? Because she thought you had parents who didn't care."

"Mom. It's done and I'm happy. Don't beat yourself up about it. I'm a fucking lieutenant now—you can't get much higher than that."

"I suppose so." Her mouth pulled sideways. "These days, you look more like my grandson than my son, you know. It's...strange."

It was true. I lifted my shoulders, let them drop.

"So," I said. "About Esposito. When did you see him last?"

"I don't know. Why don't you text him yourself?"

"I did," I said, tight-jawed. "He changed his number again."

Esposito changed his phone number as often as other people changed their shoes. And when I'd had the PI track down his new number, he hadn't responded.

"It's your fault, you know. If you treated him with any respect, he wouldn't—"

"When did you see him last?" I interrupted.

She narrowed her eyes at me.

I grabbed for my patience. "Please. I need to know."

"Why?"

"That, I can't tell you. But it's important."

She stared at me for a beat, then shrugged. "A couple of weeks ago."

"In Halifax?"

A shake of her head. "Montreal. We went out, had some fun."

"Montreal. He was gambling again, right?"

"He played a few hands of poker, yeah."

I suppressed a sigh. "How much did he lose?"

"Nothing." Her smile was triumphant. "He won—big. He bought me this." She pushed up the sleeve of her sweater to show me a delicate gold chain dotted with what looked like real diamonds.

"Huh." My stomach twisted. Esposito only gave her gifts when he wanted something.

Her mouth turned down in disappointment. "That's all you have to say?"

"It's pretty," I made myself add.

She pulled the sleeve back over her wrist again. "He asked about you, you know."

Ah. "What did he want to know?"

"How you were, that sort of stuff. I told him you were a lieutenant now, and he said to tell you congratulations."

"Tell him I said thanks," I said, to make her happy.

Esposito would be asking for more money any day now. He always needed money. Maybe he really had won big this time, although it wouldn't be the first time he'd lied to my mom about it. But even if he had, what he hadn't spent buying her presents, he would've lost at cards.

"Did he say anything else?"

"Just that he'd be in touch. He's changed, Talon. If you spent some time with him, you'd see. He wants to be a father to you."

I stared at her. If Esposito had actually changed, then I was an eight-legged kraken. But he was her weakness; she'd always see him through rose-colored glasses.

And she'd always choose him over me.

I'd had enough. I pushed back my chair and rose to my feet. "I have to go. But if you hear from him, let me know, is that clear? This is important."

She rose, too. "Sure, honey. You can count on me."

No, I can't. And I never could.

In fact, until I'd met Cain and later, Brien, the only person I could truly count on was myself. But what was the point in saying it? I'd only hurt her, and it wouldn't change anything.

I rounded the table and squeezed her shoulder. "You got everything you need?"

"Yeah, I'm good," she said, reaching for another cigarette. "Love you, sweetheart."

"Love you, too."

I'd ridden my motorcycle from the castle. She followed me onto the narrow porch and leaned against the porch rail, smoking the cigarette, as I rode off.

As soon as I was back in my apartment, I sent for Eden, then poured myself a glass of blood-wine and sank onto the couch.

Eden appeared immediately like she'd been waiting for my summons. No ripped jeans and soft blue sweaters tonight, though. Tonight she wore tight, body-hugging black—leggings and a sleeveless top that showcased her full tits.

"Hey, there." Her smile was tentative.

Holy fuck.

I stilled, the wine glass partway to my mouth.

It was Catwoman with short, dark-tipped yellow hair and a baby bump—and I'd always had a weakness for Catwoman.

Whatever Eden saw on my face made her smile broaden. She sauntered toward me.

I managed to unfreeze my vocal cords. "Hey," I returned, and without taking my eyes from her, set my glass on an end table. As soon as she was close enough, I snagged her hips and practically dragged her between my knees.

She leaned into me, her hands on my shoulders. "I went to Olivia's today. She says everything's fine."

"I know." I caressed her hips. The tight black pants looked like leather, but they were some other, shiny material. "I read her report as soon as I got up."

A nod. "She...told you it was a boy?"

"She did—and that he's healthy." And I thanked all the gods for that. "You *will* take better care of yourself going forward," I added, because it still pissed me off that she'd been too scared of me and the syndicate to get the medical care she needed.

What the fuck would've happened if I hadn't found her in time? Would she have given birth in that apartment with only Rio to help her?

She grimaced. "I will, I promise. Thanks for setting it up. I know I should've gone to a doctor sooner."

"Yeah, you should've," I returned.

A small sigh. "I'm sorry. Another thing I fucked up."

I smacked her ass. "Don't worry, I added it to the list." I was only half-joking.

She dragged her teeth over her lower lip and swayed closer, putting those tits right in my face, clouding my brain with her sweet, Eden-scent.

I fingered the zipper of her clingy black top. "Did you wear this for me?"

She dipped her chin. "D'you like it? It's vintage—one of the things I bought the other day."

"Fuck, yeah." I slid the zipper down, exposing soft breasts barely covered by a filmy black bra. "I withdraw my objection to second-hand clothes if this is what you're buying. But this outfit makes me want to do bad things to you." I teased her nipple through the gossamer fabric. "Is that why you wore it?"

Her answer was to arch her back, a hungry whimper slipping from her lips.

I gripped her throat, lightly but firmly. Her lids closed in pleasure, and beneath my thumb, her carotid artery pulsed and throbbed. My mouth watered with the need to suck on that spot, to drag another of those sexy whimpers from her, but I also wanted a straight answer from her.

No, I *needed* it. Was she trying to play me? Or was she truly sorry?

"Answer me," I told her. "Tell me why you wore it. The truth."

Her eyes met mine, her expression stark. "Because I don't want to fight with you. I want to get back what we had."

Gods, I wanted to believe her. Too much.

I stroked my thumb down her the side of her neck. "Then you shouldn't have left like that. You shouldn't have taken money to spy on Twilight."

"You're right. And I'm sorry. I promise I'll do better. I know it doesn't make it right," she added, "but I'm going to keep telling you until you believe me."

I did believe her. Jones had reported her conversation with her mother to William, the castle's steward. Eden could've made trouble for the syndicate by crying to her mom, but she hadn't. She'd come back to face me another night, not knowing what I'd do to her next.

So I believed she was sorry. That didn't mean I was ready to forgive her.

She'd humiliated me in front of Brien and Cain.

Attempted to hide my own spawn from me.

She owed me, and I intend to collect. If that made me a bastard, then I'd own it.

"You abused my trust, Eden."

"I'm sor—," she started to say, but I put my hand over her mouth, stopping her.

"Words are cheap," I said and released her.

She lifted her gaze to mine, finally understanding where I was going with this. "What can I do?" she asked huskily.

Oh, baby. So many things.

"Show me." I sat back, widening my legs. "Show me how sorry you are. Show me how you can do better." I rubbed my hand over the hard ridge my dick was making in my jeans.

She swallowed, her gaze glued to my crotch.

The woman was going to kill me. I had to clamp my molars together to stop myself from grabbing her head and forcing her face between my thighs.

I didn't, though.

An apology should come willingly—or not at all.

"Show me how sorry you are." Talon's voice was low and edged with a roughness.

It licked hotly over my skin, sending an answering tremor through me.

I'd returned to the castle with my emotions all over the place. Excited about the baby, and worried I wouldn't be a good enough parent. Upset about my mother and yet glad she knew I was okay. Eager to see Talon but sick of the tension between us.

But that all faded away when I saw him lazing on the couch, hard-bodied and wolf-eyed. In the dim lighting, his face shimmered, vampire beautiful.

In the human world, he could've been a model, the kind they photographed slouched against walls exuding testosterone and attitude. Thick brown curls cut short on the sides and long on the top. Chiseled jawline. Full lower lip.

My heart fisted. Sometimes my love for him was so strong it hurt.

I'd been lanky and awkward from age eleven to thirteen. Even after I'd filled out, I'd felt funny in my own body. Yeah, as a thrall I'd learned to hide that discomfort—wearing the short, tight dresses; applying the makeup—but that had been like playing dress up. Pretending to be someone I wasn't.

But these last two nights I'd said to hell with that. First, I'd dressed down, and Talon had still seemed to find me hot. And tonight I'd dressed sexy, but on *my* terms, pregnant belly and all.

Now I wondered if I'd been trying to prove that he didn't really want me, Eden. He wanted the seductive, eager-to-please thrall in the tight red minidresses.

If so, I'd been wrong. Maybe sex was all we had, but there was no way he didn't want this as much as I did. His cheekbones were slightly flushed, his eyes heavy with lust.

"Apologize to me, baby." Reaching between his parted legs, he slowly ran his hand up his tented jeans.

Squeezed. Released.

My nipples tightened into points. A honeyed heat slid through my belly.

Yeah, he was being kind of an asshole, demanding I suck him off as an apology. But I couldn't pretend I didn't like it in a kinky sort of way. Because I did...a lot.

And I wanted to do it, wanted to show him how sorry I really was.

"Maybe tonight I'll even let you come," he added.

Okay, that was definitely assholey behavior. My chin lifted. "How do you know I didn't come last night?"

His eyes hooded and the hard planes of his face took on a dangerous cast. "Did you?"

"No," I admitted.

His mouth curved. "That's what I thought. Now stop stalling and suck me."

My stomach contracted at the arrogant demand.

His living room was modern urban-loft—wood-and-metal tables, wide-plank floors, industrial copper lighting, a distressed leather couch. Except for the lack of windows, it could've been in New York or Vancouver.

I lowered myself to my knees on the copper-and-gray Kilim rug in front of him, and his smug expression dissolved. He stared at me with an intent, animal focus. The shark tat swimming up his neck seemed almost alive.

I undid the button of his pants, eased his zipper down over his cock. It surged against his boxer briefs.

Somebody was eager. I shot him a triumphant look up from beneath my lashes.

His chest rumbled in displeasure. "Do it."

I trailed my fingers over his hard length through his boxers. The tip had already dampened the nylon placket.

A sense of my own power filled me. Oh, yeah. He wanted this—wanted *me*—bad.

I slid my fingers into his boxers. The skin of his abdomen was vampire-cool, but not here. Here he was warm and smooth and thick.

I removed my fingers from his boxers and tugged on the waistband. "Take these off."

He grunted assent and rose to his feet, me still kneeling before him. He bent and took my mouth in a hard, wet kiss.

"Don't move," he said, releasing me.

He pulled off his T-shirt and slipped off his boxers before lowering himself to the couch in front of me again. God, I loved his body: hard-muscled and warm-skinned, his legs long and strong, his chest dusted with wiry black hair.

A liquid rush between my inner thighs made me press them together, and he noticed.

Of course, he noticed.

His nostrils flared and his lids lowered in a hungry, I'm-going-to-devour-you-little-girl expression.

My body responded, mindless and needy. The heat between my legs expanded to my belly, my breasts. My nipples pushed against the filmy bra, aching to be touched.

"Take off your shirt," he said, and waited as I wriggled out of it.

He studied my breasts for a few seconds, then, as if reading my mind, he brought his hands up, shaping them, squeezing them, toying with the nipples. I was so sensitive that it was both pleasure and pain.

"So pretty," he said, almost to himself.

He tweaked them hard, and I flinched and moaned. It hurt, but in a good way.

He cupped my chin. "Too much?"

I shook my head. "I liked it."

His thumb rubbed over my lower lip. "You look so beautiful kneeling for me. You make me want to do such bad things to you."

Yes, please.

A dizzying wave of desire gripped me. My heart thumped, its rhythm echoing the pulsing in my core.

Talon released me and sat back, spreading his arms along the couch again. His eyes snagged mine. "Suck me, pretty girl."

I fisted the base of his cock and sucked the tip into my mouth. Out of the corner of my eye, I saw his fingers tighten on the couch back. I took him as deep as I could, then pulled back before taking him deep again.

"Mm," I said, letting the words vibrate around his cock.

His groan was my reward. "That's it. Just like that."

I continued working him with my lips, mouth, and one hand. With my other hand I cupped his stones, squeezing and caressing them.

It wasn't an apology anymore. Or, it wasn't *only* an apology.

It was me demonstrating how much I loved him. A gift from me to him.

He was close now, his testicles drawn up tight and hard. He released the couch and speared his fingers into my hair, holding my head still so he could fuck my mouth. His strokes sped up, grew more forceful, although he was careful not to go too deep.

It was so hot, having him control me. I slid my free hand between my legs to ease the ache. I sucked harder—greedy for his pleasure.

He came in my mouth with a drawn-out groan. I swallowed it down, then sat back, my hands on his long, strong thighs. Talon exhaled, eyes closed, relaxed as a conqueror. Then he took my face in his hands and kissed me on the lips.

"Apology accepted," he said, drawing me to my feet.

I slanted him a cocky look. "My turn now, right? You promised."

"Did I?"

Actually, he hadn't. And my cockiness was faked.

But he had a small smile on his face as he turned me toward his bedroom. "Get in the bed."

Like the living room, Talon's bedroom was uncluttered, masculine.

Walls the color of parchment, and other than the sleek leather-and-walnut bed, the only furniture was a pair of mid-century walnut night-stands and an espresso-colored leather chair. No books, no paintings, no knick-knacks. The only art was a sinuous, hammered-metal shark that covered most of one wall.

I went willingly but veered toward his bathroom as we entered the room, saying, "I need to clean up."

And pee. Pregnant woman, here.

We took turns in the bathroom. When Talon came out, I was standing next to his massive bed, still in my panties and bra, not sure if I should lie down or not.

A few months ago, I would've crawled under the covers to wait for him, but things were different now. I wasn't sure where we stood, how much to assume.

He strolled across the plank wood floor, fully erect again. Without speaking, he removed my bra, dropping it beside the bed.

My gaze moved over his face, my insides tight with a painful yearning.

His hands covered my breasts, weighing them, fingering the sensitive tips.

He slid a hand behind my back, bringing me against his naked body. His other hand curled around my nape, holding me still while he kissed me. Slow, hot kisses that left me dazed and breathing hard.

He released me long enough to draw back the silky blue coverlet, then pressed me down on the mattress so I was on my back looking up at him.

My panties were the next to come off. He knelt on the floor and put my feet on his shoulders, my knees bent and open wide. Grasping my hips, he pulled me toward him. Cool lips touched my inner leg an inch from my sex.

Anticipation hummed in my veins. He feathered his mouth down my thigh, teasing me with light licks and nips.

"I shouldn't be doing this," he said against my skin. "I was going to make you wait at least a week, maybe longer."

I dug my fingers into the sheets. "Please don't."

He lifted his head to look at me. "Please don't make you wait?"

"Yeah. That."

"Mm." He ran his thumb down my slit. "You're so wet." His deep voice roughened. "You really do want this, don't you?"

"*Yes.*" I rocked my pelvis up toward him, desperate for his touch.

He bared his fangs at me, then scraped them along my thigh. To my surprise, he broke the skin, drawing a few drops of blood.

My breath caught. "Are you going to feed from me?"

"Not until you've had the baby. It wouldn't be good for you."

"Oh." I didn't like to think of him drinking from other thralls, but his consideration made my chest constrict. These flashes of caring—of goodness, even if he probably wouldn't see it that way—were why I'd fallen in love with him.

So much love, I had. And he didn't want it. In fact, if I gave into it, he'd sense it and pull back from me.

I swallowed and turned my face toward the wall with the hammered-metal shark.

Talon lifted his head. "Where did you go?"

"Nowhere." I put a smile on my lips and turned back toward him. "See. Still here."

"Eyes on me," he ordered...and licked the tiny wound he'd made on my thigh.

A white heat shot to my sex. He'd released some of the aphrodisiac in his saliva into my bloodstream. Even a tiny amount was a rush.

My pussy clenched. My toes curled. My brain clouded.

Talon's groan seemed to come from far away. "Gods. You taste so good."

He ran his tongue up my thigh again, this time continuing until he reached my center. He opened me with his fingers and licked into me.

I moaned and gave in to the pleasure. It had been so long, and I craved not just the sex, but the closeness. If this was all he could give me, for tonight, I'd take it. For tonight, I'd let it be enough.

He sucked on my clit and I made a needy sound and tunneled my fingers into his thick hair. I felt feverish, my thighs trembling.

"More," I rasped.

He hummed an assent and sucked hard on my clit. "Like that?" he muttered against my sensitized skin.

My hips jerked restlessly. I gripped him harder. If he stopped now, I was pretty sure I'd die.

"Yes. Just like that. But more. *Please*."

He did it again, sucking, tonguing, even nibbling. And then, holy crap, his finger rubbed at my back entrance, adding an extra sensation.

My orgasm barreled down on me like a freight train. My body bowed against the mattress. Releasing his head, I moaned and fisted my fingers in the soft sheets.

Pleading words tumbled from my lips: "More," and "Oh, God" and "Talon."

Between my legs, Talon growled in satisfaction, the low sound adding pleasure to the nearly unbearable sensations. He slid two fingers into me, stroking my pulsating inner walls while he continued to suck and tongue me until I shattered, calling out brokenly as dark suns exploded behind my eyes.

I was still vibrating when he slid his fingers from me and licked them, telling me to roll over. "Get on your forearms."

I obeyed, drugged by lust and pleasure, my bottom turned up, my breasts on the mattress.

He stroked a palm down the side of my abdomen. "You're comfortable?"

"Yes," I said, my voice muffled against the sheet. I turned my head. "It seems like a good position, actually."

"Good." He stroked my butt, then slapped it a few times. "Such a pretty, round ass."

The tingle spread to my cunt, making my inner thighs tighten.

God, I'd missed this. Talon had ruined me for anyone else.

A human man could never measure up to a vampire, and not only because vampires could fuck all night. It wasn't even because of their aphrodisiac, although that gave you incredible, mind-blowing orgasms. What gave vampires the edge was they sensed your emotions, detected every spurt of arousal. They knew what you needed almost before you did—and they knew how to withhold it until you were crazed with wanting.

And Talon was so very good at drawing out the pleasure.

He knelt behind me, his body curved over mine. Nudging my chin up, he put his mouth to my ear. "If you weren't pregnant, I'd take my belt to you for what you did."

I moaned. "Please," I breathed, not really knowing what I was asking for but so turned on by the aphrodisiac and his dominance that I would've agreed to almost anything.

He rose up and smacked my ass again. "If you hadn't accepted my blood bond, I still wouldn't have let you go. You're mine and we both know it. Say it, Eden. Say you're mine. I want to hear it."

It took a beat for his demand to register.

Unconditional surrender. That's what he was asking for.

In my dazed state, I almost mindlessly repeated it back to him.

But I wasn't ready to surrender that last little piece of me. Not when he was still deciding whether to trust me. Not when he'd made it clear that love wasn't on the table.

I surfaced enough to whisper, "No."

He swore under his breath. Taking hold of his cock, he dragged the head through my juices, a delicious friction that made me groan and press back against him, seeking more.

"Do it," he demanded, "or I won't let you come."

He wasn't using compulsion, but his will was so powerful that my mouth opened to comply. I caught myself in time, though, and closed it, shaking my head against the sheets.

Another hard slap. "I guess I'll have to fuck you until you say it."

I groaned a yes.

"Yeah, you'd like that, wouldn't you, little girl? You want it hard, don't you? You want to fight me because it feels so good when you give in."

Sometimes I hated how easily he could read me. "No," I lied.

His snarl said he wasn't happy with me, either. "Careful, baby. You don't want to piss me off."

He grasped my hips and slammed into me. I'd forgotten how big he was, how full I felt when he was inside.

Possessed.

Aching.

My nerve endings came alive, my mind and body attuned to him and the pleasure he was giving me. My pussy closed around his cock like it never wanted to let him go.

"Fuck," he gritted. "You're so tight like this. Aren't you?"

"Yes, yes," I said, not really knowing what I was responding to but wanting more. More of his cock, more of him.

"Mine," he said and thrust back inside.

I was drowning in pleasure. Steeped in Talon's earthy, outdoor scent, the feel of his hard body moving in mine.

"Sweet Lilith, what you do to me." He slowed down, keeping me on the edge for long minutes with shallow, teasing thrusts. "You're mine. Say it."

"Please," I said instead.

His body curved over mine, his fingers teasing my clit. "Mine," he crooned. "Say it or I won't let you come."

"No." Was that whine coming from me? "Please. I need to..."

"Say it." He pulled those knowing fingers away.

Lungs jerking, I thrashed beneath him ...and broke. "I'm yours, all right? I've always been yours."

It was the truth and we both knew it. My eyes pricked, and then a couple of hot tears spilled down my cheeks.

Because the opposite wasn't true. Talon wasn't mine. I'd never come first with him. No thrall would.

"Good girl." He reached beneath our bodies, rubbing my clit as he pounded into me.

My mind whirled into oblivion. I arched my body, pressing back against him as the pressure built inside me. Gasping for oxygen, straining against him. Caught between his body and the mattress.

My climax slammed through me like a rogue wave, dragging me under and tossing me around until I didn't know which way was up.

Talon kept thrusting, then groaned and stilled deep inside me. My inner muscles clenched around him, and he husked, "Fuck, baby, that feels so good," and followed me under the waves.

His head fell forward. I felt him breathing against my spine, still deep inside me. Then he touched his lips to my lower back and withdrew, flopping down onto the mattress next to me.

I turned onto my side, my head on my bent arm, flushed and loose and satisfied. Gradually my breathing slowed. I watched as Talon's hair-dusted chest rose and fell at a vampire's sluggish pace—three or four breaths per minute.

I love you.

I reached my hand out to touch him but halted halfway there and curled it next to my breasts instead.

He turned onto his side, so close I could see the gold flecks in his chocolate-brown irises. "You cried. Why?"

My eyes slid from his. "I don't know. I'm...emotional these days. Hormones. And the sex was so intense." That last part wasn't even a lie.

He grunted, and I could tell he knew I wasn't telling him the whole truth, but he let it go. "So you saw your mom today."

I grimaced. I should've known Jones would report us.

"Yeah, but it wasn't planned. I have no idea how she found out. She was just there in the waiting room after I saw Olivia."

Talon shrugged a powerful shoulder. "I didn't think you had anything to do with it, but you should've told me."

"I was going to," I said, which was the God-honest truth. "I was just waiting for the right moment." I hesitated, then added, "But now that they know I'm home, they want to see me."

A noncommittal grunt. "Did you tell your mom why you left? What you did?"

"No. There wasn't time to explain. And—" I heaved a breath, then admitted—"I was too ashamed to tell them. But I will, I promise."

"Are they going to give me trouble about this?"

"Probably. I asked Mom to hold off for a couple of weeks, but I don't know if my dad will go along with it. Maybe if you gave me access to a phone—?"

Talon had been absent-mindedly caressing my abdomen. Now he stilled. "No. And don't ask me again."

"Sorry," I muttered.

Talon rolled onto his back. I stared at his profile, wishing I hadn't said anything.

"Olivia told you I'm having a boy?" I asked.

"Yeah." His expression softened. He turned back to me, smiling. "She sent me one of the pictures she took so I could see for myself."

"Yeah? Could you make me a copy?"

"Sure."

"Thanks." I traced a circle on the sheet between us. "I guess that makes you happy, right? That he's a boy?"

A slight frown creased his forehead. "Because I wouldn't be happy if we were having a girl?"

I nodded. "You're a lieutenant—I figured you'd want a boy." Yeah, the Maritime Syndicate had a couple of females in key positions, but they were the exception, not the rule.

"Hell, I don't care as long as the baby's healthy. And Olivia said he's doing great—a strong, active little guy."

"That's how I feel." I grinned, remembering what the baby had looked like on the black-and-white screen. "And he is—he was moving the whole time."

The corner of Talon's mouth ticked up. "My mom said that when she was pregnant with me, I kicked her black-and-blue."

I blinked. "Yeah? He's not that bad."

"Yet," Talon responded.

We grinned at each other. "You're scaring me here," I teased.

"Sorry. But I'll be there to help with him."

My heart did a happy little skip. "Good. That's good."

We were still looking at each other. Our smiles faded, but that was okay, because it felt like Talon was drinking me in the way I did him.

His eyes dropped to my abdomen. "I—whatever you need to get you through this, let me know, okay?"

I dipped my chin. "Okay."

"I mean it," he said.

"All right. And thanks."

Fragile wings rustled in my chest, that hope I couldn't quite seem to shake off. For the first time, it felt like we were partners in this.

Until Talon added, "You don't have to thank me. I'm the guy responsible. It's only right that I take care of you both."

"Oh. Of course." My heart plummeted.

So that's what this was about. To Talon, me and the baby were a "responsibility." Something he hadn't asked for—or wanted—but was making the best of.

I mean, I admired him for that, but it was like he'd reached out a fist and crushed those small, hopeful wings between his fingers.

"Right." He ran a hand over his face and sat up.

He must've sensed my disappointment because I could practically see him retreating inside his walls. Adding bricks to make them higher. Reinforcing them with concrete.

He glanced over his shoulder and I thought he was going to tell me to leave, but instead, he said, "The primus and prima want to see you."

❧ 14 ❧

TALON

Eden moistened kiss-swollen lips. A dull hurt replaced the joy emanating from her. "Tonight?" she asked.

Guilt slithered through my ribs. I had the sudden, shocking urge to tell Brien to go fuck himself, which was messed up. Eden was in the wrong here. One round of hot sex didn't change that.

Even if it had been five-alarm, make-your-eyes-roll-back-in-your-head hot sex.

Even if I'd been compelled by some primitive instinct to make her admit she was mine...

"Tonight," I confirmed.

She sat up, the sheet clutched to her chest, a clear sign she felt vulnerable—and why that made my heart constrict, I didn't know. But it did.

"Why?" Her eyes pinged back and forth between mine. "What do they want?"

"Brien didn't say. Now get up—you don't want to keep them waiting."

I got out of bed, aware I was being an ass. But it seemed imperative to reassert my control over Eden. Or maybe myself, because the woman hadn't been back for forty-eight hours, and already, I was ready to go up against my primus for her. Already, I'd all but begged her to say she was mine.

I busied myself checking my phone. "Take a shower," I said without looking at her. "I'll text someone to bring you some clothes. You can't go dressed in that Catwoman outfit." For a formal meeting like this, she'd need something more subdued. An outfit like that might even be considered an insult.

Out of the corner of my eye, I saw Eden roll her lips in. Then she rose from the bed and strolled past me naked and proud as a queen.

I texted Kerry to have someone bring Eden a nice dress and a pair of heels, then put the phone down and blew out a breath.

Where were these inconvenient feelings coming from? I'd never felt like this about a thrall before. Why now? Why her?

And that was my legs moving, following her into the bathroom.

Instead of a tub I'd probably never use, I'd had a doorless shower installed with a heated towel rack and multiple showerheads. A second section with a handheld shower had a teak stool against one wall. Eden used to sit on the stool to shave her legs while I watched.

I rounded the partition between the shower and the toilet. Eden had turned on the lower five showerheads, leaving the rain shower off so her hair didn't get wet.

She stood in profile to me, eyes closed, one hand on the rough slate tiles, letting the hot water flow over her. Slippery and pink-skinned and so beautiful my heart did that constricting thing again.

"Hey," I said.

She opened her eyes and turned toward me, swiping her hands over her face. The gold cuff on her wrist glinted in the muted lighting.

"I'm done." She went to brush past me.

She'd closed down. That's what I wanted, wasn't it? A thrall who didn't make inconvenient demands for things like affection or time outside of the bedroom.

So why did it feel like she'd shoved a screw into my chest and twisted it?

I caught her arm, trapping her between my body and the tile wall.

Sea-glass eyes met mine, their color intensified by the water droplets dotting her dark-gold lashes. "What?" she asked flatly.

I stared down at her with what felt like a fishbone lodged in my throat. Slowly, carefully, I brought her wrist to my mouth, kissing the inside just below the gold cuff that symbolized her bond to me.

My intent was to remind us both who she belonged to. That this wasn't a relationship but a transaction—vampire to thrall.

But it didn't go down like that, not with her blood pulsing in the vein beneath my lips. Not with her scent enveloping me.

Heated skin.

Feminine spice.

Against my will, my fangs lengthened. I scraped the tips over that tempting blue line.

Mine.

Feed.

Without warning, the blood-hunger wrested control of my brain. I made a low, animal sound deep in my throat.

I wanted—no, needed—to bury my fangs in the clean-smelling hollow at the turn of her shoulder.

Needed to shove her up against the slate tiles.

Needed to fuck her, deep and hard, until she felt me everywhere from the crown of her head to her pretty pink toes.

She'd accepted my blood bond. She was *mine*.

She tensed. "You're hungry."

I stifled a groan. *You have no idea, little girl.*

I reminded myself that drinking from Eden wasn't an option right now. That it could harm both her and my spawn.

Just a taste, the hunger crooned.

I drew a slow breath, then forced myself to lift my head and release her. "Go," I said gruffly.

She nodded and slipped out of the shower.

I rested my forehead on the slate tiles.

What the fuck, Talon?

I hadn't come that close to losing myself to the blood-hunger since the first months after I'd been turned.

I dialed the water temperature to ice-cold—anything to cool myself—and soaped up.

When I reentered the bedroom, a black knit dress was laid out on the bed along with a half-slip, and Eden was perched on a chair in a lacy black bra and panties, pulling on a pair of sheer thigh-highs. My dick twitched, but I moved past her to my walk-in closet for a suit and a dress shirt.

Back in the bedroom, Eden was still perched on the chair. As I buttoned my shirt, she rolled up the second stocking and pulled it over her toes, unrolling it to her ankle and then up her long, lean leg.

My fingers stilled on my shirt buttons as she pulled the sheer material over the strong muscles of her calf and continued up to her thigh. Watching Eden dress was almost as good as watching her undress—and it reminded me of how much I'd missed her.

I turned away.

She fooled you once. Who's to say she won't do it again?

Her disloyalty crouched between us like a dark, ragged thing. I'd accepted her apology, but we could never go back to how we'd been.

In claiming Eden as my exclusive thrall, I'd elevated her status. She'd traveled with us, received special treatment—extra freedom, a larger suite in the thralls' quarters, bonuses in the form of jewelry and cash.

The syndicate had known what that meant. She was a weakness, one I reluctantly owned because the alternative—knowing other vampires were fucking and feeding from Eden—simply wasn't tolerable.

And in return, she'd spied on the syndicate and run from me, a sickening repeat of all the times my mom and my loser of a father had let me down.

I could forgive Eden. But I wasn't sure if I'd ever trust her again.

She put on the half-slip and shimmied into the black dress. The form-fitting knit made it clear she was round with my spawn. That, at least, wasn't a lie.

She tried and failed to reach the zipper. She cast me a look over her shoulder. "I can't—"

I was already crossing to her. Her nape was damp from the shower. She smelled like my soap and her own unique essence.

My dick pressed against my dress pants. I gritted my teeth and took hold of the dress's pull-tab. My fingers brushed her bare neck and she gave a small shiver.

Something crawled through my chest. A dark, primal yearning.

Mark her.

Claim her.

Eden licked her lips. "Something wrong?"

I inhaled, told myself it was simply the blood-hunger. I needed to feed, that was all.

"No," I lied and zipped her up. Instead of releasing her, I cupped her neck, tipping her head back so I could speak into her ear. "If you have to grovel, you'll fucking do it. Got it? I can only protect you so far."

Her chest jerked in a jagged breath. "Yes."

She was truly afraid now, her emotions so raw it was like she was shouting them to the room. I resisted my urge to soothe, reassure.

Brien was a tolerant primus and I believed Twilight was prepared to forgive and forget, but only if Eden showed the proper amount of contrition.

"Good." I bit the side of her neck—no fangs, just my human teeth. But I did it hard enough to leave a mark.

⁂

The war room was empty except for Diane. She glanced up as we passed her computer station. "Good evening, Lieutenant."

I paused. "Everything okay?"

Her eyes slid to Eden, standing straight-backed by my side, then dropped to the blood-bond bracelet, taking it in, unsurprised. Word must've gotten around.

"It's been pretty quiet," the soldier replied.

"Good." I guided Eden into Brien's office.

He was seated behind his desk with Twilight standing to his left, her long hair in its usual inky braid. No Cain, for which I was grateful. He'd made his disdain for Eden clear; I didn't need him mucking this up for her.

"Talon." Brien shut his laptop. "Thank you for coming."

"Of course." I included Twilight in my respectful nod.

Brien's gaze flicked to Eden, noting first the red mark I'd put on her neck, then the gold cuff. He met my eyes, acknowledging the message that, for better or worse, this woman was under my protection.

Eden was staring at Twilight, brow pleated.

In a short pink dress and platform shoes, our new prima appeared as lethal as a piece of bubblegum, but I'd seen her fight—the woman was good. In fact, she probably had a blade strapped to one of those lean thighs.

"A vampire," Eden said in a disbelieving voice. "You're a vampire?"

❧ 15 ❧

EDEN

My jaw dropped. Twilight was a vampire?

"You didn't tell her?" she asked Talon.

"Didn't think of it," he said.

Twilight looked back at me. "Brien turned me after you left."

"Oh."

"Eden." Talon's fingers tightened on my waist, and I realized I was gaping at Twilight, mouth ajar.

Closing it with a snap, I lowered my gaze to the polished wood desk.

But, damn. Brien hadn't just mated with her, he'd turned her.

It was a punch in the throat. Brien hadn't known Twilight nearly as long as Talon had known me. Plus, she was a freaking slayer.

She was one of them now, while I was still on the outside looking in. I felt like a teenager again, gazing up at the castle on the cliff, wondering what it would be like to live in it. A thrall's life had seemed so glamorous. Parties, clothes, expensive gifts. Beautiful, broody men who'd ruin you for any other man...

No, wait, that last part I hadn't known back then.

I wiped my face of expression, shoving my shock and hurt down deep. Otherwise, they'd all pick up on it and right now, I couldn't bear that.

127

"Answer him," Talon ordered under his breath, and I realized Brien had asked how I was doing.

"I'm good, thank you." I stretched my lips in a smile that probably didn't fool any of them.

Brien dipped his chin in acknowledgment. His dark blond hair was pulled back in a short ponytail, his lean face surfer-boy handsome. A man who'd been born a pureblood vampire and a prince, he wore his new position as primus easily, as comfortable in a ten-thousand-dollar suit as in a T-shirt and jeans.

Grovel, Talon had told me. Humbling myself wasn't easy, but I was determined to do it—and not because of Talon. I owed both Twilight and Brien an apology.

I squared my shoulders. "If I may speak...?"

"Go ahead," Brien said.

Okay. My heart banged against my chest. I had to get this right.

I wiped my sweaty palms on my skirt and let the words spill out.

"Before we go any further, I want to apologize. To you both, but especially to Twilight. I'm sorry." I met her eyes. "I never did anything like that before—I want you both to know that. That's not an excuse, by the way. There's no excuse for what I did—breaking the syndicate's trust like that, and especially, for spying on you. I'm sorry for that, and I'm especially sorry if it put you in—in any danger."

To my humiliation, my voice cracked. I dug my teeth into my lower lip, willing myself not to cry. That would be the final straw, breaking down in front of Twilight.

Talon's hand returned to my lower back in silent support. I hadn't expected that. My heart squeezed. If only we really had a relationship like that, one where he had my back, no matter what.

One where he loved me like I loved him. No matter what.

Twilight tilted her head like an inquisitive robin. She'd been pretty as a human, but as a vampire, she was breath-taking. Her skin shimmered like the inside of a shell, her dark eyes were luminous, her lips a rosy red.

"Why did you do it?" she asked.

I shook my head. "That's not important. I knew it was wrong, and I did it anyway."

"Mm." Her gaze dropped to my swollen belly, her look knowing.

Shortly before I'd left the island, Twilight had found me crying in the bathroom of the Bite Club, the castle's dance club. I hadn't told her why, but she must've realized that was around the time I'd found out I was carrying Talon's child.

My lower back was aching from standing too long. I shifted my weight and brought my hands to my sacrum. Talon's large palm went right to where it hurt the most, massaging the tightness.

"Jesus." Twilight pointed to the armchair in front of the desk. "Let her sit already."

"Thank you." Talon helped me lower myself to the leather seat.

The new prima folded her toned arms over her candy-pink bodice. "Here's what I think, Eden. Nothing you did harmed me personally. I was here under false pretenses myself." She and Brien shared a look. "So as far as I'm concerned, we're good, although I appreciate the apology."

I swallowed, nodded. "Thank you."

"But that's only me," she said. "There's still Brien and Talon."

Talon put his hands on my shoulders. "We're good. She apologized to me, too."

My mind flashed to me on my knees, taking him into my mouth, and my face heated.

Twilight's gaze flicked to my cheeks. I had a feeling she guessed exactly what form my apology had taken.

Brien leaned back in his chair, and she rested a hand on his shoulder, like one of those scary power couples from *Suits* or *Succession*.

"We let you into our castle," he said. "You were a third-year thrall, someone I believed we could trust. Talon made you his favorite. I suppose we should be grateful they didn't ask you to do anything more damaging. Or did they?"

"No!" I straightened. "That's all I agreed to—make friends with Twilight and report on what she did. And I passed one note for them. That's it. I swear that's all."

Talon's grip tightened on my shoulders. I wasn't sure if he was protecting me or making sure I stayed put.

The baby moved like he'd picked up on my agitation. I took a deep breath.

"Look," I told Brien, "you can have the money he—Eugene—paid me. I don't want it. I haven't spent any of it, just the money I earned as a thrall."

"I'll leave that up to Talon." Brien flicked a long-fingered hand, dismissing the hundred thousand dollars I'd been paid as if it were nothing. "I don't need or want your money. But you broke your contract, Eden. That, I can't forgive. You owe us."

All the spit left my mouth. The office walls felt like they were closing in on me.

"I...owe you?"

"Not money." Brien's teeth gleamed in the dim light. "A favor."

I gulped. No human with any brains wanted to owe a "favor" to a vampire syndicate.

"A favor," I echoed with a panicked glance up at Talon.

He was glaring at Brien, but he kept silent.

"What kind of favor?" I asked.

"I'll let you know," said Brien. "You can refuse, of course. But I'd think hard before I said no. Because if you do, I'll have to assume your apology is just words, won't I?"

My hands were in my lap now, the fingers so tightly interlaced, my knuckles had turned white. But I pulled back my shoulders, looked Brien in the eye. "I won't say no."

A slight smile. "I'm glad to hear that. For now, your movements will continue to be restricted. Talon will decide when the restrictions should be lifted."

Twilight took her hand from Brien's shoulder.

Behind me, I felt Talon relax. "We appreciate that," he said to his friend.

"And your spawn?" Brien glanced at my stomach. "I understand you saw the midwife?"

I had to make a conscious effort not to wrap my arms around my belly to hide it. "I did, yes."

"Olivia says they're both doing fine," Talon inserted. "Our spawn is due in mid-February. A male."

"A male?" Brien's eyes creased in a smile. "That's good news, very good news. It's been years since we had a child in the castle. Congratulations, both of you."

Talon released me. "Thank you." When I slanted a look up at him, he was smiling, too.

"Thank you," I murmured hollowly. All my fears rushed back.

What kind of life would my baby have? I don't care what Jasper said about things being better for dhampirs here on Lilith Island. The vampires still treated them like they were somehow lesser. Half-bloods, they called them.

Twilight frowned. "Why does that bother you? Aren't you happy about the baby?"

I blinked. "I—."

Now Brien was frowning, too.

Behind me, Talon said, "Answer the prima."

I couldn't lie to them, so I started to side-step the question. After almost three years as a thrall, it was second nature to suck up to vampires. To keep my head down, avoid making waves.

"Of course, I'm happy—," I started to say, but why not tell them the truth? What did I have to lose, after all? I was already in disgrace.

And maybe it would make a difference to my son. Brien wasn't an old-world aristocrat like his father. He might be open to a new way of doing things.

"I'm happy about the baby," I said. "But I'm worried for him, too. I don't know if I want him growing up in the castle."

"Because he's a dhampir?" Twilight asked.

"Yes, exactly." I nodded, surprised at how quickly she'd grasped the issue. However, as a slayer, she must've seen the inner workings of a number of vampire syndicates. "You guys look down on dhampirs."

"Eden," Talon warned.

"No," said Twilight, "let her finish. I want to hear this."

Brien was no longer frowning, but now his expression was unreadable, which was almost worse.

"Go on," Twilight told me.

I sat a little straighter. "Right now every single enforcer in the Maritime Syndicate is a vampire, and your two lieutenants—" I spoke directly to Brien—"are also vampires. I get that you're stronger and faster, but don't brains count for anything? Not one dhampir has a rank higher than soldier."

There was a short silence, then Talon said, "She's right, you know."

I slow-blinked. I hadn't expected Talon to take my side, not with the way he felt about siring a dhampir child.

"The hierarchy decides these things," Brien said. "Not me. Except for my lieutenants, of course."

"But Adrian could hold his own against the less dominant vampires," said Talon.

Brien lifted a brow. "Then why doesn't he challenge them?"

Twilight leaned a hip on the desk. "Maybe he thinks it wouldn't do any good. Even if he won, he wouldn't necessarily be promoted. That's up to the primus."

"I don't know," said Brien. "The hierarchy exists for a reason, and if Adrian receives a promotion over a vampire, there will be hell to pay."

"Then maybe," Twilight muttered, "the vampires need to get over themselves."

Brien turned his head to look at her. She smirked back.

"Tell me again why I mated with a slayer?" Brien asked the ceiling.

Her smirk deepened. "Because I think outside of the box."

"There is that..." He turned back to us. "I'll think about it, all right?"

"Thank you," Talon said, and I echoed him.

Brien pulled Twilight onto his lap. "C'mere, you."

Behind me, Talon said, "If we're done here?"

"Get out," Brien said without taking his gaze from his mate.

Talon helped me to my feet, and we exited the office. He shook his head, a smile on his lips.

"Those two," he said, then sobered. "You did good," he told me. He tucked a short strand of hair behind my ear. "I'll bring it up again," he added, low-voiced. "About the dhampirs."

"You will?"

"Yes. That's a promise."

Cain emerged from the office next door. "What's a promise?"

"Later," Talon said with a glance at Diane.

Cain followed us out of the war room, closing the door behind him. He eyed my pregnant stomach but otherwise ignored me as if I were a rock or other unimportant, inanimate object.

"So what happened?" he asked Talon.

"She apologized."

"And?" the lean blond vampire prompted.

Talon gave Cain the Cliff notes on what had been discussed in Brien's office.

"A favor, huh?" Cain's expression carefully neutral.

But when Talon turned back to me, the look Cain sent me from his ice-blue eyes made me gulp.

"I'm going to walk Eden back," Talon said. "I'll see you in a few minutes."

The fear and adrenaline caught up to me on the way back. By the time we reached my suite, my legs felt like two overcooked noodles. I made my way across the living room, sinking onto the couch.

Talon's brows pulled together in a frown. "You're hungry." He took out his phone. "What do you want to eat?"

"A yogurt." I toed off my high heels and released a sigh of relief. "But you don't have to order it for me. I have a couple in the fridge." All the thralls' suites came with a wet bar and a small refrigerator.

"I'll get it," Talon said and, going to the fridge, got me a banana cream yogurt and a spoon, then folded his long body into the green-and yellow striped armchair next to the couch as I ate.

"Brien went easy on you," he said after a while.

"Because of you."

"Maybe. But you were honest, and with Brien, that counts."

I put down the yogurt cup. "That favor," I burst out. "I won't kill someone. Or...hurt them, you know."

Talon's mouth twitched up. "Why would Brien ask you to do that when he can send a soldier—or even me?"

My lungs released like a deflating balloon. That was good, at least.

But I was pregnant now with a dhampir baby, the spawn of one of Brien's top men. A child Brien clearly was interested in.

"It won't have anything to do with the baby, will it?" I asked. "Because that's a hard no. I don't care if that pissed him off."

Talon's face lost its humor. "He'd have to go through me first. But Brien's not like his father—he doesn't take his anger out on innocents. You should know that."

"I do know that. But this baby's *mine*, first—not the syndicate's. It's why I accepted your blood bond, remember?"

A nod. "That's why I offered it."

That hurt, even though I'd asked for it. Even though it was the truth.

I looked away. "Right."

Talon's mouth flattened. "Finish your yogurt," he said and watched from beneath hooded lids until I'd eaten every bite.

"About the money," I said. "I'd like to give it to Rio."

He lifted a brow. "I'll think about it."

"Please?" I put the empty yogurt cup down. "He wants to go to culinary arts school, and a year costs as much as college. More, even, if you go to one of the top schools like the one he's looking at in New York. Plus, he'll need somewhere to live, and apartments are so expensive there. You could rent a whole house in Nova Scotia for what I was paying for that one-bedroom. That money plus the money he's making from the syndicate would mean he had enough to pay for an associate's degree and an apartment."

"I'll think about it, okay?" Talon drew me to my feet. "Walk me to the door."

I followed him into the hall. "Please. Rio deserves a break, you know? And he's such a good cook already. He—"

He considered me. "This really means a lot to you, doesn't it?"

"Yeah."

"Fine. Give me the details and I'll have Smythe—that's Brien's new PA—set up an account for Rio and transfer the money."

"You will?" I broke into a smile. "Thank you. It will mean so much to him."

And then somehow, I had my back to the wall with Talon so close that when I took a breath, my nipples in the black knit dress dragged over his suitcoat.

He put a hand next to my head. "What about you, Eden? How much does it mean to you?"

A hot shiver went over me. "A lot."

"So you'd say you owe me?"

Oh, God. At his dark tone, my panties went from damp to soaked. Without taking my gaze from his, I dipped my chin in assent.

"Good. Because you'll be paying me back."

"I will?"

"Yeah. With interest." He nuzzled my neck. "But I have to leave —work."

My head fell back against the wall. "Are you coming back?"

"No."

Don't beg. Don't beg.

But the words spilled out. I'd missed him, and I was lonely. I knew I'd gotten off easy, but the isolation was getting to me. And I was so turned on, craving sex...but also more of Talon, even if I knew I'd feel empty after.

"Please?" Sliding my hand between us, I gave his erection a suggestive squeeze. "Just for a little while."

He briefly closed his eyes and I thought he was going to give in, but instead, he took my hand and moved it back to my side. "You need your sleep."

"You could wake me up."

"It wouldn't be for hours. I have things to do."

Things. Which probably included another thrall.

I turned my head, giving him my profile. "Got it."

He drew a harsh breath. "Fuck this," he said under his breath, and palmed my cheek, turning my face toward his.

His mouth came down on mine. His body pushed me into the rough stone, his hips grinding into mine.

When he broke the kiss, all I could do was swallow. Twice.

In the flickering torchlight, Talon's face was all shadows and gold. "Get some sleep, Eden. You're going to need it."

❧ 16 ❧

TALON

When my mother sent a text saying she needed to see me ASAP, I was in my office in the war room, catching up on work. My first thought was that she'd hurt herself. It wouldn't be the first time. Last year she'd spiraled into a whiskey-fueled depression and broken an arm, and a few years ago, she'd tripped on the stairs, also while drunk, and knocked out a couple of teeth.

TALON: *You OK?*

MARY ALSTON: *Yeah. Just come, OK?*

So maybe this was about Esposito. My gut tensed, like it always did when I had to deal with my sperm donor. It had been ten days since I'd asked my mom to keep an eye out for him, but so far, he was still MIA.

Be there in thirty minutes, I responded.

Instead of putting the phone away, my fingers hovered over the screen. Maybe I should text Rio, ask him to let Eden know I wouldn't be there for another couple of hours? She'd be expecting me; I'd gotten in the habit of going to her every night around now.

Then I realized what I was doing and shoved the phone into my pocket.

For fuck's sake, Talon, she's your thrall, not your girlfriend.

I stopped in Cain's office to let him know where I was going and that I'd be back in an hour or two, then grabbed my bike from the renovated carriage house that served as the castle's garage and headed out. The cottage was a few miles south on the opposite side of the island from Bluebeard's Cove. I found my mom sitting in the dark again, this time in her living room.

"Talon." She stubbed out her cigarette in an ashtray and rose from the couch. "Thanks for coming."

"No problem." I kissed her cheek, taking the opportunity to surreptitiously sniffed her breath. But she hadn't been drinking. In fact, she appeared fine—clear-eyed and alert, if a little depressed. "So what's up?" I asked. "Did Esposito contact you?"

"No, and stop asking if I've seen him." She rubbed her neck irritably. "Because I haven't. I sent for you because I wanted to ask you something and I didn't want to do it over the phone."

I folded my arms over my chest. "Go ahead."

"Not here." She moved past me to the short hall. "Let's go for a walk—I could use the exercise."

"Sure, why not?" With a shrug, I followed her into the tiny foyer, taking her navy peacoat from the peg and helping her into it.

Pulling a striped wool hat over her short gray hair, she picked up a pair of mittens. "Ready," she said and proceeded me out the door.

The cottage was near the end of a narrow dirt road lined with bare-branched maples and oaks. We followed the road until it dead-ended onto a windy cliff overlooking the Atlantic, then walked along the edge for another five or ten minutes.

Mom paused on the scrubby grass and lifted her face to the biting salt air. "I smell snow," she said, inhaling. "We'll have two or three inches by morning."

"Yeah?" I didn't question her certainty; my mom was the island weather witch. If she said snow or rain was on the way, then it was.

"It will be December in a couple of weeks," she added, almost to herself. "Winter lobster season."

I nodded, gazing out at the heaving black waves. On nights like these, I was grateful I hadn't grown up in a lobstering family. "Anyone who takes a boat out in this weather has balls of steel."

Mom made a sound of agreement, her mind clearly elsewhere. "I hear Eden Montgomery is having a baby. A boy."

I snapped my head around to find her frowning at me from beneath the striped hat. So that's what this was about. "That's right."

"He's yours, isn't he?"

"Yes."

Her throat worked, her hurt permeating the air. "I see."

"I'm sorry. I was going to tell you."

"When?"

An icy wind buffeted me. Even for a vampire, it was fucking cold out here. I jammed both hands into the pockets of my leather jacket. "Soon."

"How long have you known?"

"Two weeks," I admitted.

Two weeks in which Eden had gradually worked her way back into my life.

Not my heart. That part of me was firmly closed to her. Reinforced with walls of steel.

But my life, yeah. I'd rearranged my schedule so I could see more of her. The woman needed looking after, in my opinion. Someone to make sure she ate meals on time and got enough rest. Someone to fuck her until she had that heavy-eyed, satisfied expression...

"Two weeks?" my mom said. "So you knew the last time I saw you?"

"Yeah."

"Jesus, Talon. I may not be much of a parent, but I'm the only mother you've got. I don't care if you've been reborn as a vampire. I shouldn't have to hear I'm going to be a grandma through the grapevine."

My jaw tightened. As far as I was concerned, she'd lost the right to pull the Mom-card when she'd started accepting my money so she could drink all day instead of holding down a job.

"I was getting around to it, okay?"

Pain flickered across her face. "I'm home pretty much every damn night. You could've told me anytime."

She was right. I hunched my shoulders. So why hadn't I told her yet?

"Look, I'm sorry," I said. "I guess I'm still getting used to the idea myself."

Wondering what kind of father I'd make.

Mom sighed, then pulled back her shoulders. "I'd like to meet Eden, get to know her. I remember seeing her around when she was a kid, but we never really talked."

Oh, fuck no. Eden was still under house arrest. And even if she wasn't, my mom was...unpredictable. What if I brought Eden over and she was drunk?

"I'll think about it," I said. "But now's not a good time."

"What d'you mean it's not a good time?"

"Just that it's not."

"She's okay?"

"Yes. She's fine. They're both fine." *Except for the not-so-little fact that she's not allowed to see anyone, even her parents.*

Mom wrapped her arms around herself. "Gigi told me, in case you're wondering—Eden's mom. She drove out here just to tell me." She paused, and when I didn't say anything, added, "They're worried, Talon. Gigi says you're not even letting them talk to her, and that when Eden's father came to the castle, you sent him away."

So now I was the bad guy? "I spoke to Montgomery and told him Eden's okay—that she and the baby are getting the best of care. If he chooses not to believe me, that's his prerogative. But it's the goddamned truth."

"Eden's their daughter. Of course they're concerned. Especially after Gwen disappeared like that."

A muscle ticked in my jaw. "This is nothing like that. Eden's fine, and they'll see her when I'm ready—and not before."

"It had better be soon." She rubbed her mittened hands up and down her arms. "I didn't know what to say to Gigi. It doesn't look good, Talon. An island girl, and she's pregnant, too. And you can tell your fucking syndicate that I said that, too."

"With all due respect, this is none of your business. But I treat her like a goddamn princess, all right?"

"Christ." Her mouth thinned. "You sound just like your father. Always telling me things aren't my business."

Anger flared in me, hot and black. I just stared at her, my teeth clamped so tightly I'm surprised they didn't crack. If anyone else had said that to me, I would've had them by the throat, demanding they apologize.

My mom's gaze dropped first. "Sorry. That wasn't fair."

"No, it wasn't. Because I am nothing like that prick." I blew out a breath through my nose. "Look, I'm not telling you what happened because it's not my story to tell, it's Eden's, all right? Believe it or not, I'm trying to protect her. She fucked up, and she's paying the price—and that's all I'm going to say."

Frankly, I didn't think Eden would want the whole island knowing what she'd done. She had to live here, and so did our son.

Mom hmphed. "How bad could it be?"

I lifted a shoulder, let it drop.

"Fine, go all syndicate vampire on me. But tell me something, Talon. Do you want this kid, really? Or is he just an obligation? Because if that's true, maybe you should just settle some money on Eden and let her go."

I eyed her, frowning. Where the hell had that come from?

One thing I knew, no way was I ever letting Eden go—now or twenty years from now—and the same went for my spawn.

An uncomfortable thought occurred to me. "That's what happened with you and Esposito, wasn't it? You got married because of me."

Mom had always said I'd been born early—a seven-month baby—and I'd never questioned it.

"Well, yeah. But I wanted you." She took a step toward me, her expression fierce—brows lowered, mouth firm. "I wanted you more than anything. And I've never regretted it. *Never.*"

I was still absorbing the fact that I was the reason my parents had gotten married. "But...did he feel the same way?"

She lifted her chin and threw my own words back at me. "With all due respect, that's none of your business."

Then he hadn't.

I swallowed sickly. It was like the cliff had shifted under my feet. I rocked back on my heels, off-balance.

So my dad had done the right thing? Or at least tried to? Until it had gotten too much for him, anyway, and he'd taken off for the mainland.

"Anyway, this isn't about me and Marco," Mom said. "It's about you and Eden. I can guess how she feels right now. And Marco loved me. That was one thing I had that she doesn't—because you don't love her, do you?"

"I blood-bonded her," I said. "To protect her and the baby."

Mom looked disappointed in me. "So it wasn't because you wanted *her*—Eden. It was because you thought you had to."

A feeling way too close to shame constricted my chest. "That's what she thinks," I admitted.

"Oh, Talon." Her tone was resigned and a little sad. "Don't..."

"Don't what?"

She heaved a breath. "Don't push her away. Make sure she knows you really want this baby."

"She knows," I said, then halted. Because did she?

I remembered how uncertain Eden seemed at times, almost too eager to please. I'd thought it was because she was trying to show me that she was sorry for what she'd done, but maybe that wasn't the only reason. Maybe she thought I didn't really want the baby. That he was just an obligation.

Mom put a hand on my arm. "These past couple of months, after she left, you missed her. Don't try to tell me you didn't. I saw how you were—closed down, angry at the world. It was like you were seventeen again—at least that part of you. You hid it well, but I know you. And I can tell Eden's more than a thrall to you. Now you've got her back, and I'd hate to see you blow it. She needs to know how you feel. She's a human, and a young one. If you care for her at all, let her know. Hell, tell her you do even if you don't. Because there's nothing worse than feeling like an obligation when you're in love with a man." Mom's voice cracked on the last few words.

A muscle jumped in my jaw. "So you want me to lie to her? Like Esposito does to you? No, thanks."

My mother sucked in a breath and released my arm. It was a low blow, and I knew it. But I didn't apologize because she'd earned every word.

"Love is a human construct," I added. "It's different for a vampire."

"Is it?"

"It is for me." I'd promised myself to live without love.

Loving a person meant you had to let them inside. Before you knew it, they were fucking with your boundaries. Making demands. Look at Brien and Twilight.

He's happier than he's ever been, though. And it hasn't made him weaker. He seems stronger, more confident.

Still, Twilight wasn't Eden. Twilight was an asset to the syndicate in a way Eden could never be.

The wind had picked up. It scraped chilly fingers over us, stinging our faces, searching for an opening in our clothes.

Mom shivered, and I took her arm. "You're cold. Let's go back."

She nodded and fell into step with me. After a while, she said, "I'd really like to meet Eden. And maybe...after the baby's born, you'll let me see him sometime?"

"If you're well enough," I hedged. "Then, sure."

Her face fell. "I understand," she said in a voice like a rusty hinge. "I'm not exactly grandparent-of-the-year material. Just think about it, okay?"

"I will."

"Thank you." She squared her shoulders. "I won't drink around the baby. That's a promise."

I grunted, because how many times had she promised something like that?

"I won't touch a drop before your hockey match. I promise."

She'd showed up drunk and tripped in the stands, hitting her head on a bench. I'd had to leave the rink to drive her to the doctor so she could get stitched up.

"I'll pick you up at the dance. Midnight, right?"

She'd never showed. I'd waited until all the other kids were gone, then hitched a ride with a teacher kind enough to drive me to our crumbling, out-of-the-way cottage on the opposite end of the island. Mom had been weeping on the couch, a couple of empty wine bottles on the floor next to her.

"They hired me at the Cove Restaurant. I'm starting as a dishwasher but if it works out, they'll promote me to server."

It hadn't worked out. In fact, she'd been fired within a week for coming to work drunk.

I looked at my mom's worn, hopeful face and forced myself to sound positive. "Okay, great."

A flurry of snowflakes dusted our clothes a powdery white. "You were right about the snow," I said, and we shared a smile, a genuine one.

Before I left, I replenished the stack of firewood on the front porch, then started a fire in the wood stove in the living room. When I came back to my feet, Mom had a cigarette out.

I watched as she lit it. "I'll see you in a few days, okay?"

She walked me to the door and gave me a hard hug, the smoke from her cigarette curling around us. "You're good to me, Talon. Don't think that I don't appreciate that."

An uncomfortable pressure banded my heart. I put my arms around her in return. A loose, awkward hug.

"Call me if you need anything," I said, and left.

Cain strode up as I reached my apartment. "What did Mary want?"

"Hello to you, too." I touched my palm to the pad, unlocking the door. "And just the usual. She wanted to see me." Cain would buy the evasion. He knew how needy my mom could be.

He followed me inside, closing the door after us. "She say anything about Esposito?"

"Only that she hasn't heard from him."

Going behind my wet bar, Cain got out a bottle of blood-whiskey. "Well, it's not a loan shark he owes. It's a casino. He dropped two hundred grand at the tables."

So much for winning big at poker like he'd told my mom. Although that was a lot of money even for Esposito.

I hung my leather jacket in the closet next to the door. "So what's new?"

"This is different. This time, he owes someone high up in the Quebec City hierarchy. When he started losing, they fronted him another hundred-fifty thou instead of shutting him down."

"Hell." My fingers flexed. In my mind, they were tightening around Esposito's throat.

"Here." Cain pushed a double shot in my direction.

I tossed it down, welcoming the burn of the whisky. Every time Esposito went AWOL, shit happened.

"You sure?" I asked.

"A friend in the QCS tipped me off."

I blinked. "You have a friend in the Quebec City Syndicate? Since when?"

Cain sipped his whiskey. "Not a friend, exactly. Let's say we have mutual...interests."

He was avoiding my eyes. What the actual fuck?

"Who?" I asked, temporarily distracted from Esposito and his problems.

"You wouldn't know her."

"Her?" I asked neutrally.

"Her name isn't important. And I promised no one would be able to trace the intel back to her."

"Okay," I said slowly. "And you trust this 'friend'? You don't think she's feeding you false intel?"

"Why would she lie about this? And it fits. It's not like Esposito would say no if someone offered him a low-cost loan."

I nodded. Unfortunately, that was true.

"If your mom knows anything, " Cain added, "you have to get it out of her. Compel her if you have to. She's not immune."

"No."

"Why the fuck not?"

I put the shot glass down on the bar a little too hard. "Because she's my goddamn mother."

Cain's pale eyes flickered. "She's a weakness."

"Maybe, but she wouldn't know anything anyway. You think Esposito tells her his secrets? The man lies about what he ate for breakfast. She thinks he won big. No, we have to find the sonuvabitch and shake it out of him."

"I'll help," Cain muttered. His expression telegraphed that he'd do more than shake Esposito, too—and this time, I might let him. "He hasn't come to you for the money?"

"No." Which, now that I thought about it, was damn strange. "It's not like him. Why hasn't he tried to squeeze me for the cash? Especially if they're leaning on him, because why else would he have gone to ground like this? Plus, I told the PI to put extra men on this and they haven't uncovered a trace of him."

"That's bad."

"Yeah." I blew out a breath. "Up until now, I figured he'd turn up sooner or later. He always has before."

Cain finished his whiskey and set it on the bar next to mine. "It's time to tell Brien."

"Fine," I snapped. "I'll talk to him tonight, all right?"

My old friend looked me over, his lean body tense, his fingers tapping on the bar's polished surface. "You're hungry. When did you last drink fresh blood?"

"I don't know. When I was in New York, I guess."

"That was what—eleven, twelve days ago?"

"Two weeks," I muttered. "So?"

I only wanted Eden. Even drinking from another thrall felt wrong.

"So you need fresh, damn it," he said. "Blood-alcohol is a stopgap, not a permanent source of nutrition. You're pale as a ghost and you're edgy. Come to the Bite Club with me. We'll grab a couple of thralls, hang out."

"Some other time, okay?"

Cain's cheekbones seemed to sharpen. "Eden can spend a night alone, you know. Might do her some good."

Damn, I was tired of him trashing Eden. "What the hell is your problem? Ever since I brought her back, you've been riding me about her. I thought you liked her."

He opened his mouth, but instead of answering, grabbed the whiskey bottle and poured us both another shot. A double, this time.

"Here." He pushed a shot glass into my hand. "Have another one."

I stared at the red-tinged amber liquid. A vampire's metabolism processed alcohol differently, making it difficult to get drunk.

Sometimes, though, I wished it were easier. But then, I might've ended up like my mom. I'd been damn close to it that night Prima Lenore had walked into the jail with her proposition.

I put the glass down without drinking.

"And I like Eden okay," Cain said. "But I don't trust her, and if you were smart, neither would you."

"Who said I trust her?"

His dark brows climbed. "I see," he said slowly.

Guilt slunk up my spine. It felt underhanded, talking about Eden behind her back like this. I wasn't even sure it was true anymore. Deep down, I *was* starting to trust her again. To believe what she said without searching for hidden meanings or evasions.

My mother's words crawled through my brain.

"She's a human, and a young one. If you care for her even a little, let her know. Hell, tell her you do even if you don't. There's nothing worse than feeling like an obligation when you're in love with someone."

"She's trying," I said. "She apologized, and she's following my rules to the letter."

And doing her best to make it up to me. The guilt increased even as my dick gave an enthusiastic salute at all the ways she'd been making it up to me.

Cain's mouth pulled into a cynical smile. "But then she would, wouldn't she?"

"Sweet Lilith, can't you just be happy for me?"

His knee started jiggling. I could tell even though he was on the other side of the bar because his whole body bounced along with it. "Happy for you?"

"She's having my spawn. The first born to a vampire in the castle in over twenty years. So yeah, I'm happy. And I'd like my best friend to be, too. Fuck that promise we made each other—we were practically kids. What did we know?"

"Of course, I'm happy about that. I'm sorry you even had to say something." He raised his glass to me with a crooked smile. "To your spawn. A boy. You're a lucky bastard."

"I know." I picked up the shot glass and clinked it against his.

He tossed his down and I took a small sip in solidarity, then eyed my friend.

"Cain?"

"Yeah?"

I drew a slow circle on the bar with the shot glass. "You ever wonder what kind of father you'll make?"

He barked a laugh. "A shitty one."

"Yeah, me too." My own laughter was hollow.

"But that's me," Cain said. "You're not worried about yourself, are you? Because you're going to make a great fucking father."

"Why?" I looked away, wondering why I'd asked in the first place. But I didn't take it back because I needed to know. I was still reeling from what my mom had said about Eden and obligations and the fact that Esposito had tried to do the right thing—and failed spectacularly.

Cain's knee stopped jiggling. "A lot of reasons, starting with you asking *why*, which means you're thinking about how to be a good father. You care, and that's gotta count for something."

"Does it? Because from where I'm standing, it means I'm scared I have no idea what I'm do—."

"Let me finish, damn it," Cain interrupted. "Let's start with the fact that you're taking good care of the kid's mom, and add in how you immediately stepped up to take responsibility—you didn't even have to think about it. You just did it. On top of that, you're already working to make things better for the dhampirs in the syndicate. And I've seen you with the soldiers—you're tough when you have to be, but you're always fair. You're a leader—people look up to you. And the kid's going to look up to you, too. You just have to be yourself."

"What if that's not enough?"

"Hell, what I know about being a father would fit on the head of a pin," Cain said. "But if I could've had you as a father, I would've thought I won the lottery. And bro? I'm going to be here for you. Brien will be, too."

The hollowness eased. "Thanks," I said gratefully. "I'm going to hold you to that."

"Hey, so we had shitty father figures. Doesn't mean we can't learn from them anyway. You can always think of what my uncle would've done and do the exact opposite." He gave me a crooked smile.

"Yeah," I said, so that his comment wouldn't hang there.

Esposito might be more like a big kid than a parent, but Cain's uncle was so much worse.

"So we good?"

When I nodded, Cain finished his whiskey, clearly done with our hearts-and-flowers moment. "Let's go get a couple of thralls. You don't have to fuck them," he added before I could object. "But you do need to feed."

I thought of Eden, expecting me. But Cain was right, I did need fresh blood.

Plus, I didn't want her getting the wrong idea about what this was. Not because I was a prick but because I was trying not to be.

"Okay, already. I'll go." I gulped the rest of the whiskey and put the glass on the bar. "Anything to stop your bitching. Just give me a minute to change."

I headed into my bedroom, pulling off my T-shirt as I went, and to put on a short-sleeve dress shirt and a clean pair of dark wash jeans.

Cain was waiting by my front door. He slammed a shoulder into me, knocking me a step sideways. "It's not bitching, asshole. It's called concern—and shove a stake into me if I'm ever concerned about you again."

I shoved him back and opened the door, making a show of holding it for him. "After you, Grandma."

His snarl made me grin.

❦ 17 ❦

EDEN

I snipped at Rio's hair. "Shorter?"

I stopped clipping as he examined himself in my bathroom mirror. I was cutting his hair because he was meeting a guy for a drink in Bluebeard's Cove. Earlier, he'd redyed his hair a mix of pink, purple and blue, then decided he wanted a trim, too.

"Just along the sides," he said. "So you can see my ears."

"You got it." I started snipping again.

At least Rio was happy. In the two weeks since Talon had found me, Rio had settled into castle life like he'd been born on the island.

As for me, I was marking time until my restrictions were lifted so I could get back to normal. Things with Talon had reached a shaky equilibrium, with neither of us doing anything to tip the balance. Each night Talon either got me himself or sent for me to come to his suite. We had sex and then he walked me back to my suite.

I suppressed a sigh. Yeah, we talked, but only about the baby and whether I was eating and sleeping enough. The distance between us was as large as it had ever been.

But what about that "mine" stuff?

He'd stopped demanding I say it back, but sometimes he pressed the word into my skin with his lips or growled it in my ear. That, I couldn't figure out. Gods, men were confusing.

At least Nathan and Jasper were talking to me again. Word had gotten out about how I'd spoken up for dhampirs at that meeting with Brien and Twilight, and they'd each made a point of thanking me. Jasper had even offered to babysit, "you know, when he's out of diapers and stuff. So he has a dhampir he can talk to about those things."

"Now the other side." Rio pointed to his right ear, drawing my attention back to him.

I snipped off more hair. "Someone's gonna get lucky," I said in a sing-song voice.

Rio hunched his shoulders under the towel I'd placed around them to catch the hair. "Shut up."

I hummed the wedding march. I'd always wanted a little brother to tease.

A flush touched his cheekbones. "See, that's why I'm not telling you his name. We're just having a fucking beer, all right?"

"Sorry." I made an apologetic face in the mirror at him. "I'm just happy for you, is all. Let me know how it goes, okay?"

He gave a very-Talon-like grunt.

I lifted a brow. "How much time have you been spending with Talon, anyway?"

"An hour here and there—why?"

"I don't know. I thought you didn't like him."

That earned me an eye-roll. "He's my boss, Eden. He's been showing me around, having me run errands for him. Stuff like that."

"So you like him now?"

Rio lifted a shoulder in a shrug. "He's okay when you get to know him. Dude can be a hard-ass, but he's a vampire, right? And if you're straight with him, he treats you right. Know what I mean?"

I nodded slowly. "Yeah. I do."

The now-familiar shame constricted my lungs. Talon had always been straight with me, too. I was the one who'd snuck around behind his back. God, I wished I could go back in time and do things differently. Tell Eugene to fuck off when he first came to me, or better yet, report him to Talon.

Rio shifted on the stool. "We done here?"

I swallowed the shame because what was done was done. I could only keep moving forward, doing my best to prove to Talon that I was trustworthy.

"Yep." I stepped back, eyeing my handiwork. "You look beyoootiful."

"Thanks." Removing the towel around his shoulders, Rio shook the colorful strands into the wastebasket, then got a broom and swept up the rest of his hair before carrying the stool back to the kitchenette.

He'd brought a clean shirt to change into. He pulled it on and struck a pose for me. "What d'you think? Pretty sick, right? I bought it right before we left New York."

"Cool." I admired the vintage Wu-Tang Clan 1992 T-shirt and its yellow bat-shape. "Wish I would've seen it first."

"Thanks." He hesitated. "What about you? You gonna be all right?"

"Yes." I made a shooing motion with my hands. "Get going already. Talon will be sending for me any minute now."

"If you're sure..." He grabbed his jacket and left.

I put on a little makeup, then changed into a cashmere sweater and the tight black maternity pants because Talon really loved my ass in them. He still hadn't come, so I made myself a mug of hot chocolate and, pulling on my puffer jacket, took it outside, where I sat on a cast-iron bench next to a koi pond, sipping the thick, sweet liquid and taking in the night sky.

Gradually, the clouds blotted out the stars. A light snow began to fall, the flakes sparkling like bits of magic under the garden's tiny lights.

Talon should've been here by now. I glanced toward the French door—again.

That's when it hit me that maybe I wasn't going to see him that night, that he was with another thrall. A jealous pang screwed its way beneath my ribcage. My stomach muscles clenched.

Stop it. Just stop it right there.

Before leaving, I hadn't seen Talon every night either. Why expect things to be different now because I was blood-bonded to him? Bottom line, I was still a thrall.

But the gold cuff on my wrist felt as cold and heavy as the boulder that had taken up residence my chest.

Who was he with? Pinky? Hanna? Lesa?

Or maybe one of the other thralls.

Yeah, back in New York, Talon had semi-promised not to fuck another thrall if I accepted his blood bond. But he hadn't actually promised, had he? He'd been too smart to do that.

And he was a vampire, his drive for blood and sex intertwined—that's why they kept thralls.

My eyes stung. I put my mug on the bench and swiped at them.

"Stupid hormones," I muttered, pretending to myself that's all it was. That I wasn't lonely and feeling fat and unattractive and...

A sob broke from me. Then another. And then I was ugly-crying, tears streaming down my face, my whole body shuddering.

I cried because it was Friday night and I was all alone. I cried because I was ashamed of what I'd done. I cried because I missed my family. But most of all I cried to relieve the grinding hurt of loving a man who didn't love me back.

Gradually, my sobs stopped. A flurry of icy snowflakes pelted me, and I was startled to see I was covered in snow, my chocolate was cold. I released a breath, emptied out but calmer.

With that calmness came clarity. This was my life now. Time to woman-up and accept it. Maybe Talon didn't love me, but that didn't mean I had to mope around like a lovesick fourteen-year-old, waiting for him to pay me some attention.

I brushed off the snow, finished the chocolate and strode back inside. I blew my nose and washed my face, then went to the walk-in closet to work on my current project, a pair of tiny overalls with matching booties that I was making from an old pair of jeans. Rio had gotten a sewing machine from Kerry and we'd set it up in a corner of the closet. I'd never sewed something so small and complicated before, and since I was working without a pattern, I made mistakes. When I did, I ripped out the stitches and started over.

The hours flew by. When the overalls were finished except for hemming the legs, I shut off the sewing machine and arched my back, yawning, hands massaging my sacrum. Then I folded the overalls and put them on a shelf along with my sewing box.

This was my dream—to give used clothes a second life. It was why I'd become a thrall in the first place, to get enough the cash to open my own vintage clothing business. When Brooklyn Vintage Exchange had hired me, I couldn't believe my luck. I'd worked hard, volunteered for whatever was needed and asked questions. Not sure if or when I'd be able to open my own store, but wanting to be ready if the chance ever came.

I grabbed a sleepshirt and went into the bathroom to get ready for bed. While I was washing up, I stopped and stared at myself in the mirror.

Who said I had to give up that dream? After things settled down, I could open a shop on the island, couldn't I? Or sell clothes online?

I'd have to clear it with Talon, of course—which chafed a little—but why would he care? He didn't require me more than an hour or two a night anyway.

I finished in the bathroom and kicked back on the living room couch to watch *Demon Slayer*. I was in the mood for a tough-ass female demon.

Then I remembered I hadn't brushed my teeth. I heaved myself back to my feet and padded back into the bathroom.

When I came back out, Talon stood in the bedroom doorway, his hands resting above his head on the door jamb, his hard body clad in dark wash jeans and a blue rayon shirt. He'd fed—and recently. I don't know how I knew except he appeared...satisfied. Satisfied and energized, his mouth a little redder than usual, his dark eyes outlined in vampire-blue.

My heart leaped inside my ribcage like an unruly puppy. Because if Talon had come to me so soon after feeding, then that meant he hadn't fucked the thrall he'd drunk from.

His gaze tracked lazily down my body, lingering on my bare legs. "You're awake."

I lifted my chin, because even though my heart was still leaping around inside my chest, I'd *waited* for this man. *Cried* when he hadn't shown up.

"Yeah, but I was just going to bed," I lied.

He lifted a skeptical brow. "No, you weren't."

"Well, as soon as I watched an episode of *Demon Slayer*."

"C'mere." He indicated the spot in front of him with his chin.

I crossed to him, and he released the doorjamb, pulling me into his arms. His mouth covered mine, his tongue sliding hotly over my mouth. When I stiffened and pressed my lips together, he slapped my butt.

"That's for lying. Now open for me."

My chest heaved, but why try to pretend I didn't want this? Why pretend I wasn't happy he'd come to me for sex like he'd promised?

I complied, sliding my hands up to his shoulders and kissing him back. When he lifted his head, I leaned into him, nuzzling his sexy, bristly jaw. "Hey, there."

He rumbled deep in his throat, a low, hungry sound that made my inner thighs tighten. "Hello."

He framed my face with his hands, his gaze on my mouth. My lids lowered and I swayed into him, waiting for him to kiss me again. Instead, he frowned and tilted his head.

"You've been crying."

How could he know that? I instinctively shook my head. "No, I wasn't."

He nipped my lower lip. "You're lying again."

My mouth firmed. "I don't have to tell you my every thought."

"When you're unhappy, you do."

I pushed against his chest. "Let me go."

He released my face, but stayed close, his hands settling on my shoulders. "I'm staying right here until you tell me what's wrong."

My instinct was to curl up like an armadillo to protect my soft spots. It's what I would've done last summer. What I'd been planning to do even a couple of hours earlier.

But how well had that worked for me? He was reaching out to me, asking what was wrong—why not meet him halfway? Maybe if I opened up, he would too.

"First," I said, "tell me how you know."

"That you were crying?"

"Yeah."

"I'm not sure." He dragged a hand over his head, mussing the dark, curly hair on top. "I've been picking up things about you. More than I used to."

"Do you think it's the blood bond?"

He frowned. "I don't know. Maybe."

So maybe the blood bond had created some kind of connection between us? I kind of liked that idea. "I didn't think blood bonds did that."

He shrugged, clearly done talking about it. "Now it's your turn. Why were you crying?"

"I missed you, okay?"

"Eden." He winced. "You know I—"

My stomach dropped. So much for opening up to him. I cut him off. "That's okay. You don't have to explain. I know how it is, all right?" I sighed. "But it's not just that. Rio's on a date, so I didn't have anyone to hang out with tonight and I miss my mom and dad. Except for that one time at Olivia's, I haven't seen them for so long and…I miss them, all right?"

There went the stupid tears again. I blinked them away, but a few spilled down my cheeks. I was officially a girl who cried. Damn freaking hormones.

"Anyhow," I said around the spiky rock in my throat, "that's why I was crying."

I tried to sidle past him, but that ended with my back against the bedroom wall. "Hey," he murmured. "It's okay."

"It's not okay," I said, bristling. "I don't have a way to get a message to them since you took my phone. I can't even tell my mom that the baby's kicking all the time now and…" I shook my head, squeezing my eyes shut.

"Shh." I felt his "shush" against my lips, soft and warm. His thumbs came to my cheeks, brushing away the saltwater tracks. "Don't cry."

That brought my chin up. "I'll cry if I want to. I'm pregnant and I want to see my mom."

I'd officially regressed to the age of a five-year-old, but I was too raw from my earlier breakdown to filter myself. Plus, it was the truth and he'd ordered me not to lie.

"Okay, cry, then." He pulled me into his chest, his arms wrapped around me. No promises, just the comfort of his body. "But I hate it when you're sad," he added under his breath like he didn't want to admit it even to himself.

I leaned into him, soaking in his earthy, Talon scent.

I needed. Lord, I needed.

His big hand stroked my back, and my muscles loosened, my eyes drifting shut. I should've been in bed an hour ago. I took a jagged breath, exhausted both physically and emotionally, and offered him a wobbly smile. "Sorry. I'm not usually so..."

"You're tired. I shouldn't have come."

"No. I'm glad you did. But I *am* tired."

I pushed at his chest and this time, he released me. I sat on the edge of the bed.

Instead of leaving, Talon lowered himself to the mattress next to me. "You fucked with us, Eden. I can't just let that go—

I cut him off. "It's okay. I accept that this is part of my punishment. You don't have to explain."

I was so damn *tired* of his walls. Of pretending that I was okay with the fact that he didn't love me.

"Yeah, well." He rubbed his cheek. "I guess I'll go. Have a good night."

I snagged his wrist before he could stand up. I blame my sleepy brain because keeping him here wouldn't change things or make this into something it wasn't.

"Don't go. Please?" When he just looked at me, I added, "Just stay until I fall asleep. I don't want to be alone. It's...wearing me down."

He rolled his lips in. "Okay. But just for a few minutes."

"In bed with me," I added, in case he hadn't understood.

He stripped down to his boxer briefs and lifted the comforter for me. I climbed into bed, laying my head on the pillow, and he followed, his long body spooning mine, his arm slung over my hips.

My breath sighed out. I adjusted his arm so it was where I liked it, right below my breasts, and shut my eyes. He brushed his fingertips over the gold cuff, then twined his fingers in mine.

My heart fisted in my chest. The kisses, the affectionate position, the entangled fingers—all of that felt like love. But he didn't love me, and it hurt. He hadn't even offered to cuddle me. I'd had to ask.

And I was a masochist for asking him to stay. For making myself vulnerable to him.

I wanted so badly to believe he had feelings me. That he'd finally realized he loved me.

But that was my heart talking, because sooner or later, Talon would recall that he was a vampire while I was a disgraced thrall.

And oh yeah, the incubator of his child. No, his *spawn*.

When my heart curled into that armadillo shape again, I welcomed it. Because if I didn't protect myself, he'd only break my heart—again. And this time, the damage might be permanent.

I shifted, putting an inch between our bodies, but he drew me back.

"Hey," he said against my ear. "Stop thinking. Relax."

I heaved a breath, but he was right. I was so *tired* of thinking. Worn out from my seesawing emotions, I closed my eyes.

❦

When I opened them again, we'd changed positions, with Talon on his back and me snuggled into his chest. I wasn't sure of the time, but at least a couple of hours had passed. I breathed him in, basking in the fact that he'd stayed.

I slipped out of the four-poster bed to use the washroom, triggering a couple of lights to come on at knee level, casting a soft glow over the bedroom. When I returned, Talon was propped on a forearm, his eyes shining in the shadows beneath the canopy.

"Thanks for staying," I said as I crawled back under the comforter, "but don't you have something to do?" He was a vampire. This was his workday.

He pulled me back into the spooning position. He'd taken off his boxer-briefs, and was thick and hard against my lower back.

His teeth scraped over my nape. "I have something to do. You."

So that's why he'd stayed. I smiled to myself even as my chest squeezed. I reminded myself that this was what I'd signed up for. Well, fifty percent of it anyway since he wasn't going to be drinking from me until after the baby was born.

Not that I was being a martyr. Just hearing him say he wanted to "do" me in that gravelly tone had me going soft and wet between my legs.

He smoothed a big hand down my front, shaping my breasts beneath the sleepshirt and sending a delicious shiver over my body.

"Stop thinking." Without warning, he pinched my nipple, making me cry out and press back against him. Then he gave the other a hard tug.

I writhed against him, my ass rubbing against his cock. His hand slid down my body to cup my mound through the sleepshirt.

"You're not wearing panties under this, are you?" His voice vibrated sensually against my ear. "Is that for me? Were you hoping I'd fuck you tonight?

I moved a shoulder.

He knocked my knee open and slapped the cotton fabric over my pussy. "Answer me."

The erotic shock jolted me clear to my toes. "Yes!" I hurried to say. "I left my panties in the bathroom."

"Because—?" Another spank to my mound.

I released a small, tortured whine, but obediently added, "Because I wanted you to fuck me."

His fingers slid lower, rubbing my clit through the soft cotton. "Are you wet for me, baby? And I want only honest answers or I'll stop right now."

"Yes. You know I am."

"Good girl. Now take this off," he said, tugging at the hem of my sleepshirt. "I want you naked.

Before I could respond, he was pulling the sleepshirt over my head, my hips and arms automatically lifting to help him. "That's better," he said with satisfaction before settling me into the curve of his body again.

One big hand slid up my ribcage, fondling my breasts. Teasing, toying, squeezing. A languid warmth spread through me, loosening my limbs. He tugged at my nipple and I moaned and arched my back, my bottom pressed erotically against his hairy thighs, coarse against my tender skin.

"You're so hot for me," he said. "So ready."

"Mm." I put my hand on his, moving it lower until it reached the juncture between my legs.

"Is this what you want?" He smoothed his fingers over the thatch of hair, delving deeper, then pulling back out.

I nodded eagerly, widening my legs to give him greater access. He draped my top leg over his thighs so that I was open to his exploring fingers. I was slick and ready for him. He hummed with satisfaction and scraped his teeth down the side of my neck.

His fingers plunged into my wet opening with a roughness I craved. My core clenched and hot tingles traveled down my spine.

He drew my juices over and around my clit. "Did you miss this? Was your pussy begging for my cock?"

God, I loved when he talked dirty. But some imp made me say, "No."

"That's a lie," he crooned, scraping his fangs over the hollow beneath my ear. He licked the small wound, and I gasped as the aphrodisiac entered my bloodstream.

"Nobody says I have to feed your ego," I managed to say.

"I'll give you that one," he said, a dark smile in his voice, "but lie again and I'll smack your pretty ass." For emphasis, he rolled me further onto my stomach and rained several stinging blows on my exposed cheeks.

I squirmed on the mattress. "What was that for?"

"Because I wanted to." He drew me back into my original position with my leg over his thigh. "And you like it."

He was right. The heat from his smacks was already moving to my sex. His hand slipped between my inner thighs again and I rocked up to meet his touch.

His teeth came to my nape, holding me still. No fangs, more like a wolf claiming its mate. His fingers spread my folds, possessing me, caressing me.

"I was with a thrall," he said.

I tensed, a cold lump of hurt settling into my stomach. Talk about a buzzkill—and why was he telling me this? "I know."

"I hadn't fed since New York, and I was hungry. But I didn't fuck her."

"Oh." I blinked rapidly. Even though I'd guessed it myself, I hadn't expected him to bring it up.

"Ask me why not." His middle finger dipped into my wetness, drew slow circles on my clit.

"Why...not?" My mind ping-ponged between his question and the erotic touches.

"Because I only want you."

The hurt lump dissolved. "Yeah?"

"I can't stay away from you." He sounded perplexed, like he couldn't understand it himself.

I turned my head so I could kiss the side of his mouth. "Then don't."

"Mm." His hand was still between my legs. He drew my slickness up and around my clit.

"More." I pressed my ass back against him, a low, inelegant sound escaping my lips.

Talon seemed to like it, though, because he brushed his fingers over me a second time. "Play with your nipples," he said against the back of my neck.

When I obeyed, he said, "Pinch them. Make them hurt a little."

I obeyed, then gasped, my inner walls constricting.

"Again. Harder." He waited until I complied before sliding into me from behind. "Good girl," he said, his mouth an inch from my ear. "I'm going to fuck you so hard because that's what you deserve. Isn't it?"

"Yes." So much *yes*.

He began to move, slow and easy. We were in our own shadowy world beneath the four-poster's gauzy canopy, the only sounds the creaking bed and my moans and Talon's rough encouragement.

His rhythm changed. He moved faster now. Deeper and so good.

Between my thighs, he touched me in just the right spot. Sparks of excitement lit up my veins like a freaking firecracker had exploded.

My eyes closed. My mouth opened, sucking in breaths.

The darkness was edged with heat; it swirled and burned in me.

I was so close. So. Very. Close.

I pushed against him, frenzied with want. I'd released my breasts, but now I touched them again. Pinching my nipples. Increasing the burn.

"That's it," he rasped. "Take what you want."

I drew in a breath, saying, "Yes," and "Please," and then all I said was his name, over and over, as the fiery darkness exploded behind my closed lids, my sex clenching rhythmically around him.

"Fuck, baby," he said harshly. "You're so tight."

He pushed deep. Then again. And again and again and again.

I gave a small scream, still climaxing, caught in a sensual haze of heat and light and pleasure. He clamped a hand on my hip and thrust, hard and fast, until he stilled, pulsing deep inside me as he came with a drawn-out groan.

His breath scraped in. Then he kissed me between the shoulders and relaxed, his head on the pillow behind mine, his arm resting on my hip. Gradually, his breathing slowed to half my rate, but somehow, we were in sync, me drawing two breaths for every one of his.

My eyelids drifted shut. I was almost asleep when he smoothed his palm down my rounded belly.

"I should leave. You need your rest."

I put my hand over his. "Stay."

The baby twisted and turned beneath our joined hands. Talon chuckled, his fingers spread over my lower abdomen. "He's busy tonight, our son."

Our son.

It was the first time he'd claimed the baby in both our names, the first time he'd called him his "son" instead of "spawn" or "the child."

I was still smiling when he rolled me onto my back so he could kiss me, long and sweet. When he lifted his head, he nuzzled my ear.

"It's almost dawn—I have to leave. But you sleep in. I'll tell them not to bother you in the morning."

"Mm-kay." I snuggled into the comforter, dimly aware of him dressing and leaving.

In the morning, there was a new phone on my nightstand.

What the—?

I snatched it up, almost afraid to find I was dreaming. But it scanned my face and opened. A text message popped up.

TALON: *This is for you. Fyi, I'm monitoring your calls and texts but use it whenever you want.*

I sat up and scooted back against the headboard, then scrolled to the contacts, where I found four phone numbers: Talon's, my mom's, my dad's, and Freya's.

I grinned and pressed the phone to my chest. It was the best gift Talon could've given me, proof that he was softening toward me. Plus, it had to mean he was starting to trust me again, didn't it?

I texted Talon a *thank you!* so he'd see it as soon as he came out of his day sleep, then touched the phone icon next to *Mom.*

It rang a couple of times before she picked up. "Hello? Who is this?"

"Mom?" I dragged in a breath. "It's me, Eden."

Cain threw a roundhouse punch at my head. I ducked and slammed my fist into his solar plexus, and he stumbled backward. I came upright to find Brien aiming a flying kick at my chest. I dodged left and he overshot me, landing in a catlike crouch on the mat.

I spun around, taunting, "You candy-asses can't take me even when you double-team me."

We were in the castle gym and I'd challenged them to a fight. No weapons except our hands or feet, which meant no claws or fangs, either. I'd needed to take the edge off. Esposito was fucking with my mind. He was clearly in big trouble. If he owed money, why hadn't he contacted me? Had he made some kind of deal with the vampire he did owe?

Brien and Cain traded looks. Then Brien smiled, a chilling stretching of his lips that would've made a vampire lower in the hierarchy freeze in his tracks. Even I felt a shiver shoot up my spine.

"What did you call me?" he asked.

I grinned. "Candy ass—." My breath whooshed out as he slammed into me, dropping me to the mat.

Cain chuckled. Brien was faster and stronger than me—he was the primus, after all—but I slithered out of his hold as we hit and slammed an elbow into his jaw before rolling back to my feet.

Cain wasn't smiling now. He circled right while Brien circled left. I glanced between them. Brien's hair had come out of its ponytail and the shoulder of my shirt was partially ripped off. Cain, on the other hand, looked like we'd been discussing the goddamn weather, his blond hair neatly in place, his T-shirt snowy-white.

I jerked my head at him. "Man's too neat," I said to Brien. "Let's mess him up a little."

His smile was evil. "Sounds like a plan."

Dropping into a crouch, Cain turned his palms up and scooped his fingers at us. "Bring it on, assholes."

Brien and I jumped him at the same time. We ended in a pile on the mat, punching and elbowing and headbutting one another like a bunch of hockey goons.

Usually it was me who called a halt to things, but this time I kept fighting until Brien shoved me off Cain, saying, "Enough, already. I don't want to have to explain to Twilight why my nose is broken."

"It'll heal by morning," I muttered, but he was right, we'd gone at it long enough.

Still, it had helped; the tension eating at my gut had eased. We formed a seated circle on the mat, giving each other tips on fighting techniques. That segued into the problem of Esposito.

"The QCS could be hiding him," I said. "It's no secret that we're related. They could think they can use him to get to me."

The idea made the skin of my nape crawl. Esposito was unpredictable. If I figured he'd zig left, then he'd zig right—or even take off at a tangent.

Cain reclined on his forearms. Fighting relaxed him, even though he'd probably throw his torn T-shirt away as soon as he reached his quarters.

"Would they be wrong?" he asked.

"No," I admitted. "If it was just me, I'd let the fucker hang, but my mom loves him."

Cain glanced at Brien. "What did Régis say?" Régis was the Quebec City primus.

Brien stretched his long legs out on the mat, one knee bent. "He swears he hasn't seen Esposito, that he knows nothing about the guy except that he's Talon's father, and I believe him. He's got too much riding on the new casino. He knows I'll pull our investment if I find out he's fucking with one of my lieutenants, especially after what Fleur's coven did to Twilight."

I swore under my breath. "So, nothing."

"Yeah." Brien moved a shoulder. "Still, how much trouble can Esposito make for us? He's only a human, after all—and we know what he looks like, where he's likely to go if he comes to the island."

I nodded. "I already told the ferry captains to alert us if they see him, and I have Chief Valente keeping an eye out, too. William and Kerry know to contact security immediately if he's seen anywhere on the castle grounds."

"Then relax," Brien said. "He'll turn up eventually, and we'll handle it then. Now if that's all..." He gathered himself to stand.

"There's something else," I said.

"Yeah?" Brien sank back to the mat.

"Eden." I turned the conversation to the other human currently fucking with my mind. "Her parents have been asking to see her. Her dad is threatening to raise hell if we don't allow it—he even came to the castle, demanding to see her."

Brien nodded. "William told me. He said Montgomery made him promise Eden was okay. Made him swear it actually."

"I know." Thank the gods for William. The castle butler had grown up on the island and people trusted him to give them the truth, no bullshit. "But it could be a problem. Since Gwen, people are edgy."

Gwen's family had been paid to keep quiet about her death, but it was a small island. Nothing could be kept quiet forever. The humans might not know that Jules had abused Gwen, then drained her blood, but they realized something bad had gone down.

"That was last week," I added. "I issued Eden a phone so she's free to call them now. She knows I'm monitoring her calls and messages, but that should keep Montgomery quiet until I'm ready to let her visit them."

"Your call," Brien said.

Across from me, Cain nodded, his expression carefully blank. But I knew him too well.

"A pregnant woman needs her mom and dad," I said. "I want to keep her happy; it's good for both her and our spawn."

Good, practical reasons.

No need to explain that I'd gotten a little panicky at how sad Eden had seemed last Friday. She'd lost her sparkle, and I hated knowing I was responsible. It felt like my mother and my old man all over again. Different characters, same story.

"She's not a suitable mate," Cain stated.

I stilled. "I know that."

"Ah." Brien lifted a brow. "The elephant in the lair."

Cain's focus remained on me. "Do you? Know, I mean?"

"Yes," I said shortly.

"She'd be problematic," Brien mused. "You could turn her, of course, but would we be able to trust her?"

I ground my molars together. "The woman made a mistake, okay? She agreed to pass a note and the little prick blackmailed her into spying for him."

"So it's like that," Brien said.

"Like what?" I demanded.

"Just that I seem to remember arguing with you about Twilight being my mate. You said she was—and you were right."

Cain sat up and pulled his legs in. His knee started to bounce.

"It's different for us," he told Brien. "You're a pureblood. Mating with Twilight doesn't affect your status, especially now you've turned her. And even if you'd had a spawn with Twilight while she was still human, you're strong—and a primus. You could mate with anyone and your spawn would still inherit your power and a fuck-ton of magic. But Talon and I made a pact that we'd only mate with other vampires."

I aimed a scowl at Cain. "I'm not breaking the damn pact. I like Eden, yeah—and I want to keep her happy."

At least that's what I'd told myself this past week, when I'd crawled into bed with Eden each night around her bedtime, holding her until she fell asleep...because I hated seeing her sad and lonely.

"But that's it," I added when neither of them said anything.

I was a planner. In the years I'd been Brien's bodyguard, I'd turned my life around. The reckless twenty-year-old had been replaced by a man who thought five steps ahead, had long-term goals. I'd already adjusted my plans to offer Eden my blood bond. I saw no reason to change them further. Mating with a vampire was the best option for both me and the syndicate.

"I'm not so sure you can control it," Brien said. "In fact, I know you can't. It's an instinct. Lilith knows I fought it, but you saw how well that worked. Not that I give a fuck." His gaze turned inward. "Twilight...completes me."

"You didn't grow up with my parents," I said. "I saw firsthand what choosing with your heart does. No, when I mate, it's going to be with a vampire who brings something to the table, someone of value to the syndicate."

Brien leveled a *dude, get-your-head-out-of-your-ass* look at me. "Even a vampire has a heart. You can't choose a mate like you'd choose a horse. Even my father didn't do that, and the gods know he was a cold-ass SOB."

"And your mother was his weakness," I returned, "and everyone knew it. No disrespect intended, of course. That's why, when they couldn't get to Jules, they staked her instead. So no, I will *not* take Eden as a mate. I'll take care of her, keep her until she dies. But I will not mate with her. A blood bond is enough."

Cain stirred. "The blood bond was a good idea, actually."

"That's not what you said a couple of weeks ago," I told him.

He shrugged. "I've been thinking, and it binds her more tightly to you and the syndicate, aside from the fact that she's carrying your spawn. Smart move."

"Glad you approve," I responded dryly.

Still, Cain was right. I hadn't asked Eden to accept my blood bond for those reasons, but from a purely cynical standpoint, it had been the best way to keep her under control.

"That's settled, then," said Brien. "When the time comes, you'll both look for a mate in the vampire world."

Cain murmured agreement, but my stomach tightened uneasily. Had I agreed to that?

"Speaking of mates..." Brien rose to his feet. "You guys have a good night. And don't bother me unless it's critical because I plan to be busy." His smile was pure sin.

Cain and I made a couple of rude suggestions, which only made his smile widen.

As he left the gym, I felt an unfamiliar clench of jealousy. Brien had mated a human, after all—a slayer, for fuck's sake. Yeah, she'd later asked to be turned, but at the time, he hadn't known she would and had claimed her anyway.

I reminded myself that I'd made that pact with Cain for a reason, and that nothing had changed. If anything, now I'd made lieutenant, it was even more critical for me to mate with a vampire. Brien—my primus—clearly believed so.

So then why did my chest feel like a boa constrictor was wrapped around it? A boa constrictor that squeezed tighter with every breath I took?

19

EDEN

"So." Rio faced me on the couch. "What're you going to name the kid? Because 'Rio' would be so dope. We can call him Rio the second."

He stretched out his long legs along the cushions, forcing me to inch closer to the far end as I hemmed a pair of tiny purple joggers (Rio's suggestion after he'd come across a bolt of purple fleece at Bluebeard Cove's craft store).

I chewed on my lower lip like I was actually considering his naming suggestion. "Uh, no."

"Why not?"

"Because there's only one you. Two Rios would be a travesty. Think what the kid would have to live up to."

His mouth hooked up. "True."

We met each other's eyes and laughed.

"Seriously, though." He rested his feet, encased in thick orange-and-blue socks, against my thigh. "What are you going to name him?"

I moved a shoulder. "I don't know. We haven't really talked about it."

"Huh. What names are on the list?"

"I like Talon."

"Not bad. It's badass, you know?" Folding his arms under his head, he contemplated the ceiling while I finished hemming the first leg and moved to the second. "So the kid would be Talon, Junior?"

"Nah—I don't like Juniors. We can give him a different middle name."

"Does Talon have a middle name?"

"No." I pushed the needle through the folded fleece. "He only uses his first name. It's not unusual with vampires."

"Really?"

"Mm-hmm. I think it's because after they're turned, they cut their human connections. Most of them, anyway. Talon takes care of his mom."

"She's still alive?"

I nodded. "She's in her sixties, I guess. I don't know about his dad —he's not in the picture."

I finished the hem and cut and tied the thread before stabbing the needle into a pincushion. "What d'you think?" I held up the tiny pants.

"Let me see," Rio said and I tossed them on his lap. He held them up in front and made a comical face. "You sure they're big enough? They look like they're for a doll."

"He's only going to be seven or eight pounds when he's born."

"That's insane."

"They grow fast."

"If you say so." He threw the joggers back to me. "They're pretty lit, though. You should make him a tiny hoodie to go with them."

"I'm going to. And mitts and booties."

"He'll be purple from head to toe. Talon's going to crap himself."

"He'll survive." We grinned at each other.

Still grinning, Rio took my sewing box and bobbled it. "Shit." He caught it before it hit the floor. When he sat back up, he returned it to the coffee table.

"I brought you something," he said conversationally. "Don't look now, though. I hid it beneath the thread."

What the—?

"You need a weapon," Rio said, his voice lower but still conversational.

A what? I stowed my pincushion in the box and shut the lid, trying not to look as shocked as I felt. I was pretty sure there were no cameras inside my rooms—just in the hall outside my door, and that one in the garden—but still...

"So." Rio picked up the TV remote. "Wanna watch a movie? My turn to pick."

"You picked the other night. And where the hell did you get a weapon?" I wanted to yell the question, but I kept my voice as low and unconcerned as his.

"Mrs. Park. She said to pass it to you just in case. Now, drop it." He turned on the TV. "And you loved that movie, by the way. You said Henry Cavill was eye-candy."

Playing along, I elbowed him in the side. "That was you. But this is crazy, you know. Just in case what? And what if they find it?"

They meaning Talon.

Rio dropped his voice again. "He's not going to look in your goddamn sewing box. Now drop it, okay?" He laughed and pushed my elbow away. "Like you don't think Henry is eye-candy, too."

I released an aggravated breath. Rio had clearly dug in—pushing him wouldn't get me anywhere.

"Henry Cavill is always eye-candy," I said. "Dark-haired, long white hair, with a beard, without—doesn't matter. It's like a law of the universe. And fine. You can pick if you make the popcorn."

"Deal." He scrolled through the choices.

"The kind with real butter and Parmesan cheese," I added. "I woke up this morning thinking about it." Like really, really wanting it. "I almost had popcorn for breakfast."

"You and your cravings. I can't wait until you pop this kid out."

I chuckled. He sounded so put upon.

Rio made the popcorn and we watched the movie—another one starring Henry Cavill.

As the credits rolled, Talon texted me to meet him at his apartment, and I texted back that I'd be there in five minutes. "Gotta go," I told Rio.

By then I'd almost forgotten about the weapon, until he hugged me and whispered, "Don't forget to look inside the sewing box. Talon's okay, I think, but I want you to be able to protect yourself."

I frowned. "Is there something you aren't telling me?"

He lifted his palms. "Hey, I'm just the messenger," he said and left.

I gave a frustrated growl, then with a shrug, took the finished pants and sewing box back to my walk-in closet, where I peeked into the box. A look beneath the spools of thread revealed a six-inch-long stainless-steel rectangle. It took me a beat to realize it was a closed switchblade.

I snatched it up and pressed the catch, instinctively keeping my back to the closet door. A long, sharp silver blade shot out.

Holy crap on a stick.

I hurriedly pressed the catch again, retracting the thin, wicked-looking blade. Heart pounding, I slipped the weapon back under the colorful spools, closed the lid and shoved the sewing box onto a shelf.

I stared at the box, breathing hard. I knew I should tell Talon, but Rio was only trying to protect me. I couldn't do that to him.

There was no earthly reason Talon would open my sewing box, but I grabbed a folded sweater and put it on the shelf in front of the box to hide it. Then I shut the closet door and crossed to the bathroom.

Why would Mrs. Park give me a switchblade? I didn't even know the woman. Plus, she was Twilight's grandmother—wasn't she on their side?

I dug the heels of my palms into my eyes, breathing noisily in and out. *Calm down, damn it. Talon's going to wonder why you're upset.*

I splashed cold water on my face and wiped it off. Then I stilled, the towel in my hands. Because the real question was why did Mrs. Park think I needed a weapon in the first place?

20

TALON

Fifteen minutes passed and Eden still hadn't shown up. When I found myself glancing at the door for the sixth or seventh time, I closed my laptop and strolled around the corner to her suite.

She was just coming out of her bathroom. She started and pressed a hand to her chest. "Talon. I didn't hear you come in."

I could hear her heart pounding from across the room. I crossed to her in two long strides. "Everything okay?"

Her eyes jittered sideways. "Why wouldn't it be?"

"No reason." I rubbed her shoulders, instinctively trying to calm her. "I didn't mean to startle you, that's all. I was wondering where you were. It's been a while since I texted."

"Oh—sorry." She made a face. "Rio was here and we watched a movie, and I was cleaning up."

"Okay." I continued massaging her shoulders, drinking her in, all pink-cheeked and soft-mouthed, her fuzzy sweater the same sky-blue as her eyes.

She sighed and rested her forehead against my chest. "That feels so good. Can you do it a little harder?"

At her breathy, suggestive words, my groin tightened. "Sure, babe."

I increased the pressure, focusing on the areas of tension, until she stepped back with a murmured thanks.

"I love sewing," she said, rolling her head from side to side, "but it's kinda like working on a computer—tough on your neck and shoulders."

"Sit with me." I took her hand and guided her to the couch. "You were sewing?"

"Yeah, before the movie."

When we were settled on the couch, I stretched an arm along the back, smoothing my free hand over her abdomen. "How are you feeling?"

These days not even the loose, oversized sweater could hide the fact that she was round with my spawn. Something primitive in me loved that others could see it; would know I was the man who'd put a baby in there. It meant Eden was mine, and not just because of the blood bond.

"Good. I have so much more energy now that I'm not working so much."

She curled into me, idly stroking my chest. My stomach muscles knotted, then eased. Before she'd left, she used to caress me like that sometimes—and I'd missed it. Setting aside all the reasons I shouldn't let myself get too close to Eden, I kissed her temple, steeping myself in her warm, sugar-cookie scent.

She snuggled deeper into me. "Rio wanted to know what we're going to name the baby."

"Name the baby?" I repeated. Somehow, I hadn't gotten that far in my thinking.

She nodded against my shoulder. "I like Talon myself. Do you want his last name to be Esposito?"

"No," I said firmly. "I want him to have his own name. And especially no to Esposito. That name means *nothing* to me."

A short silence. "Because you're a vampire?"

"No. Because Esposito's a shitty father."

"Oh." I sensed her looking at me. "So you and your dad aren't—?"

"I only see him when he wants money."

She swallowed. "I'm sorry."

"Don't be. I stopped counting on him a long time ago."

"I'm still sorry. My dad's the best, you know?" She'd stopped stroking my chest, but now she resumed her gentle petting. "So, no Esposito," she said when all I did was grunt. "But I'd still like to name him after you. Maybe Talon could be his middle name."

I shrugged. "Why don't you come up with a list and run it by me? We can choose together."

"Any preferences?"

"Nothing too fancy. I'm not saddling him with some long, pretentious name. Other than that, it's up to you."

Her chuckle vibrated through me. "Now how did I know you'd say something like that?"

I squeezed her shoulder. "Watch that smart mouth, baby, or I'll find something to keep it busy."

She giggled and relaxed against me again, her fingers toying with the hair on my nape.

"So what were you sewing?" I asked.

"An outfit for the baby. Rio bought me a yard of purple fleece and I'm making him a hoodie and a pair of joggers."

"You know how to do that?"

"Not really." She grinned up at me. "I'm figuring it out as I go along. Rio got me a sewing machine—I think Kerry had an extra."

"Can I see?"

"Sure," she said and scooted forward, preparing to stand. "I just finished the pants. They're in the bedroom closet."

I helped her rise, following her to the bedroom door. She went into her closet, returning with a pair of miniature joggers. "Here," she said, handing them to me.

"These are for the baby?" I held them up in front of me, a strange constriction in my chest.

She nodded. "I started with the pants—I figured that would be easier."

I flashed on what the baby would look like, all tiny and fat-cheeked, his little legs encased in the soft purple material. I think that's the moment when he became real for me. Even though I'd felt him move, heard his heartbeat, he hadn't been quite real. More an idea than an actual person.

Now it was like this tiny being had balled up his fist and punched me in the gut.

Me and Eden, we'd made a person together—a little boy. I was going to be a father.

My throat cinched. Because what if I fucked it up like my old man?

"D'you like them?" Eden asked.

I forced my attention back to the purple joggers. "I do, yeah."

I examined the neat stitching, trying to focus on it instead of the anxiety clogging my lungs. But when I did, I was seriously impressed.

"You're good," I told her. "I didn't even know you could sew. I wouldn't even know where to start making something like these."

Her face cracked wide with a smile. You would've thought I'd given her a little blue box from Tiffany's, not complimented her sewing.

"It's easy. I measured a pair of my own joggers—to use as a pattern, you know—and then divided by a lot." She chuckled. "I figured his waist and butt need extra room, too. Not that I don't have a big butt..."

I dropped the tiny pants on a chair and pulled her to me, filling my hands with her round, firm cheeks. "Your ass is perfect."

"Yeah?" She ran her hands up my shoulders, linking her fingers around the back of my neck.

I urged her up against my erection. "Tell me you want it 'a little harder' again."

Her mouth edged up. "You liked that, huh?"

I slapped that perfect bottom. "So it was deliberate?"

"No! It wasn't, I swear."

"What if I think you're lying?"

That long, curvy body pressed against mine. "You know I'm not."

I did, but I liked playing games with her. "Hm." I made my tone stern. "Now tell me what you want or I'll have to spank you." I smacked her ass again just for the hell of it.

She rubbed against me, back and forth, back and forth. "I want it hard," she said, sliding me a suggestive look from beneath her lashes.

Oh, baby. My dick lengthened, pressing against my zipper. "How hard?"

"Very, very hard." As she spoke, her fingers snaked between our bodies to undo my pants. She reached inside, stroking me over my boxer briefs, sending a heated bolt straight to my balls.

"Bad girl." Catching her wrist, I removed her hand. "You have to ask permission before you touch me."

She pouted up at me. "Please...Master."

The woman was going to slay me. I might as well stab a dagger in my own chest and be done with it.

Dragging in a breath, I caught her lower lip between my teeth, enjoying how her pulse sped up at the tiny pain.

"Not yet," I said against her mouth. "First I get to play."

I tugged off her sweater. Her bra followed, and then the rest of her clothes. When she was naked, I lifted her up and walked backward with her until we were at the bar in her kitchenette.

Shoving a stool out of the way, I set her on top of the smooth wood and smacked the side of her knee. "Spread your legs."

When she complied, her hands on either side of her hips, I nipped each of her nipples, enjoying how they beaded under my tongue.

She rasped my name. "Hurts..."

"Too much?" I soothed the reddened tips with my tongue.

"No." A seductive smile. "It's...hot."

Sliding an arm behind her back to support her, I sucked each of her nipples into my mouth, tonguing them as she moaned and squirmed beneath me. I gave them each a final, wet kiss.

"You're my angel, aren't you? My bad-girl angel."

"Yes..."

"Keep those hands on the bar," I ordered and trailed my lips down her rounded abdomen until I reached her center.

I swiped my tongue through her glistening pink lips. She gasped and arched her back. I did it again, then sucked hard on her clit. She was panting now. I pulled back a little so I could see her.

Her eyes were half-closed, her mouth slack with enjoyment, her nipples rosy and pointed.

My woman. My own naked, pregnant Madonna.

Mine.

Something in me stirred, something hungry. A craving that predated my being turned into a vampire. This went back to the pissed-off, edgy teenager who, like Rio, had wanted more but hadn't known how to get it.

Chest tight and achy, I slipped two fingers into her hot, slippery channel and pumped, a little roughly, showing her who owned her.

"You want me to fuck you, baby?"

Her answer was a moan.

"Tell me. I want to hear the words."

I sucked on her clit again, knowing it would interfere with her ability to speak. Meanwhile, I was still stroking her inside where she was warm and wet.

Her core clenched on my fingers, and her breath released in a shaky exhale. "I want...you to...fuck me."

"Want me to fuck you—what?"

It was no longer a game. The hunger required her to beg. Demanded proof that she was mine, body and soul.

"Please." She whimpered. "I want you to fuck me, *please*."

I rumbled in satisfaction. "Then I will. But first, I want to feel you come."

"Yes..." She swallowed, added "please" without my prompting her.

"That's it, angel."

I put my head between her thighs again and, supporting her lower back with one hand, went to work on her with my mouth and fingers —although it wasn't *work*, it was pure, unadulterated enjoyment.

I got to touch Eden, taste her, smell her. Hear her sexy whimpers.

And when she broke, I got to feel the tiny explosions that started in her cunt and shot up her spine to burst from her mouth in high, pleasured sounds.

By then, I was so hard, so hungry, my brain in an Eden-induced fog. She had barely finished climaxing when I had her in my arms and in the bedroom. I bent her over the bed and dragged off my clothes.

I grasped her hips. Somehow, I had the presence of mind to check in with her. "You okay? Comfortable?"

"Yeah." She turned her head on the mattress, gifting me with a dazed smile.

"Good." I wanted to slam into her, but I forced myself to slide in slowly.

At first she was passive, still recovering from her orgasm. I slowed even further, licking my fingers and reaching beneath her to swirl them around her swollen clit.

Raising up on her forearms, she arched her ass up to me and started to push back at me in rhythm with my strokes. The hunger clawed at me. I thrust more firmly, then stilled, afraid I'd been too rough.

"Tell me if it's too much," I said, my voice harsh in my ears.

"No, no." Husky tones. "It's good. I like it hard. You know I do."

That was all I needed to hear. "Hang on, then, baby. I'm going to fuck you so hard and deep. I want you to still feel me tomorrow. I want to be all you think about."

"Yes. Please, Talon. I need it."

Gods, I loved hearing her beg to be fucked. Loved hearing my name on her lips.

"Then take it." I thrust again, over and over, until she screamed and tightened around me, climaxing a second time.

Sweet Lilith, that felt good. My eyes closed as I pushed in again—hard. "That's it, baby. Feel me deep inside you. Feel your man."

She shuddered. Tiny muscles gripped me. "Oh my *God*."

My mind blanked, consumed by a hot, dark pleasure. I groaned, hips jerking, and followed her over the cliff.

After, I hung over Eden's back, breathing in the scent of her and salty, sweaty sex until I came back to myself enough to lift her onto the bed.

I pulled the covers around her and she snuggled into them with a sleepy smile up at me. "G'night."

"Good night."

I couldn't stay—I had things to do. But I stared down at her like my feet had grown roots, the raw craving barely satisfied.

It's the blood-hunger. She's not your mate.

Brien's words last night snaked through my brain.

"I'm not so sure you can control it... It's an instinct."

But Brien didn't really believe that, did he? Because he'd all but ordered me to look for a mate in the vampire world.

My stomach churned. I bent to kiss Eden again, this time a firm, almost angry press of the lips, and left.

❊ 21 ❊

EDEN

Ghostlike fingers of fog wafted over the enclosed garden. Bored and antsy, I followed the curving flagstone path as far as it went, then turned and went back the other way.

It was the end of November and I'd been confined to this small section of the castle for more than three weeks, unless you counted my daily walks and that trip to Olivia's. Rio was in Bluebeard's Cove again, and Talon would just be waking up. It would be hours before he sent for me—the earliest he ever wanted me was eight or nine o'clock.

I heaved a breath and kept pacing. On my fourth or fifth lap, I took a fork that ended at one of the two outer walls. My steps slowed. I considered the grape vine trellised against the rough stone.

You could cut through the forest and be at Mom and Dad's in fifteen minutes. If you make it quick, Talon will never even know you're gone.

But even if I could get my six-month-pregnant body up a five-meter-high wall, I'd still have to drop to the ground on the other side. Not to mention the wolfdogs who patrolled the castle grounds. On the other hand, the dogs knew me. And I could probably bluff my way past their handler...

I shoved my hands in my pockets. It wasn't worth it, and not just because of the wolfdogs.

Talon was beginning to trust me again—that phone he'd given me last week was proof.

And the other night, he'd opened up about his human family, even if it was only to tell me Esposito was a shitty dad. That might not seem like much, but it was the first crack I'd seen in that barrier of his.

And I wanted Talon's trust—wanted past his walls—more than I wanted a few minutes of freedom.

A tiny sound lifted the hairs on the back of my neck. I turned to find Twilight watching me from a few meters away, her face luminous in the misty light.

"You wouldn't get far," she said—and smiled, her teeth gleaming whitely against her red lips.

Goosebumps popped up all over my body. For a panicked few seconds, I wished I'd brought that damned switchblade outside with me. But it was still in my sewing box, where it had been ever since Rio gave it to me three days ago, partly because I didn't buy that I was in danger. Other than Nathan or Jasper and the maid who cleaned my suite once a week, I didn't see anyone except Talon and Rio.

Plus, there was that trust thing. If I got caught with a switchblade, I could give up any hope of fixing things with Talon.

I lifted my chin. "A woman can dream, can't she?" I was damned if I'd let her see my fear. Yeah, she could sense it, but she didn't have to *see* it.

Twilight's smile morphed into a grin. An appreciative, you're-all-right grin. Unlike me, she wasn't wearing a coat, just one of her funky, ultrafeminine outfits—short-sleeved pink sweater; tiny, pink-and-black checked skirt; chunky, lug sole loafers. A shiny brown braid fell forward over one shoulder.

"It's a beautiful garden," she said.

"It is."

I relaxed marginally, still wondering why she was here, but happy to chat. Heck, who was I kidding? I was dying for some company, even if it was the woman I'd been a first-class bitch to.

"I used to think of it as my secret garden," Twilight said. "Like that book by Frances Hodgson Burnett."

"Yeah? I loved that book when I was a kid." We shared a *you-too?* smile.

"It's interesting how the walls keep the garden so much warmer, isn't it?" I glanced around at the wet leaves littering the ground. "Most of the trees still had leaves until that storm the other day."

"I know, right?" She lifted her face to the fat, hazy moon, and I flashed back to how she used to do that with the sun. "D'you smell it?" She inhaled like she was drawing the whole island into her lungs.

"Smell what?"

"The ocean."

"Well, yeah." I'd grown up with its sharp, salty scent.

"I love the way it mixes with those pines down the hill."

My brows climbed. The pines were a half mile away. "I can't smell them."

"No?" She gave a wondering smile. "I'm still getting used to how intense everything is."

I nodded. Why was she telling me this? Actually, why was she here at all?

A thick cloud blotted out the moon, and a sudden gust of wind rattled the tree branches. I shivered and huddled into my puffer jacket.

"You're cold," Twilight said. "Come inside—I ordered you a hot chocolate. Just the way you like it—I asked Rio."

She had? I eyed her suspiciously. "Umm—thanks?"

Inside my suite, a steaming mug of chocolate waited on the wet bar next to a split of blood-wine. Hanging up the jacket, I took one of the stools and Twilight took another, leaving an open seat between us.

She poured herself a glass of wine and we faced each other on the stools like two gunslingers in a Hollywood Western.

I wrapped my fingers around the mug to warm them. "You're not going to tell Talon, are you?"

"Tell him what? That you were walking in the garden?"

I blinked, then nodded. "Thank you," I said and took a sip of the hot chocolate. It was delicious—dark, sweet, and topped with whipped cream and a dash of nutmeg. I gave a little hum of pleasure.

"Damn, that's good," I said, taking another sip. "It might even be better than Rio's, but if you tell him I said that I'll say you lied."

"You're welcome." She took a drink of her wine. "You know there's a camera in the garden, don't you? Near the French door."

"Yeah," I said with a shrug. I knew where all the cameras were.

"Although they probably wouldn't have seen you back there," she added. "Not in the dark."

Exactly. I wasn't dumb enough to say that aloud, though.

Twilight fingered her wine glass. "You like the garden suite?"

"I do, yes." She seemed to expect more, so I added, "It's very pretty. Were you the one who told them to put me in here?"

"No, that was Talon. He wanted you to be able to get outside whenever you wanted to."

"Yeah?" I smiled, liking that he'd thought of that.

She considered me. "He was messed up after you left. He wouldn't stop looking for you. The man was obsessed."

My smile faded. "Because I ran."

"No. Because he missed you. We all saw it—me, Brien, Cain."

"Huh." Her comment was like a shot of hope to my veins.

"And he didn't forget what you said about dhampirs. He's been pushing for a change in how the dhampirs are treated, starting with promoting Adrian to enforcer. Brien agreed—the announcement will be made in a few days."

"He didn't say anything to me."

"Maybe he's waiting until it's a done deal." She toyed with the stem of her wineglass. "You know, he wasn't even interested in other thralls until it was clear you'd gone of your own free will. And then he didn't seem to care who he fucked—I think he was just trying to forget you."

"You think?"

"Yeah. Every time I saw him, he was with a different thrall."

The hope expanded, spreading to my chest. Maybe Talon had cared more than I'd realized?

And then I'd ruined it by leaving like that.

"Why are you telling me this?" I asked Twilight.

"Because Talon won't."

Yeah, that sounded like Talon. "You're probably right about that. But why do you care?"

"Honestly?" She leaned back on her stool to eye me. "I'm not sure. Except that I like you for some goddamn reason."

"You do? But why?"

She lifted a shoulder, let it drop. "I like how you handled yourself in that meeting with me and Brien. You were straight with us and your apology was sincere, but you didn't let us push you around. And you're smart. For someone with no training in covert ops, you were damn hard to find."

I moved the mug in a slow circle on the bar. "That was partly Eugene Smith—he got me the fake ID. I think he wanted to use me down the road, maybe to draw Talon off the island. I'm lucky he got staked when he did. I was always on edge, thinking he was going to catch up to me—him or Talon."

I hadn't even gone out at night unless I couldn't help it.

"They wouldn't have ever let you go free. Once they have something on you..." A shadow crossed her face. "Trust me, I know. They were blackmailing me, too. That's why I was here in the first place. And Eugene didn't get staked—Brien ripped the prick's head off." Her smile was all vampire. "He made the mistake of touching me in front of Brien."

At the visual, I gave a queasy swallow, but I couldn't help being relieved that Eugene was in his final grave. Who knew what he would've forced me to do next?

"I was so damn stupid," I muttered.

"You weren't the only one. They got to Avril, too."

"Brien's PA?"

"Yeah. She's gone—Brien banished her from Maritime territory."

My eyes widened. "That's harsh."

"Not when she almost got him staked. Any other primus would've slit her throat."

"Oh." I gulped and subsided.

There was a short silence, then Twilight said, "So why'd you do it?"

I shrugged and shook my head.

"Because of the baby?" she asked.

I hesitated, but maybe Twilight deserved to know—my actions had impacted her, after all.

"Yeah. I wanted off the island before anyone found out." *Before Talon found out.* "Eugene didn't know, of course."

Just thinking about what the dhampir might've done if he'd realized I was pregnant with Talon's baby sent an icy prickle up my spine.

"You didn't want Talon to find out, did you?" When I made a noncommittal sound, Twilight let out a surprised huff. "You're in love with him. That's what this was about."

My chest compressed at hearing her say it out loud. It was *my* secret, *my* self-respect. "No, I'm not. I'm from the island, remember? I know better than to fall in—"

"You do love him." When I sputtered a denial, she held up a hand. "Vampire," she said, pointing to herself. "I can sense a lie now."

My shoulders sagged. The hope I'd been feeling collapsed like a torn balloon as I relived what I'd overheard Talon telling Cain.

"So what if I do? It's not like he cares." Bitterness leaked into my voice, but hell, it was the truth. "He wants a vampire mate. Someone powerful. Someone who will increase his standing in the vampire world. Not a human—especially a thrall who was only in it for the money."

Twilight's brows climbed. "He told you that?"

"Not straight out." I white-knuckled the mug. Six months later, and it still hurt like a knife to the heart. "But he said it. He was talking to Cain—he didn't know I could hear him."

Her brow furrowed. "That doesn't sound like Talon. He's not power-hungry."

"Yeah? Cain was talking about this pact they'd made to mate with a vampire or nobody, especially a human. And Talon said, 'Eden's a thrall, nothing more. And the last thing I want is to sire a dhampir. I want a pureblood spawn, same as you.'" My mouth pulled sideways. "And to put the cherry on the fucking sundae, I'd just found out I was pregnant."

"Jesus." Twilight ran a hand down her braid. "I'm sorry."

She pitied me. My stomach knotted with humiliation.

I put the mug down on the bar—loudly. Angry at myself for telling her so much. Angry at her for dragging it out of me.

"Look, I apologized to you. Wasn't that enough? Why are you here, really?"

She gazed back steadily. "Because I think you need a friend."

I made a scornful sound. "And you're it?"

"I'm the best you've got. Unless you count Rio, who I've gotta admit is awesome."

Despite my turmoil, that got me right in my proud big-sister heart. "He is," I muttered.

"You're thinking I feel sorry for you," she said. "Which has to be hard as fuck, especially when it's me." When I stiffened, she added, "And no, I'm not reading your emotions—it's what I'd think if I were you. We're not that different, you know."

"Yeah, right. You're a former slayer who's now a vampire, and I'm the thrall who spied on you for your mate's enemies. We have *so* much in common."

She leveled a look at me. "I thought we were friends. Was it all an act?"

I was tempted to lie and say yeah, it had been. But she'd know it was a lie, and why was I pushing her away, anyhow? I needed all the friends I could get.

"No," I admitted. "I liked—like—you too. Spying on you like that —it's not me. I got sucked in, and then I was fucked. I still feel dirty."

"Well, don't," she said. "Just focus on the fact that you're free of that slimy little reptile."

"I will," I said. "Hearing that from you helps. Even knowing I wasn't the only one he blackmailed helps."

"You weren't. And there might've been others we don't know about."

I nodded, processing that. The guilt and shame that had been weighing me down eased. I felt better, lighter.

"And you're right," I told her. "I could use a friend—and not just because you're the prima."

Twilight's lips twitched. "See, that's why I like you. You're honest."

I replayed what I'd said and gave a rueful smile. "Maybe a little too honest."

"No, I love it. Half the vampires in the syndicate are horrified that a slayer is their new prima, but they can't say anything because of Brien. It feels like no one but Talon and Cain tells me what they're really thinking. They just say what they think I want to hear."

I hadn't looked at it from her perspective. Maybe this friend-thing went both ways because it sounded like Twilight could use a friend, too. I flashed my middle finger at those clueless vampires. "Well, fuck them, then."

She burst out laughing. "My friend Renata's going to love you."

"Who's Renata?"

"Another slayer. Except now she's the Paris Syndicate princess—and mated to Zaq Kral." Twilight made a comical face. "It's complicated. Let's just say she's not the princess type."

"Well, good for her. Zaq Kral is hot." The middle Kral brother was a gorgeous, fallen-angel of a man with sun-streaked brown hair and green eyes.

"Don't tell Renata that. She's wicked good with a switchblade."

"Noted."

Twilight raised her wineglass to me. "To friends."

I touched my mug to it. "To friends."

❧ 22 ❧

TALON

I paused outside Eden's door, an insulated picnic bag in my hand, edgy as a guy on a first date. I blew out a breath.

You're thirty-nine years old, for fuck's sake, and Eden's just a thrall.

I'd stashed her in a private suite like a sultan with a harem of one, restricted her movements, confiscated her money. Yeah, it was punishment, but the vampire in me enjoyed having her on a short leash.

Now, though, I hungered to move on. To make her happy. To have her laugh with me like she did with Rio, loud and uninhibited.

Because Eden wasn't just a thrall to me, was she? She was...more.

"I want to get back what we had."

That night she'd told me that, I'd figured it'd never happen. But now I wanted it, too.

I'd always liked Eden, but her time away from the island had changed her. She was more mature, with unexpected layers. Look at how she'd more or less adopted Rio. A street rat, and she'd taken him into her apartment, housed him, fed him.

Believed in him, which I knew from experience was what he'd needed most of all.

The old Eden wouldn't have done it. At least, the Eden I'd thought I'd known wouldn't have.

And this new, more complex Eden drew me like a bee to honey. I

189

itched to peel those layers away and find the woman at their heart. Itched to know her better.

But it wouldn't happen unless I opened up a little myself. Showed her that I cared about her, that she wasn't just an obligation.

So I'd pulled Twilight aside to see if she had any ideas, and she'd suggested a picnic. Which was why I was loitering in the passageway, clutching a snack packed by Rio.

Enough.

Disgusted with myself, I unlocked the door with a wave of my hand over the sensor and went inside.

Eden was on the living room couch, frowning down at the beaded fabric in her lap. Her light blond, black-tipped hair had grown out in the three-and-a-half weeks since I'd brought her back to Lilith Island, giving her a softer, just-out-of bed look.

My dick twitched.

Picnic first, damn it.

She broke into a smile when she saw me. "Hey. You're early tonight."

I showed her the bag in my hand. "I'm taking you on a picnic."

"You and me?"

"Mm-hm. Get your coat."

"Sweet!" She did a happy little dance on the couch, which didn't help my hard cock. No, I pictured dragging her onto my lap and ordering her to do that sexy, wriggling dance—naked.

Down, boy.

"Okay, just let me tie this off." Clearly unaware of where my thoughts had gone, she finished affixing a silver bead to the filmy gray material and laid it on the coffee table.

I picked it up. It was the beaded shirt Rio had insisted on bringing from New York. "You're repairing it?"

"Yeah. Just be careful, all right? It's fragile."

I gently set it back on the table. "To wear?"

A shake of her head. "It wouldn't fit."

"So you're going to give it away?" I asked, curious now.

"Or sell it."

"To sell?"

She shrugged like it didn't matter, but I could tell it *did* matter. "I hate to see clothes like this—vintage, maybe even hand sewn—thrown out."

I frowned. "But anything you want, you just have to ask. I told Rio that. And I put the money you earned as a thrall in escrow. That's yours—I'm planning on returning it eventually. You don't have to fix up old clothes and sell them."

"I'm not doing it for the money."

"Then why?"

She looked down and I thought she was going to shrug again. Instead, she ran her palm over the beading.

"Explain it to me," I coaxed. "I want to understand."

"Someone spent a lot of time on this. This is hand beading—I can tell because of the way it was tied." She turned the hem up to show me the tiny knots on the inside of the fabric, beneath a silky inner layer. "The fabric is still good. There was a small tear along the seam and half the beads had fallen off, but I was able to find some almost like the originals to replace them. If I repair it, someone can wear it. I feel like that honors the original designer, the person who created and sewed it in the first place."

Her sparkle was back in full force, her beautiful face animated, her blue eyes gleaming. I gazed down at her, drinking in her enthusiasm like it was a glass of blood-champagne.

Something clicked. "That's why you were working at that store. You didn't need the money—you wanted hands-on experience."

"Oh, I needed the money. You know how expensive it is to live in New York City? And I was afraid to touch what I hadn't already withdrawn because—well, you know. But yeah, I went to every vintage clothing store in the city until I found one that would hire me. Someday I want to open my own store. But that was before—you know." She looked away.

"I see." But I didn't, not really.

Eden didn't need to work. On top of the money she'd already earned, she'd get more for each year she was a thrall, cash she could access as soon as I trusted her again. Plus, there was the baby. Even I knew a new mother didn't have much time.

My fingers tightened on the picnic bag. Maybe it should've occurred to me that Eden had dreams, dreams she'd never shared with me.

Not that I'd asked.

She scooted to the edge of the couch, preparing to rise, and I moved to help her. She stretched up to kiss me, her gaze sliding to my hand. "What's in the bag?"

I held it away from her. "A surprise."

She lunged for the bag, and almost got it, too. I raised it higher, out of her reach.

She pouted, then giggled. "You're no fun."

An answering smile claimed my face. I pulled her in for a one-armed kiss, then smacked her butt and released her. "Put on your hiking boots, too. We'll be in the woods."

She nodded and went into her bedroom, returning in sturdy hiking boots and a yellow down jacket. She could barely close the zipper over her abdomen.

"You need a bigger jacket," I told her, frowning. "Have Rio order it."

"I'm okay." Finally getting the zipper over her stomach, she pulled it the rest of the way to her neck. "I can wear this one unzipped with a sweater underneath."

"The hell you will. I can afford to buy you a fucking jacket." If I wanted to, I could buy the whole goddamn manufacturing plant.

Her jaw set stubbornly. "But I like this jacket, and it's only for a couple of months. After I have the baby, it will fit again. It's not because I think you can't afford it. It's because I'm against throwaway, fast fashion. That's what I've been trying to tell you."

I grunted noncommittally. I heard her, but we were on an island in the North Atlantic and tomorrow was December first. She needed something warm, something she could zip up for Lilith's sake.

In the castle courtyard, a driver was warming up a syndicate SUV for us. He exited the vehicle, leaving the key inside.

"You can go about your duties," I told him as I helped Eden into the passenger seat. "I'll return the SUV to the garage myself."

He dipped his chin. "Very good, Lieutenant."

We drove out of the courtyard under a cloudless sky. Last week's snow had melted the following day, and nothing had fallen since, leaving the streets clear except for a few dirty piles along the shoulders. I took the cliff road south. To the east, the moon floated above the ocean like a fat gold balloon.

Just before we reached the turn-off to my mom's house, I swung onto a dirt road lined with sugar maples, their smooth gray trunks skirted with a fine mist.

Eden glanced around, her pretty oval face alight with interest. "I don't think I've ever been down this road before."

"No?" I navigated the last hundred meters of mud and gravel. "There used to be a sugar shack back here. This guy named Magee owned it, and I'd help him in return for a couple of jugs of maple syrup. When he died, no one took it over."

"That's too bad. My dad had a friend who made his own, and me and Freya used to help tend the fire. It was the best."

"I used to love maple candy." My mouth watered, remembering.

"Really? Me, too. Sugar or cream?"

I slanted her a look. "Both. Why choose?"

She snort-laughed. "I like how you think."

That silly snort fell on my soul like rain on a desert. I made a mental note to have Rio grab Eden a big box of maple candy in Bluebeard's Cove.

The road ended next to an old sugar shack. The roof had caved in during a tropical storm a few years back, and all six windows were either broken or missing all together. A maple sapling had found its way inside, its branches pushing through the window frames and out the roof.

I took the insulated bag, a small flashlight and a waterproof picnic blanket from the backseat and met Eden at the front of the SUV.

"Where are we going?" she asked, pulling on her striped mittens.

"A creek I found back when I was a kid. We're not far from where I grew up." I handed her the flashlight. "There's a path—just follow me."

"Okay," she said cheerfully, switching on the flashlight.

I hesitated, belatedly questioning the wisdom of taking a pregnant woman over rough ground, but the creek was only a short walk away, and Eden was more animated than I'd seen her in a week.

"Stay right behind me, all right?" I told her. "And be careful."

She brought the flashlight to her temple in a smart-ass salute, the beam sweeping over the crumbling shack. "Got it."

I started off at an easy pace, glancing over my shoulder every few steps to see how she was doing.

"I'm fine," she told me the third time I did it. "I walk for at least an hour every day."

"That's in the daylight."

She picked up the pace, coming up next to me so she could slide her arm around my waist. "Better, Grandpa?" she asked with a side-long grin.

I wrapped an arm around her shoulders. "Behave, woman."

She chuckled and snuggled closer.

Five minutes later, we reached our destination, a moonlit glade next to the creek. A light frost glittered on the dormant grass. Some-where nearby, an owl hooted.

"*Oh.*" Eden switched off the flashlight and turned in a circle. "It's...magical."

My breath hitched. She was so beautiful, her short hair bleached silver by the moonlight, her eyes dark and soulful.

The hunger awakened in me. Just like that, I was semi-hard. I busied myself with spreading out the blanket and put the bag on top of it.

Eden slipped the flashlight into a jacket pocket and moved to the creek bank. "Did you come here a lot when you were a kid?"

"Yeah." I joined her. Together, we stared down at the water tumbling over the rocks. "It's peaceful, you know?"

And I'd needed that, especially when Esposito was in the house, stirring up my mom, oozing fake charm. Inserting himself in my life, making me and my mom count on him...and then taking off again.

Magee had been more a father to me than Esposito, so even after joining the syndicate, I'd kept coming. Carrying buckets of maple sap, chopping wood, monitoring the fire—it takes hours of boiling and 40 gallons of sap to make a single gallon of syrup—until the winter he died.

"It *is* peaceful." Eden turned and put a mittened hand on my chest. "Thanks for sharing it with me."

"My pleasure." I covered her hand with mine, happy that she seemed to like it as much as I did. "Want to see what's in the bag?"

"Yes, please."

"Sit down, then." I helped her settled onto the blanket, then stretched out alongside her.

The bag had two insulated compartments. In one was a hot chocolate, in the other was a carton of Moon Mist ice cream.

I offered her both. "What are you in the mood for?"

"Ice cream." She pulled off her mittens and took it, squinting at the label. "It's Moon Mist! How did you know?"

"Rio told me," I said. The ice cream was a Nova Scotia specialty, a blend of grape, banana, and bubblegum flavors.

She pried off the lid. "I've had such a craving for Moon Mist, but you can't find it in the States. Please tell me you brought a spoon."

Returning the hot chocolate to the bag, I dug one out. "Here you go."

She took it and dipped it into the Moon Mist. As the spoon slid between her lips, her eyes closed in pure bliss. "Oh. My. God."

Thank you, Rio.

The kid had been feeding me information about Eden for reasons known only to him. I owed him a bonus.

Eden opened her eyes and caught me looking. Her smile widened. "Don't laugh. It's so good."

The corners of my mouth tugged up. "I'm just glad you like it."

Eden licked the spoon clean and went back for more. I settled onto my forearms as she devoured half the carton. Watching her was almost as good as sex, each lick and suck going straight to my dick. I reminded myself that it was cold out—for a human, anyway—and I hadn't brought Eden out here to fuck. I'd brought her here to get to know her.

She eyed me, and then with a wicked little smile, slipped the spoon between her lips and made a show of pulling it out...slowly.

Her lips clung to the tip, then she released it with a pop. My breath shuddered in.

Sitting up, I cupped her chin, my thumb tracing the seam of her lips. "Are you going to let me taste?"

A slow dip of her head.

I leaned in. Eden's lips parted and I licked into her mouth, tasting the sweetness on her tongue. I hummed low in my throat, then with a restraint that should've won me a damn medal, pulled back.

Her dark, spiky eyelashes fluttered.

I retrieved the spoon from her lax fingers before she dropped it. "More?"

"More?" She followed my gaze to the spoon. "Oh, you mean ice cream. No, I'm full," she said with a regretful look at the Moon Mist. "I can't eat another bite."

I replaced the lid on the carton and returned it with the spoon to the bag. "There are three more cartons in your refrigerator."

"Really?" She grinned. "You're going to make me fat."

Oh, yeah, I definitely owed Rio. And Twilight, too.

"Not fat," I said, laying back down and bringing her with me. "Beautifully round."

"Good answer," she returned and snuggled into me, her head on my shoulder, one knee bent, her thigh resting on my leg.

She was soft and warm, her belly pressed against my side so that when our son shifted his position, we both felt it. The hungry thing let out a breath, content for now. I gathered her closer and gazed up at the multitude of stars, happier than I would've believed possible when I'd left for New York four weeks ago.

Eden's breath tickled my neck. "This is nice—being alone with you out here."

"You're not cold?"

"Nah. I run hot these days."

"I know." I turned my head so I could look at her. "I like it. There's nothing I like more than being buried in your heat."

She screwed up her nose and laughed like she thought I was joking with her; and I was, a little. But it was also true. I rolled her onto her back and came over her, forearms on either side of her head, my body planked above hers.

"I mean it." I teased her lips with my tongue. "You...warm me. I can't explain it. You just do. And not just when we're having sex."

I felt the shape of her smile against my mouth. "Really?"

"Really." The confession left me feeling exposed, so I kissed her, slow and deep.

No one saw that vulnerable side of me. Ever.

I didn't stop until she was breathless and moaning, her lips kiss swollen. Even though my whole body was tight with need, too, it eased the vulnerability, to see her so wrecked by me.

When I came off her, she winced and shifted on the blanket. When I eased her back onto her side, she reached beneath her jacket to rub her lower back.

My brows pulled together. "You're hurting."

She shook her head. "Just stiff."

I brushed her hand away and took over, massaging the sore spot with the heel of my hand.

"Mmm." She relaxed, resting her head on her bent arm. "That already feels better."

"Massage helps?" Kneeling behind her, I lifted the back of her jacket and continued working on her lower back.

When she nodded, I said, "You should've said something sooner. I'll have a therapist come to your suite. How many times a week?"

"That would be awesome. And I don't know—maybe once a week?"

"Twice a week," I decided. "And if you need them to come more often, let Rio know."

"Thanks," she said with a yawn.

"C'mere." Angry at myself for keeping her out too late, I scooped her up along with the blanket and the other gear and started back to SUV.

"I can walk," she said around another yawn. "Olivia says it's good for me."

"Quiet." I nipped her lower lip. "I want to, okay?"

23

EDEN

Talon struck out for the SUV with a long, easy stride. I curled drowsily into his hard body. If only it could always be like this.

Here in the woods he wasn't a tough-ass Maritime lieutenant, and I wasn't a disgraced thrall on house arrest. We were just Talon and Eden.

"You...warm me. I can't explain it. You just do."

My heart turned over when he said things like that. When he noticed I was getting tired or that my back hurt.

I kept coming back to what Twilight had told me about how upset he'd been after I'd left. *Obsessed*, she'd said.

Maybe it was true? And if so, maybe I hadn't totally fucked things up between us?

Because tonight, he'd taken me on a date. There was no other word for it. A first date, because we'd never gone somewhere like this, just the two of us.

Yeah, we'd gone places together when I'd been his thrall—to clubs or parties—but always as part of a group of other vampires and thralls. Never alone, and especially not somewhere so intimate, so clearly special to him.

He'd shown me a piece of himself tonight, a piece I suspected few people had ever seen. I hugged the memory to myself like he'd given me a bag of gold.

Maybe we were finally getting back to what we'd had? Or...even more?

We reached the SUV, and he opened the door and helped me inside, then handed me my mittens before stowing the rest of the stuff in the back. When we emerged onto the main road, the ocean was spread before us, the full moon splashing light on the dark waves.

"It's so pretty tonight," I murmured.

"You want to stop?"

"Yes, please." I turned my head to smile at him, tired but not wanting the evening to end.

"No problem." He pulled off the road onto a grassy cliff, angling the vehicle so we could look out. Fifteen meters below, the water heaved like a living thing, the surf's muted boom reaching us even through the closed windows.

"I missed the ocean," I confessed. "The salty air, the sound, the way it never looks exactly the same..."

His left brow lifted. "I thought you hated Lilith Island."

"I don't hate it. It's home, after all, but sometimes it feels so... claustrophobic. Everyone's related to everyone else. Everyone knows your business."

"I know," he said drily.

"Yeah, I guess you do."

"So you've heard the stories?"

"About you and Cain? Yes."

I was too young to have known them as kids, but I'd picked up pieces here and there. People had been a little afraid of them even then. They drank too much, got into fights, broke hearts. Beautiful, fucked-up boys.

He grimaced. "We were assholes."

I tilted my head to the side. "Back when you were a teenager, did you want to leave?"

"No. Well, maybe I would've, but my mom—" He shook his head. "Cain, though—he was on his way out of here. He'd already moved out of his uncle's house and was staying with me and my mom. Then

Prima Lenore offered us a better deal. We were in the island jail at the time, by the way."

My jaw loosened. "Seriously? Why didn't I know that?"

The deal Talon and Cain had made with Brien's mother had become part of island lore. The year they'd turned twenty, she'd offered to turn them into vampires and bring them into the syndicate. In return, they'd be Brien's personal bodyguards. They'd sworn a blood oath to protect Brien.

However, this was the first I'd heard they'd been in jail at the time.

"We don't like to advertise it." A wry smile. "But we deserved it—we were out of control. Out all night, picking fights for no reason except to prove what hard-asses we were. A little breaking-and-entering, like people wouldn't guess it was us. The chief of police finally locked us up for a month to scare some sense into us. Made us share the same cell, too, the prick. A few nights before we were supposed to be released, the cell door opened and there was Prima Lenore. Turned out she was looking for a couple of guys with our skillset."

"That's why you're helping Rio, isn't it?" I said slowly. "Because he's a kid without enough options, like you were. Maybe you hired him to ensure my good behavior, but you didn't have to hand that money over to him."

True to his word, Talon had transferred the entire hundred grand I'd received from Eugene into Rio's account.

"I didn't need the fucking money," was his growly reply. "You know that."

But I was on to him now. Unbuckling my seatbelt, I leaned across the console and squeezed his hand. "He likes you, too."

Rio's original prickly wariness of Talon had morphed into respect. The money had helped, but he clearly looked up to Talon, saw him as something of a mentor.

Talon shrugged that off to consider me. "Tell me something, Eden. When you left, why did you leave behind all your jewelry? I thought you liked it."

I retreated to my side of the SUV. "I did. I loved it. All of it."

He'd given me earrings, a necklace, a couple of bracelets—gorgeous, one-of-a-kind gold pieces studded with gemstones. Emeralds, sapphires, chalcedony, blue topaz... He'd said he liked me in blues and greens because they brought out my eyes.

"Then why not take them? You could've pawned them, taken the cash."

I rolled my lips into my mouth. "It didn't feel right."

"Why not? Those were gifts, no strings attached. You took Smith's money, and I assume you had plans to access the money you earned as a thrall."

"That's why it didn't feel right. Those were gifts—I hadn't earned them. And I didn't want your gifts."

"I see." He turned back to the ocean. With the moon lighting only his right cheek and the edge of his jaw, I couldn't read his expression, but his mouth was turned down, his body language stiff.

He was upset, but it didn't feel like anger. It felt like hurt.

Strangely, that encouraged me. Up until now, I hadn't believed I could hurt him.

"No," I said, "you don't see."

A soft, frustrated exhale. "Then explain it to me."

I toyed with my mittens. He didn't understand, and he wouldn't unless I told him what I'd overheard. My instinct was to bury it, pretend it hadn't happened. To "keep the peace." That was how my parents dealt with painful truths. Hell, burying the body—literally or figuratively—was a Lilith Island tradition.

"I—" I shifted in my seat.

"You're not comfortable." Talon reached for the gear shaft. "I'll take you back."

"I heard you and Cain," I said lowly. "When we were in Quebec City this summer."

Talon sat back. "And—?"

"At a party in Primus Régis's garden." My voice was louder now. It *needed* to be louder. I wanted him to hear every word. "You were talking about a pact you'd made."

He rolled his lips in. "Oh."

"Yeah. You said that I was a thrall, nothing more. Which I knew, I guess. But you also said the last thing you wanted was to sire a dhampir." A laugh grated from my throat. "Not what I wanted to hear when

I'd just found out I was pregnant. That was like a—well, you can see why I didn't want your goddamn jewelry."

The anger and hurt spilled out, shocking even me. I twisted the mittens in my lap, lungs burning. I filled them with a breath before finishing more calmly, "I didn't want anything from you. I just wanted *out*."

He swore under his breath. "That's why you took the money to spy on Twilight."

"That's right. Not that's it's an excuse, but I wasn't thinking clearly. And then I was in too deep." This time my laugh was sad. "The worst of it is, you weren't wrong. A dhampir son will be a drag on you."

"I didn't mean it like that."

"Then how *did* you mean it?"

"Don't move." He unbuckled his seatbelt and jumped out of the vehicle. "I want to do this face to face."

A split second later, he was opening my door and turning me toward him.

"Let's get something clear." He slapped his hands onto the seat on either side of my thighs. "I do *not* think our son will be a drag on me. I never thought a dhampir spawn would be a drag on me. This was about him, not me. I wanted to mate with a pureblood for *him*—and because it's better for the syndicate, yeah, but that wasn't my main reason. I know what it's like to have to fight your way up in the hierarchy, and it's even harder for a dhampir. But I was wrong, okay? I should've never made that pact with Cain because now that dhampir son is a reality, I don't feel the same. And I promise, our son will have every possible advantage."

A cautious happiness filled my chest as what I'd heard last summer rearranged itself. "You mean that," I stated.

"Fuck yeah, I do." His hands moved to my shoulders, his dark eyes burning into mine. "I swear it on Prima Lenore's grave. We're already making changes so things will be different for dhampirs."

I nodded. "Twilight told me."

"Then you know it's really happening."

"But what if he doesn't want to join the syndicate? What happens then?"

"I can't make any promises about where he'll be in the hierarchy." Talon loosened his grip on my shoulders but kept his hands where they were. "That's up to him—dominance isn't something you can predict, or force. But I give you my word that our son will receive the same training as a vampire spawn. And if he chooses not to join, then I'll set him up in any business he wants. Or pay for him to go to university if that's what he prefers."

"Swear it." I grabbed his wrists. "I want you to swear that, too. Swear on your sire's grave that whether he joins the syndicate is up to him. That he'll have choices."

Talon stiffened; I'd insulted him. But this was too important. It wasn't just my life, it was the baby's.

"By Prima Lenore's grave," he said, "I swear that our spawn—both this child and any future spawn—will get to choose whether he joins the syndicate. And what he does as an adult is up to him, as long as he's not sitting around on his ass...or stirring up trouble like his old man."

That last part made me smile. "Thank you," I said over the pointy lump that had gotten lodged in my throat.

With Talon—a syndicate lieutenant—in his corner, my little guy would have a powerful advocate. And I liked that Talon had brought up the possibility of more children. I wanted at least two.

That left the other part of what I'd overheard, the way he'd dismissed me like I was last week's garbage. *"Eden's a thrall, nothing more."*

I slid my teeth sideways. Wanting to ask but afraid to hear the answer.

"What?" His gaze jumped between my eyes. "Talk to me."

I let go of his wrists. "What about me? Did I misunderstand that part, too?"

He straightened from me, his hands gripping the top of the door frame. "Eden..."

That hesitation—that *I'm sorry, but...* grimace—said it all. I pressed my lips together. "Got it."

"I don't want to lie to you. You're special to me, you know that."

A special *thrall*, he meant.

The prickly lump expanded until it was pressing against my heart. "Right. That's what I thought."

"Eden..."

"Please." I lifted my hand, palm out. "I just want to go. It's late. I'm tired."

He eyed me for another beat, then expelled a breath. "Okay."

We drove back in silence. Talon stopped in front of the carriage house garage. As we waited for the doors to slide open, his fingers opened and closed on the steering wheel.

"I want to be a good father," he said. "You'll have to help me on that. I didn't have the best example, growing up."

It took a second for that to sink in. Then my breath hitched at the hint of vulnerability. He was such an alpha that it had never occurred to me that he might worry about what kind of father he'd make.

"Both of us will be learning on the job, right? Poor kid." I made a face, still hurt but trying to lighten the mood.

"You might be learning," he said, "but that kid is lucky to have you as a mom."

"You think so?"

The garage doors had opened, but he made no move to pull inside. "I do, yeah. You're going to be great. Look how you are with Rio—the kid worships you. And you have parents that acted like parents."

"What d'you mean?"

"I mean they're actually parents." He stared out the windshield, giving me his profile. "They took care of you growing up instead of the other way around. Don't get me wrong, my mom loves me. I think even Esposito loves me in his own way. They were just too young, you know? I didn't know it when I was a kid, but I was an accident."

My heart dropped to the sole of my hiking boots. "Oh," I said in a barely audible voice. "Like our baby."

"Yeah, but I want him. I did from the start." He turned to face me. "He's *not* an obligation. Neither of you are. I wanted you to accept my blood bond. I *need* you, Eden. But love..." He fingered the shark tattoo on the side of his neck. "I'm a vampire, you know? Love is so...human."

Jesus, the more he tried to explain, the worse he made me feel. "It's okay. Really."

He worked his jaw from side to side, then, with a tight nod, drove the SUV into the garage. "You've been back a month now," he said, shutting off the engine. "Go ahead and set up a visit with your parents for Saturday. I'll have Brien's PA arrange a ride for you."

Maybe he was feeling guilty, but whatever. I'd take it. I was feeling bruised inside and I really, really wanted to see my family.

"Thank you, I will."

"Don't thank me." He unbuckled his belt, then leaned over the console to brush his lips over mine. "You've earned it."

I'd earned *it?* My heart folded in on itself. *Way to put me in my place.*

He must've felt my recoil because he touched his forehead to mine. "I want you to be happy. Can you do that?"

I dragged in a breath. "I'm trying," I said.

❧ 24 ☙

TALON

I walked Eden back to the garden suite. On the surface, she acted like everything was all right, but the joy from earlier—the sparkle, the flirting—was absent. In trying to be honest with Eden, I'd only made things worse. Her effort to pretend otherwise—to make *me* feel better—was like a spike of guilt to the gut.

It reminded me of my mom when Esposito was getting restless, clearly preparing to leave again, how she'd lose the light in her eyes. I didn't want to be that guy, but I wasn't sure how not to be.

We were blood-bonded. I'd given Eden safety and security. Made guarantees regarding our spawn that no other vampire I knew would've agreed to.

And it still wasn't enough.

This is why you didn't want to bond with a human.

Now that we were blood-bonded, I felt responsible for Eden. She had needs I wasn't meeting. Couldn't meet.

I was failing her like I had my mom. Whatever I did, it wasn't enough.

I wasn't enough.

I not only didn't know how to be a father, I didn't know how to make a woman happy.

When we reached Eden's suite, I halted in the doorway, the *not-*

enough sensation pressing on my chest. "Good night," I said, deciding to leave. Having sex with her tonight felt wrong.

Eden paused in the act of unzipping the sunny yellow jacket. "You're leaving?"

When I said yes, she rolled her upper lip in.

"I'm not fragile, you know." She tossed the coat on a chair along with her hat and mittens. "I can handle a little hurt. Yeah, I wish things were different, but after I left, I did just fine on my own without you."

"Were you?" I took a single step inside her suite. She'd picked a bad time to remind me how she'd been living; thinking about it still gave me chills. "You were in that tiny apartment, working too hard. Afraid to go anywhere. You hadn't even been to an OB-GYN."

She threw up her hands. "Because I was on the run from your fucking syndicate. And I was doing all right, considering. You know I was. I would've kept going if not for the baby and Rio."

Her chin was at a stubborn angle, her hair tousled, her cheeks rosy from the cold. She'd gone from sad to pissed off. That was better, somehow—and that up-tilted chin challenged me to reach for her and kiss the fight right out of her.

Plus, she was right. If she'd kept running every few weeks, I might not ever have found her. If that Kral soldier hadn't tipped us off, she might still be missing.

"Actually," I admitted, "for someone who's never lived off-island, you did good."

"There you go! So, stop feeling guilty or responsible or whatever the hell you're feeling."

Her words were a nail gun to the heart. Because I *was* feeling guilty and responsible. I hated that I'd hurt Eden. I wanted to fix this, damn it.

She stalked toward me, determination in every line of her swishing hips. "You don't really want to leave, do you? Because you'd already be gone."

Startled, I unfolded my arms as she launched herself at me, catching her against my body.

She gripped my face. "Kiss me," she demanded. "You wanna make me feel better? Then do it. I'm horny and I want sex."

I gaped at her, still back there knowing I'd hurt her. That I'd failed her.

She didn't wait for me to catch up. Raising onto her toes, she fused her mouth to mine in a lush, ice-cream-flavored kiss.

For a couple of seconds, I was too stunned to do anything but kiss her back, my hands empty at my sides. My dick surged to attention, pushing against my zipper, and I started to participate. Eating at her mouth like a starving man. Sliding my fingers into her short hair. Gripping her ass so I could jerk her up against my erection.

Still kissing her, I reversed our positions, closing the door with one hand so I could push her up against it, my thigh against the heat of her pussy through her leggings. My hand moved from her ass to her sweater, pulling it up so I could run my thumb roughly over her nipple.

She gasped into my mouth, rubbing her crotch against me.

I broke the kiss. "That's it, angel. Take what you need. Get that pussy hot."

This much I could do for her. If she wanted an orgasm, I'd blow her goddamn mind.

"I am." Her lungs lifted and fell. "I *am*."

"Try harder." I drew back enough to drag off her sweater. "I want you nice and slippery, I'm going bury my tongue in you so deep, you'll be crying for me to let you come."

That made her back arch, a whimper escaping her lips.

"You like it when I talk dirty, don't you?" I was on my knees, removing her boots, dragging off her leggings and panties. "After you left, did you think of me when you touched yourself? Did you hear me telling you that you were a bad girl and you did it anyway? Maybe you pictured me watching you."

"*Yes.*" Her head fell back against the door. "I did. All that. And I hated you for making me want you. Christ, I hated you."

"You think I didn't hate you right back?"

Our gazes snagged.

Her throat worked. "I didn't think you cared enough to hate me."

"Then why did I come after you? No, don't answer." I reached up and covered her mouth with my hand.

Because I knew what she'd say, that I'd only gone after her to punish her, to prove she couldn't fuck me over like that and get away with it. It was what I'd told myself, wasn't it? Except even then I'd known that wasn't the whole story, that I'd have gone after her no matter what.

I tightened my grip on her face. "Just take what I'm going to give you. Because this is what you want. What you need. Every night, you need it all over again, don't you?"

She nodded beneath my hand, and I released her.

She licked her lips. "I do need it. Make me forget everything but you inside me."

"Anything you say, baby. As long as you take care of me, too."

"I will."

"Good." I slid my hand down her throat to where her breasts were encased in a satiny pink bra. I pinched both her nipples into hardness. "What about that? Does that help you forget?"

She made a small, tortured sound.

"Words," I said. "I want to hear words—and my name."

Her long, smooth throat worked, a seduction in itself. "Yes...Talon."

I grunted in satisfaction, my eyes focused on the soft, dark-blond mound inches from my face. "Open those sexy legs for me," I told her while I undid my jeans and slid the zipper down. When she obeyed, I said, "Good girl," and granted myself a few hard strokes.

She watched, her blue eyes almost black with arousal, her pretty nether lips glistening. Still grasping myself, I dragged my tongue through her slit, ending at her clit.

"Maybe I'll edge you again tonight," I said. "Make you beg for your orgasm until when you finally come, you'll be crying my name. So full of me you'll think you can't take anymore. But you will, won't you?" I swatted the side of her ass.

She whimpered and pressed herself against my mouth. "Please..."

"Oh, yeah, you will. Because you want this as much as me."

"I do. I do."

I couldn't hold out any longer. Not when my nose was filled with her salty aroma, my mouth watering to taste her.

I buried my tongue in her sex, licking through her seam to her clit. My fingers dug into the bare globes of her butt, massaging and pulling them apart while I laved her swollen little nub.

She grabbed my head, angling me so I was where she wanted me. "So close, so close…"

Drawing back a scant inch, I blew on her clit, edging her as promised. "Beg me."

"No…"

I gave her a single, light lick. "Beg me. And use my name."

She groaned, her hips writhing in my grip. "Please, Talon. Don't stop, please…I need it."

"Like this?" I went back to what I'd been doing, sucking and licking and lapping, one finger circling her back hole, teasing the delicate tissue.

Her knees locked. She ground herself against me. "Ohmigod."

I pulled back again.

"*No.*" She tried to force my head back and I let her. "Let me come. Please don't make me wait. It's so…"

"Mm." I could've kept mouth-banging her for another half hour; she smelled and tasted so good. But she was going over the cliff with or without me.

Giving her plump clit a long suck, I pushed two fingers into her, stroking her inner walls, and she gave a little scream and cinched around my fingers, thighs shaking, sobbing out my name.

I didn't stop until she went limp and started sliding down the door. Standing up, I took off her bra and urged her across the room with a hand on her lower back. I bent her over a couch arm and jerked off my shirt, popping a couple of buttons in my hurry. My shoes and pants followed.

"I need to be inside you."

Eden's breath shuddered in. She propped herself on her forearms, pushing her bottom out to me, widening her legs without me having to ask.

My stomach tightened at the erotic picture she presented. I took her by the hips, somehow managing to pause long enough to ask, "This is okay?"

A rapid nod. "Yes."

"Good." I slid into her, slow and deep, and released a primal groan.

Loving how she felt taking my length. Constricting around me as I seated myself fully inside her.

I rocked in and out a few times. "Touch yourself," I ordered.

"Can't," she rasped. "Too...much."

"You *can*." I bent forward and fingered her myself. "I'll go slow. Let you catch up."

She jerked against me, making me grit my teeth in pleasure. "No. Please, I—"

"Shh. I'll take care of you."

I released my fangs, scraping them over her shoulder, then licking the tiny marks to give her a boost of aphrodisiac.

Her back arched, her soft, warm curves pressing against my groin. "*Talon.*"

"That's who's inside you, angel." I slid out almost to the tip. "Is it still too much? You want me to stop?"

"Yes. *No.* I mean, don't stop. Don't stop."

I pressed a kiss to the center of her back and started to move, teasing her with my fingers. "You're dripping for me, aren't you? So wet for my dick."

I kept that up for a few minutes until she was with me again, pushing against me and giving hot little whimpers that I felt clear to my balls.

"Sweet Lilith," I husked. "You feel...perfect. So good I'm going to ride you all night. You'd like that, wouldn't you? You love having me in you, taking you until all you can think of is me. Don't you?"

"Yes, yes," she sobbed out.

I pinched each of her tits. When I went to finger her again, her hand was there, pleasuring herself.

I hummed in satisfaction. "That's it. Make yourself feel good for me."

She said something guttural in return.

My lower back muscles went tight. I slammed into her, balls slapping against her ass. Then again, and again. She wailed my name and started to come, her whole body strung tight, her inner walls squeezing me, over and over.

"That's my good girl. Take what you want. Empty me out."

I gathered Eden to me, supporting her belly with one hand, helping her finger herself with the other. I clung to her like she was the only thing in my world, pumping into her hard and fast. My fangs were still extended, the blood-hunger digging its claws into me.

At that moment I'd have given my left nut to drink from her. But I didn't. Instead, I touched my fangs to her neck, some vestige of sense stopping me from breaking the skin, but craving the feel of her skin beneath my teeth.

Then my own climax overtook me. My vision turned a hazy red.

"Eden," I said, the word both a groan and a prayer, and stilled deep inside her, the pleasure so intense it felt like I was being wrung out by a giant hand.

When I came back to myself, she was hanging limply in my arms, her breath choppy. I slid an arm under her thighs and carried her into the bedroom, laying her on her bed.

I tucked the covers around her, brushing my lips over hers. "You want me to sleep with you?"

"I'm good," she said with a crooked half-smile. "Thanks."

She'd been open to me while we had sex, but already she'd pulled back into herself. She seemed okay, though. Not sad, at least. Resigned.

That's what I'd wanted, right? For her to accept what we had without pushing for more.

"Okay." I stared down at her. "And for the record, I don't think you're fragile."

"But you do feel responsible for me."

I hesitated. It felt like a trick question. "Because I am."

"No, Talon, you're not—not the way you mean, anyway. Because you think you're responsible for making me happy, don't you?"

Because I am.

This time I didn't say it aloud. "If you're unhappy," I evaded, "then it's on me."

"No," she said, raising up on her forearms to scowl at me. "It's not. I'm an adult, and if I'm unhappy it's my own fault. You're responsible for the baby, not me—and then only until he's an adult. Yeah, you're responsible for me in a way—I'm going to need you to help me with the baby, especially when he's a newborn. And I hope I'll have your emotional support, too. But that's where it ends."

"You'll have it," I vowed, ignoring the "that's where it ends," part for now.

"Then we're good," she said, lying back down.

"Okay." I rubbed a hand over my chest. If we were good, why didn't I feel better about this? "You'll let me know if you need anything, right?"

She closed her eyes. "Sure."

I hovered another few seconds until she said, "Good night, Talon."

"See you tomorrow." I brushed my fingers over the back of her cheek and left.

EDEN

"So you're having a baby." My dad nudged a plate of his homemade oatcakes in my direction, then sat back in a kitchen chair, arms folded over his worn flannel shirt. "A dhampir."

Beside him, my mom cast him an exasperated look. "I already told you she was."

I helped myself to an oatcake. "It's okay, Mom."

The three of us were seated around the rustic farmhouse table that he'd built for Mom as a wedding gift, long and narrow to fit the dimensions of their 1920s kitchen. At one end of the table a hand-thrown blue pitcher was flanked by a matching teapot; Mom's day job was as a primary school teacher, but she made pottery on the side.

Dad scowled at me. "What were you thinking?"

"Wes," Mom said warningly.

"Damn it, Gigi," he said, "let me say my piece."

She shook her head but subsided.

I was visibly pregnant now. In a month, I'd gone from *thick around the middle* to *holy crap, she swallowed a basketball*. Talon and I were both on the tall side, and Olivia had told me the baby was big for his gestational age.

"You—" Dad pointed at me—"should have used protection."

"We did," I said, starting to get angry. I slathered butter and honey on the oatcake with quick, hard strokes.

My father loved me. I knew that. When I'd arrived, he'd opened the door before I could knock, then, without speaking, pulled me into a hard hug. But he was upset. He hadn't wanted this for me. He hadn't even wanted me to become a thrall, but at twenty-one, I hadn't needed his permission. I hadn't expected he'd be overjoyed to find me pregnant with a syndicate baby, but his disapproval still hurt.

"You know the rules," he said, tight-jawed. "Put in your time with the syndicate, take their money, and you're out. Now you're going to be tied to them for the next eighteen years—at the least."

"But..." I trailed off, staring at the oatcake.

But I love Talon.

My throat closed up. I set the cake on the plate without eating it.

That's right, folks. I'm the living, breathing cliché—a thrall who fell in love with a vampire.

Unfortunately, the sleeve of my sweater had somehow gotten pushed up my forearm. Both their shocked gazes locked on the gold band around my wrist. Too late, I jerked the sleeve down.

Mom gasped. "You're blood-bonded to him?"

"Jesus Murphy. I—" Dad shoved his chair away from the table and stalked out of the kitchen.

"I didn't have a choice," I blurted.

Mom's breath whooshed out. "He *forced* you?"

"No, no. I—" I shook my head. "It wasn't like that. He was trying to protect me."

"Protect you from what?" Dad loomed in the kitchen doorway, his lanky body tense.

I moved the plate aside and, resting my elbows on the table, pressed the heels of my palms into my eyes. "The syndicate."

"Why would he need to protect you from his own syndicate?" Dad asked. "Aren't they happy about the baby?"

"They are, yes." Taking my hands from my eyes, I lifted my head.

Dad's expression darkened. "Then it's Talon who doesn't want it?"

"No! He wants this baby."

I bit my lower lip. *You have to tell them the whole story.*

They'd blame Talon and the syndicate otherwise, and that wasn't fair.

God knew, I was tired of confessing what I'd done, but if I didn't, I'd have to lie to them, and I was trying to learn from this, to own my mistakes. To be someone my little guy could look up to, like I did my parents.

"I told you I messed up," I said to my mom. "What I didn't tell you was what I did. Dad, sit down—please?"

His whiskered face bunched in a frown, but he retook his seat. "Talk."

"Okay. So…" I wrapped my fingers around my mug of tea and told them the whole sorry story.

When I was finished, Mom reached across the table to pat my hand. "Oh, sweetheart. I wish you would've come to us right from the start. Maybe we could've helped."

"Maybe," I said, even though I knew they couldn't have done anything. And I wouldn't have wanted them to. I was an adult, as I'd told Talon.

I raised the mug to my lips, but it was empty. Dad refilled it for me, adding a splash of milk before pushing it back across the table to me.

He looked older, like the lines in his face had deepened as I told my story. "You're tied to them now. I can't break a blood bond."

"I know. But I don't want to. Please don't be unhappy for me. I love Talon. I want to be with him."

It was the truth, and I knew it would make them feel better. What they didn't know was that Talon didn't feel the same, but that wasn't anyone's business but mine.

The other night, I'd just…snapped. If he wanted sex without ties, then that's what he'd have. I was not a victim. I was not fragile. I was not some needy human.

Last night had been more of the same, except this time we hadn't gone anywhere, just fallen into bed as soon as he arrived. Again, I'd told him he didn't have to stay. I meant it. I didn't want him to, not if it was only because he felt guilty about me.

I could tell I'd knocked him off-balance. He wasn't sure how to handle this new version of me, which gave me a savage sort of satisfaction. Maybe someday he'd even see me as an equal—as much as a human could be, anyway.

And if he didn't, at least I'd have my self-respect.

Across the table my dad opened his mouth, then shut it. I could almost see the words, the anger that wanted to spill out—not at me, at Talon—but he swallowed it.

"Look," I said, "I know I messed up. But I hope you can be happy about the baby at least."

Mom puffed up at that. "Of course we are. You did nothing wrong there. It's not your fault the birth control failed, and if you want this baby, then we're a hundred percent behind you. Aren't we, Wes?"

"Of course we are." Dad nudged my plate back to me. "Eat your oatcake," he said gruffly, uncomfortable with all the emotion. "I made them with cinnamon and walnuts the way you like them."

Making my favorite oatcakes was his way of showing me he loved me. That and taking a day off during prime lobster season because it was the only time I could visit.

"Yeah?" I smiled across the table at him, relieved to have that behind us, and buttered another piece of oatcake, washing it down with the milky tea. "Mm. These are good."

"They're easy enough to make," he muttered, but I could tell he was pleased.

"Have another." Mom deposited a second one on my plate, adding, "Just give it time. In the end, things always work out for the best. You'll see."

Two of her favorite sayings, back-to-back. I smothered a smile. "That's what I keep telling myself."

"Good." Mom picked up the teapot and clicked her tongue. "It's empty." She rose to make a new pot. While she waited for the water to heat, she smoothed a hand down the back of my head. "You cut off all your hair. And what's with the dye?"

"I was in hiding," I said, and Mom winced.

"Should've come to us," Dad grumbled.

I fingered one of the faded black tips. It had grown out a half inch or so, but was still pretty short. "I like it like this. I'm going to keep it.

Even the dye, but this time it's going to be purple." Rio had promised to redo it for me tomorrow.

"Yeah?" Mom touched her own thick blond braid. "Well, I guess it's up to you."

The kettle whistled, and she returned to the stove.

Dad beetled his brows at me. "Talon's treating you okay? Because he'd better. If he doesn't, you let me know and I'll have a talk with him. I don't care if he's the King of England."

"He is," I assured him. "He arranged for me to see Olivia the day after we got back, and I'm getting regular massages because my back's been hurting."

"Oh, I remember that." Mom slanted me a sympathetic smile. "Yoga helps, too."

"It does. Olivia sent over a yoga DVD for pregnant persons."

Mom set the fresh pot of tea on the table and retook her seat. "Talon's all right," she said. "Look how he is with his mom. Mary, her name is. He looks after her—he even hired her a housekeeper/cook."

"I know," I said.

"When they wouldn't let us see you up at the castle," Mom added, "I went to see Mary. She didn't know about the baby. But then Mary was never much of a mother to Talon."

"Drinks too much," Dad muttered.

"I guess," Mom said, "but she was sober enough when I saw her. Anyway, you're here today, aren't you?" she told me. "Maybe she spoke to him."

"Maybe."

"Talon will take good care of you and your little boy," Mom added. "Just like he does Mary."

"Yeah." I nodded agreement, but inside, I cringed as another piece of the puzzle of Talon's family slotted into place.

I didn't want to be another of his responsibilities like his mom.

I didn't want to be taken "good care of." I could take care of myself.

I wanted Talon to be with me because it was what he wanted. That it was what he'd choose even if there was no baby.

T he rest of the afternoon passed quickly. Dad got out the Scrabble board and we played until we'd used all the tiles, razzing each other and stabbing the other players in the back whenever possible. I hadn't laughed so much since I'd found out I was pregnant.

The sun dropped over the cove. Talon texted me, asking if everything was okay. I sent him a thumbs-up in return and got to my feet. "Time for me to go."

While in Halifax searching for me, my dad had stayed with my sister and her husband. Now he took out his phone, saying, "I almost forgot, I have pictures of Freya and Devon."

He pulled up a couple of photos. Devon had his arm around Freya's shoulders. In the first photo, they grinned at the camera. In the second Devon nuzzled my sister's cheek. Her expression was so satisfied, so happy, that I couldn't help a twinge of envy.

"They look great," I said, handing the phone back.

If only I'd fallen for a human like Freya had. Life would be so much simpler.

"They'll be here for Boxing Day," Dad said. "You're coming, aren't you?"

"Of course. No way I'd miss Boxing Day."

Our annual after-Christmas celebration was when we exchanged gifts. I'd have to clear it with Talon, but he'd be sleeping anyway. Maybe by then he'd even have let me off the tight leash he kept me on.

I shrugged into my jacket and went to the front door. The SUV was idling at to the curb, the back door open. Mom and Dad followed me onto the porch.

Mom pulled me into a tight hug. "Come back next Saturday, and this time stay for dinner. I'll make my bisque."

I hugged her back. "I'll do my best. And this time, you have to show me how to make it." Mom's lobster bisque was freaking amazing —chunks of lobster swimming in cream and butter, and flavored with a dash of sherry and her special spices.

"We'll see," she said like she always did, adding (also like always), "if you knew the recipe, you wouldn't have a reason to visit."

"I'd visit anyway, and you know it."

She chuckled and kissed my cheek. "Love you, sweetheart. And Eden? You've got this. I have faith in you. You're going to be a good mom."

I hadn't known how much I'd needed her to say that until she had. "Love you back," I said around the golf ball lodged in my throat. "I'll do my best."

"I know, honey. And we're right here whenever you need us. To talk or help out, okay?"

Then it was Dad's turn to pull me into a hug. "You take care of yourself, okay?" he said. "And the little guy, too."

I nodded against his flannel shirt. "I will."

Giving him a squeeze, I jogged down the front steps and climbed into the back of the SUV. I didn't think anything of it when Mr. Jones didn't get out to shut the door after me. I could close my own doors, after all.

The locks clicked and the SUV moved off. My parents stood on the front porch, framed in the light spilling from the hallway, Dad with his lanky, scarecrow body and Mom, a head shorter and curvy. I waved at them through the darkened window, even though I knew they probably couldn't see me, then faced front.

Somehow, being with them today had renewed my hope. I wasn't done fighting.

Maybe I'd accepted Talon's blood bond because it had seemed my only choice, but if I had to do it again, I would. Everything I'd said to my parents was true. Talon was good to me.

"You warm me."

And then later that evening, he'd said he needed me. I'd brushed that off because he'd slipped that into the middle of explaining why he couldn't love me, but now it landed on my heart with an almost audible thud.

Maybe Talon wasn't ready to commit to me, but he'd gradually opened up to me, shared something of himself. That meant something, didn't it?

The more I heard about his parents, the more I realized I wasn't the problem here. Those walls had been put in place a long time before he met me. He was protecting himself, same as I did when I imitated an armadillo.

I fingered the gold bracelet.

Maybe I needed to look at this from another angle. Yeah, he'd offered me his blood bond to protect me and the baby, but he'd wanted it. He'd told me so himself. And looking back, he'd done everything he could to convince me to accept it.

He'd wanted me bonded to him. He'd wanted *me*.

He needed *me*. I *warmed* him.

A smile curved my lips. I could work with that.

❧ 26 ❧

TALON

Sunset comes early to Nova Scotia in December. When I opened my eyes that evening it was only a little after four-thirty.

I got out of bed, a vague uneasiness prickling my nape. It reminded of the last time Eden had left the island. I'd had a bad feeling then too, right before I'd discovered she was gone.

Take it easy. She's at her parents' house.

I texted her anyway to make sure everything was okay. When she replied with a thumbs-up, I put down the phone and headed into the bathroom. For a few seconds there, I'd come close to losing it. The woman was messing with my head, even if she didn't intend to.

Yeah, I wanted Eden to be happy, but there was the pact. And my long-term strategy.

That stupid pact can go fuck itself. And a strategy shouldn't be a straitjacket.

My step hitched, my brain shocked at the violent gut reaction. I scraped a hand down my face, hating this out-of-control feeling. My life had swerved onto an unexpected path and I didn't like it, hadn't planned for it.

All I knew was I sure as hell didn't like having Eden on the opposite side of the island away from the safety of the castle.

Get a fucking grip, man. It's only because of the baby. Of course, you're extra-protective right now.

But I knew I'd feel the same way even after the baby was born. Unfortunately, locking Eden up to keep her safe wasn't the solution. Even if I could get away with it, she wasn't a creature, something I could cage.

What if I didn't have to break the pact? What if I could have Eden—and a vampire mate? Or even a dhampir?

You could turn her.

The surge of relief felt like it had blown open my chest, letting in hope.

Turn Eden, and I wouldn't have to watch her grow old like my mom. Wouldn't have to live with the knowledge that next to my life, hers would be a brief flicker of a candle. I could have her for hundreds of years, not a few short decades.

Plus, she'd be stronger, less vulnerable. Because she *was* fragile, whatever she believed. Maybe not emotionally, but physically, she simply couldn't fight off a supernatural.

The hope and excitement carried me into the shower. For a whole five minutes, I let it buoy me up.

Then logic took over.

For one thing, Eden's parents would go ballistic. The locals were pragmatic about trading their bodies for money—that was an accepted way of financing your education or a new business—but they drew the line at the syndicate recruiting from their ranks. Other than me and Cain, no Lilith Islander had been turned in decades, and let's face it, everyone from the mayor on down had heaved a collective sigh of relief when Prima Lenore had taken responsibility for us.

Then there was the fact it was Eden, the thrall who'd used her position to spy on us. Would Brien allow me to turn her? It was one thing to accept her back as a blood-bonded thrall, but asking him to welcome her into the syndicate was a whole different beast.

And that supposed Eden said yes. Not everyone made it through the transition. Could I ask her to risk her life for me?

The elation cracked like a broken plate, shattering at my feet.

Because no, I couldn't ask her to risk her life for me, a man who'd never be able to give her what she really wanted—my love. That wouldn't be fair to her. It was best for both of us if she stayed human, and a thrall.

Even if the thought of someday losing Eden filled me with a sick helplessness.

I turned off the shower and toweled off like a goddamn zombie. Stiff limbed. No feelings.

I was pulling on tactical pants and a long-sleeved T-shirt when Cain came to my door. I padded across the living room in my stocking feet to let him in.

"You're up. Good." He brushed past me, clearly agitated.

"What's wrong?" The prickle of unease grew into a buzzing in my brain. "Not Eden—?"

"Eden?" He shot me an odd look before shaking his head. "No. It's Esposito. He's on the island."

It took me a few seconds to comprehend through the buzzing. Then my stomach dropped. Another part of my life I'd lost control of.

"Since when?"

"Earlier today. He came in on the ferry—the PI watched him get on it and alerted Adrian. Adrian met the ferry himself, but Esposito never got off."

"Shit." Going to the wet bar, I poured a couple of shots and passed one to Cain. "Adrian searched the ferry?"

"Yep. He called in another soldier and they went over it with a fine-toothed comb. And the ferry doesn't return to Halifax until next Tuesday. Esposito's on the island, all right."

"Someone helped him. Someone who was in the shadows." A supernatural could bring a human into the hazy gray twilight world as long as they maintained contact. Together, they could've left the ferry unseen.

Cain nodded, unsmiling. "Exactly."

"Brien knows?"

"Yeah. He wants us both to come to his apartment ASAP."

I lifted a brow. "Not the war room?"

"No. He'd prefer to keep this quiet for now."

I drained the shot glass in one gulp and put it on the bar. "Because of me." Because it was my goddamn father.

Cain lifted a shoulder, let it drop.

I shoved my feet into a pair of shoes. "Let's go, then."

Following his ascent to primus, Brien had moved into his parents' old apartment after first redoing it in a less ornate style to suit his and Twilight's taste. The living room was similar to mine, with minimalistic furniture and wide-plank floors, but more colorful, with blue-green walls and large, sensual oil paintings by a reclusive artist.

Brien was on one of the couches, a laptop open on the coffee table in front of him. He closed the lid and indicated the couch across from him. "Have a seat."

"Thanks." I sat down, hands on my knees. Cain chose to lean against the polished wood bar instead.

Brien opened his arms along the couch back and crossed one leg over the other, his ankle on his thigh in a deceptively relaxed pose. He had to be concerned; we all knew Esposito was a loose cannon.

"You hear anything else?" he asked Cain.

"No. Bastard's gone underground. If I didn't have the PI's report, we wouldn't even have known he's on the island."

Brien's green eyes narrowed. "You trust this PI?"

Cain jerked his chin in assent. "He's being paid double his usual fee, and I ran a background check on him before hiring him. I suppose for enough money, he could be convinced to lie to us, but he's smart. He knows his life wouldn't be worth fuck-all if we found out."

"So someone helped Esposito sneak onto the island," said Brien. "A supernatural, probably a vampire."

I nodded. "Whoever it was would have to be strong to bring a human with them into the shadows."

Cain's knee was moving double-time. "They had to have been on that ferry with Esposito. I'll talk to the captain, but if a vampire entered and exited in the shadows and stayed out of sight the rest of the time, the crew would've never known they were on board."

"Agreed," Brien said. "But we have to consider the possibility that the vampire was already on Lilith Island, that they met the ferry when it docked and brought Esposito off that way. Which means it could be one of us."

His shoulders were tight beneath his T-shirt, his fingers digging into the couch back. We'd thought we'd purged the syndicate of the traitors who'd tried to block his ascension to primus.

"It's possible," Cain allowed. "But I'm betting it's someone from off-island—a member of the Quebec City Syndicate, for example. Régis isn't happy about you and Twilight going after one of his top people."

Brien's lip curled. "Fleur had it coming. Régis should've handled it himself."

Fleur had been keeping blood slaves, along with Lemaire, another QCS member. Twilight herself had been caught in their net. If Brien hadn't bought Twilight at an illegal underground auction, she might still be enslaved.

"Doesn't mean Régis doesn't want revenge," Cain said, "especially if he can blame it on Esposito somehow. But my money's on Lemaire. He still hasn't surfaced."

Brien nodded thoughtfully.

"And then there's Nazaire," I pointed out.

Nazaire was an enforcer, a cold SOB who'd somehow found out that Brien was moving on the slavers in the QCS. When Brien and Twilight had broken into Nazaire's lair, he was nowhere to be found. We'd tried to locate him, but there was only so much we could do against a QCS enforcer.

Régis had turned a blind eye when Brien and Twilight had come into his territory to take out Fleur and Lemaire, but they were soldiers, relatively low in the hierarchy. Régis couldn't let us hunt one of his enforcers without retaliating. If Brien wasn't careful, he was going to ignite a full-out war.

"So, Esposito comes to the island," Brien mused, "because QCS or some other syndicate got their hooks into him."

I nodded. "Mom said the last time she saw him, he was riding high on a big win. That's when he's at his most vulnerable. He starts thinking he can't lose."

"So they use that," said Cain. "They wait until he's deep in the hole, then send him here."

"But to do what?" asked Brien.

"That," I said tightly, "is the million-dollar question. But don't worry, I'll find him." I met Brien's eyes. "I'm sorry about this."

"Why? Nobody's blaming you."

I shook my head. "I fucked up. Should've handled the guy a long time ago."

"Hey," he said, "I wasn't worried either. I thought the man was harmless."

Cain unfolded his arms. "So what now?"

"You alerted the war room?" Brien asked him.

"I did. They know what Esposito looks like—they have photos and videos. If he tries to get in here, they'll let us know immediately."

"Good," said Brien.

I rose to my feet. "If we're done here, I think I'll pay a visit to my mom."

Brien nodded, but Cain was shaking his head. "She's not going to take your side against Esposito," he said. "She'll protect him—you know she will."

"Maybe," I returned. "But I have something she wants, something to bargain with."

Cain's knee stilled. "Yeah?"

My mouth twisted. It went against the grain to use my son as a pawn. If Eden ever found out, she'd never forgive me. But Esposito had backed us into a corner.

"My spawn," I said.

27

EDEN

The man behind the wheel wasn't Mr. Jones, it was a stranger, a little younger than Mr. Jones, with thick brown hair.

Wariness sheeted up my spine. I leaned forward. "Where's Mr. Jones?"

The driver's eyes met mine in the rearview mirror. "He had a family emergency. They sent me instead. That okay?"

Something about the way he was acting made me uncomfortable. He was too casual, trying too hard to reassure me.

"Of course it is." I slid the phone from my jacket pocket, careful to keep it out of sight of the rearview mirror. "I'm sorry about Mr. Jones, though. Is everything all right?"

"Everything's fine," the driver replied, his eyes on the road again. "I'll tell him you asked, though."

I nodded and flashed what I hoped was an unconcerned smile, then turned sideways and pretended to look out the window, trying to open the phone without the driver seeing.

In the window, I glimpsed a dark shimmer. It took me a beat to realize it was a reflection, that the shimmer wasn't outside the SUV, it was inside.

With me.

My heart kicked into overdrive. A vampire, coming out of the shadows. I jerked around in time to see a man in a pinstriped suit and a short hipster ponytail appear on the backseat.

Forget hiding that I was texting. I shoved the phone in front of my face and it opened. I desperately typed a short text to Talon.

EDEN: *Help. Vampir—*

I never pressed *Send*.

With superhuman speed, the ponytailed man plucked the phone from my hand, deleted the text, and powered it off.

My lungs compressed. I lunged for the door handle, then halted. We were going at least thirty-five miles an hour.

The baby. You can't jump. Not at this speed.

I swallowed sickly. Why hadn't I kept that freaking switchblade with me? It was still in the bottom of my sewing box. But I hadn't wanted to give Talon another reason not to trust me. I'd even wondered if it could be some kind of a test.

The vampire or dhampir—I didn't know which—produced a syringe from his suit pocket.

What the—? Panicked, I worked frantically at the handle, but the child lock had been activated and the door wouldn't open.

"Let go of the door." He spoke in Québécois-accented English, low and stern.

I released the handle, my eyes on the fluid-filled syringe. "What's that?"

"Something to put you to sleep."

Every hair on my body lifted. My heart battered at my chest with small, terrified fists.

"No! You can't." My fingers fumbled with the seatbelt buckle, trying to disengage it. "Please—I'm pregnant. You could hurt the baby."

"This won't hurt your spawn." Cool fingers pried mine from the buckle.

"*No.*" I shoved at his arm. "I mean, please, I'll do anything you say. Just don't—"

My pleas strangled in my chest as he grabbed my leg, plunging the syringe through my pants and into my thigh.

"No," I cried, bucking wildly, fighting to get free. When that didn't work, I switched tactics, going for his face with my fingernails, trying to dig them into his goddamn eyes.

His hand shot up, too fast to see, corralling both my wrists. He kept them raised high above my head while he finished injecting a clear fluid into my thigh.

"Don't worry." Withdrawing the needle, he tucked the syringe back into his pocket and released my wrists. "We don't want to hurt you or your spawn."

A red-hot rage heated my brain. "You *dick*. I'll kill you for this."

I tried again to open the door handle.

A hand landed on my shoulder. "Calm yourself."

I tried to shake him off. "I will not—"

I stared at my fingers. I couldn't feel the handle anymore, or his hand on my shoulder. Fear stole my breath. Ice slid through my veins, slowly and inexorably, like a creek in the winter.

My eyelids grew heavy. I forced them open as he undid my seatbelt and eased me onto my side on the leather seat.

"Talon will—" My mouth had filled with marbles. I couldn't talk around them.

"Talon will think you ran away," he informed me in silky tones. "Again."

My stomach hollowed out. *No.*

Talon just might believe it. He might even think this was why I'd been so eager to see my mom and dad.

I shook my head against the seat. Inside, I was screaming and screaming, but all that came out was a moan.

The ice was everywhere now. I couldn't feel my legs or toes or even the leather beneath my cheek. My vision went dark but I could still hear.

The car slowed. The driver finally spoke. "What the fuck? You said you wouldn't hurt her or the kid."

The blond man growled. "Keep driving."

The darkness dragged me under.

❧ 2 8 ☙

TALON

On my way to my mom's house, I stopped by the garden suite to make sure Eden had gotten back okay, but she wasn't there. The uneasy prickle returned.

"Eden?" I asked, palming a switchblade.

The silence reverberated in my brain like a gong, drowning out everything but the need to find her.

I tore through the rooms, checking the bathroom, the closet, even beneath the bed. Back in the living room, I jerked open the French door and ran into the enclosed garden.

"Eden?" I called as I raced down the curved flagstone paths. "Are you out here?"

The only answer was an irate meow from Demon, Brien's white cat. It stalked past me into Eden's suite, tail twitching.

I closed the blade and shoved it into a pocket so I could send a quick text to Jones. He'd been instructed to have Eden back at the castle by sunset.

Calm the fuck down. She's fine. They had a flat tire or something.

But the driver didn't respond either.

The uneasiness became a swarm of buzzing, stinging bees. I was overcome by an eerie sense of déjà-vu. It was happening again, just like last August.

231

My next text was to Brien and Cain, informing them that Eden was missing and asking if they or anyone else had heard from Jones.

Cain called me right back. "Adrian doesn't know anything. Did you ask Rio?"

"No. Can you do it? I'll contact her mom and dad."

"Will do," he said. "And I'll see if Kerry or William know anything."

"Thanks."

I ended the call and started to open my contacts. Then I cursed. Why hadn't I added the Montgomery's numbers to my own phone when I'd programmed Eden's?

Then I remembered we were monitoring her cell. I opened the security app and pulled up her recent calls and texts. Unfortunately, Eden's parents didn't know anything more than I did.

"She left here over an hour ago," Gigi Montgomery told me. "She never came back?"

"That's what I'm trying to find out. She's not in her suite and no one seems to know where she is. She was coming straight back, right?"

"Well, yeah." Gigi paused. "I mean, we thought she was. We watched her get into the SUV and drive off. Have you sent someone out to look for the SUV?"

She could be lying. My lie-detector sense only worked when I was physically in a human's presence. But my gut said the woman was telling the truth—for one thing, she sounded as worried as I did.

"Not yet," I said grimly. "But I will."

"Let me talk to him," Wes Montgomery said, and a moment later, he came on the phone. "Are you saying Eden's missing?"

"I don't know. She could be somewhere on the castle grounds."

She didn't have permission to roam the castle, but this was Eden. She was resourceful, and she knew the castle as well as I did.

"Maybe she left," Montgomery said. "Maybe she doesn't want to spend the rest of her life as your goddamned thrall."

My molars clamped together. "That's between me and her," I said tightly. "If you know something, I suggest you tell me. Now."

Otherwise I'd compel it out of the man. I didn't care if he was

Eden's father or that the syndicate had an unwritten policy of not pissing off the locals. Finding Eden trumped both of those things.

A long, insulting pause, but when Montgomery replied, he confirmed what his wife had told me. "We thought she was on her way back to the castle. The last thing we saw, she was getting into one of your SUVs."

"Okay." I forced my jaw to loosen. "Contact me at this number if she turns up."

"I'm taking my truck out to look for her," he said and ended the call.

Acid ate at my stomach. I paced up and down the path near the French door.

Eden hadn't wanted to come back to Lilith Island. I'd forced her to return. Maneuvered her into accepting my blood bond.

Could she have been biding her time? Waiting for a chance to escape?

But it didn't add up. She was truly sorry for what she'd done—that part hadn't been a lie. I'd *felt* her guilt and shame. She hadn't even touched Eugene Smith's blood money. She was doing everything she could to make it up to me and the syndicate.

Plus, there was the baby. Why leave now after we'd come to an agreement about his place in the syndicate? Hell, she'd made me swear on my sire's grave that our son would have choices, that he wouldn't be forced to join the syndicate if he didn't want to.

My phone buzzed with a text from Cain: *Rio doesn't know anything & William was about to let you know she hasn't come back.*

A text from Brien popped up next. *The cams show she left & never returned. Jones isn't back either.*

Hell. I didn't know what to think. Had she left on her own or been kidnapped?

Whichever it was, I wasn't sticking around any longer to find out. I sent a quick text to William, directing him to send a soldier out to drive the cliff road to Bluebeard's Cove in case they had an accident. Meanwhile, I'd head into town to see what I could find out.

I was already moving as I informed Brien and Cain of my plans.

TALON: *On my way to the Cove. Taking my bike.*

BRIEN: *Meet you @ the garage.*

CAIN: *Same.*

They caught up to me on the stairs leading up to the ground floor. Together, we raced through the foyer and outside. As we rolled our motorcycles out of the carriage house, our phones buzzed with a message from Twilight.

Jones had been discovered wandering in the forest between Blue-beard's Cove and the castle. *Looks like he was drugged*, she informed us. *They're taking him to the clinic.*

My fingers clenched around the phone so tightly a fracture zigzagged across the screen.

Brien met my gaze, his expression somber. "Let's get over there, see what he knows."

We roared out of the courtyard, taking the shortcut through the forest south of the castle. Ten minutes later, we bumped down the stairs of the cliff that overlooked the Cove.

When we arrived at the island clinic, Dr. MacKenzie was examining Jones. We pushed our way into the room examining room, where the driver was laying on a table, eyes closed.

"Is he okay?" Brien asked, and Jones's eyes opened.

The beefy doctor nodded. "He will be. He needs rest and—"

"Has he said anything about Eden Montgomery?" I interrupted. "He was supposed to be driving her back to the castle."

"No."

I turned to Jones, watching us through heavy lids. "What do you know?"

"The man's been drugged," MacKenzie said. "I'm not sure he can tell you anything useful."

"No." Jones struggled to sit up, and I moved forward, supporting him with an arm around his back. "I can talk. I'm sorry, my lord." His gaze swung to where Brien stood at the foot of the examining table. "I didn't see them." He swallowed hard. "I'm sorry," he repeated.

"All right," Brien said calmly. "Take your time and tell us what—"

"Eden," I said, unable to wait while Brien coaxed it out of the man. "She's missing. What do you know about it?"

"Eden never came back?" Jones turned his head in my direction, then winced and rubbed his temple.

"No," I said.

He briefly closed his eyes. "Jesus. I was afraid of that."

"Easy," the doctor told him and tried to elbow me aside. "Lieutenant, if you give him some space, he—"

I hissed and bared my fangs. "Eden Montgomery is missing and this man can help. Now shut up or leave the fucking room."

MacKenzie moved back a foot, arms folded over his broad chest. "I'll stay."

"Talon," Brien said with a warning look.

I gave a curt nod and withdrew my fangs.

Brien turned his attention back to Jones. "So you saw Eden Montgomery to her parents' house," he murmured in soothing, almost hypnotic tone. "Then what happened?"

"I'm not sure." The older man's shoulders drooped. "All I remember is that around four o'clock, I texted my wife to bring me a sandwich and a thermos of coffee. I didn't want to leave Eden unattended, and my house is just a block from the Montgomery's."

"And then what?" asked Brien.

"My wife got there about fifteen minutes later, and I got out of the car. She stayed for a few minutes while I started eating, and then she left. But I didn't get back in the SUV. My right knee had stiffened up, so I walked up and down the sidewalk until it loosened up. It was dusk by then, and I knew we had to get back. I finished the sandwich and poured the last cup of coffee and started toward the Montgomery's house. The next thing I knew, I was on my back, staring up at an oak tree."

Cain stirred. "How many people—one? Two?"

The older man's chest heaved. "I'm not sure. I didn't see or hear anything."

Cain, Brien and I exchanged a look.

"Vampires," muttered Cain.

Brien nodded.

Whoever had attacked Jones had probably been in the shadows.

Could it be the same person or persons who'd helped sneak Esposito onto the island? My stomach folded in on itself.

Because if the answer was yes, Esposito was part of this.

Jones touched his left thigh. "I felt something sting my leg."

MacKenzie moved forward. "Can I have a look?"

"Sure," Jones said, and I eased him back onto the examining table, watching as the doctor helped Jones out of his pants.

MacKenzie examined the faint bruise on Jones's thigh, a bruise with a tiny hole in the center. "You were definitely injected with something. Fast-acting from the sound of it."

Jones glanced at me. "I'm sorry, Lieutenant. I should never have gotten out of the SUV."

I blew out a breath. "Not your fault. I should've had you take backup."

But I hadn't thought Eden was in danger. Not on Lilith Island.

"If that's all," said the doctor, "he should rest now."

"Let us know if you remember anything else," Brien told Jones and we left the examining room.

Mrs. Jones was pacing the waiting room. It must've started raining because she was soaked, her short brown hair matted to her head, her sweater dripping.

Her attention shot to the three of us. "How is he?"

"He's shook up," Brien said, "but he should be all right."

Her hand flew to her mouth. "Thank God."

"Dr. Mackenzie's with him now," Brien added. "You can go in."

"Thank you, my lord," she said and hurried past us.

Outside we paused on the clinic's front porch. I stared into the driving rain. It was barely above freezing. By morning it could turn to sleet or snow. The thought of Eden out there somewhere made me feel like I was being sliced with sharp silver razors.

"She's a human, and pregnant," I said. "She can't survive for long on a night like this."

Brien and Cain exchanged a glance.

"Eden's okay," Brien told me. "They wouldn't have gone to this much trouble if they wanted to hurt her."

"We'll find her," Cain added. "Whatever it takes, we'll do it."

My jaw worked. "Thank you," I said, my voice rough with emotion.

"You have to consider the possibility that your father has something to do with this," Brien said.

Blackness edged my vision. I threw him a savage look. "He is not *my father*."

Brien dipped his chin. "Esposito, then."

"Hey." Moving up on my other side, Cain bumped my shoulder with his. "Take it easy. We're on your side, bro."

I grabbed for the ragged shreds of my control. "Sorry," I told Brien. "That was out of line. And yeah, that occurred to me. That he's in this somehow."

"Call Mary," Brien said. "Maybe she knows something."

"Good idea. Should've thought of it myself."

Unfortunately, my mom knew nothing, either. "You're saying your dad is on the island? I haven't seen him—I swear I haven't. But he wouldn't have anything to do with this, either. I know it. He's not violent—he wouldn't hurt Eden. He—"

The buzzing in my head was back. "I have to go," I said, cutting through her stumbling defense of the SOB. "Call me if you see or hear from him. But if he gets in touch, I want to know. Is that understood? You let me know *immediately*."

"Yes. I—"

I didn't hear the rest because I ended the call. "You guys heard?" I asked my friends.

"Yeah," said Brien.

"What if—?" I swallowed over something acrid. "What if Eden left on her own? What if she planned this?"

Cain spoke first. "No fucking way. Don't let yourself go there. Maybe that's what they want you to think, but that woman loves you. Even I can see that."

I stared at him, shocked that he of all people was defending her. But it helped quiet the buzzing, especially when Brien added, "Why would she leave now? She's due in February—that's what, ten or eleven weeks from now? She wants that baby. Even if she hated your guts, she'd stick around until after he was born."

"Yes. She would." I dragged a hand down my face, reminding myself that it didn't add up.

"So we'll go on the assumption she was kidnapped," Brien said.

Kidnapped.

Hearing someone say it out loud was like throwing a match on the gasoline fire of my fear. Brien and Cain were still talking but I couldn't hear them. I could only stare into the rain, horrified that Eden was out there somewhere. I almost wished she *had* left willingly. At least then she'd be safe. Dry. Warm.

"Talon," Brien said sharply. "Focus, damn it."

He's right. Don't think about it. Focus on getting her back.

I nodded. Shoved the cracked phone into my pocket.

"Okay. Okay." I somehow made myself switch into planning mode. "One of you wake up the mayor, get her to mount a search along with us. Eden's a local, and they'll want to help—and who knows, maybe someone will get lucky. Meanwhile, I'll start at the marina. If they're thinking of taking her off island, it would be by boat."

A helicopter would be noticed, but the locals took boats in and out all the time. One more wouldn't be remarked on.

"Go," Brien said. "I'll get some of our people on it, too. They can search the woods and the beaches."

I was already heading for the porch steps. Icy raindrops pelted my face, drenched my T-shirt and pants. I noticed the needle-like sensation, but from far away as if the rain—and my body—were on the other side of a window fogged with dread.

Behind me, Brien and Cain were working out which of our people were available to search. Brien was going all out to find Eden, even if it meant leaving the castle only lightly guarded, and I was grateful to him, and Cain as well. For their support. For their willingness to put aside what Eden had done and help find her.

But it was still like looking for a needle in a fucking haystack. And that was assuming Eden was still on the island.

29

EDEN

I curled onto my side, clinging to unconsciousness like a security blanket.

I hurt. My head. My hip from the cold, hard surface beneath me.

My eyes were crusted with sleep, my tongue thick and swollen.

I swallowed and choked on my lack of spit, which brought me fully awake.

My eyelids popped open.

The baby. *Jesus, the baby*.

They'd kidnapped me. Knocked me out with some unknown drug. Had they hurt the baby?

Tears trickled from my eyes. I spread my fingers over my abdomen. No pain or cramping. That was good, right?

Please, please let him be okay.

I turned my attention to my surroundings. Pitch-black and musty. Hard-packed dirt, not concrete.

I waited for my eyes to adjust but it remained dark. So, a basement or cellar...or a crypt.

The fine hairs on my arms stood on end. Had they left me here to die?

Deep breaths.

Deep. Breaths.

I pushed myself to sitting with my palms against the cool, gritty surface. I wasn't tied up, and I was still dressed in the clothes I'd worn to my parents' house. They hadn't molested me. Another good thing.

But who...? And why...?

My mind supplied the answer.

"Talon will think you ran away."

A chill crawled up my spine. My nape tightened.

This wasn't about me. This was about Talon.

A few meters away from me, the air seemed to shift. I froze, concentrating on the spot.

The seconds ticked by. Then a glowing face appeared. A vampire, a male one. It was too dark to see anything but his face and throat, but he appeared to be seated on something because his face hovered three to four feet above the ground.

Lean, angular face. Prominent cheekbones. Short dark hair. And dressed in a suit from what I could see of his neck, which sported a buttoned-up collar and the knot of a necktie.

Against his paper-pale skin, his lips appeared to have been drawn on with black ink, his eyes dark holes like a nightmare come to life.

The inked-on mouth moved. "You're awake."

I didn't want to be awake. I wanted to curl up and pretend I was still asleep. But that wasn't an option, so I drew my legs in, knees bent, feet on the dirt floor and wrapped my arms around my bent knees, grateful for the warmth of the puffer jacket.

I didn't try and stand up. That seemed too chancy on my jelly legs.

Rubbing the crust from my eyes, I croaked, "Who are you?"

"You can call me M'sieur." A French accent, but not French Canadian like the dhampir in the SUV. This man sounded colder, more cultured.

An older vampire then. Typically, the longer a vampire lived, the less they recalled they'd been human once, too.

Panic coated my insides. I swallowed thickly.

"You're thirsty." He bent forward, then came upright again. I heard a cap being unscrewed from a plastic bottle, the sound loud in the hush. "Would you like water?"

"Yes, please," I said as meekly as I could. If I had to kiss this man's ass, I would. Whatever it took to keep my baby alive and well.

"M'sieur," he corrected.

I dug my nails into my palms. "M'sieur."

A thin smile. "That's better. You can have this water, but first, you have to do something for me."

I licked dry lips. "What, M'sieur?"

"You will record a message for me."

"What message?" This time, I didn't tack on the *M'sieur*, but he didn't call me on it.

"Tell her, Esposito."

I jolted. Someone else was in here, too?

"She needs a drink, first." A male voice.

"A sip, no more."

"Got it."

Footsteps in the darkness, coming in my direction, then Esposito hunkered down before me. Human—his skin didn't have that moon-like glow. I couldn't make out his features, though. Actually, I hadn't even seen him crouch; I'd sensed his motion.

"They're not going to hurt you or the baby as long as you do what you're told," he told me.

Yeah, right.

I lifted my chin. "Water, first."

"Here."

Something cold touched my arm and I flinched, until I realized it was a water bottle. I grabbed it and took a couple of gulps before he snatched it out of my hand.

"Just a sip, I said," he muttered.

"I was thirsty," I said as contritely as I could, adding, "Thank you."

I sensed rather than saw his shrug. "I have a phone here. He wants you to make a video."

The camera came on, set to film a video selfie, painfully bright in the darkness. I had to close my eyes for a few seconds.

When I opened them again, the light illuminated enough of Esposito's face to see his deep-set eyes and curly dark hair touched with silver. I was pretty sure he was the man who'd been driving the

SUV. He looked familiar, but maybe he was from Lilith Island, someone I'd seen but never met. About 15,000 people lived on the island, too many to know everyone personally, especially a man thirty or forty years older than me.

Esposito noticed me eyeing him and withdrew his head further into the darkness. That was encouraging, actually. If he didn't want to be recognized, then he believed I'd be alive to identify him.

On the other hand, he was only a human servant. Who knew what the vampire intended?

"A video?" I asked.

"To send to Talon. Instructions."

"Instructions?" I repeated, my brain still fuzzy. "But why?"

The vampire answered. "Because if you don't, I will drain every drop of blood from your body and leave you and your spawn here to die."

My swallow was loud in my ears.

A bright blue line had flared to life around the vampire's irises. His tongue flicked out, like he was literally tasting my anguish.

The prick was aroused by my pain and helplessness.

"Do I have your agreement?" he asked.

"Yes," I bit out.

"Yes, who?"

My jaw tightened. "Yes, m'sieur."

"Good girl. Tell her what we want her to say," he told Esposito.

Esposito.

That's why he seemed familiar—he looked a little like Talon, especially around the eyes. They both had that sexy, hooded-eyelids thing going.

Could this be the shitty father, the one Talon saw only when the man needed money? Something told me not to say anything, though.

"Okay." Esposito's mouth turned down like he didn't like being part of this, but he dutifully gave me the words I was to say.

When he was finished, I swallowed queasily. Making this video might break Talon's trust in me forever.

"Ready?" Esposito asked.

Behind him, a small smile played on the vampire's inky lips.

He could've compelled me to obey him, but he hadn't even tried. No, he wanted to force me to do it on my own so he could watch me squirm.

Well, fuck you, too.

Anger pushed through the helplessness, energizing me, making me determined to do whatever was necessary to survive and escape.

I straightened my spine. "Let me hear that one more time."

We tore that fucking island apart looking for Eden.

In addition to a dozen vampires and dhampirs, the searchers included hundreds of humans, including Eden's parents, and, to my surprise, my own mother. The mayor and the local police worked with Cain to coordinate the search, starting with the marina and fanning outward through Bluebeard's Cove and then to the rest of the island.

Vampires combed through the woods and the island's caves, using their superior senses to hunt for Eden in places humans would be handicapped by the darkness. The rain had stopped, but unfortunately, it had washed things clean.

When Cain tried to track Eden's phone, he discovered it had been shut down, its last known location a few hundred meters from the Montgomery's house. The only clue was the SUV, which had been abandoned on a beach near my mom's cottage.

Eden had been taken off island—nothing else made sense. Probably by a local who knew a good hiding place. Esposito, for example, because that beach near my mom's house had a shallow cavern that could've concealed a boat.

Rio attached himself to me, his skinny body wrapped in a long black raincoat like something out of the *Matrix*.

"I'm going back to that beach," I told him.

"I'm going with you," he said, and swung onto the bike behind me without waiting for permission.

I considered tossing him off, but the kid had grown on me, and who knew, maybe he could be of help. "Hang on," I told him and accelerated out of town.

We left the bike on the cliff, making our way by foot down the rocky path to the cavern. The tide was coming in, making it even less likely I'd find anything, but I wasn't leaving without trying. There must be something we'd missed. A clue. A trace of Eden—a footprint, a strand of hair—that would miraculously point me in her direction.

Rio trailed me into the cavern, swinging a flashlight methodically from side to side, but we both came up empty. When we reached the entrance again, I paused on the thin strip of sand and rocks that hadn't been eaten by the tide, staring out at the Atlantic.

Rio stopped a few feet away, fury radiating from him like his heart was burning up. I knew how he felt. I even guessed some of his anger was for me, and I accepted that.

He turned off the flashlight and shoved it into his coat pocket. "Why the fuck did you make her come back here? Why couldn't you just leave her alone?"

Guilt pressed on my chest. "You think I'm not asking myself that?"

"So then why, damn it? She was happy. She was doing okay. I would've helped her after the baby was born."

Because she's mine, damn it. And so is that baby.

That wasn't a good enough answer, though, was it? And it wasn't even the whole truth.

I'd gone after Eden because without her, nothing had seemed to matter. Not the syndicate. Not my promotion to lieutenant. Not even the respect I got these days from all the islanders who'd written me off as a troublemaker.

Rio sniffed, clearly fighting not to cry. He covered it by swiping at his nose with the back of his hand. "This wasn't supposed to happen. You motherfuckers are supposed to protect her."

My jaw worked. "I know. But I'm going to get her back."

"You'd better."

Dawn was creeping closer. I noticed with that part of me that was always aware of the coming daylight, but otherwise ignored it.

"I will," I said, as much for myself as him. "Or go to my final grave trying."

He speared me with a look. "Good."

Brien texted me, ordering me to return to the castle ASAP. I swore, resenting the weakness that prevented me from continuing the search. But letting the sun burn me to a crisp wouldn't bring Eden home.

Up until now, I'd kept my fear for Eden at bay, but as the darkness lightened, I wanted to drop back my head and howl at the sky like an animal in pain.

"We have to get back," I told Rio.

I didn't recall the ride back to the castle. Somehow, I ended up in the war room, Rio still stuck to me like a burr. Brien and Twilight had already returned, and Cain walked in seconds behind me.

I could tell by their faces that the news wasn't good, but I asked anyway.

Brien grimaced. "Nothing. I'm sorry."

"We won't give up," Cain said. "Tomorrow night we expand the search."

I tugged on my hair, fighting that urge to howl again. "That's too late. We need to find her *now*."

The pair of soldiers in the war room shifted uneasily, their gazes carefully aimed at the floor. Brien pulled me into his office. Twilight and Cain followed, closing the door on Rio and the soldiers.

"You have to chill," Brien told me. "We'll keep the search going. Aiden is standing by to spearhead it."

I drew a deep breath. Normally, I was the coolheaded one, the man who calmed everyone else down. Well, fuck that.

I shook off his hand. "This is on me. If she's gone missing, then someone kidnapped her to get to me. Because she's carrying my spawn."

Twilight propped a hip against the desk. "I think you're right. But why—what do they want from you?"

"That's a good question," I said slowly.

Brien massaged the bridge of his nose. "Gods, I wish we knew more. I hate flying blind like this. But maybe we should move the search to the mainland."

I jerked my head in assent. "Now. Before we sleep."

"We'll have Aidan take point on that," Brien agreed with a yawn. He scrubbed a hand over his face. "We all need to get to bed—and soon."

"Ten minutes," said Twilight. "Maybe less."

Cain took out his phone, saying, "I'll have Aiden meet me at my apartment."

The four of us set off at a fast pace for our respective quarters. Aiden jogged up as Cain and I turned down our corridor. The two of us brought the lean, dark-haired dhampir up to date.

"If you find her," I added, "don't wait for us to wake up. Get her the fuck out of there unless you think it would put her in more danger."

"Will do." Aiden squared his shoulders. "And I just want to say, I appreciate your trust in me. I won't let you down."

"I know," I said and watched as he strode back in the direction of the war room.

Cain touched my back. "Go to bed. We'll find her—or they'll contact us. One way or the other, we'll know more soon."

"Yeah." I nodded and went into my apartment. For a beat, I slumped against the closed door. Gods, I was exhausted. And hungry. It had been too many nights since I'd had fresh blood.

But I'd run out of time. I headed into my bedroom, yawning and shedding clothes as I went. As I set my phone on the nightstand, my phone buzzed.

A message from Eden.

My stomach lurched. I snatched the phone up, but my eyes had already closed.

I fought the day sleep with everything I had but my body was shutting down. The phone dropped back to the nightstand, and I fell sideways onto my mattress like a goddamned tree in a windstorm.

❧ 31 ❧

EDEN

Esposito took the phone back and the two men left. A door opened, and before it closed again, I got a look at my new quarters. The cellar was larger than I'd realized, about the size of a small basement, and sparse—concrete block walls and a dirt floor.

I needed to pee. I scrambled to my feet a little too fast and the darkness spun around me. I leaned against the wall, breathing through my nose, until the dizziness passed. Then I felt my way around outside of the cellar, one hand on the wall, until I reached the exit.

The door was locked, the thick wood reinforced with metal bands, probably silver. Confirmation (if I needed it) that I was in a vampire lair. That heavy, silver-reinforced door wasn't to keep vampires out—it was to keep vampires in. A prison.

I gave an involuntary shudder. But really, what difference did it make? Silver bands or not, I couldn't bust through a thick wood door.

"Help!" I jiggled the handle one more time. Banged my fist on the wood. "Somebody, please help. I need to use the washroom. *Please.*"

I yelled until I was hoarse, then leaned my forehead against the door. Had they sent Talon the video yet? I pictured him watching it, how pissed off he'd be. Would he believe I was working with these assholes?

A tear trickled down my face. Then another and another, and then

I was crying—deep, wracking sobs. I slid to the dirt floor, my back to the wall, and gave into them until I had no more tears left.

Digging out a tissue, I blew my nose and hugged my knees to my chest, thighs wide to make space for my pregnant belly. Drained and feeling more alone than I'd ever been in my life.

The baby shifted and kicked, protesting the cramped space.

With a shaky laugh, I relaxed my grip on my knees. "Trust me, I want out of here as bad as you do."

Still, knowing he was awake and moving around settled me.

You're not alone.

I had this small, fragile being in here with me, and it was up to me to protect him. I spread my fingers over my abdomen.

"Your daddy will come for us," I whispered. "And if he doesn't, I will get us out of here. I don't know how yet, but I will."

Talon had come for me last time even before he knew I was pregnant with his spawn. There's no way he'd let me go now, even if he believed I'd run away again, that I was part of this thanks to that stupid video.

At least, that's what I told myself because if I didn't, I was going to curl up in a ball and start sobbing again.

You have to hang on. Have a little faith.

The door opened and I straightened. It was Esposito, silhouetted against the dim light from the hallway.

I couldn't make out his expression, but his chin dropped and I could tell he was looking down at where I sat against the wall. "I brought you something to eat."

My gaze locked on the foil-wrapped sandwich in his hands. "Thank you."

I came onto my hands and knees and started back to my feet. He watched a second, then with a loud exhale, grabbed my arm, hauling me the rest of the way upright.

"Here." He thrust the sandwich at me along with a bottle of water.

"Thank you." I hugged them to my chest, the scent of bread and meat and something Italian making my stomach growl. "Thank you so much. But can I use the restroom first?"

He frowned. "I don't know."

"Please," I said. "I'm hurting here."

With a muttered curse he pulled his shirt up over his nose, hiding his face, and ushered me into the hall. "C'mon, then."

I followed him, bringing the food with me, afraid to let it out of my sight. We were in a short hall with four closed doors. If this was a vampire's lair, it was a small one.

Esposito opened the nearest door, revealing a small bathroom with white tile walls. "Five minutes," he said, closing behind me.

I put my precious sandwich and water on the counter and hurried to the toilet. That taken care of, I washed up, wishing for a toothbrush or even some toothpaste. Then I gathered up the food and opened the door.

Esposito had the T-shirt pulled up in front of his face again. He didn't speak, just indicated that I was to proceed him down the hall.

"How long am I going to be here?" I asked as he opened the cellar door.

He eyed me, a deep groove between his thick black eyebrows. "Not long. They don't want to hang around for more than a night or two. This is too close to Castle Leclerc for them."

So we hadn't gone far, which meant we were probably on one of the uninhabited islands near Lilith Island.

He made to close the door, but I stuck out a foot, blocking it. "Wait. Can I have a light?"

"No. Inside." He gave me a gentle push out of the way.

I shook my head. "Why are you doing this?"

He made a tortured sound. "Look, I'm sorry, all right?"

"Then help me get out of here. I'm Talon's thrall. You know that, don't you?" I gestured at my belly. "This is his baby. If you get us out of here, he'll pay anything you ask."

His gaze darted around the dark space like he was looking for an answer. He licked his lips and I held my breath.

Then he took a step back. "I can't."

My lungs compressed in a crushing disappointment.

The door shut and my fear flooded back, almost worse than before. The walls seemed to close in on me.

I don't know how long I stood there, fighting for calm.

Don't panic. Don't panic.

My stomach growled, bringing me back to myself. I laughed—an unhinged, horror-movie kind of laugh—and found my way to a wall, where I slid to the floor, legs crossed yoga-style.

"Okay," I said, speaking aloud because the silence was getting to me, "let's eat. You'll feel better with some food in you."

Esposito had brought me a meatball sub. It was still warm and smelled like heaven. I moaned in pleasure as I bit into a fat, juicy ball of ground meat smothered in cheese and tomato sauce.

I wanted to cram the whole thing into my mouth, but I made myself eat slowly, making it last. I briefly considered saving half for later but decided I should fill my belly while I could. When I was finished, I licked my fingers clean, folded the foil wrap and placed it on the floor beside me.

How much time had passed? I wasn't even sure whether it was day or night.

I finished the water and curled up on the hard dirt, my head on my arm. I was drifting off when my eyes popped open.

Esposito hadn't seemed surprised that I was Talon's thrall. He'd known it already, known I was carrying Talon's baby.

I swallowed, surer than ever that he was Talon's dad.

Jesus Murphy. What kind of man would do something like this to his own son?

I shivered and curled tighter into myself.

※ 32 ※

TALON

My phone was in my hand before my eyes were fully open. I sat up, swinging my feet to the floor as I pulled up Eden's message. A short video loaded.

Eden stared unsmiling into the camera in a dark room, eyes big in her face. "We want Twilight. You'll be contacted telling you where and when. And Talon? Bring her yourself, and do *not* tell anyone. That means Brien and Cain, too." She took a jagged breath. "We—we'll be watching."

Her gaze moved off-camera. Then the phone was taken from her and the video cut off.

My blood pounded in my ears, slow and heavy. For a second—but only a second—I wondered if she'd betrayed me. Again.

But it didn't ring true. I replayed the video, this time focusing on nuances.

"*We* want Twilight." Someone had made Eden say that.

Her tone had been so flat, not like her at all. I didn't believe for a second that she was involved in a plot to kidnap or stake Twilight.

Eden loved me. I hadn't needed Cain to tell me. She'd made herself vulnerable to me, over and over again. Every time we were together, her love had radiated from her, bathing me in its warmth. I'd told myself it was only the afterglow from good sex, but that was me lying to myself. So, yeah, I'd known she loved me even before she'd left the first time, but I'd pretended I didn't because then I'd have to deal with it. Gods, I was a coward.

Eden would never have left like this, which meant she'd been forced to make that video. Her kidnapper or kidnappers wanted me to believe that she was involved.

A muscle worked in my jaw. The only conclusion was that someone on the inside was part of this. Someone who'd known Eden had betrayed the syndicate once.

Hell, they'd told me that straight out.

"We'll be watching."

A second message popped up, also from Eden's phone. A crude map of a small, unnamed island about ten kilometers northwest, accompanied by additional instructions.

Leave T on the shore. You have until dawn or else your woman and spawn will be forfeited.

An X marked a narrow inlet on the island's west side.

Fear clawed at my chest. I stared at the cracked screen for long seconds after it went black, torn between my loyalty to Brien and the need to rescue Eden whatever the cost.

As a lieutenant and a made man in the Maritime Syndicate, I should go straight to Brien, show him the video and the map. But what if he decided it was too dicey?

Twilight was his mate. How could I ask him to risk her?

But if I didn't, I'd lose Eden...and our son.

Phone forgotten in my hand, I dug the heels of my palms into my eye sockets. For the first time ever, I considered lying to Brien.

My friend and primus.

The man who, while still a teenager himself, had befriended an angry, moody twenty-year-old and by believing in me—by *trusting* me —had taught me to believe and trust in myself.

Think, damn it.

One thing was clear. I'd do whatever it took to save Eden—and not because she carried my spawn, but because if I lost Eden, my world would go dark.

She was my priority. Compared to her safety, nothing else mattered.

Not my honor.

Not my position in the syndicate hierarchy.

Not even my long friendship with Brien.

Nothing.

Bringing my hands down, I eyed my phone. Maybe I could ask Cain to try again to track Eden's phone? They might have forgotten to power it off after sending the texts.

Or would they know if we tried to track her? That might piss them off and make things worse. Plus, Cain would wonder why I was asking. If he got suspicious, he might go to Brien.

I couldn't fuck this up. Eden's life depended on it.

I tapped out a return text. *Eden comes with me or no deal.*

The message was marked as *sent*, but not delivered. So her phone *was* off.

The SOBs weren't even giving me the chance to negotiate.

The claws dug deeper into my chest, squeezing the oxygen from my lungs. They'd already had Eden for over twenty-four hours. Were they keeping her in some musty, airless cell? Was she allowed to move freely, or had she been restrained?

Had they fed her? I recalled how she'd fainted that night in New York. Worse, had they fed *from* her despite the danger to her and the baby?

My fangs elongated. I growled and surged to my feet, angrily pacing the bedroom floor.

I grabbed my head.

Focus, damn it. If you lose it, you'll just make things worse.

But if they'd fed from Eden, I wouldn't just stake the bastards. I'd rip their goddamned limbs off and feed their bleeding remains to the sharks.

My phone buzzed. My heart leapt, but it was Cain, texting me to meet him and Brien in the war room ASAP.

I pulled on some clothes—a long-sleeved Henley, tactical pants, combat boots—and chugged a half-bottle of blood-wine. Nourishment to keep me going until I could spare the time to feed. The last thing I did before leaving my apartment was to slide a switchblade into my back pocket. My favorite dagger went into a pocket on the side of my thigh.

The war room was empty except for Brien's PA. I eyed him, frowning. A thirty-something dhampir who'd been recommended to the syndicate by Brien's friend Zoe Tremblay, Smythe didn't have clearance to be the war room.

One look at my face, and he jumped to his feet. "Lieutenant."

"What're you doing here?" I demanded.

"I—" Smythe scraped a hand over his longish dark hair, his narrow face anxious. "The primus cleared me to be here. I'm taking over some of Adrian's duties while he's on the mainland. I—"

His words tasted of truth.

"All right," I interrupted. "Any updates? Has Adrian found her?"

"No, sir. Sorry, sir. Adrian says that..." He kept talking, but I listened with only half an ear. The bottom line was that Eden was still missing and we had no clue as to her whereabouts.

Brien and Cain entered the war room in time to hear Smythe's report. Brien took me by the shoulder, waiting until I met his eyes.

"You have to have faith, bro. We'll find her, I promise."

"Yeah," I said and even managed a thanks, even though we both knew he couldn't promise that.

We filed into Cain's office and waited while he contacted the island's chief of police to see if there was any news. Cain put the chief on speaker phone, and I forced myself to pay attention as he ran down what the islanders learned that day, which again, was nothing helpful.

Whoever had kidnapped Eden knew what they were doing. But then, I'd already surmised that.

The phone call over, Brien propped a hip against his desk and looked at us. Cain was already on his feet, and I hadn't sat in the first place, choosing instead to hover near Cain as he spoke to the chief.

During the conversation, though, I'd come to a decision. I'd talk things over with Cain first, see what he thought. Then, if he agreed, I'd go to Brien.

"She'll turn up," Brien said now. "They'll make a mistake, and we'll have them."

I grunted, Eden's video burning in my brain, uneasily aware I was lying to my primus by omission.

"You're sure your mom hasn't seen Esposito?" Cain asked.

"Yes," I said. "I asked her flat out when she arrived to help search, and she swore she hadn't."

In fact, she'd broken down crying when I'd threatened to cut her off permanently from her grandson. She'd even offered to call Esposito in front of me to prove he wasn't involved. When he hadn't answered, she'd stubbornly insisted he'd call her back. "And then you'll see," she'd told me.

I'd left her then, because if I hadn't, I might have done something I regretted.

"All right." Brien opened Cain's door. "I'll be in my office. Keep me updated."

"Will do," said Cain.

Hanging back, I caught Cain's eyes and jerked my head in the direction of my own office, letting him know I wanted to talk privately. I didn't know Smythe well, and Nathan was now in the war room next to him. Until Eden was safely back in the castle, I wasn't trusting anyone but Cain with that video.

As soon as I was safely in my office behind a closed door, I scribbled a note to Cain and waited for him to come to me.

Five minutes passed, five minutes that felt like an eternity, while I stared at what I'd written, paralyzed by uncertainty. Was I doing the right thing, bringing another person into this?

If I fucked up, Eden was dead. They'd either kill her outright or leave her to starve to death in whatever dark place they'd concealed her in. That's if they didn't sell her and the baby as blood slaves.

I even toyed with the idea of kidnapping Twilight. So what if Brien staked me when he found out? At least Eden and the baby would live.

The door opened and Cain stuck his head inside. "You free?"

At my nod, he closed the door and took the chair across from me.

With a heavy sigh I pushed the note across my desk. "Maybe you're right. Maybe the bitch ran again." They'd expect me to say something like that, and for all I knew, my office could be bugged. At this point, I trusted no one except Cain, Brien and possibly Twilight.

Cain scanned the note and slid it into his pocket, frowning. I'd told him that Eden had been kidnapped, that the kidnappers wanted Twilight in exchange.

"I told you she couldn't be trusted." The words were contemptuous, but his steady gaze told me he was playing along.

"Yeah."

"What d'you want me to do?" His mouth firmed, and I knew that whatever he thought about Eden personally, he'd go to the wall to help me get her back.

I shook my head, pretending frustration when what I really felt was a killing fury. When I spoke, my voice was rough with anger.

"Just keep doing what you're doing." I pointed at the ceiling and waited for Cain's nod. "I'll be in my apartment if you need me. I want to follow up a few leads from there."

We'd done this before. Cain would meet me in the west tower, away from the video cams and any hidden watchers. A tunnel connected to the west tower led from a hall near our apartments. A tunnel which everyone but me, Cain and Brien seemed to have forgotten existed.

When I reached my apartment, I stepped inside long enough to enter the shadows out of sight of the nearest camera, then left, slipping around the corner to the tunnel. I dropped out of the shadows long enough to open the door, then slipped through, leaving it ajar for Cain.

I remained in the physical world, waiting in the unlit tunnel until he joined me a few minutes later. We both faded back into the shadows until we reached the tower's top floor. We had to leave the shadows to speak, of course.

By unspoken agreement, we moved to the tower's dark side, avoiding the moonbeam slanting through a narrow window.

"Talk," Cain demanded, his voice barely above a whisper. "The kidnappers contacted you?"

I nodded grimly. "Through Eden. They made her record a video."

I had him watch the video, then showed him the map and the accompanying instructions.

When Cain got angry, he went still. Now he went so motionless he was like a dead man standing. "Those motherfuckers. Are you going to tell Brien?"

I appreciated that he asked rather than demanding. As Brien's other lieutenant, I wouldn't blame him if he insisted on going straight to Brien.

"I don't know." I returned the phone to my pocket. "One part of me thinks he can help. The other part is afraid it's too risky. If I do something and Eden gets hurt..." I shook my head, throat tight.

Cain glanced at the moonbeam, sliding his lips to the side. I waited, giving him time to think.

"I think you should go to him," he said after a few seconds. "They want you to keep this from Brien, to come alone with Twilight, which means they plan to overpower you and either kidnap or stake Twilight. At that point Eden might be expendable."

"That's my guess, too. But I can't risk Eden. And let's face it, she's..." My voice faltered. "She's expendable either way. If I come with Twilight or if I don't."

"Not if I come, too."

"You'd do that?"

A pissed-off snarl. "You have to ask? Of course, I'll come."

I briefly closed my eyes. "Thanks, man."

"Hey. Together, right?" He raised his fist.

I bumped mine against it. "Together," I said past the obstruction in my windpipe.

"We'll get Eden back or go to our final graves trying. But if you want some advice—?"

"Please. I can't think straight. I keep picturing her with some SOB who thinks of her as a pawn, not a person." I dragged in a breath. "And she's pregnant."

"I know, bro. I know." Cain pulled me into a one-armed hug. An awkward man-hug. But I felt the love and it choked me up even more.

"You know why she left?" I asked gruffly. "She heard us talking. Heard me say she was only a thrall. I keep thinking about that, how hurt she must've been. She loves me—you said it yourself. And I didn't want to know. Didn't want her to *complicate* things. Gods, I'm an ass."

"Stop that. We'll get her back, and you can make it up to her—

understand?" He slapped my back and released me. "Okay, then. So we tell Brien—"

"Yeah."

"Maybe Twilight doesn't have to come," he said. "One of us can assume a glamour."

"But they'll know it's not her as soon as we say something." A glamour didn't change your voice, only your outer covering.

"So we won't say anything. Now, how do you want to do this? Do you want me to send Brien up here so you can tell him?"

I met his eyes. "I'm not going to tell him. You are."

"Ah." Comprehension flickered across his face. "So you think they really do have someone watching you?"

"Yeah. Think about it—they know too much. Like how did they know Eden would be visiting her parents yesterday afternoon? And why are they trying to make me think she's on their side?"

Cain nodded thoughtfully.

"So, you talk to Brien, and I'll arrange the boat. It's less than twelve hours until dawn. We have to move." I was already fading into the shadows. "Not the Cove marina," I added. "They could be watching it, too. The cavern under the castle."

Brien kept a speedboat in the cavern that only we knew about. Might as well keep them guessing as to whether I was coming or not.

"Got it," Cain said and followed me into the shadows.

❧ 33 ❧

EDEN

Time passed with a dreamlike slowness. I slept in fits and starts, unable to get comfortable on the packed dirt. I was cold and my lower back ached.

The next time I was awake, I explored the cellar, working my way around the outside and counting off my steps until I returned to the door again. My prison was a 10-by-15-meter rectangle (give or take a meter) with a neck at one corner that led to the door and the hall beyond.

On the far side of the cellar, I came across a pair of metal cuffs fastened to the blocks. Lower down I discovered another, single cuff, this one attached to the wall by a thick chain. I shivered, guessing they were silver cuffs. God, vampires could be cruel. No one—even a blood-mad vampire—deserved to be chained up in the dark, unable to move freely.

I needed to pee again. I made my way back to the door and hammered on it until Esposito responded.

"Here." He thrust a plastic bucket and a roll of toilet paper at me. "Take this. And be quiet, damn it," he added in a harsh whisper. "I'll bring dinner when I can."

"When?" I whispered back, clutching the bucket and toilet paper.

"Two, maybe three hours." He glanced around and lowered his

voice even further. "It's almost sunset—they'll be up soon. Try not to draw attention to yourself."

I blocked the door before he could shut it. "Please—I need water. I'm so thirsty..."

He blew out a breath. "Fine. I'll get you another bottle but you have to let me shut the door."

Could I trust him? But what choice did I have? I stepped back and he closed the door.

I put down the bucket and toilet paper and leaned against the wall, waiting. The minutes ticked past. I'd almost given up hope when he returned with two bottles of water.

"Stay quiet, okay?" he muttered in a strained voice as he handed them over. "They're up. I heard them moving around."

"Got it." In the hours I'd been in here, I'd calmed somewhat, but seeing how anxious he was, my fears came roaring back.

With the light behind him, I couldn't see his expression, but he ran a hand down his face in a very Talon-like gesture. "I'm sorry about this. I didn't mean—" He shook his head and shut the door.

I stood there, limbs icy, chest heaving, the water bottles clutched to my chest for I don't know how long.

The vampires were up, so Talon was, too. He'd have seen the video by now.

What if he didn't come? Even if he wanted to, Brien might forbid it. Twilight was Brien's mate, after all—and I was only a thrall. Why would they choose me over Twilight?

It was the baby moving that brought me back to myself. That, and the urgent need to pee. I took care of that first, then drank a half bottle of water, conserving the rest for later, even though I was still thirsty.

Beads of sweat prickled my face. I swiped a hand over my forehead.

You could die in here.

They wouldn't even have to kill me. They could simply leave me here to starve.

I had the horrible feeling that Talon's father—because I was sure now that the man helping me was Talon's father—was the only reason

I'd been given food and water. If something happened to him, I was fucked. If only I was some kickass slayer like Twilight. I would've given every penny I'd earned as a thrall for that switchblade in my sewing box. Why hadn't I kept it with me?

But I'd been taking a syndicate SUV to my mom and dad's house. Why would I think I'd need a freaking weapon?

I sat on the floor, arms wrapped around myself. God, I hated being this helpless. Hated having to depend on someone else to rescue me.

Talon will come for you.

I had to keep telling myself that, had to keep my shit together.

Surrendering to the fear was letting them win. And they would *not* win.

❧

Time inched past. I did some yoga, paced back and forth. When Esposito returned, I was curled up on the dirt floor again, half-asleep, but the door opening snapped me awake.

I scrambled to my feet, blinking against the weak light from the hall.

"Here's your dinner." He thrust a baguette and an apple into my hand. His mouth touched my ear and I flinched, but he was only trying to tell me something. "Talon's on his way," he whispered. "I'll come back for you as soon as I can."

I grabbed him. "What's going on?" I whispered back.

A shake of his head. "I can't talk. Stay ready." Then he was gone.

I put the apple in my coat pocket and sat back down, breaking off a piece of the baguette. It was stale, but I took a sip of water and gamely chewed.

There were really only a couple of reasons why Esposito would help me escape, and they all boiled down to a single conclusion.

He didn't believe Talon would be alive at the end of this.

❧ 34 ☙

TALON

I eased Brien's boat out of the cavern under a hazy third-quarter moon. When we were away from the cliffs, I set course for the island on the map, increasing speed until we were running wide open, the pointed bow cutting through the waves like a knife through butter.

Brien and Cain were concealed below deck in the small cabin. At the bow, Twilight frowned into the night, the wind whipping her black braid around her shoulders, oblivious to the sea spray hitting her face.

She'd realized something was up and demanded to know what. When she'd heard a rescue mission for Eden was underway, she'd insisted on coming even before she knew they'd demanded her in exchange. At that point, not even Brien could've stopped her from coming.

She'd dressed in something similar to Eden's Catwoman outfit, although her sleeveless top was blood-red and her black leggings included hidden pockets for weapons. Her eyelids were done up in some sparkly shit, her lips the same red as her shirt. Trust Twilight to wear makeup to an ambush.

Although when I thought it over, I understood. It was camouflage, just like her cover as a social media influencer had masked her activities as a slayer.

263

"We'll get her back," she told me, unconsciously echoing Brien and Cain. "That's a promise."

I grunted. I wouldn't relax until Eden was safely back at the castle. "You want to go over the plan?"

"I think I've got it." Twilight turned so her back was to the rail. "When we're five minutes out, you're going to put those fake silver cuffs on my wrists."

"I'll have to let them take you." None of us liked this part, especially Brien. "If they suspect this is a setup, we'll never see Eden again."

She pointed a thumb at her chest. "Former slayer, remember? I notched a dozen kills—before I was turned. Those assholes don't know what they've gotten themselves into."

My brows climbed. "Okay, then."

"Yeah." She flashed a hint of fang. "Anyway, you'll refuse to let them have me until they hand over Eden. We make the exchange, and Brien and Cain will follow me in the shadows. But if these bloodsuckers won't give you Eden, then you have to leave, Talon. I know you don't like that part, but unless we can figure out where Eden is right off the bat, they have to think they've won. It's the only way they'll give away where Eden is."

I scowled. Twilight was right, I hated that part of the plan. I wanted to tear apart the whole damn island the instant we landed. Unfortunately, this scheme was the best we'd been able to come up with limited intel and on a short timeline.

Twilight's expression softened. "Eden will be okay. She's smart, and she knows vampires."

My fingers tightened on the wheel. "I don't care how smart she is, she's seven months pregnant. What kind of SOBs kidnap a pregnant woman?"

"SOBs who want me," Twilight said. "Their mistake, right? Because we *will* get Eden back, and then we'll rain fucking hell down on their asses."

Guilt clogged my throat. Eden had been targeted because she was carrying my spawn. They must've guessed I'd do anything to get her back safely.

"But I'm the bastard who got her pregnant. I'm the one who brought her back to the island. If I hadn't, she'd be safe right now."

I hadn't forgotten what Rio had said. The knowledge that this was all my fault pressed on my chest like a hundred-pound weight.

Twilight was silent for a long moment. "Have you told her you love her?"

I just stared at her. Because of course, I loved Eden.

Admitting it even to myself was like a full moon suddenly emerging from behind the clouds, dazzling me with its radiance.

Sweet Lilith, I was an idiot. I'd had my head up my ass for too damn long. My gaze slid from Twilight's.

"No," I admitted. "I didn't know myself. I didn't want to know."

◈

The ocean grew rougher as we neared the other island, the waves threatening to swamp us. I was forced to focus on keeping the small boat upright and on course.

"Need a hand?" Twilight asked, leaving the bow.

"I've got it," I said as we climbed a wave and slammed down on the other side. I gave her a grit-toothed smile. "Here's betting Brien and Cain are cursing me out down in the hold."

But they were vampires. They probably wouldn't even bruise.

"Do vampires get seasick?" she asked. "Because I feel fine."

"Nah. But Cain and I never got seasick, even as kids. And Brien is a born sailor. I've never seen him get sick, either."

She nodded, and we continued talking about not much of anything until suddenly, the island loomed before us, a hulking shape in the night. I eased back on the throttle.

"Time to cuff me." Twilight held out her arms, wrists together.

I took the fake cuffs from a small bag attached to my belt loop and snapped them around her wrists. "You sure you can break out of them?"

"Yep." She grinned and gave me a double thumbs-up. "Let's kick some ass."

Despite my worry, a corner of my mouth twitched up as I retook the wheel.

"There's the inlet." She indicated it with her joined hands. "To our right."

"Got it." I was already turning the boat to starboard.

As we entered the island's lee side, the wind died. We continued up the narrow inlet. Up until now, we'd been running with all lights off. Now I flicked our navigation lights on, getting as close to shore as possible before dropping anchor. We'd have to take an inflatable dinghy the rest of the way in.

"Brien?" I asked under my breath. "You guys up here?"

"He's here," Twilight said.

I nodded, not questioning her certainty. She must've sensed him through their mate bond.

A single figure appeared in the shadow of a cliff. A man, the darkness masking his features. He couldn't hide his gleaming eyes, though, or his faint, supernatural shimmer.

"Not a human," murmured Twilight.

"Yeah. But there's only one of him."

"That we can see," she muttered.

The plan was for me and Twilight to go ashore in the dinghy. Brien and Cain would swim in our wake, still in the shadows, to observe the exchange. If the SOBs hadn't brought Eden, Brien would stay with me and Twilight while Cain slipped off to search the island.

I lowered Twilight into the dinghy. She pretended to resist, keeping up the fiction that she was my prisoner. I gave her a small shove and jumped in after her, undoing the tow line and tossing it onto the deck. The short distance wasn't worth firing up the dinghy's small motor, so I rowed us to shore.

The man had moved closer. He waited on the rocky shore, legs braced apart, his long black hair pulled into a ponytail, his sinewy body clad in an expensive suit.

I stiffened in recognition. "It's Pascal," I said in an undertone.

"You know him?" Twilight said.

"Yeah—a QCS soldier."

"Lemaire," she breathed.

"Looks like it." Our intel had linked Pascal to Lemaire and Fleur, but since he hadn't been part of their coven, we hadn't followed up on the connection. I'd been racking my brain, wondering who wanted Twilight so bad they'd go to so much trouble. "Although I didn't think Lemaire would be stupid enough to go up against us after we destroyed his lair."

I palmed a switchblade and hopped into the surf, dragging the dinghy onto the rocky shore. Taking Twilight by the upper arm, I pulled her out of the boat.

Pascal came forward. "I'll take her."

I pressed the switchblade's catch, released the long silver knife. "The thrall, first. That's the deal."

Pascal flicked me a look. I had the impression of a sharp mind, ticking through the possibilities. "You're not in a position to bargain."

"Then we'll leave." I moved backward toward the dinghy, bringing Twilight with me.

A pointed silver dagger jumped into the other vampire's hand. "I don't think so."

I flashed my fangs. "Try and stop me."

Cain would already be searching the island. The longer I kept this asshole engaged, the more time he'd have to find Eden.

"The thrall is pregnant," Pascal said. "With your spawn. Oh, yes, we know. Even if you feel nothing for the thrall, I imagine you won't want your spawn harmed."

It was as I'd thought—they knew too much about me and Eden. My guilt turned to a cold fury. "Then you know I won't leave without her."

Without warning Pascal lunged at me, dagger out. I knocked it aside and released Twilight. He stumbled past me and I lowered my shoulder and slammed into him, knocking him to the ground. I straddled his waist, pinning the hand holding the dagger to the beach. With my free hand, I ripped open his coat and dug my own blade into the sweet spot beneath his rib cage. One hard shove, and the sharp silver point would be in his heart.

"Where is she?" I said between clenched teeth.

He had the balls to sneer at me. "Stake me and you'll never find her."

Twilight grunted. Out of the corner of my eye, I saw she'd broken the cuffs apart.

"Key's in my back pocket," I told her.

Pascal's gaze darted between me and Twilight.

"No worries." She already had the cuffs open, an open switchblade in her hand. She dropped the cuffs on the beach and crouched beside us. Wrapping an arm around Pascal's head, she touched the knife point to his right eye.

"Tell us where we can find the thrall or I'll carve your eyes out. They'll regenerate, but I hear it's a long, painful process." She pursed her lips in mock sympathy. "Meanwhile, you'll be blinded. I wonder how long you'll last if we toss you to the sharks."

Pascal was no longer smiling. He moistened his lips. "You'd risk your spawn?" he asked me.

I growled and pressed the point deeper. Blood oozed, staining his white shirt. "If Eden dies—hell, if you motherfuckers even put a bruise on her—I'll carve off your goddamn balls. Slowly."

Pascal paled but he managed to curl his lip at me. "What makes you think I came alone?"

"Yeah? Then where are they? Looks like they left you to twist in the wind."

Brien stepped out of the shadows, dressed like me in a long-sleeved Henley and tactical pants. He kicked the dagger out of Pascal's hand and scooped it up. "Want me to take over?"

"No."

I needed to do this. Needed someone to vent my rage on.

Meanwhile, Pascal's gaze had shifted to my primus. "Fuck," he mouthed.

"Yeah," I told him. "Turns out, I didn't come alone either."

On cue, Cain appeared to Brien's right, his pale hair shining in the moonlight. At my hopeful glance, he shook his head.

"I thought I caught Eden's scent, but as far as I can tell, there's no one else on the island." He considered Pascal with a jaundiced eye. "This prick hasn't told you anything yet?"

"No." My patience evaporated. "Talk." Jerking up the other vampire's bloody shirt, I screwed the blade deeper into the hole I'd made. "Where's Eden?"

Brien and Cain came to stand on either side of us. It seemed Pascal had finally grasped the hopelessness of his position because he erupted, fighting to break free of me and Twilight.

I released my switchblade and grabbed his wrists, slamming them to the beach on either side of his hips. "Where...is...she?" I demanded between gritted teeth.

Pascal glared up at me, thin-lipped.

Cain had drifted down to Pascal's lower body. I heard a couple of muffled, crunching sounds, and our prisoner shrieked in pain. When I glanced over my shoulder, his feet were turned at odd angles from his legs.

Twilight sighed. "You should know I'm not a very patient person. It's a fault."

That was the only warning before she sliced her blade across his eye. Blood spurted, leaking down his cheek.

He sucked in a breath, throwing himself from side to side, trying to break free of me. He was strong, but I had a killing fury on my side. I quickly subdued him.

Twilight bared her fangs. "Ready to talk yet, bloodsucker?"

Brien dropped down on Pascal's other side. "I'd talk if I were you," he said in a conversational tone. "She's a former slayer, and she still has this thing about vampires who don't play nice."

"Fuck this. Restrain his wrists," I told Brien.

"Good idea." He produced a pair of silver handcuffs.

"Give me a minute with him," I told Twilight.

She released Pascal's head, and I rolled him onto his side while Brien snapped the handcuffs on him. He hissed as the silver burned his wrists.

Retrieving my switchblade, I nudged Pascal onto his back with my foot. "She's not kidding about your eyes," I told him. "But let's make it more interesting for the sharks, shall we?"

I kicked his legs open and crouched down, ripping the crotch of his pants open with my blade.

Fear tightened Pascal's face. He glanced down, then back at me. "You sons of bitches," he spat out.

"Talk." I tapped his balls with the knife.

Pascal's lungs heaved. He cursed, then said, "Lemaire has the thrall."

"Where?" demanded Twilight.

His mouth set. "I don't know."

"Not good enough." I pressed the point into his scrotum.

"No…" He thrashed on the rocky ground.

I shoved my face into Pascal's. "*Talk*, you sonuvabitch," I said, putting all the force of my dominance behind the question. "I'm through playing games."

He was desperate and close to me in dominance, but I was fighting for Eden. The woman who meant more to me than anything in the world.

He wavered, then caved. "The south side of the island. There's an old fishing shed—that's the lair entrance."

Cain growled. "Try again, mofo. I already searched the shed. There was no sign of a lair."

"The entrance is hidden."

I rose to my feet. "Then I guess you'll have to come with us and show us where it is."

"I've got him." Cain slung Pascal over his shoulders in a fireman's carry. "You guys go. I'll be right behind."

❦ 35 ❦

EDEN

The silver-reinforced door creaked open. My heart thumped against my ribcage.

"Time to go," Esposito said, low-voiced. He grabbed my arm and urged me out the door. "Something's up. If they see us, let me do the talking, okay?"

I dipped my chin in acknowledgment, blinking rapidly. Even the dim light in the hall was too much after so many hours in the dark. For the first minute, I had to rely on him to guide me.

When we reached a staircase, he mouthed, "Follow me," and jogged up the narrow metal steps, me scrambling after him as best I could.

The door at the top of the stairs stood open. Esposito sniffed, shooting a frowning glance at me over his shoulder. That's when I smelled it—the faint, acrid scent of smoke.

"That's the only exit," Esposito whispered, indicating a thick wood door at the far end of the hall. "We have to chance it. I'll go first. Wait for my signal, then follow."

For the first time I got a good look at his face. Yeah, this was defi-nitely Talon's father. Same dark curls (although Esposito's were streaked with gray), same full lower lip, same deep-set eyes. But this man's features were softer, weaker, the face of a man who usually took the easy way out.

"Got it," I mouthed. "And thank you."

With an odd little smile, he shoved his hands into his pants pockets and sauntered into the hall. *Nothing to see here, people.* The man could've been an actor.

He cast a casual glance around, then jerked his chin at me to follow.

I counted three doors ahead of us, two behind. If this was a vampire's lair, it was a small one, and by vampire standards, bare bones. The walls were white-washed stone, the floor rough planks, the only lighting a half-dozen sconces shaped like hanging bats, electric tea lights cupped in their upside-down wings.

Esposito inched forward, me creeping after him. We passed the first door. The second.

The smell of smoke increased. At the end of the hall, a gray wisp snaked under the door and curled lazily through the air.

We were almost to the third door when it was thrown open. I froze. Esposito cursed and grabbed my arm, dragging me backward.

A blur of motion, and the vampire from the first night, his face a mask of fury, halted in front of us. I gulped. The contrast between his terrifying expression and elegant navy suit was disorienting, like an accountant had been possessed by the spirit of Cujo.

Esposito released me and raised his hands, palms out. "Lemaire. I—"

The thin, dark-haired vampire hissed. grabbed Esposito's throat and squeezed. "Where do you think you're going?"

Esposito scrabbled at Lemaire's wrists. "Take it easy," he choked out. "It's not what you th—"

The vampire shook him like a rabbit. "It's exactly what I think."

"Run!" Esposito hissed at me out of the side of his mouth.

I nodded rapidly and backed up.

Silver flashed. Blood spurted from Esposito's throat.

I moaned and clapped a hand to my mouth as he kicked wildly to be free.

Lemaire's fangs extended. He zeroed in on Esposito's bleeding throat. I could practically feel his craving, like a pulsing in the air.

Run, my brain screamed, but my feet had grown roots. I was lost in horror, unable to look away as Lemaire bent Esposito over an arm, mouth open, fangs glistening. His eyes met mine over Esposito's writhing body, and his focus shifted to me.

The glowing blue around his irises brightened. He lifted his head, that vampire-hot gaze trained on me. He was going to try and compel me. I knew it as certainly as if he'd told me aloud.

Esposito made a heartbreaking sound, somewhere between a groan and a whimper. Lemaire glanced at him again.

My muscles unlocked. I wrenched my gaze from the men and bolted back the way we'd come.

Please let Esposito be wrong. Please let there be another exit.

I tried the first door. A bedroom.

I kept going, tried the second. Another bedroom.

My breath sobbed in.

Esposito had been right. The only exit was behind Lemaire.

The door with a fire burning on the other side.

I halted, lungs heaving, and risked a look at the two men. Lemaire had latched onto Esposito's throat. He hunched over his victim, an urbane spider feeding on his prey. Mercifully, the other man was no longer moving. I prayed he'd lost consciousness.

Behind them, the hall was filling with smoke. It's not easy to kill a vampire by fire, but if the fire's hot enough, it's possible. Was this Lemaire's doing, or part of a plan to rescue me?

Whatever. Time was running out.

I couldn't stay here, but I didn't think I'd get past Lemaire, even distracted as he was.

I had to try, though. I'd die if I didn't.

Fragments of how to escape a fire flitted through my mind.

Stay low.

Cover your mouth and nose.

If you catch on fire, stop, drop and roll.

Pulling my sweater up over my face, I sidled back down the hall, knees shaking, heart threatening to beat out of my chest. Lemaire remained intent on his meal. I held my breath and kept going.

Just when I thought I'd made it past him, he flicked me a look. My stomach dropped and I sped up.

He reached out almost casually, backhanding me across the mouth. A bright pain exploded in my brain. I slammed into the wall, the breath leaving my lungs in a whoosh. The coppery taste of blood filled my mouth. Stunned, I brought my hand to my cheek, working my jaw back and forth.

Lemaire dropped Esposito and straightened, his striped tie spattered with red. He removed a silk handkerchief from his breast pocket and wiped the blood from his mouth and chin, his gaze never leaving mine.

I swallowed queasily and brought my hand down.

Blue-rimmed eyes snagged mine. "Don't move," he said, and hit me with a compulsion so hard I froze in the act of turning to run, one foot planted, the other knee bent, the ball of my foot ready to push off.

I struggled against the compulsion, but only managed to make a small, frightened sound. The smoke grew thicker. Stinging my eyes. Burning my throat.

"I wouldn't fight it," Lemaire said. "There are two ways out, and one is blocked by fire. Stay behind, and you'll die." He moved closer and put a hand on my belly. "That would be a shame, wouldn't it?"

I shuddered at the possessive touch.

His blue-touched eyes glowed impossibly bright. "You're going to come with me, Eden Montgomery. You'll stay within a meter of me at all times. Say 'yes, master' if you understand."

Against my will, my lips moved. "Yes, master."

"That's my pet." Taking my arm, he strode back to the stairs to the lower level, pulling me onto the landing and locking the door behind us.

He released me and reinforced the compulsion by repeating that I was to stay within a meter of him, then ran lightly down the metal steps. The compulsion tugged at me like I was attached to a rope with him at the other end, forcing me to follow at the same speed so that I remained within a meter of him. I jogged down the steps after him, a hand on the rail, praying I wouldn't trip and fall.

When we reached the bottom, he turned in the opposite direction of the cellar where I'd been imprisoned. This hall wasn't lighted. I had to feel my way along the wall, helpless against the compulsion's pull, my legs moving as fast as they could despite my attempts to slow down.

Fortunately, we didn't have far to go. When Lemaire halted, I nearly ran into him.

"Stop," he ordered absently, his attention on something in front of him.

Metal groaned, then slid to the left. A metal gate.

Lemaire took me by the arm and pulled me through an opening. The gate slammed shut behind us.

"Keep following." He set off again, at a slower pace this time.

I found out why when I felt rough stone on either side of me. We'd entered a narrow tunnel. The damp air had a salty bite, and somewhere ahead, the surf boomed.

I trudged behind my captor, feeling my way along the uneven, pitch-black passage, trying not to panic. What if the cavern narrowed further? Lemaire was lean as a weasel. He might not have calculated for my pregnant body.

Events had happened so quickly that I'd been moving on autopilot, fueled by terror and adrenaline, my focus on surviving at any cost. Now I steadied—and noticed that the compulsion to follow him had lessened.

My step hitched. The adrenaline kicked in again.

Run.

I actually took a small step backward until I realized I had nowhere to go. The way behind us was blocked by the gate. The only way out was forward.

And yet... Lemaire didn't seem aware that I was no longer bound to him as firmly. If I could fool him into thinking I was still under his compulsion, I might be able to escape.

I kept walking.

The sound of the surf grew louder. A light breeze teased at my nostrils. I drew a deep breath, filling my lungs with the fresh ocean scent. After two days in a dank cellar, it smelled like freedom.

Gradually, the darkness lightened. Somewhere ahead, light sparkled on an expanse of water, and then we were out of the tunnel and in a sea cave, its walls carved by the ocean. Moonlight slanted through the large opening, illuminating a small motorboat floating inside the cavern, its glossy black hull barely visible against the night sky beyond.

Lemaire ordered me to get into the boat and leapt the half-dozen meters to the deck, leaving me to wade through waist-deep water.

The ocean surged, lifting me off my feet. I lunged up for the mooring line, fighting to remain upright as the icy liquid receded, sucking at my legs. The nylon line stretched, and I almost went under. Somehow, I managed to stay upright, but the shock broke Lemaire's compulsion for good.

Clinging to the line, I waded the last couple of meters to the boat. The water was up to my armpits now. The last few steps I was half-walking, half-pulling myself along the line until I reached the metal cleat it was fastened to.

I had to stretch up to grab the cleat. I clung to it, my other hand on the hull, as the ocean tugged at my water-logged clothing.

"I need help," I told Lemaire, careful to wipe my face of expression.

Muttering under his breath, he fastened cool fingers around my wrists and swung me aboard. "Sit." He pointed at a short bench on the boat's port side.

My sweater and jacket were soaked, my short leather boots filled with water. I sloshed across the deck and lowered myself onto the bench.

Lemaire leapt back to shore, where the mooring line was attached to a sturdy metal pole. A tug, and the line came free. He tossed it onto the deck and followed.

"Talon brought the prima," he told me. "They were spotted a few minutes ago."

My head snapped up. Hope surged. "He's here?"

He came.

Lemaire sneered. "He must think I'm a fool to believe he'd exchange his prima for a thrall, even one pregnant with his spawn."

"But...that was the deal."

"What deal? The instructions were for Talon to bring Twilight himself. No deals were offered."

I mentally replayed the message I'd been forced to record.

"We want Twilight. You'll be contacted telling you where and when. And Talon? Bring her yourself, and do not tell anyone. That means Brien and Cain, too. We'll be watching."

Lemaire was right. My heart sank.

"Then why would he bring the prima?" I asked.

Lemaire sniffed and straightened his lapel. "No doubt he thinks to outwit me. My guess is he brought a couple of men in the shadows—that's what I would do. What he doesn't know is that I expected that. We're playing a little game, he and I." An unpleasant smile. "The fire is only the first obstacle. We'll see if they think you died in the fire... or went with me willingly. You ran once, after all."

Doubt poked at me with bony fingers.

I clasped my hands between my knees. *Stop it. He's messing with you. The bastard enjoys seeing you sweat.*

On the other hand, I *had* run once, and Talon had only just started to trust me.

If Talon's here with Twilight, then they have a plan to save you. You have to believe that.

"You hate me," Lemaire said, clearly amused. "You'd kill me if you could. The man who bought you will beat that out of you. He prefers well-trained, obedient thralls."

The man who bought me would beat it out of me?

I rolled my lips into my mouth, afraid and angry—and yeah, hating Lemaire with every cell of my body.

Lemaire went to start the boat, but it coughed and sputtered before falling silent. Face set, he tried again. This time it didn't make a sound. He cursed and tried a third time, and when it still didn't start, removed his suit coat, rolled up his sleeves and went to have a look at the engines.

My wet clothes were no match for the wind off the North

Atlantic. The cold seeped into my bones. Miserable and shivering, I hugged my arms around myself, watching him out of the corner of my eye.

He'd forgotten to renew the compulsion. If he hadn't been distracted, he probably would've noticed by now.

This was my chance, except, again, where would I go? Even if I made it outside the sea cave, my only options would be to swim for it or climb the cliff I could just make out beyond the entrance. Lemaire wouldn't even have to work hard to recapture me.

He grabbed a couple of tools from a toolbox and went back to work, his back to me.

"The man who bought you will beat that out of you."

I swallowed and decided to try anyway. It's not like I had anything to lose. He was talking about blood slavery. And they wouldn't own just me, but the baby.

Lemaire cursed and banged on one of the engines with a wrench.

Now.

I slung a leg over the rail and eased into the water. Somehow I managed to stay upright long enough to get to shore. I headed for a tumble of boulders, hoping to crouch out of sight.

Water squelched from my boots. I could no longer feel my toes. I shuffled forward because stopping wasn't an option.

"Eden Montgomery." Lemaire's voice lashed at me like a whip. *"Come back here."*

My shoulders pulled up around my ears. I fought an urge to obey, to give in.

No.

I would *not* go back. I was fighting for not just my freedom, but the baby's.

The compulsion increased. *Stop. Turn around. Look into my eyes...*

I strained against the urge to obey.

"No!" This time I said it aloud, and then I screamed it. *"No! Leave me the fuck alone!"*

My scream echoed in the cavern. The compulsion weakened, then abruptly broke. I stumbled forward, falling to my hands and knees on the gritty cavern floor, but kept going, crawling across the cavern floor toward the protection of the boulders. Although what good that would do with Lemaire watching me, I didn't know.

But turning back would be giving in. And I would *not* give in.

"Eden!" A deep voice made my breath hitch.

I lifted my head. "Talon?"

Was it really him or was I dreaming?

"Hang on, baby. I'm almost there." Powerful arms scooped me up. When I startled, he said, "Easy, now. It's me, Talon."

"Talon?" I brought a hand to his cheek, even though my fingers were blocks of ice, too numb to feel anything. "It's...you? You're really here?"

"Oh, sweetheart." His lips touched my temple. I was so chilled they felt warm to me. "It's me. I've got you. You're safe now."

"You came." Emotion swamped me. I sucked in my lower lip and took a hard breath through my nose, then grabbed his shirt and burrowed my face into his neck. "*You came.*"

He tightened his grip on me, raining kisses on my face. "Of course, I did."

For a couple of heartbeats, I clung to Talon, breathing him in, floating in a delirium of love and relief.

But there was something I had to tell him. Something important. I pulled a little away. "Lemaire, he..."

"What?"

My brain felt like it had been packed in cotton. I gave my head a shake, trying to remember what Lemaire had said.

"He t-told me," I said through chattering teeth, "th-that this is a tr-trick. He's s-set a trap."

"The fire in the lair?" Talon asked.

Shivering uncontrollably, I worked an arm around his neck. "N-no. I m-mean, that's just the f-f-first. There's m-more."

"All right. We won't go back through the lair. We can't anyway—it's an inferno up there."

A grunt drew my eyes to the boat. Brien was fighting Lemaire on the small deck. Blades clanged, the two vampires moving in a flurry of motion too fast to follow.

"Brien's here?" I asked.

Talon nodded. "And Cain and Twilight, too."

"They are? All of them? But—"

"They know how important you are to me. We had most of the island searching for you, the syndicate included."

"Yeah?" I tried to smile, but my teeth clicked together. "I'm s-so c-cold."

Swearing under his breath, Talon retrieved his phone from his pocket. "Twilight? Get the boat around to this side of the island ASAP. We have Eden."

He described our location, then carried me to the side of the cavern out of the wind. He gently cupped my injured cheek. "Lemaire did this?"

"Yeah. And...he forced me to go with him. A compulsion. I mean, I would've gone with him anyway. I couldn't stay in a burning building." My throat worked. "Why d-did he have to do that? I felt so h-h-helpless."

Talon's face darkened. "He's vermin," he said, tight-jawed. His lips touched my bruised flesh, soft as a butterfly's wings. "He's going down. I promise."

"G-good," I said fiercely as another shiver racked my body.

"Hang on," Talon crooned, rocking back and forth with me. "Can you do that for me, baby? I'd light a fire, but Twilight will be here with the boat any minute now."

"But w-what about B-B-Brien?" I asked.

"Don't worry," Talon said without looking away from me. "He's winning."

"But—" I blinked rapidly, my chilled brain uncomprehending. "Sh-shouldn't you be h-helping him?"

A groove formed between Talon's thick dark brows. "You're my priority. You and the baby. Brien can take care of himself."

I still didn't understand—everyone knew Brien came first with Talon. "B-but the blood oath—"

"Look at me." Talon nudged my chin with a finger, waiting until he had my full attention. "Fuck the blood oath," he said, slowly and succinctly. "You're what matters. You're more important. To me, you're everything. Understand?"

When I nodded, he buried his face in my neck. His shoulders heaved. "Don't ever get kidnapped again. I mean it."

I actually chuckled through my chattering teeth. "I d-didn't do it d-deliberately."

"I know. But...just don't, okay? I don't think I could survive it."

❧ 36 ❧

TALON

I'd thought I'd lost Eden.

I don't think I'd ever forget the terrible fear that had clogged my chest when we'd spotted the fire in the distance, red-hot fingers clawing at the midnight sky.

Eden was human. She couldn't survive long in a blaze like that.

"That's the lair." Pascal had somehow summoned a smug smile from where he was draped over Cain's shoulders. "Lemaire must've set a fire to keep you bastards out."

I covered those last few hundred meters in two of my heartbeats. The fishing shed walls had caved in. Flames shot out of the roof, licked at the charred framing. A section of the ground had collapsed, revealing a metal staircase leading down into the flames.

Brien and Cain caught up again with Pascal. I pulled him off Cain and shook him like a rag doll. "Is there another way in?"

Pascal's face contorted, but only a single, pained grunt escaped him. He stared at me, hatred in his remaining eye. "No. That's the only way."

We all knew the prick was probably lying—a vampire lair always has at least two exits—but there was no time to beat the information out of him. He might not even know where the other exit was.

I tossed him away and turned back, muscles bunched to dash through the flames. Brien caught my arm. "Hang on—we need a plan."

I shook him off. "Eden's in there. The plan is to fucking extract her before the whole damn place collapses on top of her."

I didn't wait for an answer. Filling my lungs with oxygen, I shot forward, scrambling over and around the burning debris. When I reached the steps, I kept going, taking them in a single leap and landing in a crouch in front of the burning door at the bottom.

My shirt and pants had caught fire. I slapped at the flames to extinguish them. My skin was scorched, but the pain seemed far away. I noted it and moved on.

I'd heal. Eden wouldn't, not if she was in that inferno.

Still holding my breath, I rose to my feet and examined the door blocking my way. The fire had eaten deep into the wood. A single hard kick, and I was through.

Brien caught up with me in the hall. Flicking a smoldering ember from my shoulder, he said, "Twilight went back for the boat. Cain's seeing if there's another way in."

I tested the smoke-filled air with a shallow inhale. There was enough oxygen for my needs, although I couldn't see more than a meter or two in front of me.

"What about Pascal?" I asked.

"I staked the motherfucker."

"Good."

We hadn't gone three meters when we came across a man lying face down in a pool of blood. Nice clothes, dark hair touched with silver.

The hairs on my body lifted. Beside me Brien muttered a curse.

I crouched, turning the man over. Esposito stared unseeingly up at me, his throat torn, skin ashy from having his blood drained.

A muscle jumped in my cheek. "I think we found Eden's kidnapper."

"Yeah." Brien shook his head. "I'm sorry."

An impotent rage coiled in my belly. Too bad the SOB was already dead because at that moment, I could've killed him myself.

"Don't be," I returned flatly, rising to my feet. "He got what was coming to him. But where's Eden?" The terrible fear slashed at my chest again.

I squinted into the dense smoke, but all I saw were a couple of open doors. "I don't sense her on this level."

We moved forward, me in the lead, until we came upon a flight of narrow metal steps. "You take the lower level," Brien said. "I'll check the rooms on this floor, just in case."

"Thanks." I surged forward, descending the stairs in two giant steps.

The smoke wasn't as thick on the lower level, giving me hope that Eden might still be alive. After noting the gate at one end of the hall, I did a quick search of the bathroom and the place where Eden had clearly been kept prisoner; her scent was strong.

The bastards had locked her in a windowless cellar without even a cot to lie on.

Brien poked his head inside the open door. "No trace of her upstairs." He took in the waste bucket with a grimace. "Bloody Lilith. This is where they were keeping her?"

"Yeah," I said grimly, coming out of the cell. I indicated the gate. "Lemaire must've taken her out that way. Hurry."

The gate was locked, but fortunately, it was constructed of iron, not silver. Brien and I each took hold of two iron pickets and tore it off its hinges. We tossed the gate aside and took off down the narrow, twisting passage.

We reached the main cavern in time to see Lemaire fumbling with the motor and Eden creeping away. A dizzying relief crashed through me.

"Shadows," I mouthed at Brien.

He nodded, already graying at the edges, as I followed suit.

"I'll take care of Lemaire," he said before he disappeared completely. "You get Eden."

I sensed rather than saw him flit across the cavern toward the boat. I sprinted along the water's edge to Eden.

And then I was stepping out of the shadows and gathering her into my arms.

Now Eden's eyes met mine, large and dark with emotion. Her short hair was matted, her face bruised and dirty.

It didn't matter.

To me, she was the most beautiful sight in the world, and at that moment I knew she'd always be.

Twenty years from now.

Fifty years from now.

Forever.

So when I said she was what mattered—that she was *everything*—I meant it with every fiber of my being.

I'd almost lost her. Everything else paled—my honor, my blood oath, my position in the hierarchy—beside that single, heart-stopping fact.

I tightened my grip on her shivering body, face buried in her hair, and breathed her in, needing to assure myself she was okay, that we'd reached her in time.

"I didn't...," she rasped. She halted, shook her head.

"What? Tell me. Please."

She lifted her gaze to mine. "I didn't w-want to make that video. You know th-that, don't you?"

I consigned the brief doubt I'd felt to the garbage bin where it belonged. Eden didn't deserve anything but my unwavering support.

"Of course, I knew."

"Yeah?" she asked.

"Yes," I said firmly.

A couple of tears leaked from her eyes, leaving muddy tracks on her dirty cheeks. "I was so a-afraid you'd b-believe I *wanted* to go with them. Lemaire said... He kn-knew stuff about me." She drew a ragged breath. "That I'd run from the s-syndicate before. He was sure you'd think I'd d-done it again."

"Forget what he said." I kissed each eye in turn, taking the salty liquid into my mouth. "It was all lies. He was fucking with you."

Her soft mouth trembled. "That's what I th-thought, but I was alone and I w-wasn't sure..."

"Be sure." I rubbed my lips over hers. "I trusted you. I ripped the island apart looking for you. I thought I'd go crazy when we couldn't find you."

"Oh." Biting her lip, she gifted me a wide smile, followed by another hard shiver.

I withdrew deeper into the cavern to protect her from the wind. A flash of silver had us both turning to look at Lemaire's boat. Brien had the other vampire on his back on the fiberglass deck. Both men were bloodied, their fangs extended.

Brien raised his blade above his head with both hands. The silver glinted in the moonlight. His lips peeled back in a feral grin.

Eden swallowed audibly. I immediately turned away, blocking her view with my body.

"No. I w-want to see him die." She pushed at my shoulder, craning her neck to look around me.

I turned back; she had the right to see this through to the end. Together, we watched as Brien drove his silver blade into Lemaire's chest.

Lemaire jerked and released his own weapon, pushing feebly at Brien's hands, blood spurting from the wound. His flesh was already blackening. The sickening odor of burning flesh drifted to us.

Eden gagged and slapped a hand to her mouth.

"That's enough," I said, angling my body so I blocked her view again. Swamped by guilt, I nuzzled her temple. "I'm sorry you got dragged into this."

"Not your fault," she muttered.

I grunted, not so sure about that, but this wasn't the time or place to discuss it. "Twilight should be here any minute now. Can you hang on a little longer?"

"Of course." She removed the hand from her face and glowered at me. "I told you, I'm not fragile."

My mouth widened in the kind of smile you give when you're so goddamned relieved you'd smile at anything. "You're not, sweetheart. You're tough as goddamned nails. And I thank Lilith for it."

Twilight arrived soon after. The water was too shallow to bring the motorboat in, so she set anchor and started rowing toward us in the dinghy.

Cain appeared on the cliff above, scrambling down the rocky face and landing on the beach a few meters away from us. He took one look at Eden, wet and shivering in my arms, and said, "What can I do?"

"Help Twilight bring the dinghy in."

"On it." Cain waded into the surf, grabbing the small boat by a D-ring on its side and towing it the rest of the way onto shore.

Twilight leapt out and hurried toward us. "You okay?" She frowned at Eden's bruised cheek.

"Y-yeah," Eden said.

"She'll be okay, but she's cold." Cuddling Eden to my chest, I strode past Twilight to the dinghy. "I need to get these wet clothes off her as soon as possible and warm her up."

Brien rinsed the blood from his face and hands and joined the others on the shore as I climbed into the dinghy with Eden.

Twilight pointed at Eden's cheek. "You stake the bloodsucker who did that to her?" she asked Brien.

"Yeah." He jerked his chin at the pile of ashes on the boat deck. "That's what's left of him."

Twilight's smile showed a little fang. "Good man," she said, and, grabbing Brien by his blood-soaked shirt, pulled him in for a kiss.

Meanwhile, Cain shoved the dinghy back into the water with me and Twilight in it. "I'll take you to the boat," he said, swinging over the side and taking up the oars. To Brien, he said, "The dinghy's too small for all of us. We'll come back for you two."

Our primus took his mouth from his mate's long enough to say, "We'll be here," before going back in for another kiss.

"Careful," I called. "Eden says there may be another trap."

He waved a hand in acknowledgment.

On the cliff the fire danced, a gleeful red and orange. The harsh smoke scratched at my nostrils. A sudden burst of wind caught the embers and scattered them like confetti over the dark waves. They sparkled gold, then winked out.

My mouth turned down. "Esposito's body is in there," I told Cain.

"Yeah?" He shook his head and kept rowing. "Nobody got out. I waited, just in case."

"He was already dead when we found him. They drained him."

Eden stirred. "He was your father, wasn't he?"

Sperm donor. "Afraid so."

"Lemaire," she said. "It was Lemaire who drained him. He k-killed your dad because of me. B-b-because he h-helped me."

"So Esposito was part of this?" Cain asked.

"H-he was the d-driver," Eden said, shaking so hard her teeth knocked together. "But he helped me—"

"Shh." I tucked her head into my shoulder. "You can tell us later."

Cain put the oars down and stood up, grabbing the motorboat's rail and bracing his feet apart to steady the dinghy. Shifting Eden to one arm, I pulled myself one-handed over the rail and onto the deck.

Cain went back for the others while I took Eden below deck and stripped off her sodden clothes, leaving her in her underwear. Dragging off my henley, I put it on her, then wrapped her in a couple of wool blankets. She sank onto the cabin's lower bunk, watching listlessly as I removed my wet socks and combat boots.

The listlessness scared the piss out of me. I sat on the bunk with her on my lap, my back against the wall. I would've liked to turn on the heat, but on a small boat like this, the heater didn't work unless the motor was running.

Eden's shivering increased. I took her feet in my hands beneath the blankets, trying to warm them. They felt icy even to my vampire-cool skin.

On the deck above, I heard the other three bringing the dinghy aboard. The engine sputtered to life and the boat swung around, heading back the way we came. I left Eden long enough to fire up the heat, then lifted her back onto my lap.

Twilight popped into the cabin to check on us. She frowned, seeing Eden's shivers. "She needs a hot drink." The lithe, dark-haired vampire moved around the tiny galley, opening and shutting cupboards.

"Don't bother," I said. "This boat's not set up to cook while we're running. Things'll go flying as soon as we hit a rough patch." As if in emphasis, the boat crested a wave, landing on the other side with a bone-jarring thump.

"How about another blanket then?" Twilight dug one out of the storage chest and tucked it around me and Eden. "And water." She handed Eden a bottle and she drained it.

Meanwhile, Twilight uncorked a bottle of blood-wine and passed it to me. I accepted it gratefully; I could barely recall the last time I'd fed. I drank my fill and handed the bottle back.

"Anything else?" she asked Eden.

"No, thank you." Eden closed her eyes and rested her head against my bare chest. Her teeth had finally stopped chattering, although she clutched my shoulder with one hand like she was afraid I might vanish if she didn't hang on tight.

Something unknotted inside me.

It felt like I could breathe deeply again. Like my heart could beat the way it was supposed to. Like the world could resume turning.

Eden was back. She was in my arms where she belonged.

The rightness of it filled my chest with an almost human warmth.

I glanced up to see Twilight's mouth hitched in a knowing smile. "I'll leave you two alone, then."

"Thank you," I said, my gaze returning to Eden, who'd closed her eyes.

I stroked her matted hair and murmured soothingly, telling her she was going to be all right, that we'd have her home in an hour or so. She nodded sleepily and relaxed against me. We sat that way for long minutes, her drowsing in my arms, me trying to come to terms with that feeling of rightness.

That warmth.

Hell, yeah, you're in love with her.

I hadn't really believed in love, figured it was more a mating urge than anything else.

I'd told myself I'd never fall in love. Love made you stupid or weak or both. I only had to look at my mom to see how it could fuck your life up.

When I mated, I'd choose wisely, leaving messy emotions out of it.

My throat closed up. I sipped in a breath—and gave into those messy, inconvenient emotions.

I loved Eden, and yeah, she was my mate. It was time to stop resisting, to admit that I wanted forever with her. If she'd died, I would've wanted to plunge a stake into my own heart.

The small cabin warmed rapidly. Eden's shivers finally eased. She stiffened, her hand flying to her abdomen.

My brows lowered in a worried frown. "What's the matter?"

"The baby...he moved." She gulped. "I haven't felt anything since we came aboard, and I was afraid."

"They...they didn't hurt you, did they? Other than your cheek?" The question scraped out of my throat.

"No. Not like you mean. I even had food and water—your dad made sure of it."

I feathered my fingertips over her swollen cheek. Sending Lemaire to his final grave as part of a fair fight had been too good for the SOB.

"As soon as we dock, I'll call Olivia and have her check you both out."

She nodded her thanks and fell silent again. Her breath deepened and she fell asleep. A few minutes later, the boat slowed, and she stirred.

"We're back?"

"I guess so." I frowned. It seemed too soon. "Current must've been with us."

Eden sighed. "I've been dreaming about a mug of thick, sugary hot chocolate. And after that, a bowl of fish chowder."

I brushed my lips over her forehead. "Anything you want, angel."

Rapid steps sounded above, accompanied by urgent voices. My chest tightened. "Something's the matter."

"I'll get them," Twilight said at almost the same time. She threw open the door. "The boat's going to blow. We have to get Eden into the dinghy. *Now*."

What the fuck? I swung my legs to the floor, Eden in my arms, and jogged up the steps.

The air reeked of fuel. My stomach tightened. This must be Lemaire's second trap.

"You go with Eden," Brien told me as Twilight approached with a life jacket. I set Eden down long enough to bundle her into it, then pulled the blankets around her again and swung her back into my arms.

Eden hooked an arm around my neck, watching everything with dazed eyes. The gods damn Lemaire anyway. There must've been at least one other vampire on the island. Pascal hadn't been lying after all.

"How far out are we?" I asked as they helped us into the dinghy.

"A quarter mile. You can't start the motor here—everything could blow." Cain waited until I'd settled Eden on the seat opposite mine, then handed me the oars and shoved us off with his foot.

The smell of fuel grew stronger. I snatched up the oars and dug them into the heaving water, rowing away from the motorboat as fast as I could.

Twilight, Cain and Brien pulled off their boots and dove over the side into the ocean. Instead of striking out for Lilith Island, the three of them lined up along the stern and started to push the dinghy.

On the motorboat, a couple of small fires ignited. It wouldn't be long now.

"Get down," I ordered Eden, "and hang onto my legs."

She immediately lowered herself into the bottom of the dinghy, sliding her ass toward me and locking her arms around my calves.

"That's it." I rowed harder, aided by the three swimmers. "Whatever you do, don't let go."

Eden's fine-boned jaw set. She turned her head to look at the motorboat. "I won't."

An eerie silence fell, unbroken except for the slap of water against the dinghy's hull.

I tensed. *Here it comes...*

I dug the oars into the waves and pulled.

Dug, pulled.

Dug, pulled.

I found myself counting: *one, two, three...*

On *four*, the motorboat blew apart in a fiery ball. Burning chunks shot skyward, arcing over the ocean. Then the shock wave hit, nearly throwing us out of the dinghy. Salt water sloshed over the sides and debris rained down around us, miraculously missing the dinghy except for a few glowing ashes.

Bracing my bare feet against the polyester hull, I pulled the oars into the dinghy, clinging to them with one hand and to Eden with the other while we rode out the waves. In the water, Brien, Cain and Twilight never stopped kicking.

When things calmed down again, I set Eden on the bench next to me. "There's too much water in the dinghy," I called to my friends. "I'm going to have to empty it before I start the motor."

"We'll keep pushing," Cain returned.

Grabbing a cut-off plastic jug tied to the back ring, I bailed as fast as I could until we were riding higher again, then moved to the bench at the stern.

Twilight was closest to the small outboard motor. "I'm going to fire the motor up now," I warned her.

She released the dinghy and popped up a few feet away. "Go ahead."

Brien took in the situation—there wasn't enough room for all three of them to push and steer clear of the motor—and told Twilight to get in the dinghy. She nodded and pulled herself on board in a single ninja-like movement, dropping down on the bench next to where Eden was huddled in the blankets, shivering.

Twilight rubbed Eden's knee. "You're doing great."

"T-trying," she said with a brave smile.

It took several tries before the motor started. "C'mon, c'mon," I coaxed, my gaze on Eden, who'd slumped against Twilight.

She was fading fast. Twilight had both arms around her, holding her so she wouldn't slide off the seat. Fear sank hooks into my gut. This was too much stress for a pregnant woman. Eden could go into early labor, stroke out—hell, I didn't know. But women died from things like that, didn't they?

In desperation, I smacked the motor and, mercifully, it sputtered to life. Gripping the rudder, I aimed us in the direction of the castle. Even with Cain and Brien assisting, we cut through the waves at a maddeningly slow pace until at last the castle appeared, its four towers silhouetted on the cliff against diamond-bright stars.

That's when I saw the fins. Three great whites, keeping pace with the dingy. They didn't usually attack vampires—something about our scent turns them off—but these seemed a little too interested in us.

"You guys see the sharks?" I called.

Brien gave me a thumbs-up. "We'll keep them away from the dinghy."

Twilight and I exchanged a look. Normally a vampire could outswim and outfight a shark, even a great white, but Brien and Cain had to be getting tired.

She pulled out a switchblade. "Want me to spell one of you guys?"

"No way," Brien ground out. "You're the youngest by a long shot. Stay in the damn dinghy."

Twilight rolled her eyes but stayed put, staring out at the circling predators, one arm around Eden, the other hand keeping the blade at the ready.

I aimed the dinghy at a cove a little south of the castle. If we'd still been in the motorboat, we could've returned through the sea cave. Unfortunately, the 10-hp motor didn't have the horsepower for the maneuvers required, which was kind of like trying to thread a needle while bouncing on a trampoline.

If I failed, we'd be dashed against the rocks.

The small motor started losing power. I eased off on the throttle, but a few minutes later it stuttered and died, out of fuel.

I cursed and started rowing again.

✤ *37* ✤

EDEN

T he trip to Lilith Island passed in surreal flashes.

Flames splashing the night in copper and gold, burnishing the ocean and Talon's tense face.

The dinghy rising and falling like a roller coaster until the after-shocks finally eased.

Shark fins, pale in the moonlight, inscribing circles around the dinghy.

Me swaying on the bench, exhausted and shivering, head nodding against Twilight's shoulder—and when had she gotten on board?

And then I was floating free somewhere above the ocean, looking down at Talon and myself and the others. Detached and no longer cold. That was good, right?

It was Talon's voice, his *will* that pulled me back. "We're almost there. Hold on, angel. Can you do that for me?"

I mumbled, "Yes," my tongue so thick in my mouth I barely understood myself, and came to myself with a jerk.

Across from me, Talon rowed for shore, mouth set. I'd never seen him like that before. His eyes burned into mine, the irises outlined in cobalt like a corona flaring around a dark sun. He looked...wrecked. Terrified. For me.

Awe spread through me, warm and sweet. Filling up every corner of my soul, pushing out the anger, healing the hurt.

I really was important to him. I *mattered* to him.

We fought to land through the crashing surf. The ocean threw us forward. Dragged us back. Talon swore under his breath and rowed harder, his motions a blur.

"C'mere. If we hit a rock, you might pop out." Twilight moved me to the floor, braced me between her legs, and wrapped her arms around me.

My hands were numb, but I held onto her as best I could, trying to do my part. On either side of us, Brien and Cain kept pushing, under-water more than they were above it.

And then the dinghy bottom scraped against sand and pebbles. Tossing aside the oars, Talon scooped me into his arms and leapt onto the beach.

His deep tones vibrated against my cheek. "I'm taking Eden to my quarters. Someone contact Olivia and get whatever she needs to the castle."

"You don't want to take Eden to the clinic?" Brien's voice.

"She's in bad shape. I don't want to risk moving her across the island. We need to get her warmed up ASAP."

Safe.

I could let go now.

My brain clouded over, my eyes drifting shut.

When I opened them again, I was on Talon's bed, wrapped in a big towel, the heat cranked up. Taking a washcloth, he gently wiped the mud and dried salt from my face. He rinsed the cloth in a bowl of warm water and continued cleansing the rest of me, lifting a small part of the towel at a time and patting me dry with a second towel.

I gave a hard shudder, and he dragged his teeth over his lower lip. "Almost done, baby."

I nodded mutely.

When I was as clean as he could make me, he bundled me into a sleepshirt and tucked two thick blankets around me, topping them off with his silk comforter.

"Drink." Supporting me with an arm around my shoulders, he

brought a cup of hot broth to my lips, feeding me sips until it was gone.

Only then did he leave me for a quick shower. He reappeared dressed in clean clothes and climbed into bed with me, pulling my chilled body against his.

I slipped my hand beneath the covers, fingers spread over my abdomen. The baby hadn't moved for hours. Panic wrapped a fist around my windpipe.

"The baby?" I rasped.

Talon stroked the hand on my abdomen. "You're okay—both of you. I can hear his heartbeat. He's resting, that's all."

"Really?"

"Really. But Olivia's on her way."

"Good. I mean I believe you, but I want to be sure."

"Of course, you do." He feathered his lips over my temple. "Whatever it takes, I'll do it. If I have to fly a specialist in, I will. I won't lose you now—either of you."

I rested my head against his cheek. "Thank you."

My toes and fingers started to prickle. I gave them a tentative wiggle, wincing at the pain.

"What is it?" Talon asked. When I told him, he brought my right hand to his lips, kissing the fingers one by one. "That's good. It means they're not frostbitten."

I nodded and burrowed into his chest. "This feels so good. To be close to you."

His arms tightened on me. "Get as close as you want."

I drew a jagged breath.

He nuzzled the side of my neck. "What's wrong, baby?"

"It still doesn't feel real. I keep thinking I'll wake up and I'll still be in that cellar." I shuddered. "Lemaire...he said he'd sold me to another vampire. He was taking me to whoever it was. The baby would've been born a slave."

Talon swore roughly. "Did he say who?"

"No. All I know is that it was a man. Lemaire said 'he.'"

He was silent for a couple of beats. "There aren't that many vampires who keep blood slaves any longer. We'll track the SOB down. In fact, I may know who—" He broke off, shaking his head, and I knew that was all I'd get out of him. "Anyway, it will be handled. That's a promise."

Olivia arrived, dressed in pink joggers and a yellow hoodie, a cheerful, very capable whirlwind. The first thing she did was check my pulse, then hook me up to an IV, "for dehydration," she said.

Next she whipped out a special stethoscope and listened to the baby's heart. She examined me internally, too, then pulled my sleepshirt back down and tucked the covers around me again.

"He's got a good, strong heartbeat. We'll keep an eye on things, but he should be fine."

I let out a breath and met Talon's eyes. He was smiling, his relief clear. He squeezed my shoulder and pulled up a chair next to the bed. "And Eden?"

"She's doing great," the nurse-midwife said.

"Good." His jaw worked. "That's good."

My brain had cleared enough by then to realize my parents must be worried sick. "My mom and dad," I asked Talon. "Do they know what happened?"

"They were the first ones I called when you went missing."

"Oh, God. You have to tell them I'm all right."

Talon took out his phone. "Brien or Cain probably already contacted them, but I can text them anyway."

"Please," I said.

"Everyone knew," Olivia said. "Talon had the whole island out looking for you. The man didn't rest the whole time you were gone."

"Yeah?" I eyed him, stupidly pleased. He'd said something like that earlier but it was still dawning on me how much he cared for me.

Talon glanced up from his phone, giving me the same intense, burning look he'd given me in the dinghy. "Hell, yeah," he said, all growly vampire.

Olivia patted my leg. "I want you to take it easy for the next twenty-four hours, okay? Just rest and a little gentle exercise. We'll monitor you both to make sure everything's okay."

Talon's phone pinged. "It's your mom," he said, showing me the screen.

She'd sent me their love and a string of heart and hug emojis, then told me to rest now, they'd call tomorrow.

Talon pocketed his phone. "I'll have Smythe set you up with a new phone," he told me as a knock sounded on the outer door. "That will be your food," he said.

He left the bedroom, returning with Rio and a wiry older woman in a black T-shirt and white jeans, her nut-brown hair cropped short and streaked with gray.

"This is Mrs. Park," Talon said.

So this was Twilight's grandmother. There was a family resemblance—the same honed muscles, the same confident stride. The wooden tray she had tucked beneath one arm seemed somehow wrong; those strong hands seemed like they'd be more at home with a weapon than something so domestic.

"Hello." I struggled to sit up in bed, almost pulling my IV out.

Olivia clucked in dismay, but Talon was already there, lifting me up and tucking a large pillow behind my back.

"It's nice to meet you," I said when I was settled again. "I've heard a lot about you from Rio."

Dipping her chin in dignified acknowledgment, Mrs. Park unfolded the tray's legs, placing it over my lap. She took the containers from the insulated bag Rio carried along with a plate, bowl and silverware, and in moments, I had a bowl of steaming chicken wonton soup and two slices of toast before me.

My water glass was refilled and I was told to drink, the baby needed it. When I obeyed, Mrs. Park indicated the soup. "Now, eat."

"Yes, ma'am," I said and dug in.

Rio stood at the foot of the bed watching me. He looked like he hadn't slept since I'd gone missing. He had dark smudges beneath his eyes and his pink, purple and blue hair was matted down in some places, sticking up in others.

"You okay?" he asked after I'd taken a few bites. "Really?"

"Yep." I gave him a reassuring smile. "Just hungry."

He glanced at Olivia, who nodded. "She'll be fine, love. She needs food and rest, that's all."

His shoulders eased. "That's all right, then."

"Now off to bed with you," Olivia told him. "You look like you need sleep as much as she does."

He yawned and nodded, rounding the bed to pat my shoulder. "I'll see you in the morning, okay?"

"Sounds good."

He shifted from one foot to another, still staring at me like he couldn't believe I was really all right. Then he crouched and hugged me, careful not to jostle the half-eaten soup. "You scared the shit out of me," he said against my temple.

My heart constricted. I reached up, squeezing his forearm. "I scared the shit out of myself."

A rusty chuckle escaped him. "I'm so glad you're okay. You're like family, you know?"

I turned my head and kissed his cheek. "Back atcha, little brother."

"Right." He cleared his throat and with a last hug, came to his feet. "Let me know if she needs anything," he told Mrs. Park.

"I will," she told him, and he nodded and left.

Talon had left the room for a few minutes to have a low-voice conversation with Brien and Cain. Now he returned and pulled a chair up to the bed, watching as I resumed eating.

"MinJi has volunteered to keep an eye on you," Olivia said with a nod at Mrs. Park. "I'll stay another hour just to make sure everything is all right, and then she'll take over for the rest of the night. I'll be upstairs if you need me, though."

I frowned at Talon. "Why can't you watch me?"

"I can't, sweetheart." He curved his hand around my nape and rubbed his lips over mine. "I have to leave, but you'll be fine with Mrs. Park here." He exchanged a look with the former slayer and straightened, adding, "There will be a guard stationed in the hall, too."

A guard? My brow furrowed. "What's going on?"

Talon rolled his lips in.

I put down my spoon. "Tell me. I deserve to know, don't I?"

He considered me another few seconds, then nodded. "If you could leave us for a minute?" he said to Olivia.

She nodded and exited the room, closing the door behind her.

Talon turned back to me. "We're pretty sure there was someone else on that island. Someone who stayed in the shadows while we were searching for you. Somebody rigged our boat to explode, and if Lemaire was with you, it couldn't have been him. We know there was a second vampire—we took care of him. But there must've been a third."

"You could be right," I said slowly. "Your father was worried about more than one vampire. He kept saying 'they're.'"

Talon nodded. "Whoever it was, they're probably not still on the island, but we'd like to check it out anyway. Meanwhile, I want to be extra careful with you."

"All right," I said, although he wasn't really asking for my agreement.

He brushed the back of his fingers over my bruised cheek. "I love you," he said, low-voiced, and strode out of the bedroom, leaving me staring after him, mouth ajar.

Olivia took the chair Talon had vacated. "Whew," she said, smiling and shaking her head. "What a night you've had."

"Yeah." I closed my mouth, still back there with Talon saying he loved me—and then leaving. "First time the man tells me he loves me, and he runs out the door before I can even say it back."

"He's afraid," Mrs. Park said from the doorway.

My brows climbed. "Of me?"

"Not you so much," she said. "What you represent."

"And what's that?"

"Vulnerability. Someone hurts you, and they hurt him. We saw it ourselves. He wasn't himself while you were gone. He wasn't just upset and angry, he felt guilty."

I nodded slowly. It made sense, especially with parents like his. He was used to being the problem solver, the protector, the hard-ass.

Mrs. Park indicated my tray. "Finish your soup," she said in a firm but kind voice. "Rio made it himself."

❧ 38 ❧

TALON

Outside the castle walls, two syndicate helicopters were standing by. Brien, Cain and I climbed into one, and three enforcers piled into the second.

As I'd told Eden, our motorboat hadn't sabotaged itself. There had been at least one other person on the island. Fortunately, that had occurred to Brien, too, and while he and Twilight were waiting for Cain to come back with the dinghy, Brien had disabled Lemaire's boat.

Whoever it was wouldn't have an easy way off. Yeah, they could swim, but it was a long, energy-draining trip, even for a vampire, and the closest inhabited land was Lilith Island. Most likely, they'd either called for pick up or were swimming in our direction. Either way, we might still be able to capture them before they slithered back into whatever hole they called home.

Cain and I took the seats in the back, and Brien took shotgun next to our pilot, a soldier named Gianna. We donned our headsets and Gianna took us up, the second bird immediately after.

The wind off the ocean buffeted us. Gianna cooly steadied the small aircraft and swung northwest. The other pilot followed, keeping a distance of about a hundred meters. Both pilots flipped on their searchlights.

I leaned forward trying to see something, anything—a swimmer, another boat, even a helicopter. In the seat ahead of me, Brien did the same. He muttered something under his breath.

"What was that?" asked Cain.

"Just wondering how the fuck Lemaire established a lair this close to Lilith Island without us realizing it."

Technically, this was Maritime Syndicate territory. The entire Maritime Provinces were. But our focus was on the mainland, as it had been for Brien's parents before us.

"It wouldn't be a smart use of resources to monitor every uninhabited island," Cain pointed out. "There are too damn many."

He was right. In fact, there were close to three hundred islands within a twenty-five-kilometer range.

"This island was different," said Brien. "Jules took me there once when I was still a kid. He even showed me that lair, but I'd forgotten all about it until tonight. That was our lair, originally—Jules had it built back when he first came to North America. He was planning to establish his base there until he struck the deal for Lilith Island. It was bigger, and a little farther from the mainland. And, of course, Bluebeard's Cove is wider and deeper than any cove around."

"I never stepped foot on it before tonight," Cain said.

I nodded. "Same here."

"Might be worth rebuilding," Brien mused. "A backup lair in case of emergency."

Cain and I murmured agreement, then fell silent, our full attention on the search again.

I'd told Brien and Cain that Lemaire had sold Eden to someone as a blood slave. The vampire who came to mind was Nazaire, the QCS enforcer who'd tried to buy Twilight at a private auction. In fact, the whole setup reeked of him.

Take Twilight and Eden and he'd have the two women most important to us. It was ingenious, really. The SOB could strike a blow at the heart of our syndicate while at the same time feeding his addiction for unwilling females.

"Whoever bought Eden," I said, thinking aloud, "whether it was Nazaire or someone else, he wasn't on the island. Lemaire was taking her somewhere by boat."

"I wish I'd known Lemaire had sold Eden into blood slavery," Brien said. "I'd have kept him around long enough to get a name out of him."

"The buyer could even be on a nearby island," Cain said.

If he's not on Lilith Island itself.

I shook off the stray thought, telling myself not to be paranoid. But Lilith Island wasn't impregnable—it was too large for that. Yeah, we restricted access, but it wasn't a fortress. And even the most secure fortress can be breached. Brien's mother had been slain within sight of Castle Leclerc.

Uneasiness whispered up my spine. Maybe I shouldn't have left Eden.

They can't get to her. She's not even their main target.

Somehow, I wasn't reassured.

❧

Our destination came into view and Gianna spoke into her mic. "Where should I put her down, my lord?"

"There." Brien pointed to the smoldering shed. "Near the fire. We'll start at their lair and work outward. There may have been an exit or tunnel we missed."

"Very good, sir." She touched down on a flat patch of grass about fifty meters from the building's charred remains.

"Keep the motor running," Brien ordered. "We may have to leave in a hurry."

"Roger that."

Brien, Cain and I ripped off our headsets and jumped out. As Cain shut the door, he told Gianna, "This door stays shut, understand? We don't know how powerful this bastard is. He could be lurking in the shadows, waiting to hitch a ride."

"Yes, sir," she said.

The second bird touched down and three enforcers, all vampires, exited. We divided the island into six sections and set off at a run.

Twilight pulled a chair up to the bed where I lay staring at the ceiling. She'd taken a shower and changed into baggy joggers and a cropped silver tee. She looked fresh and rested while I probably looked like crap.

"My halmoni says you're having trouble sleeping."

I scooted higher on the pillows, bringing the duvet with me. "She shouldn't have bothered you. I'm fine, really."

Just tense and afraid to sleep because they might come for me again. I knew it wasn't rational. I was safe now, the castle on high alert. There was a guard stationed in the hall outside Talon's apartment, and Twilight's intimidating grandmother in the living room. No one was going to hurt me or the baby.

Twilight tipped her head to the side. "Did you get any sleep at all?"

"Not really."

"Wanna talk about it?"

I started to say no, then changed my mind. "Yeah, maybe. Lemaire..." I took a ragged breath. "He told me he'd sold me and the baby. Talon—Talon wouldn't have known where we were. He would've thought I left him—again. That I didn't want to be with him. And the baby would've been born a slave."

"Well, fuck that." Twilight sat next to me on the mattress and pulled me into a hug. "You're safe, and Brien and the guys will get whoever it is."

"I hope so. I would've killed myself first."

"No, you wouldn't have. You would've thought of the baby."

"You're right." I pinched the bridge of my nose, horrified at myself. "I can't believe I said that."

"Hey." She squeezed my shoulders. "It's okay. It's only me here and I understand."

MinJi Park appeared in the bedroom doorway. "You're not supposed to upset her."

"I didn't." Twilight lifted her head to look at her grandmother. "Fucking bloodsucker sold her to a slaver."

That surprised a laugh out of me. "You know you're a bloodsucker, too, right?" I asked, then winced. "Sorry, I didn't mean to say that out loud."

"I'm a vampire," Twilight returned. "There's a difference. A bloodsucker just takes and takes like the leech they are. I know what it's like to be treated as less than human. I will *never* be a bloodsucker."

My jaw set. "You're right. Lemaire was a bloodsucker."

"And he's in his final grave," Twilight said. "If anyone else tries to get to you, they'll join him. Nobody's going to hurt you or that peanut of yours. I mean, how else do I get to be Auntie Twilight?"

My mouth twitched. "Is that what you want him to call you?"

"Why not?" she said.

Mrs. Park sat on my other side, rubbing my back. "Feel better?"

"I do, yeah."

Twilight nudged me with her shoulder. "You did okay, you know? You should've seen her," she told her halmoni. "She never lost it, even when we put her in a little rubber dinghy with everything exploding around us. We were in the middle of the goddamn North Atlantic and she kept her head."

"It's not like I had a choice," I mumbled, a little embarrassed. In my family, you didn't pitch a fit over things you couldn't help.

"But some people would've lost it. No judgment—we can't always help how we react, especially someone with no training like you."

Mrs. Park patted my thigh. "She's got lady balls."

Twilight chuckled, but I was incredibly complimented. I beamed at the older woman. "Thank you."

"I'll tell you what," Twilight said, returning to the leather chair, "after you have the baby, I'll teach you some self-defense moves. You'll feel better if you can defend yourself."

"Seriously?" At least if a vampire ever tried something like that again, I could do some damage.

"Absolutely. Some knife work, too."

"Then, hell, yeah. But you know thralls can't carry weapons," I felt obliged to point out.

"Don't worry, Talon will be on board for this. You should've seen what he was like when we realized you'd been kidnapped. Even I was afraid of him."

"Yeah?" I liked the sound of that, not that I believed for a second that Twilight had been afraid of him.

"Hell, yeah. The man went all Bruce Willis on us. And after that video came, I think he actually considered kidnapping me if that's what it took to get you back."

"Jesus." I couldn't help smiling, though. It was still sinking in that Talon loved me. That I came first with him.

Mrs. Park stood up. "You can talk about this later. You—" she pointed at me—"use the bathroom. I'll help. Then you will go back to sleep. Now, come."

She pulled me to my feet. Behind her back, Twilight made a rueful face at me. I suppressed a grin. Mrs. Park was clearly used to being obeyed, but you couldn't help liking her. I could see why Rio adored her.

When I returned to the bedroom, Twilight was still on the leather chair. "Why don't you go to bed?" she told her halmoni. "I can take over now."

Mrs. Park looked doubtful. "I don't know...," she said with a glance at me.

"I'm fine," I said. "I'm pretty sure I can fall back asleep now."

"Go. I can watch her sleep the same as you—and I'm not the one who was up all day." Twilight urged her halmoni toward the door.

"Sunrise isn't until a little after seven. If you come back at six-forty-five, that gives you almost five hours."

They had a whispered discussion and then Twilight appeared in the doorway and dimmed the lights. "Unless you want them completely off?" she asked.

"No." The thought made my throat cinch. "Leave them on."

Darkness gave *them* an unfair advantage. They could see me, but I couldn't see them. I hadn't forgotten that first night when Lemaire had been in the basement with me and I hadn't even known it.

"And please close the door." A vampire in the shadows could slip through even a narrow crack.

"Gotcha," said Twilight. "Try and get some sleep, okay?"

"Okay."

I waited until I saw and heard the door close completely, then snuggled deeper into the soft bedding.

To distract myself, I pictured those burning looks Talon had given me.

How he'd had everyone out looking for me.

How he'd held me on the boat like he'd been terrified he'd lose me if he didn't keep me close.

How he'd chosen me over Brien, because even though Brien probably hadn't needed help, Talon had made it clear that I was his priority.

Not his primus. Me.

He loves me.

In my chest, the love I'd repressed for so long unfolded its wings.

Talon. Loves. Me.

The wings flapped, eager to be set free. So I let them soar.

❧ 40 ❧

TALON

By the time I circled back to the meeting point, a patchy fog covered the island. I found Brien contemplating the shed's blackened remains.

"Any luck?" he asked.

I shook my head. "You?"

"No."

Cain jogged up in time to hear us. "Same here. We've been over every inch of this island. Hell, I turned over rocks in case the bastard's burrowed into the ground."

The three enforcers arrived from different directions. They hadn't had any luck either. The person or persons who'd rigged our boat to explode had vanished.

Brien's mouth compressed. "It's like these motherfuckers are always one step ahead of us."

"Yeah." I fingered my switchblade's smooth ebony handle. I'd had it out the entire time we searched. If I'd seen Nazaire, I would've struck first, asked questions later—or not.

Answers didn't matter. What mattered was keeping Eden safe, and I wouldn't rest easy until Nazaire—or whoever was behind this—was in their final grave.

"Let's go." Brien jerked his chin at the waiting helicopters. "We're cutting it close as it is, and this fog doesn't help."

I jogged forward with the rest. Something about this didn't pass the smell test. The urge to return to Eden, to assure myself she was safe, was a monkey on my back now, impossible to shake off.

On the flight back, Brien and Cain discussed strategy. I listened through my headset without joining in, Brien's comment chewing at me.

These motherfuckers are always a step ahead of us.

I straightened up. "Why tell me to bring Twilight?" I interrupted.

My friends stopped talking to look at me.

"What d'you mean?" asked Cain.

"Why would Nazaire—or Lemaire, for that matter—want Twilight? She's a vampire now. Vampires don't make good blood slaves. To keep her under control, they would've had to chain her in silver, keep her half-starved."

I'd never kept a blood slave, but a half-starved anyone simply didn't taste as good. That's why the dark SOBs like Nazaire turned their thralls into addicts. Much easier to control someone when their "fix" was you drinking from them.

"That's a damn good question," Brien said.

"I figured it was to draw Brien out," said Cain.

"But they told me not to tell anyone," I pointed out, "especially Brien."

"Maybe the plan was to weaken him," Cain said. "Slay his mate, and it's as good as taking him out, too. He might even go blood mad like..."

Cain trailed off, but he didn't have to finish. We all knew he was thinking of Brien's father, who'd never been the same after losing his mate.

"That's what I figured, too," I said. "But what if we're wrong? What if this wasn't directed at Brien? What if it's always been about Twilight?"

"But why kidnap Eden?" Cain asked.

"Because she's carrying my spawn. They can't easily kidnap Twilight. She's a vampire, and Brien's with her most of the time anyway. And you don't have a mate. Eden was the easiest one to grab. They knew I'd go after her, if only to save my spawn."

Cain winced. "Hell."

Brien's snarl ripped through the headphones. "And we left Twilight in the castle while we're an hour away chasing our goddamned tails."

My throat worked. Because Eden was in the castle, too. "I might not have it right."

"Or you might have it exactly right," Brien returned. "Pick up the pace," he ordered Gianna. "I'll text Twilight." His thumbs moved over the screen. "She isn't responding," he said a minute later.

Cain had his own phone out. "Jasper's in the war room," he reported. "He says everything's quiet."

White lines appeared around Brien's mouth. He leaned toward Cain. "Where's Twilight? Ask him."

"Texting him right now," replied Cain. A few seconds later, he swore. "He says she's with Eden and the cams just went down in that section."

"No." My stomach dropped through the helicopter floor and kept dropping until it hit the ocean and sank below the waves, taking my heart along with it.

Why the hell had I left Eden? She was bruised, exhausted, dehydrated. She couldn't take much more.

And that was if they allowed her to live.

Eden had been kidnapped to use as a bargaining chip. If we were right and they really wanted Twilight, Eden wasn't any use to them except as a slave.

"Twilight's tough," Cain said. "She won't be easy to take. And she'll look out for Eden. That's how she's made."

I shook my head, fear eating at my insides, tunneling into my brain.

Brien leaned forward, staring out the windshield like he wished he could sprout wings and fly the rest of the way.

I knew exactly how he felt.

❧ 41 ❧

EDEN

I started awake, heart slamming in my ears.

The bedroom door opened. "Bad dream?" asked Twilight.

I sat up, took a deep breath. "Yeah."

"Lights up. Daylight glow," At her command, the lights brightened. "That better?"

"Yeah. Just give me a minute. What time is it, anyway?"

"A little before four. You've been asleep for a couple of hours."

"It was like I was still in that cellar with Lemaire watching me. But I couldn't see him." I drew a jagged breath. "I tried but I just couldn't."

"That's normal," she said matter-of-factly. "You're processing what happened. There were vampires I saw in my dreams for years."

"Really?"

"I was trained to compartmentalize the bad stuff, but it still bothered me."

I fingered the duvet. "Does it get better?"

"Yeah. And if it doesn't, we'll find you a therapist to talk it over with."

"Thanks." I heaved a sigh. "It helps, knowing I'm not the only one."

"You're not, trust me. So don't feel bad, okay?"

I nodded and pushed the duvet down. "I'll be right back."

"You have to pee?"

"Yeah, but I can do it myself." I swung my legs to the floor.

"I'll just go along with you to make sure." She stayed close, rolling the IV stand across the room for me, then after making sure I was okay, left me alone in the washroom. When I was finished, she helped me back into bed again.

I sat up against the headboard. "Talon will be back soon, right?"

"I think so. I haven't heard from them."

"I think I'll stay up until then."

"Want some company?"

"Sure. But could you get my sewing box first? It's in the closet in the garden suite. And bring the blue shirt on top, okay? I just want to do something...normal, you know?"

She nodded and left, a short time later. She handed me the sewing box but kept the tiny blue tee, examining the white shark appliqué pinned to the front. "You made this for your baby?"

"Yep." I rooted through the sewing box for white thread, careful not to dislodge the switchblade from its hiding place, even if I was pretty sure Twilight wouldn't care if she saw it. "I cut it down from an old T-shirt of Talon's. He doesn't know, by the way—it's a surprise."

"I won't tell him," she promised. "But wow, this is really good. Are you selling these?"

"I'd like to." I hesitated, then added in a rush, "When the baby's older, I want to start an online business."

"You totally should." She passed me the little shirt. "Want some help? I can take photos and we can put them up on Instagram. My last cover as a slayer, I was an influencer with over a million followers."

"Are you kidding?"

"True story. I kinda miss it, actually."

"Well, then, I'd love your help."

"Good." She grinned. "We can use your little guy as a model. We won't show his face, of course—you don't want his likeness out there where anyone can see him—but we can show him from the chin down."

"Sounds good." I threaded a needle. "How about some music?"

Twilight pulled up some chill electronica on Talon's system, then perched on the leather chair, arms wrapped around her legs, watching as I sewed the shark applique to the shirt.

"I never figured I'd have a baby," she said.

My gaze snapped to her. "Are you—?"

"No." A self-conscious smile tilted the corners of her mouth. "But we might start trying."

"They could play together," I said before stopping to think, then bit my lower lip. I pulled out a pin, sticking it into the apple-shaped pin cushion I'd picked up in New York. "I mean, if that's okay with you and Brien."

"Of course, it is. Even if I didn't like you—which I do—Brien and Talon are best friends. Your baby is going to be so spoiled."

"You think?"

"Yes." Leaning forward, she gave my wrist a quick squeeze. "Give them time. Brien's already coming around, and Cain will, too. Those three are like brothers, you know? Your little guy is going to have two powerful uncles, not to mention a great father."

I smiled. "He will, won't he?"

I'd been feeling better ever since Talon promised that our son could choose his own path, but it was good to hear Twilight's perspective. And I already knew Talon would make a good father, even if he didn't think so. He was calm, controlled, protective, the type of father who'd set clear boundaries, but also explain the "why" behind his rules. Our baby was going to adore him.

I slid Twilight a look. "So why did you think you'd never have a baby? Don't slayers have kids?"

"Some do. Most of us don't live that long."

"Oh." I tried not to show my shock; she said it so easily, like dying young was no big deal. "Your halmoni did, though."

"True, but she's a badass."

I chuckled. "That's what Rio says."

Twilight grinned. "She likes him, too." She fell silent, watching me sew. After a while she said, "My mom was a slayer, too."

"Was?"

"She died when I was still a teenager. An op went sideways and…" She gave a sad shrug.

"I'm so sorry," I said, my heart hurting for her. "That must've been hard."

"It was a long time ago."

"So? If it was my mom, I'd still miss her."

"I do miss her, but it was my halmoni who raised me. Mom wasn't around much even before she died. She was a legend in SI. They still talk about her in training camp. Same with my halmoni." She played with the end of her long brown braid. "Kinda hard to live up to, you know?"

"I bet you lived up to them both okay."

"You think?" A pleased smile flashed over her face. "I tried, anyway. My last real job—not the thing with Brien, but before—was basically a suicide mission. When that went south, I got out—or tried to, anyway. So, yeah, I figured I was the last of my line. I guess I still am. It's not like my spawn will grow up to become a slayer."

"Does that bother you?" I tied the thread and snipped off the ends, then removed the rest of the pins, sticking them in the pincushion.

"Kind of, but SI has changed. I'm not sorry to be out of it. Plus, I could never have mated with Brien if I hadn't left."

"You're lucky," I said. "I've seen how Brien looks at you, like you're the best thing that ever happened to him."

"That's how Talon looks at you."

I shook my head. "It's not the same thing."

"Sure looks like it to me."

"We're not mated."

"Yet," she said.

I dug my teeth into my lower lip. I was still getting used to the fact that he loved me. I hadn't even said it back. "He won't mate with a human."

"Then ask him to turn you."

I just stared at her. I'd thought about it, of course. But hearing someone speak it aloud made it real, in a way that was scary and exciting at the same time.

Twilight made humming sound, clearly reading my emotions. "You want it, I can tell."

"I do and I don't," I admitted. "It's a big step, you know?"

"I always wanted it," she said with a far-off look. "But you don't have to become a vampire. You could become a dhampir, too."

Like the baby.

But more importantly, I could be with Talon for hundreds of years. He was young for a vampire. Stay a human, and I'd die centuries before him. If we weren't mates, he'd move on eventually. Find a true mate.

Something primal and possessive sprouted teeth and claws.

No fucking way. He's mine.

"Think about it," Twilight said.

"I will." I closed the sewing box and put it on the nightstand, the T-shirt on top of it.

We kept talking clothes, and I told her about how I repaired vintage clothing, too. It turned out that Twilight had been a stylist in one of her other lives.

"It was all part of my cover as an influencer," she told me. "I liked it, you know—putting outfits together for other people. Maybe you could even let me help. Or we can go thrifting together."

"You're officially my best friend," I said fervently, and we grinned at each other.

Her phone buzzed. "It's Smythe," she said, glancing at the screen. "He says Brien's been trying to reach me. He has a message. He wants to give it to me personally. I'll be right back."

She left the bedroom. I heard the apartment door open, and her voice as she stepped into the hall. Then everything went silent.

My nape tightened. Something seemed off.

The door. I hadn't heard it shut.

"Twilight?" I slid my hand into the sewing box, closing my fingers around the switchblade. "Is everything okay?"

"Yeah," she called back. "Go to sleep. I'll be right back."

Fear tripped up my spine. Why was she telling me to go back to sleep when I'd clearly told her I wanted to stay up? And wasn't she supposed to stay with me until Talon came back?

I couldn't go into the living room with a knife in my hand, though, so I stuck it into the back of my panties as the apartment door closed with a thud. I opened my mouth to say something, then shut it again, swinging my feet to the floor.

The damn IV tugged at me. I slid the needle from my forearm and pressed a tissue to the small wound before creeping forward to peek around the door frame.

In the living room, a man I'd never seen held a wicked-looking silver blade to Twilight's throat. Blood seeped from a small hole in her shirt where he must've stabbed her first.

I froze. Both their gazes swung to me.

"Get back in the bedroom," Twilight said tightly. "And shut the door."

My chest seized. I swallowed and lifted my forearm in a lame attempt to pretend nothing was wrong. "I pulled out my IV."

The man looked like Loki in an I'm-going-to-fuck-you-up mood—chin-length dark hair, deep-set eyes, a sharp chin. spoke in a scarily calm voice. "You shouldn't have come out here," he told me calmly. "Now I can't let you live."

"No, you can, really," I said—ridiculously polite, but it was the first thing that came to my head. "Pretend I'm not here."

I threw an agonized look at Twilight and inched backward. I didn't want to abandon her, but I had the baby to think about.

The Loki-lookalike flashed a pair of sharp fangs. "Get the fuck over here."

"Run, Eden!" Twilight slammed an elbow into his side.

He grunted and hung on, dragging the knife across her throat. She gasped but kept struggling as I stared, horrified at the thin red line the knife had left on her creamy skin.

"Don't move," he told her, digging the knife point into the base of her throat for emphasis. To me, he said, "Come here—now—or I'll stab this into her jugular. You know what silver does to a young vampire? She's already weak."

He pressed the point deeper into the base of Twilight's throat. She arched in pain, her hands clawing at the air.

"I bet your veins are burning, aren't they?" he said. "Traitor. I know what you did."

"What I did?" she rasped.

"I'm Stygian," he said.

"Fuck." Twilight's eyes widened.

"That's right," he told her and jerked his chin at me. "You—get over here. *Now*."

"Don't listen to him," Twilight mouthed, her eyes pleading.

I moistened my lips, torn between helping her and saving myself and the baby.

"I'll get you either way," Stygian said.

He was probably right. Talon's inner doors weren't reinforced with silver, except for his sleeping vault, which I hadn't been cleared to enter, and the intruder was obviously either a dhampir or a vampire. Even if I locked the door, he'd just kick it down.

But that wasn't the only reason I obeyed him.

If there was a chance to save Twilight, then I'd take it. I couldn't live with myself otherwise. Twilight was going to have her baby, that baby who would grow up to be best friends with my little guy.

And on a purely personal level, I was sick and tired getting pushed around by vampires, dhampirs or whatever the hell this man was.

Playing the helpless pregnant woman, I shuffled forward, a hand under my sleepshirt, pretending to massage my lower back. My fingers closed around the switchblade's handle.

Stygian narrowed his eyes. "Put your hands where I can see them."

Damn. "Okay, okay."

Releasing the handle, I brought my hands up and kept going.

Feverish color splotched Twilight's cheeks. Her eyes darted around the room, like she wasn't sure where she was. "So hot." She focused on my throat and electric-blue rimmed her irises. "I need..."

My heart thudded against my ribcage, but I kept going. "Snap out of it, Twilight. It's me, Eden."

"Eden..." She drew my name out, then blinked and focused on me. "*Run*. I'll stop him."

"The fuck you will." Stygian gave Twilight a vicious shake. "The bitch stays."

For a few seconds, his attention was on Twilight. It was the chance

I'd been waiting for. Palming the switchblade, I stumbled forward, pressing the catch. The switchblade snicked out. I kept going.

Twilight tried to catch me. Stygian swore and dragged her backward.

I kept going. His gaze flicked to the switchblade, and he shifted Twilight to his other side, leaving his attention torn between us for a crucial second.

I lunged forward, aiming for his stomach, but he managed to twist so that the blade sank into his upper thigh instead. His breath hissed in. He shoved me away, and I let go of the switchblade, leaving it in his thigh.

This time I stumbled for real, arms flailing, and smashed into the coffee table. I started going over but managed to wrench my body around so that I sat down—hard—on the wood-and-copper tabletop.

Twilight erupted, snatching Stygian's weapon, flipping him over her shoulder to the hard wooden floor and staking him with his own blade. He slid to the floor, the hole she'd made in his chest already smoking with an unearthly fire.

She took a couple of steps toward me. Then her hands went to her head, her face contorted in pain. "Hurts...everywhere."

I started to go to her, then groaned and doubled over as pain shot up my side.

She stumbled forward one more step, then collapsed to the floor in slow motion—knees, hands, body, head—and went limp.

A broken doll of a person.

"Twilight? You okay?" My body started to shake. Pressing a hand to my side, I lifted my head, willing her to answer me. "Please tell me you're okay."

When she didn't move or speak, I gritted my teeth and tried again to stand.

That's when the apartment door slammed open. Talon burst into the living room, Brien and Cain on his heels.

❧ 42 ❧

TALON

"Talon?" Eden swayed on her feet, a hand to her side.

My heart ricocheted into my throat. "I've got you."

I scooped her up and sat with her on the couch as Brien shot past us to where his mate lay crumpled on the floor.

"Are you okay?" My gaze went to where Eden pressed a hand to her abdomen. Shards of fear scraped my lungs. "Please, angel. Tell me you're okay."

"I'm not sure." She leaned against me, and I felt her trembling. "But I think it's just a pulled muscle."

"Okay. Okay. Take it easy." Easing an arm around her shoulder, I sent a desperate look at Cain. "Get Olivia back down here."

He nodded and whipped out his phone.

"What the fuck happened?" Brien lowered himself to the opposite side of the couch, Twilight cradled in his lap. "Drink, love," he crooned. When she didn't respond, he gently cupped the back of her skull, pressing her mouth to his throat.

"Stygian," Eden told Brien. "He stabbed her."

Cain finished his quick conversation with Olivia and looked at Eden. "Stygian? Who's that?"

"No idea," she said. "But Twilight seemed to know who he was."

"SI," Brien said under his breath.

I met his eyes over the top of Eden's head. "Could be. Working with Lemaire?"

Brien made an angry sound. "Wouldn't be the first time. Did this Stygian mention anyone else?" he asked Eden.

"No. It—it all happened so fast."

"I want the castle searched," Brien told Cain. "Nobody goes in and out until we know if this guy was working alone.

He waited for Cain's nod and went back to trying to wake Twilight up enough to drink from his vein.

While Cain made a second call, I lifted Eden's forearm. "What happened to the IV?"

"I had to take it out so I could move around."

"And meanwhile, we were chasing our tails on that fucking island."

Cain put his phone away. "Olivia will be here in ten minutes, and James is coordinating a search of the castle," he said, naming one of the enforcers who'd accompanied us to the island.

Cain crouched next to Stygian's smoking bones and ashes. He plucked two switchblades from the charred remains. "This is Smythe's. I recognize the raven." He indicated the bird engraved on the ebony handle of one of the switchblades.

"Smythe?" Brien's mouth tightened. "Bloody Lilith."

"Yeah. Twilight staked the mofo with his own weapon." Cain's tone was admiring.

"Good," Brien said shortly. "Saves me the trouble."

Cain cleaned both blades and closed them. Then he hefted the second switchblade. The plain, stainless-steel one.

"But I don't recognize this one." His gaze slid to Eden.

She tensed. Still trembling, but now she looked scared on top of it. Her throat worked. "The other switchblade is—"

"Mine," I interrupted. I looked at Brien over her head. "I gave it to her because I was afraid something like this would happen."

I sensed Eden's surprise, and I'm sure Brien and Cain did, too. I locked gazes with Brien, daring him to contradict me. He gave me a considering look, then with a shrug, went back to coaxing Twilight to drink.

Cain put the blades at the end of my bar and poured himself a blood-whiskey. "So you stabbed Smythe, too?" he asked Eden.

"I—" Eden nervously licked her lips.

"It's okay," I said. "You saved Twilight, didn't you?"

Eden straightened. "Yeah. And I did stab him—in the thigh. He had a switchblade to her throat, and he'd stabbed her three times, maybe more. She was hurt—she looked like she had a fever. But when I stabbed Stygian or Smythe or whatever his name was, she managed to get his blade away from him and stake him. Then she collapsed."

Cain lifted his glass to her. "Good for you, love."

"Yeah. You're a hero." I brought her hand to my mouth, kissing her fingers. "My hero."

"Yeah?" Her beautiful eyes creased in a smile. "I love you," she said.

I knew she loved me, but finally hearing it aloud was like absorbing a body blow. Three little words, but they squeezed my heart. Pulled all the oxygen from my lungs.

I touched my forehead to hers. "I love you, too. So much."

A noisy sucking made us pull apart. Twilight had finally revived enough to drink from Brien. She'd be okay, then, although she'd feel like crap for a few days. Silver poisoning hurt like a sonuvabitch.

"That man," Eden asked. "He was actually Smythe? Brien's PA?"

"That's what Cain thinks," I replied.

Cain left the bar, stopping a few feet away from us. "What did he look like?" he asked Eden.

"Kinda like Loki on that TV show—you know the one I mean? Narrow face, shoulder-length brown hair."

"Tom Hiddleston," Cain said. "I've never seen the show, but I met him once in London."

"Oh. Well, anyway, that's who he looked like. He wasn't British, though." Eden's gaze turned inward. "He had faint European accent, even though I'm pretty sure he was North American—maybe even from Canada."

"Sounds like Smythe," Brien said. "He told me he'd been a PA in Paris for five years or so. But why attack Twilight?"

"And what about the guard who was supposed to be on duty?" asked Cain.

"And MinJi Park?" I added.

"I don't know about the guard, but Twilight sent Mrs. Park to bed," Eden volunteered. "That's why she was here."

Cain had his phone out. "James says Smythe sent a message to the guard," he said, his eyes on the screen, "telling him Brien wanted him in the war room. It seems to be legit. The man showed James the message."

I frowned. I'd told the guard not to leave his position until I returned. "Have James confine him to his quarters until I've had a chance to talk to him."

Twilight stirred. "Smythe told me straight out that he was Stygian. I never met him in person, but I know he was with SI. He was my alpha's PA, in fact."

"Ah," said Brien. "But why—?"

"Because he *knew*," she responded with a sideways look at the rest of us. "When he grabbed me, he said, 'This is for Crow, you bitch.'"

"So this was about revenge?" I asked. I didn't know the whole story, but I knew Twilight had had a falling out with her former alpha, and then her alpha had disappeared. Permanently.

Twilight's eyes closed. She looked better, if feverish, her face lined with pain. "Yeah," she said, resting her head against Brien's shoulder.

"And somehow, he hooked up with Lemaire," said Cain. "Who was also out for revenge."

"And Nazaire, too," I added. "I still think he's in this somewhere."

"I may be able to find out more about Nazaire." Cain cleared his throat. "That...contact I have in the QCS."

Brien's eyes blazed blue. "Do it. I want whoever is behind this stopped, damn it. If this had worked, it would've been a win-win for those SOBs. Take out my mate and it's as good as staking me. Because—"

He halted, shaking his head, but I heard what he didn't say.

It would've broken him.

I understood. Losing Eden would've left me not just broken but shattered into jagged pieces.

Brien rose, Twilight in his arms. "If you two have this handled, I'm taking Twilight back to my apartment."

"Go," I told him.

Brien paused next to us. Eden had stopped shaking, but at his scrutiny, she tensed up, until he said, "Consider your debt to us repaid in full."

Her jaw dropped. "Yeah? Wow. Thank you."

"No," he said. "*I'm* thanking you. And I'll make sure the syndicate knows you saved the prima's life."

Twilight lifted her head from against Brien's chest. "She saved us both. She could've barricaded herself in Talon's bedroom. I *told* her to do that, actually. But she didn't."

Eden moved a shoulder like she hadn't done all that much, but she was smiling.

I kissed her temple. "Mine," I mouthed at Brien—and I didn't mean she was my blood thrall.

He understood. He dipped his chin in acknowledgment and left.

"I can talk to the guard," Cain told me. "You stay with Eden." His gaze shifted to Eden, his ice-blue eyes warming. "You did good," he told her. "That kid's lucky to have you as a mom."

It was high praise, coming from Cain, and Eden knew it. She gravely thanked him.

He offered her the stainless-steel switchblade. "I believe this belongs to you."

Her swallow was audible. Then she lifted her chin. "It does, yeah," she said, and took it from him.

With a curt nod at the rest of us, Cain left, and I carried Eden back to my bedroom, where I placed her on the bed, her back against the pillows to wait for Olivia. Eden was still clutching the switchblade. With a glance at me, she slid it under the pillow.

"It's yours," I said. "You earned it."

"And I'm going to learn how to use it," she said. "I never want to be that helpless again."

"Fine by me," I said.

When Olivia arrived, she confirmed that Eden had pulled a muscle in her side but was otherwise fine. "I won't hook her back up to the

IV," she added. "As long as she's drinking all right and able to urinate, she's good."

She handed Eden a glass of orange juice and ordered her drink it. "You're not to move a step today," she told Eden in a no-nonsense voice, "unless it's to go to the bathroom. And this time, I'll be right here, making sure you follow orders."

"Thank you," I told Olivia. I lifted a brow at Eden. "But you will follow orders, won't you, angel?"

She brought her fingers to her temple in a salute. "Yes, sir."

Olivia suppressed a grin. "I'll stay anyway."

Dawn was less than an hour away. Cain had reported that Smythe appeared to be working alone. The castle would stay on alert, but for now we were fairly sure there wasn't another traitor in our midst.

I tossed down a shot of blood-whiskey, then closed the door to the living room, where Olivia was reading a magazine, and got undressed, climbing into bed with Eden and pulling her against my naked body. She yawned and snuggled deeper into me.

My chest contracted. I tightened my grip on her, my fingers spread over her belly.

Mine.

The almost savage sense of possession was tinged with vulnerability. I should wait, romance Eden like she deserved with hot-house flowers and Moon Mist and over-the-top jewelry. I wanted to adore her and fuck her senseless—and *then* ask her to be my mate.

But to Hades with that. Eden was mine. The romance could come later. If she needed it, I'd romance her every night for the next decade.

Right now, though, I was claiming her.

I teased her earlobe with my tongue. "You're my mate," I told her, the words tumbling from that hungry, possessive, vulnerable place.

Her cheek lifted in a grin. "Are you asking me or telling me?"

"Both." Beneath my fingers on her belly, a tiny elbow or knee pushed back. Our son apparently approved.

"Don't I have to accept?"

I growled and bit down on her lobe. "Don't make me punish you. I can be all kinds of creative."

She shivered in that way I loved, then giggled. "Okay, okay. I accept."

And damned if I didn't feel a punch in my chest. At the same time, Eden arched against me, a throaty moan tumbling from her.

"Holy shit, Talon."

"I feel it, too," I said hoarsely. "I didn't know it would be so...physical."

"Yeah." She swallowed hard. "Like we're connected now." She took the hand I had resting on her abdomen and brought it to her lips. "I love you. So much."

The words branded themselves on my heart, digging hooks in so deep I'd always be connected to her.

"I love you, too."

She kissed my hand again. "I know. I feel it, same as you feel me."

My dick pressed against her lower back. Gods, I wanted to take her, to claim her in the most primal way.

"I want it too," she said, wriggling against me, which didn't help one iota.

"Not until we get Olivia's okay." I kissed the side of her mouth. "Now go to sleep."

"Are you always going to be this bossy?"

"Yes."

I waited until she dozed off, then reluctantly left the bed to lock myself in my vault so that Olivia would be free to come and go. It felt like I was tearing myself away from my own soul.

But it was okay. No, better than okay.

Because when I woke up tonight, Eden would still be here.

43

EDEN

That first day Olivia watched over me like a mother hawk, urging me to eat and drink, monitoring my vital signs and those of the baby.

She encouraged me to rest but I woke as soon as Talon left the bed. When I finally dropped off again, I landed back in that damn cellar. I jerked awake, heart pounding.

In the vault off the bedroom, I could swear Talon turned over, restless because I was. He must've sensed it through our mate bond.

Talon loves you. He claimed you as his mate.

A wave of happiness hit me, washing away the unpleasant, scratchy residue of the nightmare. I curled up again, and this time, when my eyes drifted shut, my dreams were nightmare-free.

I woke up a few hours later, ready to eat. I ate a good meal and called my mom and dad with the new phone Rio had arranged for me, then flipped through copies of *Vogue* and *Elle*.

Olivia had said no visitors for now, but Rio must've made a pest of himself because she let him in around noon. He stomped into the bedroom, skinny body tense, dark eyes wild. "What the hell's wrong with this place?"

"Oh, Rio." I held out my arms.

He looked at Olivia. "Is it okay to hug her?"

"Gently," she replied, adding with a maternal look that encompassed both of us, "Thirty minutes, that's all," before returning to the living room.

Rio pulled the leather chair closer to the bed. "Jesus Murphy," he said, making me smile because I knew he'd picked that up from me. "I can't leave you for more than a couple of hours without you getting yourself attacked. Again."

"It's not me, it's them."

He rolled his eyes, fighting a grin.

"I owe you," I said. "If it hadn't been for that switchblade you gave me, that guy might've gotten away with it."

"Yeah?" He sat taller. "Well, what about you? Mrs. Park says you stabbed the guy, that the asshole had a knife to Twilight's throat."

"He did." I shuddered, recalling how Smythe had kept pricking Twilight with it, trying to poison her, to weaken her enough for him to kill. "Although I think she might've fought back harder if I hadn't been there. She was trying to protect me. She wanted me to lock myself in the bedroom, but I couldn't."

"There you go," Rio said. "You know, Twilight says the first time she saw you she thought you were a Valkyrie. You have that whole tall, curvy blonde thing going on."

"Yeah?" I kind of liked the sound of that. "Wait, do Valkyries save people or kill them?"

"Hell if I know. But you saved me."

I shrugged. "All I did was give you a place to stay."

"Eden." He scraped a hand over his multi-colored hair. "I was barely surviving. I was even thinking of selling myself to one of the pervs who were always coming around the subway tunnels."

My heart dropped into my stomach. "I didn't know."

"No judgment on the guys who do, but—" He closed his eyes, shook his head. "Anyway, I just needed to know someone cared whether I lived or died. And you did. You saved my goddamned life. Don't you know that?"

I rolled my lips into my mouth. "Rio..."

He jabbed a finger at me. "Don't cry."

"I'm not." I swiped at my eyes before the tears spilled over.

His brown eyes were suspiciously wet. He pointed at them. "See what you did?"

"C'mere." I held out my arms again and he lunged. We enfolded each other in a tight hug, both of us sniffing. "I love you, you know."

His arms tightened on me. "Love you back."

We stayed that way for a beat, then he sat back with a lopsided smile. "Anyway."

I grinned back. "Anyway." I reached for my water and he handed it to me.

I drank and he put it back on the nightstand for me. "Something I've been wondering," I said. "Why did Mrs. Park want me to have a switchblade in the first place?"

"She said that you should have a weapon, that she had a bad feeling about some of the people in this castle. Her nape was prickling, and that's always a sign something was off."

"Why didn't she tell Twilight, then?"

"I think she did. Twilight was keeping an eye on you, wasn't she?"

"I suppose so."

"In the end, you helped each other, didn't you?"

"Yeah." My smile spread across my face.

"And guess what? Mrs. Park's going to teach me some basic self-defense, including how to use a switchblade. I want to be able to defend you."

"That's nice," I said, touched. "But I don't want you to get hurt because of me. And you don't have to defend me. Twilight's going to teach me some moves, too."

"That's good, but it's not up to you. And you're not going to send me home, either. I have a contract, and I like it here. For now, I'm staying."

I nodded slowly. Rio was an adult, and to be honest, in New York, he'd been the streetwise one, not me. Still, up until now, I'd thought of myself as his defender, not the other way around. Maybe not his savior like he seemed to think, but I'd definitely been taking care of him.

Still, it was odd, having him take charge like this. Like déjà vu, only in reverse. This was what it would feel like when my baby grew up.

I quirked a brow. "You think they'll let Mrs. Park give you a switchblade?"

"Are you kidding?" He chuckled and sat back. "No one tells that woman what to do."

⌘

After that, Olivia and I played cards, then I took another nap and went for a short walk, Jasper accompanying me around the castle courtyard. I was back in bed, reading, when Talon finally emerged from his vault.

"Olivia says you're having nightmares." He sat on the edge of the mattress, brows drawn together.

I wrinkled my nose. "I keep dreaming I'm back in that cellar."

"Oh, baby." He pulled me onto his lap, and I leaned my head against his chest.

"Actually," I admitted, "in the dream I was giving birth with no one to help me."

On the dirt floor in that cold, dank cellar.

Talon's throat worked. "You know you're safe now."

"Yeah. But..." I shrugged.

"Hey." He ran his fingers through my short locks. "You survived because you kept your head, did what you had to. You're okay, and the baby's doing fine. I'm fucking impressed. We all are."

"Yeah?" That made me smile. "Mrs. Park did say I have lady balls."

Talon chuckled. "You do. I'm so sorry you got sucked into this. So goddamned sorry. Lemaire had it out for Brien and Twilight—you were just the easiest way in. Because of Esposito and what he is to me." His voice iced.

"Your father." I swallowed queasily, flashing on how the poor man had hung in Lemaire's grip as the vampire drained him of blood. "I saw him die. Lemaire...he was so fast and I couldn't have stopped him even if I tried. It was awful—"

"Shh. If you'd tried to interfere, Lemaire probably would've drained you as well. As for Esposito, he brought it on himself."

"I'm still sorry. He didn't deserve that."

"No?" Talon's tone was hard. "Then he shouldn't have helped kidnap you in the first place."

I pulled back, frowning. "He tried to save me—you know that, don't you? That's why we were in the hall. Lemaire attacked him because he was helping me escape. And even before that, he did his best to protect me."

"He shouldn't have taken you in the first place," Talon asserted. "The worst part is he was only in it for the money. He got in too deep at a Quebec City casino. My guess is, Lemaire lured him in, then lent him the money to gamble. He would've known Esposito was my father —it's not a secret, not if you dig a little. And now that I'm a lieutenant, that made Esposito valuable. And I knew that. I had him under surveillance, but I never thought he'd sink this low."

I relaxed against Talon again, stroking his chest. I could feel his emotions through the bond now, and I knew he needed soothing, even if he pretended like he didn't give a damn about his father.

"I suppose. But I think he was sorry, that he hated himself for it. I heard him arguing with Lemaire, saying he'd promised that me and the baby wouldn't be hurt."

"Yeah? Well, he didn't have to do it. He could've come to me as soon as he realized what they wanted him to do. But if it makes you feel better to think of him as the good guy here..."

"He was," I said. "In the end, he was."

Talon made a noncommittal grunt.

"Have you told your mom?" I asked.

"No. There wasn't time. I'll tell her tonight." His chest heaved beneath my hand. "I don't know what to say. There isn't even a body to bury."

I kissed his jaw, running my lips over the faint, dark bristles. "Tell her he did his best, okay? That he took care of me and the baby. She doesn't need to know the rest."

"You want me to lie?"

"You don't have to lie. Just...don't tell her the whole story, okay?"

"I'll think about it." Tucking me back into bed, he stood up and stretched.

Muscles rippled and his shirt inched up, revealing a slice of wash-board abs. I guess I was feeling better because my insides tingled.

This man was my *mate*.

He'd *claimed* me.

Damn, I was lucky. And not just because he was hot as hell. He was the whole package, as far as I was concerned, the perfect blend of tough and caring.

"I'm going to shower," he said, "then I'll be back."

"Okay," I said absently, my gaze still on those tasty abs.

Bringing his arms down, he eyed me back, his expression taut. "Hold that thought, all right? Or I'm going to fuck you, and Olivia will chop off my balls."

I blinked, then smiled. I had power over this man, and I liked it.

"Don't give me that look," he warned.

I widened my eyes, messing with him. "What look?"

"That cat-who-swallowed-the-canary look." He put a hand next to my head, sliding the other beneath the sheet to cup me between my thighs over my panties.

"I can't do anything right now, but as soon as you're cleared..." He lightly spanked my mound.

I mock-pouted. "Now you're just being mean."

"That's right." He stroked me over my panties. "Tell me you love me."

My eyelids lowered. I arched my back, pressing myself against his teasing fingers. "I love you."

"Again." His middle finger toyed with my clit.

I exhaled noisily. "I love you. I love you."

He swallowed my words with a deep kiss, then lifted his head. "I love you, too. And I promise I'll be right here the rest of the night, okay?" He nodded at the leather chair. "Working."

"Mm."

When he came out of the shower, I curled up facing him so I could watch him work, enjoying how his dark brows drew together or lifted; how his sexy mouth flattened or pulled sideways; and how at times he sat back, obviously reading, while other times he hunched over the keyboard, typing rapidly.

This man is yours.

So much had happened. I was probably going to have nightmares for a while, but this right here was special and I let the awesomeness of it seep into me.

When I finally closed my eyes, I slid into a deep, nightmare-free sleep that lasted for hours.

Later that day, Olivia pronounced me fit for regular activities, but Talon waited another night, waking me up an hour before dawn the following morning. Drawing off the camisole and panties I'd worn to bed, he licked and sucked and fingered me until I came, then arranged me on his lap, my thighs spread on his.

His eyes caught mine, his amber irises outlined in hot blue. He entered me slowly, holding my gaze the entire time.

When he was seated deep inside me, we both expelled a breath. He gripped my bottom. "This is me loving you, Eden."

Hands on his chest, I lifted up and sank back down on him again. I teased his flat nipples with my thumbs, and he groaned.

"And this is me loving you, Talon."

We made love like that, slow and easy until we were both shaking with the need to climax. I slid a hand down between myself, rubbing my clit, as he sped up his thrusts, lifting me and bringing me back down. Firm but also careful.

That carefulness drove me crazy. The best kind of agony.

He kept it up until I begged him to take me harder. "I need..."

"Touch your tits," he gritted, and when I did, his eyes flashed blue.

I pinched my nipples, so primed. That was all it took. A lick of white lightning flashed up my spine, blanking my mind, sending me over the edge. I kept riding him, my inner walls convulsing around him.

"Fuck, Eden." He gave a last, hard stroke and spilled hotly into me.

After, he curled around me on the bed, pressing kisses to my cheek, my temple, my nape. I expected him to leave and lock himself into his vault, but he stayed until his breath slowed to almost nothing, his body cooling. Deep in his day sleep, a wordless expression of trust.

I stayed another few minutes, so happy my heart felt too big for my chest. Then I kissed him and left the bed to shower and dress.

❧ 44 ❧

TALON

Eden slid me a look. "You okay?"

"Yeah. Why?"

"You're white-knuckling the steering wheel."

She was right. I relaxed my grip.

We were on our way to my mother's cottage. As soon Eden had Olivia's okay, she'd insisted on meeting my mom. To tell the truth, I was glad to have her. Mom hadn't taken the news of Esposito's passing well, and I was crap at comforting people.

Mom didn't have any close family on the island, either. She'd been an only child and her parents were dead, and most of her friends had dropped her years ago. So I'd thrown money at the problem instead, paying Denise, the lady who came twice a week, to come five days instead. At least I knew my mother was eating and taking showers.

So I'd zipped Eden into the new down coat I'd bought her—because she could restore, rework and reuse previously owned clothes if that was her dream, but I was damned if my pregnant mate was going to run around in a Nova Scotia winter wearing an unzipped coat —and bundled her into the SUV.

I pretended to focus on rounding a small bend in the road. Snowflakes drifted down, sparkling under the SUV's headlights. "There's something I should tell you about my mom."

"Go on," Eden encouraged softly.

I flexed my fingers on the wheel. "She's an addict, okay? A drinker. She may not be sober."

"I know—and it's okay. I still want to meet her."

"You knew?" I shook my head. "I guess it's not a secret."

"No. And it's also not a secret how you take care of her."

"She's my mom."

"I know, and you're doing everything you can. The rest is on her."

I nodded. "I know."

"Do you, Talon? Do you really know that? Or do you think you should be able to fix her?"

I downshifted, taking the turn onto my mom's road.

I should be able to fix her. But I can't. I'm not enough. I was never enough.

"Talon?" Eden asked.

"We're here," I said gruffly.

She settled back, her disappointment filling the small cab. "I'm here," she said. "When you're ready to tell me."

"Wait for me to help you out." I rounded the car and opened the door—and pulled her close. "I love you so fucking much," I said against her striped wool hat.

"I love you, too." She stroked my nape. "Remember that."

Mom stood on the porch, arms hugged around her too-thin waist, her face lined and weary. "Thank you for coming," she told Eden.

My new mate pulled her into a hug. "I would've come sooner, but they wouldn't let me."

My mom stiffened, then clung to Eden for a long moment. When she finally stepped back, her gaze moved over Eden's face, pausing at her bruised cheek. The ugly marks Lemaire had left were still visible, if faded.

Mom gently touched the largest bruise. "They did that to you?"

"Yeah." Eden straightened her shoulders. "But the vampire who did it is in his final grave, so, you know, fuck him." She screwed up her nose. "Sorry for the language, but that's how I feel."

"Don't apologize. The sonuvabitch deserved it."

"He did," Eden agreed.

Mom turned to me. "Thanks for bringing her."

"She insisted." I touched my lips to her cheek. Her scent was free of alcohol.

She must've heard me sniff, because she said, "I'm sober. I wanted to drink, but I haven't—and I won't. I'm going to AA meetings, too. Denise takes me."

Eden eyed us, a tiny frown between her fine dark brows. "It must be so hard," she said to my mom.

"It is." Mom's chest heaved beneath her thick wool sweater. "But come in—it's too cold to stand out here."

Inside, I helped Eden out of her coat, hanging it along with mine in the foyer.

Mom led the way into the kitchen. "Can I get you a cup of tea? Something to eat?"

"Tea, please," said Eden. "If you have decaf."

"Mint tea okay?"

"Perfect, thanks."

"Coming right up." Filling an electric kettle at the sink, Mom plugged it in, then took out two cups and a wood box of teabags in various flavors. "Two more months, right?" she said with a glance at Eden's stomach.

"Yeah." Eden smoothed a hand down her loose black tunic and grinned. "He's up right now, as a matter of fact."

My mom dug her teeth into her lower lip, a look of longing on her face, one I couldn't interpret, but Eden apparently did, because she beckoned to her.

"Would you like to touch—?"

"Oh, yes. I would." Mom hurried forward. "If you don't mind…"

"You're his grandma, aren't you?" Eden said. "There. Do you feel it?" She took my mom's hand, placing it on the upper left side of her abdomen. "That's a foot, I think."

"Yes." Mom's mouth trembled. "Oh, I wish Marco could be here for this."

Putting a hand on my mother's shoulder, Eden touched her forehead to Mom's. Together, they looked down at Eden's pregnant stomach.

"I wish things could've been different," Eden said. "I'm so sorry about what happened. I can't imagine how you feel."

My mom drew a shaky inhale. "It's so hard. He was my best friend."

Eden drew her closer. "I know. I know."

I swallowed over something sharp and rough-edged and glanced around the small kitchen. The killing rage that had consumed me when I'd realized that Esposito had helped kidnap Eden had subsided, but I was still furious with him, and my mom by association.

And yeah, I knew she hadn't had anything to do with Eden's kidnapping. But she'd carried the man emotionally for years, and before I'd started giving him money, she helped him out financially, too, even when she didn't have the money to give. If she'd cut him off years ago like she should've, he might've left the area altogether. I reminded myself he'd tried to do the right thing when he'd got my mom pregnant, but...

The women separated, Mom giving Eden's stomach a soft caress. "You'll let me see him, won't you?" she said with a sidelong glance with me.

"Of course." Eden's brow pinched in confusion. "You're his grandma. I want him to know you."

"As long as you stay sober," I inserted.

Understanding dawned on Eden's face. She opened her mouth, then shut it at the hard stare I gave her.

"I will. I will." My mom swiped at her eyes and lifted her chin in my direction. "I've changed, Talon. You'll see."

Gods, I wanted to believe her. But how many times had she told me that or something like it? "Let's take it a day at a time."

"Fair enough." Mom cleared her throat and turned toward the kettle. "The tea's almost ready. Why don't you two sit down?"

I pulled out a kitchen chair for Eden, then sat next to her. "Thank you," I mouthed, taking her hand and pressing it to my lips.

I meant it. I might be mad at Esposito, but I hated seeing my mother in pain, and Eden's gesture had eased it. She'd known exactly what to say and do.

She was a good person. Warm where it was easy for me to be cold.

If Esposito were here right now, I had no doubt she'd have forgiven him, too. It made me want to protect her from herself at the same time I hoped she never changed, because if she did, she wouldn't be Eden. The woman I loved.

Mom put a tea bag in each of the mugs. The kettle beeped and she poured the hot water into the mugs, then carried them to the kitchen table and took the chair across from Eden.

"You sure I can't get you something to eat?" she asked.

Eden shook her head. "I just had supper."

My mom nodded. "Tell me how you're doing," she invited. "You and the baby are okay?"

Eden assured her they were both doing great, and the two of them fell into one of those conversations that women have about babies and pregnancy and the nursery that Eden was putting together with my and Rio's help.

I let their conversation flow over me, content to listen.

Eventually, though, Esposito came up again. "He saved my life," Eden told my mom.

Mom's gaze darted to me for confirmation. My jaw clenched but I nodded in agreement. I'd said something along those lines when I'd first broken the news to her, but I probably hadn't been too convincing.

Mom's chest heaved. "He helped them kidnap you, didn't he?"

My brows climbed. I hadn't thought she'd put it together.

"Well, yeah," said Eden. "But he was sorry. I know he was."

Mom was looking at me. "Why else would he have been there? He got in too deep, didn't he?"

I shrugged a shoulder.

"Gambling." Her face fell. "Let me guess—he owed them money?"

I nodded. "A lot, from what I can tell."

Mom sighed. "That sounds like him. Getting in too deep, then not knowing how to get out. I'm sorry," she told Eden.

"You have nothing to apologize for," said Eden. "*He* did it, not you."

Mom gripped her mug with both hands. "If only he'd said something to me. Maybe I could've talked him out of it... But he didn't. I'm sorry."

Eden reached across the table to touch her wrist. "He knew you would've gone straight to Talon."

"Yeah. I would've." Mom's mouth twisted. "And Marco knew it. He wasn't a bad man," she told Eden. "Just weak."

My jaw dropped so I probably looked like a goddamned fish. All these years, I'd thought my mom had rose-colored glasses where Esposito was concerned.

Mom slanted me a sad smile. "I knew what he was, but I loved him anyway. That's what you never understood. But maybe now you do?" Her eyes slid in Eden's direction.

I closed my mouth, nodded slowly. Loving Eden as I did—needing her as I did—maybe I'd forgive her over and over, too. I liked to believe I wasn't that weak, but deep down, maybe I wasn't so different from my mom after all.

It would've been fucking scary, actually, if I didn't trust Eden like I did. If I didn't know in my very bones that she was nothing like my father.

"Well," said Eden, "Lucky for me Esposito was there. He brought me food and water, and he died trying to help me escape."

Mom's eyes filled with tears. She took out a tissue and noisily blew her nose. "Thank you for telling me."

"It's the truth." Eden chewed her lower lip, looking like she might start crying herself. "He put himself in between me and the vampire who kidnapped me, trying to buy me some time to run. It almost worked, too, except I had nowhere to run to."

Mom's face went tight with horror. "I'm so sorry, sweetheart. For everything you went through."

Eden managed a smile. "I'm fine now, though. Good thing I'm tough."

Suddenly, I couldn't bear her being even a few inches away from me, so I pulled her onto my lap. "Yeah. She is. Although if I could stake that bastard all over again, I would."

Eden brought her mouth to my ear. "Can we tell her?" she asked in an undertone. "She could use some good news."

I nodded.

Eden turned to my mom. "We're mated. Talon claimed me, and I accepted."

"Oh, honey." Mom's mouth dropped open. Then she was on her feet, teary-eyed but beaming. She rounded the table and enfolded us both in a hug. "I'm so happy. I never thought I'd live to see Talon claim anyone."

"You'll come to our mating ritual?" Eden asked. "It will be in the spring, after our little guy is born."

Mom straightened, her face crinkled with joy. "Oh, baby, I'd be honored to."

"But don't tell anyone, okay? Even my mom and dad don't know. We want to tell them in person."

"I won't," she promised.

We left soon after that. Eden was silent on the drive to the castle, but as I helped her out of the SUV, she rose on her toes, framing my face in her hands.

"Talon? I want you to listen. Are you listening?"

I eyed her, puzzled. "Yeah."

"I am not your mother, and you are not your father. We get to write our own story. We may mess up, but that's on us."

I gripped her wrists, my gaze moving over her earnest face. Gods, I loved this woman. No, I fucking adored her.

Sincerity poured from her. I felt it in my soul, where our bond was anchored. In that moment, I realized I still hadn't let go of that last, small doubt.

I swallowed thickly—and let myself believe. In Eden. In us. In our future.

"I will," I said. "I will."

She gave a satisfied nod and brushed her lips over mine. "Good," she murmured.

I dragged her closer, eating at her mouth, drinking in her sweet Eden taste. When I released her, it was only so I could get her somewhere private and kiss her some more, only this time, we'd both be naked.

"How'd you get so wise?" I asked as we walked up the castle steps, hand in hand.

"Is that wise? Seems like common sense to me."

"Then I wish everyone had your kind of common sense. Because you're absolutely right. This is our story, and you're the only one I want to write it with."

"Oh." She sucked her lower lip in. "You say such nice things."

"It's not nice when you mean every word."

"Then what is it?"

I brought our joined hands to my mouth and kissed her fingers. "The truth."

Talon guided me down a hall on the castle's second floor. "Where are we going?" I asked.

His lips curved in a mysterious smile. "You'll see."

It was February 13th, and the baby was due any day now. Talon had arranged a candlelight dinner in a library on the castle's second floor with salmon in a creamy Tuscan sauce for me and blood-wine and chocolate for him. We'd both dressed up, and he looked way too sexy for my nine-months-pregnant self in a dark suit and white shirt open at the collar that set off his sculpted features, his strong chin dusted with dark stubble.

The food had been delicious but I'd only picked at it. My back ached and I couldn't seem to get comfortable.

Talon stopped at a door at the end of the hall. "Shut your eyes."

I put a hand on my sacrum, trying not to be cranky. "What is it?"

A boyish grin. "A surprise."

"Yeah?" Temporarily forgetting my discomfort, I smiled back—he looked so pleased with himself—and obediently closed my eyes.

Talon kissed my nape. I'd kept my hair short and he loved it, telling me everything about my neck was erotic, even the back of it. "I can't wait to fuck you again," he said against my ear.

I snort-laughed. "You've got to be kidding me. I have circles under my eyes and I'm so fat I can't put on my own shoes."

He ran his tongue around the shell of my ear. "Not fat, pregnant—with our son. And that makes you beautiful and sexy and so, so fuckable."

I hmphed. Because...cranky. I hadn't had a good night's sleep in two weeks.

Talon had moved me permanently into his apartment. He'd purchased a massage table and, after getting the therapist to show him how he could help, gave me nightly massages. They helped, but between my aching back and the fact the baby seemed to be curled up on top of my bladder, I woke up every couple of hours.

The door opened and Talon drew me inside. "Can I open my eyes now?" I asked.

"No." He nipped my lower lip and released my hand.

I heard a rustling sound; someone else was in there, too. "What are you up to?" I asked, stifling a smile.

"Open your eyes," he said.

When I did, Rio and Twilight yelled, "Surprise!" Rio wriggled jazz hands for emphasis.

We were in a large room with a row of windows along one wall. A top-of-the-line sewing machine perched on a table. Built-in shelves held scissors, thread, buttons and other sewing notions. An ironing board leaned against a wall next to a dressmaker's dummy. There was even a cutting table. The other half of the room held several racks of clothes next to a half-dozen empty racks.

I brought a hand to my mouth. "Oh. My. God."

"It's a workshop-slash-showroom," Rio stated proudly.

My gaze swung to Talon, watching me with his hands in his suit pockets, a smile on his lips. "You did this?" I asked.

He nodded. "You like it?"

"Heck, yeah." I grinned so wide I was probably giving off happiness sparks. "It's...wow. Perfect." I crossed to the sewing machine, caressing it possessively. "This thing costs an arm and a leg. I can't wait to test-drive it."

"Let me give you the tour." Rio pulled me toward the racks of clothes. "Me and Twilight flew over to Halifax and bought up a bunch of used and vintage clothes for you to work with."

I fingered a black velvet dress. "I can't wait."

"That's not all." Twilight threw open a door, revealing a small room with painted blue sharks swimming over cheerful yellow walls. "You can bring your little guy with you. There's a crib and a changing table. Oh, and a washroom, too."

"You guys thought of everything." I looked around at their smiling faces. "Thank you. I'm...speechless."

"If you want to make any changes," said Talon, "let us know."

"I will, but I can't think of anything right now. I *love* it." I twined my arms around his neck and kissed him. "It's the best gift you could've given me."

He ran a hand up and down my spine. "I want you to be happy, angel."

"It was Talon's idea," Rio said, "but me and Twilight put it together."

"You did a great job," I said, releasing Talon to hug first him, then Twilight.

She took my arm. "You have to see this vintage dress I found. I want you to fix it up for me."

I went with her to the rack she indicated. The deep-pink cocktail dress would be perfect for her. We were discussing how to make it over when the ache in my back moved around to my front, a light but definite squeeze.

I blinked and brought my hand to my abdomen.

"You okay?" asked Twilight.

"Yeah, but—" I looked past her to Talon. "Umm...Talon?"

He was across the room in a heartbeat. He took my hands, his Adam's apple working. "What?"

"I think I'm in labor."

"You had a contraction?" He sounded calm, but his eyes were wild.

I took a deep breath. Nervous and excited, adrenaline pumping through me. "I think so."

"I'll call Olivia," said Twilight. "You take Eden to the birthing suite."

Rio's mouth had dropped open. "Fuck." Then he straightened his shoulders. "I mean, you've got this. What do you want me to do?"

Twilight answered for me. "Why don't you hang out for a few minutes while we get her ready, then come along to the birthing suite, okay?"

The birthing suite had been added to the castle's lair at Twilight's instigation. Together with Olivia, Twilight and I had designed a comfortable place for labor and delivery in soothing blues and greens with dim lighting and state-of-the art equipment including a hydrotherapy tub.

The first thing I did was go to the bathroom while Talon hovered outside the door. He barged in the moment I flushed. "Twilight says Olivia's on her way."

I was still on the toilet. I pushed down my underpants and leggings as far as I could reach. "I want a shower."

"Maybe you should wait for Olivia."

The leggings got stuck around my ankles. "Please, Talon."

He pressed his lips together and knelt to pull the leggings the rest of the way off. "Two minutes, that's all."

He turned the tap and waited nearby, a towel in his hands, while I washed up. "Twilight's letting Brien and Cain know, too," he said, "and I'll text your mom and dad after we get you settled."

I flashed him a smile. "Thanks."

The past couple of months, Twilight and I had grown close. She was smart, funny and more of a rebel than I'd realized. We'd clicked, bonding over a shared love of anime and eighties dance-pop.

When she'd offered to be part of my support team during labor and delivery, I'd beamed and thrown my arms around her. "Yes, please. I wanted to ask, but..."

She seemed taken aback by my hug, but after a tiny pause, she squeezed me back. "But what?" she demanded as I released her.

"You're the prima and I'm just a thrall."

She rolled her eyes. "Do I seem like I give a fuck about that? Besides, you're not a thrall anymore. You're a lieutenant's mate. That's practically royalty."

Now I turned off the shower. Talon patted me dry and helped me into a clean dress. That's when a large hand fisted around my abdomen.

"Whoa." Bringing a hand to my belly, I sent him a stunned look.

He gulped. "What's wrong, baby?"

"A...big one," I gasped out.

"All right." He gave me his arm, and I grabbed it with my free hand. "You've got this," he said, his tone low and soothing. "Lean on me and breathe. Slow, deep breaths. Like yoga breaths, remember?"

I nodded.

"And relax," he added. "Don't fight it."

"Trying," I gritted.

Talon had done four birthing sessions with me under Olivia's supervision. He'd been so serious, like this was a test he didn't intend to fail, which made me love him even more. He had that serious expression now. A calm, I've-totally-got-this vibe emanated from him. If he was still nervous, he hid it well.

My own tension eased. I closed my eyes, focusing on breathing into the contraction instead of straining against it, as Olivia had taught me to do.

"Good girl." His free palm settled on my back, moved in soothing circles until the contraction eased. "It's over?"

I realized I had a death grip on his hand and released it. "Yeah," I said, straightening up.

That's when I saw his taut expression. He must've been feeling the contraction along with me.

I chuckled weakly. "You look like crap. You'll never last. You have to close yourself off."

"You're my mate," was his reply. "I'm going to do this with you."

That fist moved from my abdomen to my heart and squeezed. Hard.

God, I loved this man. But— "At least block some of it. I need you to be calm for me. It doesn't make me feel any better knowing you're suffering, too. Please?"

"I'll try." He gathered me to him with a gentleness that made my throat clench.

Twilight arrived, and then Olivia. Another contraction hit, this one fairly easy to handle. After it receded, she helped me onto the bed so she could check how the labor was progressing.

She grinned up at me between my spread knees, which was pure Olivia. "You're already six centimeters dilated. Let's hook you up to an IV, just in case," she said, proceeding to do just that. "If you feel like walking, that should help things along."

"I do," I said, and Talon helped me off the bed, he and Twilight falling in on either side of me as I paced slowly back and forth.

Rio arrived as I was breathing through another contraction. "How's it going?"

I felt Talon shake his head at Rio, and my friend took a pace back, eying me like I was a lit bomb that might go off at any moment.

"Good," I said, tight-lipped.

When the contraction eased, he threw himself on the couch. "I'm going to be an uncle! Tio Rio!"

Twilight laughed aloud at that, and I chuckled.

"How soon can we dye his hair? A baby would look super-cool with pink hair, don't you think? Or maybe purple."

"No," Talon said firmly.

"Not until he's old enough to have an opinion," I chimed in, adding, "I'd like to sit in the rocking chair now."

Talon helped me lower myself to the seat, and I rocked back and forth. Olivia put on soft electronica and pulled out her knitting needles and a half-finished sweater. She sat on a chair, knitting one of the arms.

Rio's hand shot into the air like he was in a classroom. "It's not too late to call him Rio the Second. We can call him Two for short.

Only Rio could make me giggle in the middle of a contraction. Talon just shook his head.

"We have a name," I said.

"And?" asked Rio.

I paused in my steady rocking to nod up at Talon. "Tell them."

He caressed my nape. "We're calling him Jude," he said. "Jude Talon Montgomery Esposito."

It had been me who'd talked Talon into giving our son his family name. I firmly believed that if Esposito hadn't kept me supplied with water and sandwiches, I might've lost the baby. Lemaire might've even preferred it—easier to sell me as a blood slave without the encumbrance of another man's child. And Talon and I both liked the name Jude.

"I like it," Twilight said.

Rio screwed his mouth to the side, considering. "I suppose two Rios would get confusing."

Twilight's eyes sparkled with laughter. "Plus, they broke the mold after you were born."

"I know you're dissing me," he returned. "But you ain't wrong."

I chuckled and started rocking again.

After that, the contractions grew more intense. "Someone's in a hurry," Olivia muttered. She shooed Rio out—not that he tried to stay; the poor guy was looking green around the edges—and had me strip and get into the birthing tub with Talon and Twilight's help.

The warm water helped. Olivia moved her chair and knitting to the side of the tub and told me how great I was doing.

An hour passed. Talon supported me through my contractions, and Twilight fed me ice chips in between. I wanted out of the tub, and Talon lifted me out while Twilight dried me with a fluffy towel.

I got back into bed, and Olivia stowed her knitting and checked me again. Her gray eyes crinkled up at me. "You're ready to push, love."

The contractions had taken over my body by then. I groaned something incoherent and bore down when she told me to, and at three thirty-seven a.m. on Valentine's Day, Jude Talon entered the world with a tiny version of his dad's growl.

Twilight said, "Aw," and I exchanged a smile with Talon while Olivia cleaned Jude up and wrapped him in a blanket so that he looked like a cuddly, Maritime-blue burrito.

She handed him to Talon. "Say hello to your son."

Talon swallowed. "My son," he repeated, joy spreading like a sunrise over his face. He gazed down at Jude, one large hand palming his small head, the other holding him close to his chest.

"Hello, little guy." He pressed a kiss to the baby's still-moist forehead, then looked at me, his heart in his eyes. "Thank you. He's beautiful."

"He is, isn't he?" I was aware of Olivia urging everyone else from the room, but all I could see was my two guys, their dark heads close together. "He has your hair," I told Talon.

"Mm. I hope he gets your eyes, though. They're blue right now. Well, kind of bluish-gray."

"Mom says they'll probably change." I held out my arms. "Can I hold him?"

"Of course." Talon gave Jude another kiss and laid him in my arms.

I nuzzled his cheek, inhaling his sweet, newborn scent. He settled against my breast with another cute growl, rooting around until he found my nipple.

"That one's going to be a handful," Olivia murmured from the foot of the bed.

Talon and I grinned at each other.

A few final contractions, and Olivia declared that I was all done. She cleaned me up, brushed my hair and helped me into a soft nightgown that buttoned up the front, a gift from Twilight.

"You can send everyone in," I told the midwife.

Talon had taken Jude. He placed the baby back in my arms as a mix of humans and vampires crowded into the birthing room.

Twilight returned with Brien and Cain, all three appearing pleased at the new edition to the syndicate.

My parents came next, Mom with an armful of flowers and Dad with a tin of my homemade cookies. They'd received special permission to enter the syndicate's underground lair. They hugged me and Rio, who'd become an unofficial member of the family.

Talon rubbed my shoulder, then shook Brien and Cain's hands, accepting their congratulations with a smile. Champagne was uncorked, both blood-infused and the human kind, along with orange juice for me.

Glasses were raised and Brien toasted first me, then the baby, then Talon. Then it was Cain's turn. I was surprised to see him here, actually. Nazaire had surfaced in Quebec City again, and Cain had spent the last couple of weeks off-island, doing some sort of hush-hush investigation.

For once, Cain's lips didn't have that cynical twist. He appeared genuinely happy for both me and Talon. "To my best and oldest friend," he told Talon, "and your beautiful mate. Your baby is blessed to have you as parents. I hope you'll let me be an honorary uncle."

He directed the question to me. Talon was already nodding, but I raised my orange juice to Cain. "Of course."

Cain's gaze moved to the baby in my arms, and his face softened. For a few seconds, he looked almost human.

My mom finished her champagne and held out her glass out for more. Rio obliged, and mom raised her glass to me. "A Valentine's Day baby—that's lucky."

Everyone drank to that, then Mom handed off her glass to Rio and snapped several shots of me and the baby to send to Freya.

Talon sat on the bed next to me and took my left hand in his. "Eden, you already accepted my mate bond."

I eyed him, puzzled. "Yeah—?"

"But I've been waiting until tonight to give you this." He produced a gorgeous ring—a flawless oval sapphire on a simple gold band—and slid it on my left ring finger. "It reminds me of your eyes," he murmured.

I rolled my lips in and blinked rapidly. I hadn't cried in weeks, and I wasn't going to now.

"Sweetheart?" My beautiful, broody vampire looked panicked. "What? Why are you upset?"

I pressed a kiss to his mouth. "I'm not upset. I'm happy."

His arm came around my shoulders. "I love you too. And I was thinking about what you said," he said in an undertone.

"About turning me?" He'd been reluctant at first, worried about the danger to me, but I'd convinced him it was what I wanted.

"Yeah. Whenever you're ready."

I nodded. I'd already made up my mind that I wanted it soon. When Jude Talon wasn't nursing anymore. The stronger I was, the less likely someone would kidnap me again to use me against Talon and the syndicate.

Talon was worried that my parents would object, but it wasn't up to them, was it? And they'd come around. This was my world now and we all knew it.

I leaned my head against Talon, smiling around at everyone as my mom and Twilight approached to admire the ring.

"I think we need another round of champagne," Rio said.

Talon's chest rumbled in laughter. "I like how you think, kid. Order it."

Rio pulled out his phone. "On it, boss."

Cain grimaced. "Sorry, but I can't stay." He raised his fist and Talon bumped it.

"When will you be back?" Talon asked.

Cain gave him an odd-half smile. "Can't say."

Brien followed him to the door, and the two men conversed in low tones, Talon frowning at them. When they were finished, Cain slipped out the door. Everyone else stayed for a second toast, then filed out, even Olivia, until it was just me, Talon and my parents.

My father stuck out his hand for Talon to shake. "You take care of her, you hear? Both of them."

"I will, Mr. Montgomery. You have my word on it."

They exchanged an unreadable, very male look, then my dad released Talon's hand and clapped him on the back. "Call me Wes, son. Maybe I'll take you out night fishing sometime. I could use a strong back, and I bet you see real good in the dark."

I rolled my eyes. "Dad! He doesn't have time for—"

"No, it's okay," Talon told me. "I'd like that," he told my dad.

"Call me when you're free," Dad said, and Talon nodded.

But it was my mom who had the last word.

"See," she said, leaning forward to kiss first me, then my sleeping infant. "I told you that in the end, everything would work out for the best."

"You did." I smiled over her head at Talon. "You did."

ALSO BY REBECCA RIVARD

Thanks so much for reading!

Want to be the first to hear about my vampire romances and other steamy paranormal romance books? Sign up for my newsletter: www. rebeccarivard.com/newsletter

In return, I'll gift you with "Lir's Lady," a short story from my Fada Shapeshifters world.

THE VAMPIRE SYNDICATE

Sexy, twisty vampire mafia romance

Tempted

Pursued

Craved

Taken

Fallen

Hunger

VAMPIRE BLOOD COURTESANS

Steamy vampire romance set in Michelle Fox's Blood Courtesans World

Ensnared: Star

Compelled: Cerise

Learn more: www.rebeccarivard.com/vampires

THE FADA SHAPESHIFTERS

Dark shifters, seductive fae...

- *Stealing Ula*
- *Seducing the Sun Fae*
- *Claiming Valeria*
- *Tempting the Dryad*
- *Lir's Lady*
- *Shifter's Valentine*
- *Sea Dragon's Hunger*
- *Saving Jace*
- *Charming Marjani*
- *Adric's Heart*

Learn more: www.rebeccarivard.com/shapeshifters

ABOUT REBECCA RIVARD

USA Today bestselling author Rebecca Rivard read way too many romances as a teenager, little realizing she was actually preparing for a career. She now spends her days with vampires, shifters and fae—which has to be the best job ever. When she's not writing, she walks and bikes in the Chesapeake Bay area with her guitar-playing, story-telling husband.

Rivard's stories have received numerous awards, including the prestigious PRISM, the RONE, and the Paranormal Romance Guild Reviewer's Choice Award.

In addition, eight of her books have been awarded the coveted Crowned Heart Review from *InD"Tale Magazine*.